2020 £3.00

Genesis

Genesis

Mark Morris

PIATKUS

Copyright © 1999 by Mark Morris

First published in Great Britain in 1999 by
Judy Piatkus (Publishers) Ltd of
5 Windmill Street, London W1

This edition published 1999

The moral right of the author has been asserted

A catalogue record for this book is available from the British Library

ISBN 0 7499 0436 4

Set in Times by Phoenix Photosetting, Chatham, Kent
Printed and bound in Great Britain by
Biddles Ltd, Guildford and King's Lynn

Thanks to Mike Slater for police stuff and Phillip Edge for guns. And thanks to Nick Royle for once living in *that* flat.

This one's for Steve and Mel Laws, for friendship and wonderful hospitality.

PART ONE: MERCY

One

Behind the band, random images flashed up on a big screen. Crowds rioting; children starving; women crying; cities burning. Occasionally the images were punctuated by single-word slogans, red on black. EXORCISE, DEGENERATE, GODLESS, SUFFER.

Nick looked at the kids, sweaty faces rapt, fists punching the air, heads nodding vigorously in time to the music, and allowed himself a smile: not of superiority, but of nostalgia, even affection. At the age of thirty-five he had seen this reinvention, this reclamation, several times over. It was comforting in a way, each successive generation claiming rebellion as their own, rehashing fashions, attitudes, techniques, even words like 'cool' and 'cosmic' and 'happening', and breathing new life into them.

This thing with the big screen, for example. He'd seen the concept used before, many times. The first time had been at the Electric Circus in Manchester, twenty years ago, when the Buzzcocks had played in front of dozens of stacked TV sets, all showing the same image. He guessed that the Buzzcocks had borrowed the idea from some other band, who had probably nicked it from someone else before that . . .

Not that it mattered. Image was the important thing. If a band was considered hip or street-cred, then the screen would be seen as audacious, retro-cool, a bold kiss to the past. If, however, the band were regarded as hoary old has-beens (or never-will-bes), then the screen would be viewed as nothing but a hackneyed stage effect, an apt symbol for a bunch of tired old tossers with nary an original idea between them.

3

It was Nick's job, in part, to instruct the public as to which bands should be given the seal of approval and which the snort of contempt. Nick was a music journalist, freelance, though most of the stuff he wrote was commissioned by the *NME*. It was a great job, and tonight was a great night. Thunderhead were so new they had still to release their first single, though they were currently making waves on the live circuit, and with good reason. Their songs were short and powerful, full of rage and catchy as hell. They put them across well too; their set was tight and the band themselves full of the kind of swagger that people either hated or loved Liam Gallagher for. Watching them, Nick silently predicted that a year from now the face of their lead singer, Martin Keefe, would be adorning the bedroom wall of every teenage girl in the country. Keefe was a Mancunian Brad Pitt look-alike, who weaved like a snake onstage and wore even sillier hats than Jamiroquai. Right now he was bent almost double, barking the chorus of 'We're not gonna do that' over and over into his microphone while Mark (Mazz) Johnson on bass stood splay-legged beside him, thrashing frantically at the strings of his guitar.

Just for an instant Nick felt a pang of envy, thinking of what might have been. Sure he had a good life, was as happy as he could ever remember, but it was true what they said about music journalists, film critics and book reviewers: most of them were failed rock stars, actors or novelists. They did what they did in the hope of catching a little reflected glory. Half his life ago, Nick had been lead guitarist in a band that had attracted enough attention to have Virgin sniffing at their heels. But then, somehow, he had managed to piss it all away.

No, scratch that. There was no 'somehow' about it. Nick knew exactly what had happened. He had been weak – too weak to face his responsibilities, too weak to resist temptation – and so, after blaming everyone else for his misfortunes, he had started taking drugs to escape them. Within a depressingly short time, the escape route had become a trap, a net that had wound itself tighter and tighter around him, until eventually he had been unable to move, to breathe, to make any decisions beyond those that would fulfil his need, satiate his hunger.

He had sold his guitar, quit the band, and moved into a squat with a bunch of other smack-heads. They had fed one another's addictions, called themselves anarchists, but the truth of the

4

matter was, they had been nothing but no-hopers, passengers on the Oblivion Express. *Pretty vacant, maaaan . . .*

The crowd went wild as the song came to a crashing halt. Keefe bared his teeth at the audience like a baboon and Nick consulted his watch. Eleven twenty. Good as Thunderhead were, he decided to head off; he had already stayed for longer than he had been planning to. He was due to interview the band the day after tomorrow (he was taking a photographer with him and they had arranged to do some shots in an abattoir in Putney) and he had come along tonight simply in order to get a taste of their live show. There was a time, not so very long ago, when he would have stayed until well after the encore, used his influence to get backstage and then taken the boys on a tour of London's after-hours drinking dens. These days, however, he preferred to head back to his nice, warm flat, stick some music on, make himself a mug of tea, and chill out. If he was feeling particularly energetic, he might sit at his computer for an hour or two, tinkering with bits of work or surfing the Net.

'This is our last one tonight. Everybody say "aaahh",' Keefe announced.

You're just a crazy party animal, Nick told himself wryly, turning away as the crowd offered up the dutiful response. Joss Nyland, on lead guitar, cranked out the first savage chords of 'Kleptomaniac' and the crowd surged forward as Keefe stage-dived, fingers hooked into talons like a pouncing tiger.

The Camden Gridlock was like a million other dives Nick had frequented over the years – black scabrous walls, tiny bar lit like a hooker's booth selling warm, overpriced beer in plastic glasses flimsy as polythene. Shouldering his way through the sauna-hot crowd, he decided to go for a pee before heading out into the darkness. It was only two stops on the tube from Camden to where he lived in Belsize Park, but he had once been mugged at knife-point by two guys in Fulham after an evening spent gigging and ligging, and now he had a thing about never walking around London at night with a full bladder.

He headed for the Gents, towards the back of the room. As the heavy toilet door swung closed behind him, the music became a distorted fuzz of drums and bass. On the left-hand wall were a row of crazed sinks and cracked mirrors, taps dribbling like senile old men. Someone had vomited copiously into and around the steel

5

urinal on Nick's right. Grimacing, he headed for the cubicle in the far corner of the room, his feet splatting across a tiled floor awash with water and piss.

As he relieved himself, taking care not to let the sleeves of his leather jacket brush against the shit-smeared walls, he idly read the obscene messages marker-penned on the walls. Beneath the shaky declaration, I SUCK FAT COCKS, someone had responded, I NIBBLE THIN HENS. Nick grinned, zipped himself up and flushed the chain.

He walked out of the cubicle into carnage.

The first thing that registered was the blood, The shocking redness of it, like an assault on his senses. It was everywhere – on the floor, spattered up the walls, on the ceiling. Lying in the middle of the still spreading pools were two bodies, limbs at odd angles like broken dolls, heads replaced by what looked like a pulp of scarlet papier mâché tangled with hair. One was a woman's body, her coral-coloured sweatshirt soaked with blood, a pair of espadrilles dangling from her otherwise bare feet.

The other body was a child's, a little girl's. She was lying on her back, one of her arms twisted awkwardly beneath her body, the other outflung, fingers curled inwards as though to catch a ball. She was wearing a school uniform and very shiny patent leather shoes. A Hanson badge was pinned on her breast pocket. Blood speckled her bare legs and white ankle-socks.

Strangely, the man – the killer – was the last thing that registered in Nick's mind.

The man was in his late thirties, a little overweight, balding on top. His hair was fluffed up on one side as though he had been lying on it. He was gripping a shotgun in both hands, holding it slightly awkwardly as if unused to doing so. Despite his crazed, empty eyes and the drool glistening on his lips and chin, he wore a business suit and a white shirt with a neatly-tied tie. His brown shoes were almost as shiny as the little girl's.

He looked at Nick, his eyes seeming to slide in their sockets. His face was filmed with sweat. He looked ill.

'Genesis,' he croaked. 'It's breaking through . . .'

Then he put the shotgun in his mouth and pulled the trigger.

Two

The shotgun blast was like a physical force that spanked Nick's ears and thrummed in his chest. He stood, frozen, as the man's head erupted in an outspray of blood and brains and bone, some of which hit the mirror behind him, some of which fountained into the air and fell like thick red rain. Oddly, the sight sparked a scintilla of memory in Nick's mind: a friend of his, an ex-police photographer, had once shown Nick a selection of his snaps of suicides and murder victims. Nick had been disturbed by them primarily because they looked so unreal: the dead had looked like half-finished mannequins, their faces slack and inhuman, their injuries like clumsy special effects. It was the *knowledge* that they were the real thing – real human beings – that had made them horrifying.

Such was the case now. Nick watched as the man's body, virtually headless now, folded up in slow motion, like a piece of furniture. Still holding the gun, the dead man dropped forward on to his knees, then tilted backwards, and then, finally, rolled round and landed heavily on his side, the stock of the shotgun clunking against the floor and skidding from his grasp.

Nick's ears unblocked. Suddenly he could hear again the toilet cistern filling, the thump of music from outside. A single thought, peculiarly calm and rational, crystallised in his mind: *If someone were to walk in here now and see this, they would think I'd done it.*

Then, abruptly, whatever barriers his mind had erected to deal with the scene crumbled, and he ran on stumbling legs to the door, gasping and blubbering. He crashed out into the dark din of the club, and instantly it was as though the band and the crowd sucked his energy out of him to use for themselves. He wanted to get away from this place, but he couldn't move another step. His legs felt soft, hollow.

He stumbled away from the toilet door and collapsed against the wall, which felt cold and greasy against his back, even through his shirt and leather jacket. Though he was shuddering deep inside, his skin, by contrast, was sizzling, as though ice were forming churningly in his stomach, spreading outwards, forcing the heat to flee his flesh.

All at once the ice seemed to bubble upwards into his gullet. He leaned over and opened his mouth, and a second later that night's pasta and beer was gushing out of him. He continued to retch even after his stomach was empty, until his head felt like a squeezed orange, liquid running from his nose and eyes.

Finally the urge to vomit subsided, and he slumped back against the wall, panting and shaking, utterly enervated. He wasn't sure how long he sat there – time seemed to slide away from him for a while, just as it had done in the bad old days – before a woman's voice, close to his ear, asked, 'Are you all right?'

Nick didn't realise his eyes were closed until he opened them. Even so he smelled the woman's perfume before he saw her. He breathed the fragrance in, grasping it with his senses as if it were a lifeline. At first the woman herself was merely a close physical presence, her face a collection of shadows. Then she moved back, shifting into focus. Nick had to resist an urge to reach out and touch her cheek, just to confirm that she was real and warm and alive.

'Are you all right?' she asked again, shouting above the music.

Nick began to nod, then shook his head. 'No. In there . . . there's a man with a gun. He's killed a girl and a woman. Blood everywhere.'

The woman was in her late twenties. She had short dark hair, large brown eyes, delicate features. She was slim, athletic-looking. Her sleeveless purple mini-dress and dark stockings were a little too elegant for the Gridlock. She frowned.

'What do you mean?'

Nick gesticulated, a little wildly. '*In there*! They're dead! Blood up the walls, on the ceiling. There was a man with a gun. He killed them, then he killed himself.'

The woman looked at him hard, clearly unsure how to take this.

A little desperately Nick said, 'I'm not drunk. And I haven't been doing drugs. I don't.'

He'd been about to add 'any more' – but wouldn't the over-emphatic denial actually have the opposite effect?

Coming to a decision, the woman said, 'I'll go and see.'

'No!' Nick grabbed her arm, shaking his head. 'You don't *want* to see. It's horrible. Maybe we should just call the police.'

She pulled her arm from his grasp gently but firmly. 'You just try and relax. Sit here, put your head between your legs and take deep breaths. I'll only be a moment. I'll just stick my head round the door.'

Nick nodded, too shaken to argue further. As the woman stood up, he did what she had instructed, closing his eyes and taking deep breaths, trying to convince himself that he could not smell blood, only smoke and sweat.

The woman was back within seconds. She crouched in front of him again. 'There's nothing there,' she said.

Nick looked at her. 'What do you mean?'

Her face was deadpan. 'There's nothing there. No bodies, no blood – nothing. It's just a normal toilet.'

'But . . . it can't be,' Nick said. 'I saw it! It was real.'

'Go and see for yourself,' the woman said.

Nick thought of the little girl's patent leather shoes, the way the man's body had folded forward before thudding to the floor like a sack of coal . . . 'No,' he said, 'I can't.'

'I'll come with you,' the woman said calmly. 'Look, I'll even hold your hand.' She took his hand firmly in hers, meshing their fingers together.

In any other situation, Nick might have told her not to treat him like a child, but now he was grateful for the human contact, and almost absurdly moved that she was prepared to share this experi-ence with him. He squeezed her hand and, with her help, hauled himself to his feet. He had seen some bad things in his time, but it was hard making himself walk back towards that toilet door again. He found it difficult to catch his breath.

The woman reached out to the door; before pushing it open she turned to him. 'Ready?'

He nodded, trying to look determined.

She pushed the door open and led him inside.

As he stepped forward, Nick felt his breath rise and solidify in the base of his throat. Light rushed into his vision, over-bright, as if someone had woken him by shining a torch full into his face. Momentarily blind, he faltered, but felt a tug on his hand and tottered forward a couple more steps. Then the glare drained away and he was blinking around at the room that just minutes before had resembled an abattoir.

The woman was right.

There were no bodies. No blood. Nothing to suggest anything remotely out of the ordinary had taken place here.

For a few moments Nick could only gape, unable to say or do anything. The woman watched him patiently, apparently content to let him come to terms with the situation in his own time. Finally he cleared his throat, though his voice still felt thick and clogged.

'I don't understand this,' he said. 'I know what I saw.' He looked at the woman and said firmly, 'I'm not mad.'

'I never said you were,' said the woman, a little indignantly.

Nick raised a hand in apology. 'No, you didn't, I'm sorry. You've been really kind and understanding. I mean, I could be anyone . . .' He attempted a laugh, but didn't quite manage it. A little desperately, he asked, 'What do *you* think I saw?'

The woman shrugged. 'There is a theory that buildings retain the energy of violent events, and that sometimes, when the atmospheric conditions are right, those events are re-enacted.'

'Ghosts?' said Nick.

She shrugged again. 'Well, that's one way of putting it, I suppose.'

Nick thought for a minute. 'Maybe I ought to try and find out if what I saw did happen here once. But then again . . . I don't know . . . those people were wearing modern clothes.' He sighed and shook his head. 'Oh, I don't know. I probably just imagined the whole thing.'

'Why? Are you prone to imagining things?'

'No, but . . . well, what I said before – about taking drugs. I don't do them now, but I took a lot of drugs when I was younger. I mean, a *lot* of drugs. I was such a mess I would take anything, and half the time I didn't know what I was taking. If someone gave me a pill I would swallow it; if they gave me a needle I would stick it in a vein. So maybe what I saw was some kind of flashback or something. I mean, I've been clean for fifteen years,

10

but LSD flashbacks can happen years later. Maybe I've just had my first one.'

'Is that likely?' said the woman. 'I mean, I don't know anything about drugs—'

Nick shook his head. His shock and tension was ebbing away now, leaving him exhausted and depressed. 'I don't know. Look, thanks for all your help and everything, but I think I just want to get out of here.'

'I'll drive you,' said the woman. 'My car's just outside.'

'You don't have to do that.'

'I want to,' she said. 'I was about to leave anyway, and I don't like the thought of leaving you to tube it by yourself, not after what you've been through. Where do you live?'

'Belsize Park,' said Nick.

'Then it's on my way,' said the woman. 'I live in Hendon. Let's go now, before the crowds start piling out. The band must be on their second encore.'

Nick sighed. 'Okay. My name's Nick, by the way. Nick Finch.'

The woman smiled and squeezed his hand which she was still holding. 'Jenna Trenchard,' she said.

Three

'Here,' said Nick.

Jenna squeezed her maroon Fiat Uno into a space between a grey BMW and a white Citroën. Latimer Street, where Nick lived, was wide and tree-lined, the terraced houses – around half of which had been converted into flats – tall and narrow, with minuscule front gardens, most of which were paved over, and steps leading up to their front doors. Nick lived at number 40, where an overhead lamp threw a cone of light across the entrance porch like an invitation.

He had spoken little on the drive back, except to give Jenna directions in monosyllables. Though he felt better than he had in the Gridlock, he couldn't rid himself of the judder of reaction deep in his belly, or the sense of depression – almost despair – that had come over him after the initial shock of what he had witnessed (or *thought* he had witnessed) had faded.

Evidently sensing his mood and understanding what was required, Jenna had kept up a steady, though never irritating, stream of casual chatter. She had supplied Nick with information about herself which, though it hadn't exactly taken his mind off his experience, had at least managed to divert it a little.

She was twenty-seven years old. She had moved to London from Colchester five years ago, and she worked as PA to a literary agent in Chelsea. When the one-way conversation threatened to flag, Jenna had reached across Nick into the glove compartment, pulled out a tape and slotted it into the cassette player, turning it up just loud enough to allow them still to talk without raising their voices.

The tape proved to be an early Manic Street Preachers album,

Gold Against The Soul, which got them talking about music. Jenna had a large collection of CDs and tapes and went to a lot of gigs – often alone, because most of her friends only listened to 'bland, unoriginal drivel'.

'I mean,' she said, 'how you can listen to Celine Dion without being lobotomised first is beyond me. And as for Robson and bloody Jerome . . .' She stuck out her tongue and made a gagging sound.

When she switched off the engine – the music cutting out halfway through Nick's favourite track, *Life Becoming A Landslide*, and the tape jumping from its slot – silence invaded the car. Nick felt it rushing at him, engulfing him. Then Jenna leaned over and briefly patted his leg. 'I'm not usually this pushy, but I think you need a coffee and someone to talk to.'

Nick briefly considered telling her that she'd done more than enough, that he'd be fine now, but for once the thought of going up to his top-floor flat alone didn't appeal to him. 'I'll make *you* a coffee,' he said, and attempted a smile. 'I think it's the least I can do.'

Entering his flat was like finding sanctuary; he didn't think he had ever found familiarity so comforting. As always he had left a lamp burning, and an album – this time *Becoming X* by the Sneaker Pimps – softly playing on repeat to greet him when he got home.

Jenna recognised the music immediately. She followed him along the narrow hallway, past the two doors on the left, bathroom and bedroom, to the main room.

'Nice flat,' she said.

It *was* a nice flat. Small, but it suited Nick's needs very well. Because it was on the top floor, the ceiling in the main room sloped at both ends to accommodate the roof. One side of the room contained his sofa, coffee table and TV; the other his desk, filing cabinet and music system. The walls were lined with shelves which were packed with books and magazines and videos, with vinyl LPs and singles, CDs and tapes. Any spare inch of wall-space that was not covered by shelving was decorated with framed covers of music papers and magazines, or with photographs of rock stars – performing live, posing, partying. Some of the photographs included Nick. There he was with Nick Cave; there with Keith from The Prodigy; there with The

13

Stranglers' Jean-Jacques Burnel; there with Elvis Costello, there with Supergrass, there with Courtney Love.

'How come you've met all these people?' Jenna said, raising her voice as Nick entered the small kitchen leading off from the main room.

'It's my job,' Nick said, filling the kettle and selecting the two mugs which were least disfigured by tannin stains. 'I'm a music journalist.'

'Really?' She appeared at the kitchen doorway, eyes shining. 'Wow, that's something I'd *love* to do. How did you get into that?'

'By accident, really. I started off as a photographer, but my photos weren't that good – I was barely scraping a living. One day I was commissioned to take some pictures of the Happy Mondays to go with an interview that a friend of mine was doing, but my friend got held up in traffic and I ended up doing the interview as well as the pictures. It sort of snowballed from there.'

'Wow. Sex and drugs and rock'n'roll, eh?'

Nick grimaced. 'To be honest, there's been little of the former, and I had more than enough drugs to last me a lifetime before I got into journalism. But yeah – the music's still good. I never lose the buzz of discovering a new band. And it's great talking to people whose work you admire, finding out what makes them tick.'

Whilst Nick finished making the coffee, Jenna asked him a stream of almost breathless questions about the people he'd met; some of them fleetingly, some of them often enough for them to become acquaintances, even friends. As Nick answered her questions, telling her of wild nights spent with Blur, with Shane McGowan, with Shaun Ryder, he felt the judder of reaction in his belly lessen a little, felt the despair that had set in earlier slowly being overlayed by the pleasure of this woman's company.

They re-entered the main room and sat on the sofa, Nick clearing aside issues of *Q*, *Time Out*, *NME* and *Loaded* to make room on the coffee table for their mugs and a tin of chocolate digestives. They munched and drank and talked, mostly about music. When the coffee was finished, Nick said, 'I fancy something stronger. I've got some red wine in the kitchen. Would you like a glass?'

Jenna looked thoughtful. 'Maybe just one. I'm driving, remember.'

'It's Australian,' Nick said, returning from the kitchen

14

moments later and handing her a receptacle that was more goblet than glass. 'Cheeky but not impertinent; fruity but not saucy.'

Jenna smiled. 'You seem to be feeling better.'

'Do I? Well, you have to learn to shrug off bad experiences or they take you under.'

'You sound like an expert.'

'Not really. I've seen and done some bad things, I suppose.'

'Such as?'

'Oh, you wouldn't like me if I started telling you my life story. You'd be looking for the quickest way out of here.'

'What does that mean?'

Nick smiled and shook his head. 'You'd wonder what sort of person you'd got yourself involved with.'

Looking frustrated, Jenna took a gulp of wine. 'I'm very open-minded. Besides, you've got me intrigued now.'

Nick laughed. 'I'll tell you what – have some more wine with me and I'll tell all. How does that sound?'

'It sounds like the sort of line someone who was trying to get a girl drunk would come out with.'

'Oh shit, does it? I didn't mean it like that. I just meant, if I'm going to start pouring out my life story to a complete stranger, I'd like us both to be equally sozzled. Just so I don't feel like a tosser in the morning.'

'And what about the fact that I've got to drive home?' said Jenna teasingly.

'I'll pay for a cab. Hendon's not that far away.'

She took another sip of wine, appearing to consider it. 'You seem very keen on telling me all of a sudden. Three minutes ago you were being Mr Evasive.'

'Yeah, well, I suppose I'm psyched up for it now. Besides, it's . . . oh, this is going to sound so dumb.'

'Go on.'

'Well, I'd just . . . really like you to stay for a while. I know I said you've got to put bad experiences behind you, but I don't want to give what happened tonight the chance to get into my head. I want someone to talk to, and I want to get blind drunk while I'm doing it, so that when my head finally does hit the pillow I'll go spark out – no nightmares, no bad memories, nothing.'

'That's a very mature approach,' Jenna said, deadpan.

'Yeah,' said Nick. 'I thought so too.'

'But what about tomorrow? How will you feel then?'

'Hungover, I should imagine.'

'I mean, about what happened tonight.'

Nick shrugged. 'I'll be okay by tomorrow. It's just tonight I need to get through.'

She said nothing for a long moment. Then, abruptly, she held out her glass. 'Go on then. I'm prepared to make any sacrifice for a good cause.'

Glasses refilled, they sat at opposite ends of the sofa, Nick with one leg up on the coffee table. 'Where shall I start?'

'You said you got involved in drugs when you were younger.'

'Yeah.'

'So start there.'

'Okay. Right. Well, I was eighteen when I started getting into drugs. I was in a band and we did regular gigs at this real dive called the Ace of Spades, in Deptford. There was this guy called Spike who used to come to our gigs, and I got to know him quite well. He really used to love our band. He'd come up to us afterwards when we were putting our stuff away, and tell us that we were the best band in London, and that when we got on *Top Of The Pops* we were to remember him and give him a wave. He looked about sixty-odd, but he was probably younger than that. He was always drugged up to the eyeballs, and he had really long grey hair and a little wizened face as if he'd been left out in the sun too long. The other lads used to avoid him, leaving Muggins here to talk to him. We used to joke – behind his back – that he was really the head of EMI, and that any day now he was going to offer us a recording contract.

'What he did offer me one day, though, was some speed. I took it off him because I wanted to look cool, and although I didn't use it for a while I didn't throw it away either. And then things started getting really heavy in my private life, and one day I just thought, "Fuck it."' The speed made me feel fantastic, took me out of myself, made my problems seem trivial.

'Of course, once that wore off I wanted more, to make me feel good again. It wasn't long before Spike was supplying me with stuff on a regular basis. I started selling things that I owned – my records, my bike – to pay for what he got me. Finally I sold my guitar and quit the band, and – to cut a long, sordid story very short – moved into a squat in Dagenham with Spike and a load of other smack-heads.

'I was hooked on heroin by this time. My whole life was centred around getting money for my next fix. Eventually I was so desperate that I held up a petrol station with a plastic gun. What I *didn't* do, because I was too fucked in the head, was cover my face, and so I got caught on the security cameras and arrested within three days of committing the robbery. I was sent to prison for five years. They let me out after three – good behaviour.

'I cold-turkeyed in prison, got off the drugs for good. When I got out twelve years ago I was clean as a whistle. I've stayed clean ever since.'

He leaned forward and grabbed the wine bottle to avoid looking at Jenna. He poured more wine for both of them. 'So now you know.'

'Yes,' she said, her voice betraying nothing, 'now I know.'

He risked a glance at her. She was not recoiling in horror, or edging away from him, or looking at him as if he were the Anti-Christ; she was simply sitting there, drinking her wine.

'So what do you *think*?' he said.

She raised her eyebrows and pressed her lips together. 'What do you want me to think?' she asked.

'Well, aren't you . . . horrified? Worried? Surprised?'

'I'm not horrified,' she said, 'or worried. Why should I be? It's not as if you're a serial killer or a rapist, is it? You got into trouble when you were younger and you paid for it. It's all in the past.'

'A lot of people get put off when they find out what you're capable of, though. Then there're the people who suck up to you because they think it's cool to be friends with a criminal. They're even worse.'

'Yeah, well, that's their problem,' Jenna said. 'I don't judge people by what they've done, I judge them by what they're like.'

'And what am I like?' asked Nick.

'Awful,' she said, straight-faced, then laughed, almost spilling her wine. 'Sorry, but you asked for that one.'

He grinned. 'I guess I did. I'll go and open another bottle.'

Whilst Nick busied himself with the corkscrew in the kitchen, Jenna browsed through his CDs. 'Mind if I change this music?' she called. 'It's a good album, but it palls a bit after you've heard it twenty-six times in a row.'

He told her to go ahead and she selected a Tom Waits album. 'Mood music,' she told him as he reappeared with the wine. When they were both sitting down again and he was tilting the new bottle towards her glass, she said abruptly, 'So this thing that happened to you tonight – nothing like it has ever happened before?'

Nick didn't answer her for a moment, and when he did he said, 'You surprise me.'

'Do I? Why?'

'Well, it's just that you haven't asked me what it's really like in prison. Most people – those who don't run off screaming – are dying to know.'

She gave a small, secretive smile. 'How do *you* know I don't already know what it's like?' she said.

Nick blinked. 'Do you?'

'Well . . . no, but . . . Oh, I don't know. I suppose I didn't want to be predictable. I've already done the whole gushing pop-star thing – you must get that all the time as well. I thought maybe you wouldn't want to talk about it, or that you'd tell me in your own time.'

That phrase lingered between them for a moment. Was Nick reading too much into it, or was Jenna intimating that she would like to continue their relationship beyond this evening?

He smiled. 'I don't mind talking about it. It wasn't a nice experience, but it was a long time ago. It hasn't traumatised me for life or anything. But to answer your earlier question: no, nothing like what happened tonight has ever happened to me before.' Then he frowned and murmured, 'Though having said that, I have been feeling a bit – odd lately.'

'Odd? How do you mean?'

His frown deepened. 'It's hard to explain. I keep feeling as though . . . as though I'm on the verge of remembering something really important, but before I can grasp what it is it slips away. Also I've been having these recurring dreams . . . nightmares, I suppose you'd call them.'

'Really?' she said. 'Related to what happened tonight?'

'No, I don't think so.' He looked down into his glass, then took a long swallow.

'Do you want to tell me about them?' she asked gently.

'You don't want to hear them. There's nothing more boring than listening to other people's dreams.'

18

'No, really, I'm interested. I'm not just being polite.'

'Well . . . okay, then. In one dream I'm one of a group of children. We're sitting in the back of an army jeep being driven by soldiers. They're not English soldiers, they're . . . I don't know . . . Middle Eastern, perhaps. They're all carrying machine guns and wearing sweaty, short-sleeved green shirts and big boots, and they're all talking together loudly in this foreign language.

'There's a real sense of . . . threat. Danger. We're all huddled together, trying to look as anonymous as possible, trying not to draw attention to ourselves.

'Eventually the jeep stops and the soldiers jabber together for a minute, then make us all get out at gunpoint. It's hot and bright. We're on a dusty road in the middle of an area of scrubland. The soldiers are pointing ahead, as though they can see something on the road. We can't see it. They make us all get into a line and then they send the first child ahead, a little girl. They shout at her, jab her with their rifles, use their fingers to make her understand that they want her to walk in a zig-zag pattern. She starts to do so, looking unhappy and confused. Then suddenly there's an explosion and the ground erupts beneath her feet. When the dust clears, there's nothing left of the little girl except a red tangled mess.

'Suddenly I realise what we're being used for. The road is booby-trapped with land mines and we're being sent ahead to set them off, to make the way safe for the jeep to pass. One by one we're made to walk in front of the jeep in the same zig-zag pattern as the little girl. As one child is killed or maimed, another is pushed forward to fill its place.

'Not all the children are killed outright. Some have their feet or legs blown off and because their injuries are so massive they can't even scream or cry properly. They just lie there, staring and shaking and convulsing, making little keening or whimpering sounds like a sick animal. The soldiers ignore the injured children – they're nothing to them. At one point a soldier raises his rifle, presumably to end the misery of a little boy who has had both of his legs blown off, and the other soldiers jabber at him. I don't understand their language but I understand the meaning of what they're saying: Leave him. Don't waste your bullets. The child will be dead soon enough.'

Nick seemed to have descended into a trance-like state during the telling. Now he looked up at Jenna and shuddered.

'That's horrible,' Jenna breathed as Nick quickly gulped the wine from his glass and poured more for himself. 'How does the dream end?'

'I always wake up before it's my turn,' Nick said. 'I get more and more terrified until eventually it yanks me awake.'

'Are your other dreams just as bad?' she asked.

'There's only one other one. It's pretty bad, yes, but it's not as long. In this one I'm strapped down in a chair, like a dentist's chair. I can't see anything because there's this really bright light shining in my eyes, but in the background I can hear a high-pitched whirring sound and people talking, though I can't hear what they're saying. Then the whirring comes closer and all at once I can feel something cold and sharp against my head. I try to open my mouth to scream, but my mouth is taped up. Just as I feel the sharp thing start to cut into my head I wake up.'

Jenna was stretched out like a cat now, relaxed by the wine, her dark-stockinged legs crossed at the ankles. 'Have you any idea what these dreams might mean?' she asked.

Nick pulled a face. 'I'm not sure they *mean* anything. Aren't nightmares supposed to be just a manifestation of everyday anxieties or something?'

'Have you been particularly anxious lately?' asked Jenna.

'Not really,' said Nick, then smiled. 'No more than normal.'

This was not strictly true. Recently he had been unable to shake off the feeling that he was being watched and sometimes even followed. Once or twice he had seen a grey unmarked van with blacked-out windows parked in the street below. However, he elected not to tell Jenna this, deciding that there was only so much he could reveal about himself before he would begin to sound completely crazy.

'Are you hungry?' he asked suddenly.

Taken aback, Jenna said, 'Er . . . not especially. I've stuffed myself full of biscuits. Why?'

'I'm starving,' said Nick. 'It must be all this soul-baring. I've got these really delicious turkey sausages from Sainsbury's. Do you fancy a sandwich?'

'At half past one in the morning?' she said.

'Yeah, why not? Let's live a little. I'll open another bottle of wine.'

She laughed. 'Go on then.'

Nick jumped up from the sofa and loped into the kitchen. 'Put some more music on if you like,' he called over his shoulder.

She did so, then browsed around the room, examing the effects of Nick's life. She picked up a framed photograph that was sitting on Nick's untidy desk; the photo showed an attractive blonde girl wearing a baggy white T-shirt. 'Who's this?' she asked, carrying it into the kitchen. 'Your girlfriend?'

The sausages were sizzling under the grill; Nick glanced at the photograph as he buttered slices of wholemeal bread. He laughed. 'I'll take that as a compliment. No, it's my daughter, Sasha.'

She raised her eyebrows. 'Your *daughter*? You must have married very young.'

'Sasha's mother and I never married. She got pregnant when we were both seventeen. It was just a one-night thing, but she decided to keep the baby. That was one of the reasons why I got into drugs – not that I'm blaming her. I just couldn't handle the situation.'

'You must have stayed in touch, though.'

'Yeah. Sasha's brilliant – we get on really well. She lives in Muswell Hill with Linsey – her mum. We see each other once or twice a week. Even Linsey and I get on okay. It's a good situation.'

'She's very beautiful,' said Jenna.

'Takes after her father,' replied Nick, and opened the cupboard above the sink. 'Jenna, do you mind if I ask you a very serious question?'

'No, of course not,' she said a little cautiously. 'Ask away.'

He turned and looked at her, his face grave. 'Would you like brown sauce or ketchup on your sausages?'

Four

'What's the situation?' asked DI Baker, opening the car door and sliding into the passenger seat.

DS Leyland, sleeves rolled up, tie loosely knotted, bullet-proof vest visible beneath his white cotton shirt, was hunched forward in the driver's seat talking into a two-way radio. The quiet suburban street, containing houses with festoon blinds at the windows and BMWs parked in gravel driveways, had been cordoned off. Beyond a line of police barriers manned by uniformed PCs a curious crowd was already gathering, despite the fact that dawn had broken barely half an hour earlier. Leyland glanced at Baker and spoke into the radio. 'The DI's here now, Ian. I'll just bring him up to speed. Keep in touch.' He put the radio aside, then twisted round to face his superior, puffing with the effort.

Leyland was not yet forty, but already he had the bloated, mottled, sweaty look of a man whose staple diet consisted of plentiful amounts of alcohol, tobacco and saturated fat. Baker, by contrast, though ten years Leyland's senior, was slight, almost scrawny. He had a gingery fuzz of hair, hollow cheekbones, a neat moustache and eyes that were sharp as diamond chips.

'Thirty-seven-year-old businessman, sir,' Leyland said without preamble, 'name of Michael Mercy. It seems he's holding his wife and seven-year-old daughter hostage at gunpoint. The next-door neighbour heard what she claimed was Mr Mercy shouting at approximately three thirty a.m. and went to investigate. She said that after ringing the doorbell several times, Mr Mercy, looking distraught, stuck his head out of an upper-floor window and shouted, "Go away. Leave us alone." When the neighbour – a Mrs

22

Murgatroyd – offered to help, Mercy pointed a gun at her. She got the message and buggered off back home. Then she called us.'

Baker listened to this with a pained, almost disapproving look. 'Has Mercy got any previous?'

Leyland shook his walrus-like head. 'No, sir. Not so much as a parking offence.'

'Any recent family problems?'

'Doesn't seem so, sir. Most of the neighbours we spoke to seemed to think the Mercys were an ideal couple – well-suited, very happy. They said the little girl was no trouble either.'

'Hmm,' said Baker. 'What about Mercy's medical history? Any indication of mental illness, depression?'

'Not as far as we're aware, sir.'

'Okay,' said Baker. 'I assume the area has been cleared.'

'Yes, sir.'

'Good. So what sort of weapon are we dealing with here, Mike?'

'Well, the next-door neighbour only got a quick look at it, but Mercy does own a twelve-bore. He's had it since '89. He's a fully paid-up member of a local gun club. We've been trying to rouse the president for his assessment of Mercy's character and recent state of mind, but he's not answering his phone.'

'I'm not surprised,' said Baker. 'It *is* only six o'clock in the morning. Why do the people who do these things always pick such anti-social hours?'

Leyland grinned in sympathy and used a forefinger to flick sweat from his brow. 'Fancy some tea, sir? From the way things have been going it looks like we could be here for the duration.'

'Yeah, go on then. I don't suppose you could rustle up a slice of toast while you're at it, could you?'

'Sorry, sir,' said Leyland, plucking a thermos flask from between his feet and unscrewing the lid. He poured his superior a cup of tea and handed it across.

Taking it, Baker said, 'Our man not talking then, I take it?'

'No, sir, hasn't spoken a word to us. First time we tried to ring him he cut the wires. Geoff and Jayne are out there now with the megaphone, but he's not having any of it, sir. Hasn't even looked out the window.'

'Stubborn bugger,' said Baker, sipping his tea. 'How many men have we got at the house?'

23

'Six, sir. Two at front and back, one at each side.'

'How many exits?'

'Two, sir, front and back, though there's also a connecting door from the kitchen to the garage. Ian Wilkie at green says there's a red Peugot parked in there. We haven't confirmed the registration, but the Mercys do own one. Their BMW is parked on the drive.'

'Right,' said Baker, finishing his tea. 'Well, I'd better wander over there, give it a go with the megaphone, though I don't suppose for a moment it'll do any good. I take it there have been no sightings of the Mercys since this Mrs Murgatroyd spoke to them . . . what . . . nearly three hours ago?'

'Not even so much as a twitching curtain, sir.'

The words were barely out of Leyland's mouth when the two policemen heard a crack, and then another, like fireworks going off. Instantly Baker pounced on the radio and snatched it up. 'Ian? This is Baker. What's happening?'

The reply, laced with static, was urgent though not panicky. 'Two shots from inside the house, sir. We're going in.'

Baker tossed the radio on to the dashboard. 'Come on, Mike, let's get over there.'

He shoved the car door open, leaped out and began running up the street, the crowd at the barrier pushing forward, craning their necks to see. Leyland puffed gamely after him, cheeks purple, sweat sheening his face.

Mercy's house was around the next corner, number 84 Primrose Gardens. Crouching down behind a low wall at the corner, their heads bobbing up to see what was going on, were Detective Sergeants Geoff Beaumont and Jayne Firbeck. Firbeck was holding a megaphone. She half-turned when Baker came scurrying up, Leyland panting a dozen yards behind him.

'What's happening?' asked Baker.

'They've just gone in, sir,' Firbeck said.

'Which is Mercy's house?'

'That one across the road, sir, with the postbox outside it.'

It was a large detached house, set back from the road, with a high hedge running along the left-hand perimeter. It would have looked like a perfectly ordinary suburban home in a quiet, affluent, middle-class neighbourhood, if it hadn't been for the fact that the green front door was hanging off its hinges.

24

There was another bang, this one louder, causing Baker and his colleagues instinctively to duck. The echoes of the sound, sharp and ringing, seemed to bounce back from the surrounding buildings. In this setting, the sound of gunfire was incongruous, and therefore seemed all the more terrible.

'Shit,' Baker muttered. 'What's *happening* in there?'

As if in answer to his question, a man wearing a bulky padded jacket and a peaked cap appeared at the shattered front door. He was carrying a rifle, though was holding it in a casual fashion. It was because of this, and his general air of dejected defeat that Baker felt the cold grind of dread fill his belly.

The man raised his arm and slowly waved, giving the all-clear. Baker and his colleagues rose from cover and began to trudge towards the house. None of them said anything.

The flowerbeds fringing the front lawn of the Mercys' house were a riot of colour. Baker didn't know much about flowers, but he recognised snowdrops and peach-coloured tulips and the frilly yellow bonnets of daffodils.

Ian Wilkie, head of the SWAT team, looked so impassive that the grind of dread in Baker's stomach intensified, becoming almost painful. 'What happened?' Baker muttered.

'They're all dead, sir,' said Wilkie, neutrally. 'They're in the front room. Mercy shot his wife and daughter and then killed himself, right in front of us.'

'Shit,' muttered Baker, sickened, then hissed out through his teeth as though the horror of the news could be expelled that way. 'Did he say anything before he pulled the trigger?'

'Yes, sir, but it didn't make much sense, he looked pretty far gone. He said, "Genesis. It's breaking through." '

'Genesis? What does that mean?'

Wilkie shrugged. 'Search me, sir.'

Baker sighed deeply. 'All right, I suppose we'd better take a look. Geoff, can you organise everyone, get them down here?'

'Right away, sir,' said DS Beaumont, and slipped away gratefully.

Baker, Leyland and Firbeck entered the house, following Wilkie down the hallway. They were still several paces away from the half-open door of the front room when Baker smelled the blood. It was an alien, invasive smell: the smell of madness. *Yes*, he thought, his mind focused, oddly calm, as it always became at

25

these moments, *madness came into this house this morning and did its terrible work.*

On the threshold of the lounge, Baker had to pause to work out exactly what he was looking at. Blood was everywhere; the sight of it assaulted his senses. For a few seconds he could see nothing *but* blood; the spatters and stains and speckles and streaks made everything else meaningless. He looked again and saw the little girl, the woman and the man, their bodies sprawled unnaturally so that they did not look quite human. Their faces were gone, torn away by the gunshots that had killed them. A maroon porridge of brains and bone and hair and flesh textured the blood on the walls and floor and furniture.

Though the room was silent, it seemed to scream with the madness of what had taken place here. Wilkie's voice came like a jolt, an intrusion.

'Have you noticed the walls, sir?'

For one ludicrous moment Baker thought Wilkie was referring to the fact that they were covered in blood. Nevertheless, he gazed at the walls. And suddenly, as though something indefinable had come into focus, he saw what had been written in pencil there.

It was a list of perhaps two dozen names, repeated over and over, covering every square inch of the pale wallpaper from floor to ceiling. Astounded, Baker began to read the list to himself, his lips moving silently. Jason Westmoreland. Julie Lean, Rebecca Butcher. Greg Lousada. Mark Cotto. Nick Finch . . .

Five

Whoever thinks that vegetarians are pale, weedy creatures in need of a good steak meal ought to be introduced to Sasha, thought Nick, turning on to Marshall Street. In the clear early October sunlight, his daughter, standing waiting for him outside Roots 'n' Fruits, seemed to glow, to be suffused with light like some divine presence. Men always paused to stare at her, and to look at Nick with envy when he was with her, which roused strange emotions in him – pride and amusement, and an instinct to gather her to him, protect her from the predators. Once Nick had asked her whether she was aware of the admiring glances she attracted wherever she went, and she had sighed and said in that eminently sensible way of hers, 'I'm not blind, Dad. The thing is to ignore it, not play up to it. What you've got to realise is that every half-decent-looking girl gets the same treatment.'

Sasha, however, was considerably more than half-decent. She was beautiful. Her wheat-coloured hair fell in a cascade of natural ringlets around her shoulders and down her back; she had huge blue eyes with long lashes, a wide, smiling mouth, flawless skin and an amazing figure. She had not inherited Nick's height, but was small like her mother, no taller than five foot four, which made Nick's heart ache sometimes when he watched her striding away from him, back into the big, bad world. She would have laughed at his concern had he voiced it, would have rolled her eyes and said, indulgently, 'Dad, I'm quite capable of looking after myself.' She was a confident, intelligent and well-balanced seventeen-year-old. It was as though she had observed her parents falling into their various traps along the way and had learned from

27

their experience to sidestep them judiciously, picking her route with care and common sense.

Nick was fifteen minutes late, which was not unusual for him. He felt horribly hungover; the light seared his eyes and lanced into his head, and his stomach was a revolving ball of acid. When Sasha saw him, she waved and grinned. Then, when he got closer, her expression became disapproving. 'Dad, you look terrible!'

'I love you too,' he said, putting his arms around her waist and kissing her on the cheek. She smelled fresh, newly minted. She was so full of vibrancy that her hair seemed to fizz against his skin.

'Do you think you can manage something to eat, or will you throw up on me?' she asked.

'Do I really look that bad?'

'I've seen cabbages that aren't as green as you.'

'Sorry. I had a bit of a heavy night last night.'

'So what's new?' she said affectionately.

'Hey, it's not what you think. I'm not the wild man I once was. It's normally slippers and cocoa and a bit of telly before bed these days.'

She smiled. 'So what was last night? A momentary lapse?'

'No, last night was . . . different. Odd.'

'In what way?'

'Come on – I'll tell you inside. It'll probably make me feel better to nibble a lettuce leaf or two.'

They went inside and queued up with their trays, waiting to be served. Though the food looked and smelled delicious, Nick remembered the perilous state of his stomach and reluctantly eschewed the more exotic-looking dishes in favour of a bowl of tomato and bean soup, a small green salad and an apple juice. Sasha, who had inherited not only her father's love of good food but also his enviable ability to stuff himself silly on a regular basis and still remain slim, opted for curried lentil bake, a huge bowl brimming with various types of salad, a potato soda-bread roll, a peppermint tea and a generous slice of pecan pie.

The seating area, busy with chatter and clinking cutlery, was like a bazaar, all low ceilings and pillars. The walls were painted in autumnal swirls of olive green, mustard yellow and brick red, festooned with South American textiles. There were booths along both walls of a corridor leading to the toilets, one of which Nick

28

and Sasha slid into, Sasha taking a while to transfer her various plates and bowls from tray to table.

Nick gingerly sipped his apple juice. After initially shocking his belly into a cramp that made him wince, it acted as a balm, soothing and cooling his roiling guts. Sasha broke her roll open with her fingers and began to butter it.

'So,' she said, squashing the fat down into the bread with her knife, 'what happened last night?'

Nick ate his soup slowly and told her what he had seen in the toilet of the Gridlock. He kept his voice low and avoided meeting her eyes, as if the vision, or hallucination, was something to be ashamed of.

Sasha listened, her eyebrows arched in concern. Though she didn't interrupt she let out shocked murmurs – 'My God' and 'Jesus, Dad' – during natural pauses in the narrative. When he finished, tailing off at the point where he crashed out through the toilet doors and collapsed against the wall, she put down her fork, reached out and squeezed his hand.

'God, Dad, what do you think would make you *see* something like that?' she asked wonderingly.

He shrugged. 'Who knows? I thought it might be some sort of LSD flashback. That or ghosts.' He offered her a tight smile to show that he didn't really consider that a serious possibility.

She frowned. 'Maybe you ought to see a doctor about it.'

'What for?'

'Well . . . just to get checked over. I mean, I don't want to worry you, but maybe there's something wrong with your brain . . .'

'Wrong? In what way?'

She looked flustered, then said, too casually, 'Well, I don't know. Maybe you ought to check that you haven't got a tumour or something.'

'A tumour!' he said, loud enough to make heads turn. He leaned forward and hissed, 'I haven't got a tumour!'

'I know that,' she said firmly, 'but it wouldn't do any harm to see a doctor, would it?'

He shrugged. 'I feel fine. There's nothing wrong with me.'

'No, I know, it's just that people don't normally have hallucinations, not like you did. If I'd seen that, I'd want to know why.'

He was silent for a moment, contemplating his soup.

'Tell me more about this hallucination,' she said. 'I mean, what

29

was it like? Did the people seem real and solid, or was it like a dream? I mean, did you feel as though you were fully awake, or kind of spaced out?'

'I was completely compos mentis,' he said. 'I'd only had one beer, and the people seemed as real as you and I.' He shook his head. 'Don't worry about it. Like I said, it was probably just some kind of flashback. An isolated thing. It won't happen again.'

'This *is* the first time something like this has happened, isn't it?' she asked.

He hesitated before answering, 'Yes.'

'You don't sound too sure.'

'Of course I'm sure. It's just that I've been a bit uptight lately. Overworked, I suppose.'

'I don't see the connection,' she said.

'There *is* no connection,' replied Nick, feeling uncomfortable. Sometimes Sasha could seem like his mother rather than his daughter. Sometimes her questioning became more like an interrogation. She liked to know he was looking after himself and not falling into bad ways.

'Why did you bring it up, then?' she asked. 'Why did you infer that there *was* a connection?'

He sighed. 'You're going to make a great lawyer, you know. I bet you're top of your class, aren't you?'

She smiled. 'It's only because I care about you, Dad.'

'I know,' he said, 'but you don't have to worry about me. I'm okay.'

'So why did you hesitate when I asked if anything like your hallucination had ever happened before?'

'Oh, it's just that recently I've been feeling a bit . . . paranoid, I suppose. I've had this weird feeling that people are watching me. Following me.'

'Have you actually seen anybody?'

'No, but I've noticed this grey van. Sometimes it's parked across the street from my flat. It's got blacked-out windows and no registration plates. I don't know what it is about it, it just . . . unsettles me.'

She shook her head and sighed. 'You must look after yourself, Dad.'

He shrugged sheepishly. 'Like I said, I'm fine. Anyway, last night wasn't all bad. There was one good thing that came out of it.'

'Oh yeah, what was that?'

'I met somebody.'

She blinked, and paused in the act of bringing a forkful of pasta and mango and pumpkin seeds to her mouth. 'How did you manage that?'

He told her about Jenna, how she had helped him at the club, insisted on driving him home, sat up with him half the night, talking.

'She ended up spending the night,' he said innocently.

She gaped. 'I don't believe you! You have this terrible, traumatic experience and you still end up on the pull!'

'She slept on the couch,' he said, grinning. 'She was too pissed to drive home. I didn't let her leave without getting her address and phone number, though.'

Sasha laughed. 'You're incorrigible, Dad.' She chewed for a moment, reflectively. 'All the same, I think you should see a doctor. Promise me that you will?'

'Yes,' he sighed in exasperation, fully intending to keep putting it off until she forgot about it.

The conversation drifted on to other things – Sasha's studies, her on-off relationship with her boyfriend, Dan, and finally Linsey, Sasha's mother.

As soon as Nick mentioned Linsey's name he saw Sasha's shoulders stiffen.

'You two still not getting on well?' he asked.

She sighed. 'I don't seem to be getting on with anybody at the moment – present company excepted, of course.' She looked down at her plate. 'I don't know – we just get on each other's nerves so much lately. It's getting to the stage where I'm thinking of moving out.'

'And going to live with Dan?' said Nick, trying not to show his relief when she shook her head.

'No, that would be an even bigger mistake. I'd probably move in with Ceiron. She's got a really nice place in Shepherd's Bush with a spare room. I'll have to see how things go. I'm not sure whether I'd be able to make enough to pay my half of the rent and keep up my studies at the same time. If I think my studies are going to suffer then I'll stick it out with Mum until next year when I'll be starting my degree course and able to apply for a student loan.'

Nick shook his head in wonder. 'Your common sense never ceases to amaze me. Where do you get it all from?'

'Sainsbury's,' she answered brightly. 'Intelligence counter. One forty-nine a pound.'

He grinned; the soup, combined with Sasha's company, were making him feel much better. 'God, when I was your age I was . . . no, perhaps it's best not to tell you what I was doing when I was your age.'

'I know *exactly* what you were doing. You were in one of the most promising young bands of your generation.'

'Slight exaggeration,' he murmured, then sighed. 'A whole sewer-load of sludge has passed under a thousand bridges since then.'

Her perfectly shaped eyebrows creased in concern. Once again she put down her fork and reached out to stroke the back of his hand. 'You *are* all right, aren't you, Dad?'

He smiled. 'Course I am. Oh, I've got some CDs for you. Promo stuff. Neneh Cherry and Mansun and The Charlatans.'

'Oh, Dad, thanks. That's brilliant.'

'And I've managed to wangle us some tickets to see Portishead next week at the Academy.' He hesitated for a moment. 'Would you mind if I asked Jenna to come along?'

'Of course not,' Sasha said. 'You know I like to vet all your women, make sure they come up to the high standards I have for you.' When he didn't immediately respond, she said gently, 'That was a joke, Dad.'

'What?' he said. 'Sorry – I was looking at your pecan pie. You know, I'm feeling a bit better now. I think I might just be able to force down a slice.'

He said goodbye to Sasha twenty minutes later and made his way through the busy, sunny streets of the West End before plunging into the darkness of the Underground at Oxford Circus to catch a train to East Putney. His photographer was waiting for him outside the abattoir when he arrived, sitting on a low wall and picking his nose, his camera slung around his neck like a baby monkey clinging to its mother.

Thunderhead rolled up in two cabs twenty minutes later, loud and lively and full of cheeky aggression, like playful puppies who might nonetheless be capable of a nasty nip. The A & R man who had travelled with them from World Records was a fussy, nervous individual called Nigel, who offered Nick a damp, boneless hand to shake. Inside the abattoir, the band did their best to keep up their rapid-fire repartee, but Nick noticed that a couple of them looked a little green at the sight of the skinned and dismembered carcasses.

Surprisingly, he himself felt fine. He had thought that after last night an abattoir would be the last place he would want to visit; but the mess and chaos of his experience in the Gridlock made this display of neatly rendered and largely bloodless meat harmless by comparison.

The band perked up again when the photographer, Pete Wickham, pointed his camera at them. They clowned and mugged and posed while Nick watched, already structuring the introduction to his article in his head. PRIME BEEFCAKE would be the headline, he decided, followed by the strapline, *Thunderhead slaughter all opposition.*

When the shoot was over they all made their way to the nearest pub and did the interview, A & R Nigel tagging along like a bad smell. Off-stage Martin Keefe, who today was wearing an orange felt hat that would have looked ridiculous on anyone other than him, turned out to be Thunderhead's quietest member. However, he was also the most thoughtful; intelligent and charismatic, he often cut through the knockabout blather with a sly and incisive comment. It was clearly he who gave the band their identity, their focus. Without him Nick felt sure the group would be just another bunch of no-hopers, banging out Clash covers in the garage on a Sunday afternoon.

The drinking went on until late into the evening, long after the interview was finished. There was a time when Nick would have stayed with it until the bitter end, would have pushed himself to his limit and beyond, but round about ten thirty he excused himself, good-humouredly resisting all attempts to get him to stay. He told the band that he had to do some work on the article tonight, that his deadline was tight and that if he didn't deliver by Friday some other bunch of young pretenders would grab their column space. That shut them up, and he left the pub with their thanks and the promise of eternal friendship ringing in his ears.

He felt only a little guilty as he trudged to the tube station. He didn't really need to work on the article tonight; he'd do it tomorrow easily and have it e-mailed to Stewart by six.

33

Thunderhead had been a decent bunch of lads, and Nick had enjoyed their company despite feeling like their father – or their schoolteacher – at times, but right now he wanted to be on his own. Since prison, when he had been forced to share a cell with two, three, sometimes four other men, he relished his solitude.

His head buzzed pleasantly as he made his way through the dark, quiet and less than salubrious streets. Twice he thought he sensed movement behind him and turned to look, but on each occasion there was nobody there. Both times he shrugged blithely and walked on, the alcohol in his system deadening the unease he might otherwise have felt.

The station was devoid of people, as was the carriage he got into after the train came clanking along the rails and groaned to a halt. As it moved off, Nick looked at his reflection in the black mirror of the opposite window, above a splotch of grease where a day's worth of passengers had rested their heads. *Yeah*, he thought. *For a raddled old rock'n'roll junkie you don't look too bad, Nick old boy. You don't look too bad at all.*

He dozed for a while, slumped in his seat, eventually coming to with a jolt. For some reason he had the confused impression that he had been asleep for hours, that the train was long past its desig- nated destinations and was now roaring through an uncharted area of blackness, far too fast, out of control. He struggled upright, his back sticky with sweat, his long legs – which had straddled the aisle – made clumsy by the numbness in his buttocks. It was only as he rubbed a hand across his face to enliven it that he realised he was no longer alone.

At the far end of the carriage, sitting next to one another, were a man and a woman. They sat primly upright, staring straight ahead, not talking, their hands folded in their laps. They were dressed smartly, in suits and matching grey overcoats. They were both in their late twenties, both blandly attractive. In a crowd, Nick might not have glanced at them twice, but right now they gave him the creeps. He sensed no immediate physical threat from them, yet he couldn't shake off the feeling that they were *too* anonymous, *too* bland. He felt like leaning towards them and asking them how many more stops to Stepford, just to see if they got the joke.

He tried an experiment; he cleared his throat loudly and abruptly, to see what their reaction would be. He half-expected

34

them to turn their heads slowly in unison to look at him, but in fact they showed no reaction at all. They merely continued to stare straight ahead like incredibly life-like robots, waiting for someone to switch them on.

The train plunged through darkness. Nick wished it would come to a station so that he could shake off the clinging feeling of disorientation, unreality. The train clanked as it took a corner and the lights in the carriage flickered. *In the darkness they'll make their move*, Nick thought involuntarily. He licked his lips.

Then light bled into the tunnel and suddenly they *were* in a station. For an instant it seemed like a mirage, the ivory-tiled walls glaring with brightness, blurred clots of shadow dotting the platform. Nick's eyes managed to snag the destination sign – Notting Hill Gate – and it felt like casting out an anchor, dragging the train to a screeching halt.

The blurs on the platform solidified into people. Normality settled inside him, and with it a sense of amused self-reproach. As he stood up and made his way to the door, so did the smart young couple. Nick glanced at them, and indeed they now seemed like nothing more than conventional city types who had gone to the pub or the cinema or a restaurant after work and were now heading home. Just like he was. The fact that they had not exchanged a word during the last few minutes was not all that unusual; the tube was noisy, and Nick knew talking was sometimes too much of an effort. Well, they might even have had an argument, have sunk now into that post-fight, fuming, silent state of introspection.

Nick stepped on to the platform and made his way towards the Central Line exit. It was relatively busy here and he looked straight ahead as he walked. He was not aware that the young couple were behind him until they appeared on the eastbound plat-form approximately fifteen seconds after he did. Though he studied them surreptitiously, Nick was not unduly worried. They didn't look around for him, didn't so much as glance at him; indeed, they each seemed preoccupied with their own thoughts. Casually Nick turned his back on them and began to stroll along the platform, putting distance between him and them. When he finally stopped and turned round to look, the young couple hadn't moved. They were still standing in the same position, still staring straight ahead, unspeaking. The man was rocking backwards and forwards ever so slightly on his heels.

The train arrived three minutes later, and six stops after that Nick was at Tottenham Court Road. As he stepped off the train he glanced back along the platform, but it was too busy with tourists and people going home after chucking-out time to tell whether the young couple had also left the train.

Feeling a little foolish, Nick stooped in the hope that he would be lost in the crowd. He hurried to the Northern Line exit; There were far fewer people on the northbound platform, but a train was waiting for him, its doors open. Looking neither right nor left, Nick loped across to it and stepped in. He hadn't even reached a seat when the doors hissed closed.

If he knew for sure that someone really *was* following him, Nick wondered what he'd do. Pretend he hadn't noticed them? Drop all pretence and run? Turn and confront his fate?

Even as he considered these possibilities, Nick knew that for him the last option was really no option at all. Despite his size and the various occasions in prison when he had been forced to defend himself, Nick did not like confrontation. Neither had prison accustomed him to violence; on the contrary, it had made him hate it. Each time he had witnessed it or been on the receiving end of it, it had only served to underline how sickening and terrifying it was, had only acted as a reminder that modern man was not that far removed from primitive savagery.

He shuddered, remembering Tony Craig, a Glaswegian who had been as tall as Nick but who had outweighed him by maybe a hundred pounds. For three endless, soul-destroying months Nick had shared a cell with Craig. On their third or fourth night together the two of them had been playing cards when Craig had abruptly pointed a fat finger at him. 'When they shut the doors tonight, Nicky boy, you and me goan have us a fight.'

Nick looked at him with a half-smile on his face, but at the big man's words his guts immediately began to contract. 'Don't be daft, Tony,' he said, amazed at how light and unconcerned his voice sounded, 'I'm not going to fight you. You'd kill me.'

Craig looked at him with his strangely flat eyes, his face neither hostile nor friendly. 'You and me goan have us a fight,' he repeated as if Nick hadn't spoken. 'I'm goan toughen you up, sonny.'

'I'm tough enough,' Nick said, trying to sound it, but the big Glaswegian simply rubbed at his forehead with the heel of his

36

hand as if the idea that had just sparked to life in his brain was causing a little tickle there. 'Oh, aye,' he said, and this time he spoke as if he were doing Nick a big favour, 'I'm goan toughen you up.'

That night Craig's first sledgehammer blow had cracked at least two of Nick's ribs. Nick had collapsed to the ground, trying to make as little noise as possible; the last thing he wanted was to attract the attention of the screws. To gain a reputation as the sort of man who got his cell-mates into trouble would have been disastrous.

As soon as he collapsed, holding his ribs and trying to protect as much of the rest of his body as he could, Craig dropped to his knees beside him. 'Och, I'm sorry, pal,' he said, sounding genuinely remorseful. Then he sat back on his haunches, put his arms behind him and squared his shoulders. 'Here you go, son. Gimme your best shot.'

It hurt Nick simply to breathe, but he managed to gasp out, 'What?'

'Gimme your best shot. Hit me as hard as you can. Go on – I deserve it.'

Nick shook his head. 'I'm not going to hit you, Tony. No way. You'd kill me.'

'No, I wouldnae,' said the Glaswegian.

'You would. You'd beat the shit out of me.'

'I'll kill you if you *don't* hit me,' Craig said reasonably. 'I promise you that.'

'Oh, fuck,' Nick groaned, curling around the pulsing, red-hot pain in his ribs. With an effort he shuffled into a sitting position and reluctantly squeezed his hand into a fist. Then, as hard as the pain in his side would allow, he pistoned the fist out, hitting Craig right in the centre of his wide, fleshy face. There was a smacking sound. To Nick it felt like striking a stone bust covered with a thin layer of latex. This time he almost *did* scream, as fiery hands reached down into his left lung and scraped burning fingernails across it. But again he managed to bite back the sound, reducing it to a kind of choking gasp.

Craig barely moved. He simply twitched his nose as if he had snorted a few particles of dust and grinned. 'There you go. Now we're even.'

For the next twelve awful weeks, until Craig was transferred to

Strangeways, Nick had had to put up with the Glaswegian's nightly 'toughening-up' sessions. There was no respite from it. Each night, without fail, Craig would beat Nick black and blue, and Nick would have to do his best to defend himself.

He was not a particularly good pupil, but then Craig never passed comment on his prowess. Rather than toughening Nick up, the nightly beatings wore him down, whittled away his sense of worth and hope that every prisoner had to cling to if he was going to get by on a day-to-day basis.

Towards the end, Nick became so depressed, so pummelled into submission, that he began to neglect himself, to let himself go. Knowing what was waiting for him at the end of each day, he saw little point in trying to make the best of things. If Craig had not been transferred when he had, Nick thought he might have gone under completely.

For his part, Craig never seemed to notice Nick's decline, never seemed to realise what effect his 'toughening-up' sessions were having on his cell-mate. Throughout those twelve weeks, despite the violence, Craig never showed any actual hostility towards Nick. Indeed, he had genuinely seemed to believe that he was doing him a favour . . .

The train whined to a halt at Belsize Park, snapping Nick out of his reverie. He stood up to get off. There were only three other people left in his carriage: a dozing black girl, a fat Chinese businessman whose black-framed glasses made his eyes look like images on twin TV screens, and a skinny, spotty teenager with long hair, torn jeans and an Iron Maiden T-shirt. As Nick stepped from the train, he glanced to his right and his heart skipped a beat. Three carriages further along, the young couple were getting off too.

Coincidence, Nick thought desperately as he lunged for the exit, hoping he looked as though he were not fleeing but merely hurrying. As he stomped up the escalator, two steps at a time, he told himself that the couple were not following him simply because they had disembarked from the train at the same time that he had. And then, as he was wondering whether the footsteps he could hear behind him belonged to someone else or were merely the echoes of his own, another thought came to him: *They know where you live*.

That almost caused him to stumble, the strength draining from his legs, but he managed to recover and carry on. He reached the top of the escalator, glanced quickly behind him and saw no one, and rushed out of the station, past the unmanned ticket booth.

He jogged across the road and round the corner, the dark and deserted streets with their tall, densely packed houses making him feel more vulnerable than usual. It was quarter to midnight now and the pubs had disgorged the last of their customers and locked their doors. Nick used every piece of cover he could find to make him appear less conspicuous: postboxes, shop awnings, scaffolding like so many zimmer-frames which supported a crumbling and descrepit terrace of houses.

Again the words rose in his mind as he turned on to a street no more than two minutes' walk from his own: *They know where you live*. Suddenly, as if the thought were an incantation that had summoned dark forces, he heard the clatter of rapid footsteps – footsteps that seemed to belong to more than one person – behind him.

He ducked into Rab's Kebab, a narrow place squeezed between a laundrette and a driving school, whose grimy front window boasted: DONER KEBAB, CHICKEN, BURGER, FRIES, SALAD, in sloping, red, self-adhesive letters. The whole place seemed sweaty, the tiled walls tarnished with grease. A thin, moustached Cypriot behind a formica counter looked at Nick suspiciously and asked, 'Yes, sir?'

Nick wanted to ask whether he could just wait inside for a few minutes to see if some people went past, but he didn't think that request would go down well. He looked at the chunk of grey meat rotating slowly on its vertical skewer, dribbling fat into the tray below. 'Doner kebab, please,' he said automatically.

As the man began to slice the steaming, dripping meat, Nick stared intently through the big front window, half-expecting to see the young couple go sprinting past. But, in the minute or so it took the man to construct the kebab, Nick saw no one.

The man wrapped the doner and handed it to Nick; Nick paid him, wished him goodnight, and left.

He stood for a moment by the entrance to the shop, looking back along the street. There was no one in sight. The sound of footsteps could not be heard.

Imagination, Nick thought, and began to walk home, feeling both relieved and foolish. By the time he had reached his home, and was standing on the porch looking for his key, he had eaten half his kebab without even thinking about it.

He found his key and was about to insert it into the lock when a voice behind him spoke. 'Mr Finch?'

Nick whirled round. Most of the meat and the salad shot from the pitta bread in his hand and landed with a plop on the shoes of the stranger standing at the bottom of the steps behind him.

The man – fiftyish, scrawny, with fuzzy hair that looked ginger beneath the street lamps – glanced with distaste at the mess on his shoes and carefully shook it off. Then he looked back up at Nick, his face deadpan. 'Mr Finch, I'm Detective Inspector Baker. I wonder if I might have a word?'

Six

As soon as Sasha closed the door, Linsey called her name. There was nothing in her voice, no sharpness, to suggest that she was angry, but Sasha sighed nonetheless, certain that she knew what was coming.

'Yeah, Mum,' she called, and walked slowly down the stairs of the spacious basement flat in Muswell Hill that she and Mum had lived in ever since Sasha was a little girl. Intermittently Linsey had talked about buying a house, but had somehow never quite managed to get enough money together to commit herself to a mortgage.

It was only recently that Sasha had become aware how disenchanted with her life her mother really was. Reading between the lines, Sasha knew that Linsey considered herself a failure, considered the road she had travelled to be a dead end, the route marked with a myriad of bad decisions and wasted opportunities. Sasha had no doubt that, despite their recent difficulties her mother loved her; but she also knew – though Linsey had never said so outright – that deep down her mother believed her first mistake had been to keep the baby she had been impregnated with at the age of seventeen, that it was this more than anything else that had held her back, dragged her down, prevented her from achieving her ambitions.

When she had become pregnant Linsey had been a budding actress. Sasha had no idea whether her mother had been a *good* actress, or whether – if the situation had been different – she would ever have made a career of it. What she *did* know, from talking to Gran, was that Linsey believed she had lost vital ground in the months leading up to and immediately after Sasha's birth.

What Sasha had further learned was that, over the course of the next few years, her mother had turned down a number of good parts because the hours were too demanding, because she was not prepared to spend that much time away from her infant daughter. Gran had helped all she could, but Linsey, despite the battering her career was taking, had been a proud and fiercely independent parent, determined not to shirk her responsibilities.

Eventually, inevitably, the worthwhile parts had begun to dry up, and she had been left simply with walk-ons, parts that required little time and effort, which she had further had to supplement with a series of dead-end jobs. Sasha was not sure, but she suspected Mum had been in at least one, and possibly several, porn movies. In the end Linsey had abandoned acting altogether. Now she worked as a researcher for a local radio station; and although it was an interesting job, it was evident from the bitterness and the resentment Mum sometimes showed that it came nowhere near the sparkling future she had once envisaged for herself.

Sasha loved and respected Linsey and never once had her mother directed any resentment towards her, but just recently the two of them could not see eye-to-eye over anything. Sasha knew all too well what lay at the heart of the problem. She was seventeen years old – the age Mum had been when she had been conceived – and was fast outgrowing the old homestead. Though she loved her mother, the two of them simply had different ways of looking at life. Sasha guessed that much of Mum's anger came from her realisation that sooner rather than later she was going to have to let her daughter go. Maybe she was scared of that prospect. Maybe she was already feeling lonely and abandoned. Or maybe Sasha's not-so-slow burgeoning into womanhood was making her feel old. Not that Linsey *was* old, nor even middle-aged, but sometimes she talked as though she was. Sometimes she talked as though her life was virtually over, and all she had to look forward to was a slow, sad decline.

All of this passed through Sasha's head in the time it took her to descend the stairs, walk along the hallway into the huge kitchen and through the arch into the sitting room. Linsey was sitting on the settee with her knees drawn up, eating cheese and chive Pringles. The heavily woven cotton throw with its beaded fringe was rucked around her like a nest. In one corner Sid, the blue budgerigar, was edging sideways along his perch; in the other the TV was playing host to a chat show that seemed to be going for the Most Hideous Set of the Year Award.

'Hi,' Sasha said, half-hoping that if she pretended not to notice her mother's scowl the two of them could at least be civil to one another.

Linsey was small-boned, with straw-like hair which had been dyed too many times. When she was tired or annoyed – like now, – her eyes became deep-shadowed and her lips grew tight, emphasising the lines around her mouth.

'Where have you been?' she asked.

'Just out with a few friends from college,' Sasha said, trying to keep her voice light.

'*Where?*'

'Nowhere in particular,' Sasha said, her irritation building rapidly despite her best intentions. 'To the NFT, to see a Woody Allen film. I left you a note.'

'I didn't see one.'

'Well, I *left* you one. I stuck it on the fridge, under the Gromit magnet.'

'And how was I supposed to see it there?'

'Did you try using your eyes?'

Linsey's legs shot from under her, her feet slapping the floor, as if she were about to jump to her feet. 'Don't you talk to me like that!'

'Well, it's not my fault if you didn't see my note,' Sasha retorted, struggling to keep her voice steady.

'Why didn't you just *tell* me where you'd be going? Or, more accurately, *ask* me if you could?'

Sasha rolled her eyes. 'Mum, I'm old enough to make my own decisions about what I do and where I go.'

'Says who?'

'Oh, come on, Mum. I'm not a child.'

'And how the hell do *I* know what you get up to on an evening?'

'Come on, Mum,' said Sasha again. 'You ought to know me better than that. I'm not stupid.'

Linsey hissed out her exasperation. The argument had hit a cul-de-sac, but she was eager to continue it by exploring another avenue. 'I made you some pasta,' she said. 'It'll be ruined now.'

Sasha pulled a face; her mother was being childish. 'That's not my fault. If you'd read my note, you'd have known I wasn't coming back to eat.'

'So *have* you eaten?'

'Yes. I had a big lunch with Dad. I *told* you I was having lunch with Dad,' she added hastily, before her mother could comment. 'And I got a sandwich this evening. Okay?'

'And how is your *beloved* father?'

'What's that supposed to mean?'

'Oh, only that you seem to prefer to spend time with him rather than me, despite the fact that I've fed you and clothed you and struggled to keep a roof over your head these past seventeen years.'

'Yeah, and can you blame me?' retorted Sasha, so angry now that her mouth was running before her mind. 'At least he doesn't hassle me all the time!'

'He doesn't know you like I do. He doesn't know how selfish and bloody-minded you are.'

'I've had enough of this,' said Sasha, turning away. 'I'm leaving.'

For the first time Linsey looked alarmed. 'What do you mean, *leaving*? It's twelve o'clock at night.'

'And what do you care?' said Sasha. She stomped out of the room, across the wooden kitchen floor and into the hallway.

Linsey jumped up and came running after her. 'Where the hell do you think you're going to go at this time of night?'

'Anywhere but here,' retorted Sasha, running up the steps to the door, fishing for her keys as she did so. She unlocked the door with a trembling hand and pulled it open, then looked back down at her mother's pinched, pale face in which the eyes appeared too big, full of anguish and sorrow. Sasha hesitated for a moment, then said, 'See you around, Mum.' Then, less than three minutes after coming home, she went back out, pulling the door shut behind her.

Seven

'Coffee?' said Nick. 'Or . . . er . . . a beer?'

DI Baker sat in Nick's grey armchair, his hands folded almost primly in his lap. He reminded Nick of a bird – watchful, expressionless. In spite of himself, Nick couldn't help feeling nervous.

'No, thank you,' Baker said, and Nick almost expected him to add, 'Not while I'm on duty.' Nick considered getting a beer for himself, but then thought better of it. He'd only drink it too fast and betray his nervousness; besides, he wanted to keep a clear head for whatever it was Baker had come here for. On the doorstep, Nick's first thought had been that something had happened to a member of his family, but Baker had quickly allayed the fear. 'No, sir – it's nothing to be alarmed about. I want to ask you a few questions, that's all. It's purely routine.'

All the way upstairs Nick's mind had been whirring: if it was a routine matter, why had Baker come to see him at midnight? Was he suspected of some crime, perhaps because of his previous record? He sat down on the sofa beneath the window, leaning back to give the impression that he was relaxed. 'So what can I do for you, Inspector?' he asked, trying to sound casual.

Baker leaned forward a little, causing the springs in the chair to creak. 'Mr Finch, does the name Michael Mercy mean anything to you?'

Nick felt Baker's eyes on him, alert for the faintest flicker of reaction. He felt his cheeks beginning to get hot and he shook his head, a little exaggeratedly. 'I don't think so, no.'

'Are you quite sure? I would urge you to think hard, Mr Finch. Could he be a business acquaintance, perhaps?'

'I don't really have business acquaintances,' Nick said, and

45

waved a hand at the framed pictures on the walls. 'I'm a writer, a music journalist. Who is this guy, anyway? What's he done?'

Baker paused, as if wondering how much to reveal. 'Michael Mercy is on the international sales team of UX Computers, based in North London. Or at least he was. He committed suicide this morning.'

There was a short silence. 'Oh. Well . . . I'm sorry, but what's it got to do with me?'

Baker let out a long breath. He was silent for such a long time that Nick began to think he'd offended the policeman in some way. He was wondering what to say to break the silence when Baker did it for him.

'Michael Mercy didn't just commit suicide,' he said. 'Before taking his own life, he killed his wife and seven-year-old daughter.'

Nick went cold. The beer and the kebab he had consumed that evening seemed to harden in his gut. 'My God,' he said. 'When did this happen?'

'This morning, just after six a.m. Mercy held his wife and daughter hostage for around three hours before killing them.'

Six a.m. Around seven hours after Nick's experience in the Gridlock. When he asked the next question his faltering voice seemed to come from far away. 'How did he . . . how did he kill them?'

'He shot them both in the head with a twelve-bore shotgun. Then he reloaded and killed himself the same way.'

Cold, greasy sweat broke out on Nick's body and his head began to pound. It felt as if he had been injected with a virus whose effects were instantaneous. He wasn't sure whether he wanted to curl up on the sofa or go to the bathroom and be sick. In the event he put a shaky hand up to his head and wiped the sweat away. 'Oh, God,' he moaned.

Baker watched him for a moment without expression. Then he said evenly, 'For someone who claims not to have known Michael Mercy, Mr Finch, I must say I find your reaction rather extreme.'

Nick licked his lips, swallowed, tried to bring himself under control. 'I didn't know him, but . . . I think I saw what happened,' he said.

Baker frowned. 'You *saw* what happened? I'm sorry, I don't follow.'

Brokenly, Nick told Baker about his experience in the Gridlock the previous evening. Baker listened, his face unmoved. When Nick had finished, he said, 'So what are you telling me, Mr Finch? That you had some form of premonition?'

Nick shrugged. 'I don't know. All I know is what I saw. I don't have any explanation for it. I thought at the time it was some sort of . . . flashback.' He grimaced. 'When I was younger, I took a lot of drugs. I thought what happened last night might have been related to that in some way.'

Baker raised his eyebrows. For the first time he looked at a loss.

'Why did . . . why did the killings lead you to me?' Nick asked.

Baker spread his hands, pressed them back together. Again he seemed to consider for a moment, then he told Nick about the list of names that Mercy had written over and over again on the wall of his lounge.

Nick felt a chill inside him. He thought of Mercy writing his name, not just once but many times, before putting the shotgun to the head of his seven-year-old daughter and pulling the trigger. He wondered who Mercy had killed first – his wife or the child. Either way the prospect was appalling, the thought that one had had to witness the other's death, that it had been the last sight they had ever seen.

His mouth was dry as blotting paper. He licked his lips, but could generate no moisture. In a croaking voice, he asked, 'But how did you know I was the right Nick Finch? There must be lots of Nick Finches. It's surely not that uncommon a name.'

Baker told Nick about computer profiling. 'We feed the information in and what the computer gives us back enables us to target the most likely suspects in a given situation. We've already eliminated several Nicholas Finches from our enquiry.'

'*Suspects*?' said Nick. 'I'm not a suspect, am I? You surely don't think *I* had anything to do with what Mercy did?'

Baker held up his hands. 'Simply a turn of phrase, Mr Finch. Nothing to get excited about.'

The phone began to ring. Nick looked at it for a moment, hoping that the answerphone would pick it up, and then he thought better of it and climbed unsteadily to his feet. He didn't think he'd be able to stand the prospect of sitting there silently with Baker, listening to Sasha or perhaps Jenna burbling happily on about nothing in particular. He reached the phone halfway through its

47

fifth ring, just as the answerphone was getting ready to jump in. He picked it up. 'Hello?'

He was expecting a female voice to reply. He was surprised when a male voice said, flatly, 'Don't tell him anything. He is not what he seems.'

'What?' said Nick, but the caller had already rung off. As he replaced the receiver, the words that the man had spoken soaked into his head. He glanced at Baker.

'Quick call,' remarked the policeman.

'Yeah,' said Nick. 'They . . . er . . . they rang off without saying anything.'

'How odd,' said Baker, his voice even.

Nick shrugged. 'Wrong number, I expect.' He crossed the room, feeling dazed, almost drunk. He rounded the coffee table, trying not to stagger, and sat back down on the sofa.

Baker leaned forward, holding something out to him. Nick thought at first that it was a handkerchief or a tissue, something to wipe his sweaty face. Then he realised it was a photograph. He took it from Baker, the celluloid slippery beneath his damp fingers.

'This is a photograph of Michael Mercy,' Baker said. 'Perhaps if you could confirm that this is the man you . . . um . . . saw, Mr Finch, it might help us understand a little better what exactly is going on here.'

Nick looked at the photograph. Michael Mercy was wearing an open-necked shirt and smiling. Behind him was what appeared to be a boating lake. The photograph had been taken on a sunny day; there was a flush of sunburn on Mercy's cheeks.

Nick found it hard to equate this smiling, sane-looking man with the drooling, sick-eyed creature he had seen in the Gridlock last night. Nevertheless he had no doubt that this *was* the same man. He thought of the calm, authoritative voice on the phone: *Don't tell him anything. He is not what he seems.*

'Well?' Baker said.

Nick handed the photograph back. 'No,' he said. 'I don't think it's the same man.'

'What?'

'It's not the same man. He looks totally different.'

Baker stared at Nick with incredulity. 'I don't expect the Michael Mercy you saw looked quite so relaxed as he does here,' he said curtly. 'Please look at the photograph again, Mr Finch.'

48

Nick felt a trickle of sweat run down the side of his face. 'I don't need to. It's not the same man. Like I said before, what I saw was probably some kind of . . . flashback or hallucination. I was drunk and confused. This is all a big mistake. A big coincidence.'

'Rather an incredible one, don't you think?' Baker said, his voice cold.

Nick shrugged. 'Look, I've never met this man. I can't tell you anything about him. I've no idea why he wrote my name on his wall.' He was trembling now, unnerved not just by the fact that he appeared to have had a bona fide premonition of a terrible event, but also by everything else that had happened tonight: the couple on the train, the phone call, Baker's frosty persistence. Baker was staring at him now with suspicion and disappointment, like a father whose beloved son has been arrested for shoplifting. Nick put his head in his hands. He had had enough. He wanted everyone and everything to go away and leave him alone.

Partially granting his wish, Baker sighed heavily. 'All right, Mr Finch – we'll leave it there for now. But I may want to talk to you again. I'd be grateful if you could remain available.'

Nick nodded and heard Baker stand up. He made no effort to do so himself; he couldn't even raise his head to look at the policeman.

'I'll see myself out. Goodbye for now, Mr Finch.'

'Bye,' Nick said.

Only when he had heard Baker walk across the room and down the hallway, heard the front door of his flat slam shut, did he lift his head from his hands. For a moment his surroundings looked unreal. He rubbed his face, breathed deeply, tried to bring his spinning mind under control. He wondered again about getting himself a beer from the fridge, but realised that not only would he be unable to keep it down, but it would almost certainly only serve to cloud the issue, make him more confused than ever.

What was he – some sort of psychic? And what link did he have with Michael Mercy? Why had this man, whom he had never met, written his name over and over on a wall before violently and inexplicably ending the lives of himself and his family?

He wondered who had phoned him that evening. Evidently someone who had known that he was talking to DI Baker. Didn't that suggest, therefore, that his suspicions had been correct, that he really was being watched?

49

But if so, why? What possible interest could he be to anyone? And was it true what the caller had told him? Was Baker really not what he seemed? Then who the hell was he?

Nick was scared. More than that: he was terrified. He might well be in danger without knowing why. He wondered again who was watching him. Could it be the police? Ought he to ring them up, demand to be told exactly what was going on?

He was so confused he didn't know what to do for the best. He crossed to the phone, hesitated, then saw Jenna's address and phone number on the pad beside it. One thing he did know was that he needed someone normal to talk to, someone who could help him to get his head straight, someone he could trust.

He picked up the phone and was about to dial Jenna's number when he heard a series of sly clicks. Not for the first time that evening his mouth went dry. Were his calls being monitored too? Maybe his whole flat was bugged! Carefully he replaced the receiver in its cradle and looked around, half-expecting to see tiny cameras pointing at him from every corner of the room.

Crossing to the window, he leaned over the sofa and peered down into the street below. Across the road, tucked in the shadow of a tree between a builder's lorry and a blue Mazda with a crumpled front wing, was the grey unmarked van he had seen a number of times recently. Nick pulled back from the window quickly, feeling trapped. He couldn't stay here, not tonight. He thought for a minute, then grabbed his jacket, picked up his keys and hurried along the hallway to the door of his flat.

He listened for a moment, but there was no sound from the landing outside. Gritting his teeth, he pulled the door open an inch and peered out. No one there. He left the flat, pulling the door closed behind him, wincing at the audible click it made. He leaned over the stairwell, still listening and watching, but the entire building seemed empty and silent. He descended the stairs almost on tip-toe. When he reached the bottom of the stairs, he headed not for the front door but the back, a heavy-duty door with reinforced glass panels and a sign above it reading FIRE EXIT in red letters. Nick twisted the catch, pulled the door open and slipped outside.

At the back of the building was a path leading through an area of unlit lawn to a small car park. Nick crossed the car park and passed under an arch on to an altogether quieter street than the one at the front of the house. He prayed Jenna would be in, hoped she would be pleased to see him; he hadn't planned his first visit to her flat to be quite like this. He began to jog up the street, heading vaguely in the direction of the tube station, hoping that somewhere along the way he would be able to flag down a cab. As he ran, sweat making his head itch, he glanced constantly behind him. The street seemed deserted, but that didn't prevent him feeling observed every step of the way.

Eight

The cab driver spent the entire journey rhapsodising about the birth of his daughter. Ordinarily Sasha would have revelled in his overwhelming enthusiasm for the miracle of childbirth and the joys of fatherhood, but on this occasion she would have preferred a less gregarious companion. It was evident from the way he had launched into his narrative as soon as she sat down that the cabbie had spent the three weeks since the birth relating his story again and again, honing it to perfection. A little uncharitably, Sasha wondered how many of his passengers during that time had told him to shut the fuck up.

Not that she could ever have been so cruel. Nevertheless, she was relieved when they finally arrived at the house Dan shared with three other guys, just off the Finchley Road. To make up for her foul mood she gave the cabbie – who had told her his name was Errol – a bigger tip than she would normally have done and told him in as warm a voice as she could muster to give little Ella a kiss from her. Errol grinned from beneath a baseball cap emblazoned with the legend CHICAGO. 'I'll do that, miss,' he said happily. 'It'll be a real pleasure. You have a good night now.'

He drove away, no doubt eager, like the Ancient Mariner, to relate his story to his next passenger. Sasha turned and walked through a creaking front gate, through an overgrown garden choked with rubbish, to Dan's front door. Dan was nineteen, in his second year of a philosophy degree course at City University. He and Sasha had been going out for seven months. At first it had been great, but gradually Sasha had come to realise just how unreliable and immature Dan really was. All the same, it was him she wanted to see right now. Although Dad would probably have been .

52

more understanding, she had always made a point of never moaning about one parent to the other. Such behaviour smacked of manipulation, betrayal. There was no way Sasha could have procured the sympathies of one to the detriment of the other and felt good about herself afterwards.

Dan's house was in darkness. For a moment Sasha thought that not only was the place empty, but also that she did not have the key that Dan had had cut for her. 'Great,' she muttered, rummaging through her pockets, already rehearsing the conversation she would have with Dad if she ended up having to stay at his place after all. *I've had a row with Mum. Can I stay here tonight?* If he pressed her, she would be firm. *I don't really want to talk about it, Dad. I didn't come here to get you on my side against Mum. That wouldn't be fair to anybody.*

She was bracing herself for the fifteen-minute walk – she couldn't face another Errol tonight – when she came across the key in the buttoned-down left breast pocket of her jacket. She unlocked the door and went into the hallway; the house smelled of curry and damp. If Dan was out she'd simply get undressed and get into his bed; it would be a nice surprise for him when he got home.

As she walked along the threadbare hall carpet to the foot of the stairs she heard music playing softly. She recognised it as a CD she'd bought for Dan a couple of months earlier, *Trailer Park* by Beth Orton, and smiled fondly. She imagined him sitting at his desk, slaving over an essay he'd been assigned weeks ago which had to be in by nine a.m. tomorrow, but which he'd only just started. Dan was like that: always leaving things till the last minute. She'd go into his room and he'd look up at her, bleary-eyed and a little alarmed. 'It's okay,' she'd say. 'I'm not going to hassle you – I'll just sit here quietly while you finish your work.'

She ascended the stairs, reluctant to call out; the house was so quiet that if the rest of the household were not out partying they were almost certainly asleep. Dan's room was at the far end of the landing, beside the stairs that curled up into the fourth bedroom in the attic. His door was very slightly ajar and there was a dim light shining from beyond it. 'Dan,' Sasha murmured as she pushed the door open and entered. 'Dan, are you awake?'

Her eyes flickered from the unoccupied desk to the bed. There were clothes strewn on and around it – a pair of jeans, a V-necked

T-shirt in orange, green and white stripes, a pair of navy blue leggings, a black bra. On the floor beside the bed were several crumpled up tissues and a used condom. Dan and the girl sharing his bed were both asleep and naked, the duvet pushed down to their waists. Dan was cuddled up to the girl's back, his arm curled around her, hand cupping her right breast. The girl was small and pretty with short dark hair. She had a rose tattooed on the shoulder that Dan's face was resting against.

For a moment Sasha stood and looked at them, not knowing what to do, feeling a strange sense of both disbelief and inevitability. It occurred to her with black humour that this was not turning into one of her better nights. She had just decided to exit the room quietly and walk round to her dad's flat – dropping Dan's key down a drain on the way – when Dan opened his eyes, turned his head and looked straight at her.

'Sash,' he said wonderingly.

'You bastard,' Sasha muttered, then turned and left the room.

If he didn't come after her, she thought she could remain calm. She heard him call her name as she was halfway down the stairs; she increased her pace, wanting only to reach the front door and get out of the house before he could catch up with her. If she could get out into the street it might discourage him from following her. But as she was pulling the front door closed behind her, she heard him shout her name again and come pounding down the stairs. She didn't turn round, though, not until she heard his footsteps slapping the street behind her. When she finally did it was to encounter Dan clad in nothing more than a pair of bright red boxer shorts.

'Sash, come back,' he moaned, hugging himself against the cold.

'What, so that we can have a nice cosy threesome?' she replied acidly.

'*No*,' he said as if she was being unreasonable. 'Look, I'll tell her to leave. I was drunk. I didn't know what I was doing.'

Sasha didn't know what she was doing either until she did it. She took three steps towards Dan, drew back her fist, and punched him as hard as she could in the face.

His nose crunched, then he was on his back on the pavement, holding his face and writhing. Sasha was both appalled and exhilarated by what she had done. She took another step forward.

'That's it, Dan. Finished,' she said quietly. 'Don't bother trying to call me.'

She threw the key to his house into the overgrown garden, then turned and walked away briskly, leaving him lying there. She was two streets away when the events of that night suddenly over-whelmed her and she began to cry.

Nine

Acutely aware of how late it was, Nick hesitated before pressing the buzzer bearing Jenna's name. He had still not shaken off his nervousness; indeed, he had spent almost the entire cab journey glancing in the side mirror to ensure that he wasn't being followed. His mind had been busy since leaving his flat, turning over recent events, trying to bring them into some sort of perspective. He kept telling himself that there had to be some straightforward explanation, but he couldn't for the life of him imagine what it might be.

Jenna lived in an apartment block so modern that the white walls still shone like bone. Upon arrival, Nick had to pass through a wrought-iron gate, down a set of stone steps to a paved area below ground level and up another set of steps at the side of the house. This suited him; at least he didn't feel exposed. He pressed the buzzer a second time, and then, after a short pause, a third. He assumed Jenna was in; her car had been parked on the street outside. If she wasn't he didn't know what he'd do. Slump against the door and wait for daylight, perhaps. Maybe even doze a little if the adrenaline that was rushing through his system allowed him to.

He was about to press his thumb on the buzzer a fourth time when a rush of static preceded a sleepy voice saying, 'Hello?'

'Jenna?'

'Yes?'

'Jenna, it's me, Nick. Nick Finch. Look, I'm really sorry about this, but something's happened. I need to talk to you. I didn't know who else to turn to.'

There was a short pause, during which Nick realised how desperate, how crazy, he must sound. He expected her to reply cautiously, 'Nick, it's almost one in the morning. Can't this wait until tomorrow?' But instead she said, 'Come on up.'

Nick pushed the door open as it buzzed at him, then clicked it shut firmly behind him. He began to climb the stairs, then realised he couldn't remember whether Jenna lived in Flat 5 or 6. There was no need to worry; she was waiting for him outside the door to Flat 5 wearing a blue dressing-gown. Her feet were bare and her hair was tousled. Despite everything, Nick couldn't help thinking that she looked lovely.

'You're white as a sheet,' she told him, putting a hand out to touch his arm. 'What's happened?'

'Can we go inside?' he asked, unable to prevent himself from glancing over his shoulder once again.

'Of course.'

Her flat was neat and compact, decorated and furnished in light, summery colours and fabrics. She had a lot of CDs and a lot of well cared-for plants. The pictures on the walls were mostly abstracts, though there was also a reclining nude in delicate pastel and a large black and white photograph of an old man with an incredibly weather-beaten face. She directed him to a pine settee with plump blue cushions. 'Can I get you anything?' she asked. 'Coffee? Wine?'

Nick asked for wine, though he was not sure his system would be able to handle it. Jenna left the room, reappearing less than a minute later with a bottle of Australian Shiraz, two glasses and a corkscrew.

'So what's been going on?' she asked, opening the bottle.

'What *hasn't* been?' Nick said, trying to produce a smile and feeling it quivering like palsy at the corners of his mouth. He accepted a glass of wine while he collected his thoughts. Then he said, 'I suppose I'd better start with the couple on the train – though I admit that might have been my imagination. The rest of it wasn't, though.'

He told her everything that had happened that evening, gulping wine at intervals to prevent his mouth from drying up. As he heard the words emerging, sounding oddly flat and distant, he began to feel scared all over again. Scared of being linked in a way he didn't understand to Michael Mercy's crazed and inexplicable act; scared of not knowing who he might be up against, what they might want from him and how far they might go to obtain it;

57

scared even of Jenna's reaction – he couldn't deny that his story sounded like the delusional ravings of a madman.

She sat at the opposite end of the settee, listening with an expression that was serious but unreadable, leaning forward with her elbows on her knees, taking occasional sips of her wine. She said only two words the whole time Nick was speaking. When he repeated what Baker had revealed about Michael Mercy, she murmured, 'My God.'

'So what do you think?' he asked when he had finished. 'Am I bonkers, or what?'

His attempt at flippancy sounded hollow. Jenna reached out and stroked his arm gently, as if trying to placate a nervous animal. 'Of course not,' she said. He twitched a grim smile. 'So what do you think's happening?'

'I don't know. Something very strange.'

'You don't think I'm imagining it all, then?' he said, probing for reassurance.

'Do *you*?'

'Of course not! But I wouldn't blame you if you did. I mean, you hardly know me.'

She smiled. 'I already feel that I know you well enough to trust that you're telling me the truth.' Her smile became a thoughtful frown. 'One thing occurs to me, though.'

'What's that?'

'Well, the most amazing thing in all of this is that you do seem to have had a genuine premonition. You appear to have actually seen something happen before it did. But you only have Baker's word on that. What if he was lying to you? What was it the voice on the phone said? "He's not what he seems"?'

Nick nodded.

'So maybe he made all of that Michael Mercy stuff up. Maybe he was trying to catch you off guard so that he could draw information out of you for some reason of his own.'

'But Baker showed me a photograph of the man I saw in the Gridlock. And besides, how would he have known about my . . . my premonition? The only people I've told are you and Sasha.'

She pursed her lips. 'I hadn't thought of that. Anyway, I suppose we'll find out tomorrow whether Baker was telling you the truth, won't we? If Michael Mercy *did* kill his wife and daughter it will almost certainly be all over the papers.'

58

'I suppose so,' said Nick, then sighed wearily. 'God, I can hardly think straight. What do you think I should do? Go to the police?'

She shrugged. 'What if it's the police who are bugging your flat? Following you?'

'Then at least I could ask them why they're doing it.'

She pulled a face. 'If it is them, they're hardly likely to admit it, are they? We'd need evidence; something to confront them with. I think we should go back to your flat in the morning and search it thoroughly. If we do find any bugs or anything suspicious we'll take them to the police and make them tell us what's going on.'

Nick thought about this, then nodded slowly. 'Yeah – okay. Thanks, Jenna, for being so understanding.'

She smiled. 'No problem.' She put down her glass and held out her arms. 'Come here.'

'What?'

'You look as though you need a hug.'

He returned her smile and moved across the short gap between them. Jenna put her arms around him, and he reciprocated. It had been a while since Nick had embraced a woman. He luxuriated in her warmth and softness, in the scent of her skin and hair. Immediately he began to feel calmer. He felt her breasts pushing against his chest and his penis stirred in his jeans. The two of them remained in that position for several minutes. Then Jenna gently disengaged herself from him and reached out to take his hand. 'Come on.'

She stood up. Nick allowed himself to be led to the bedroom, where a single small lamp burned beside the brass-framed bed. The two of them walked across to the bed and sat down on it, turning to face each other. Jenna reached out and stroked Nick's cheek, then leaned forward and kissed him on the lips.

They sank on to the unmade bed. When they began to caress one another, they did so in unison, as if each were taking their cue from the other. They removed one another's clothes just as cautiously, Nick trying to rein in his passion, trying to channel it into a show of tenderness rather than a display of reckless hunger, trying not to overstep the mark and reveal the depth of the need for physical intimacy that boiled inside him. He wanted to lose himself in Jenna so completely that it would temporarily wipe the

59

past twenty-four hours from his mind, but he was anxious not to frighten her.

It was only when they were naked, slowly and gently exploring each other's bodies, that either of them spoke. In a hesitant whisper, Nick said, 'I . . . I'm afraid I haven't got anything. I never thought—'

'It's okay,' Jenna murmured, smiling, 'I have. In the drawer next to your side of the bed.'

Their love-making, though tender, was indeed needful, even intense. Afterwards Nick's flesh tingled as if a mild electrical current were flowing beneath his skin. The tension between them broken, he and Jenna became playful, giddy, as if absurdly proud of themselves. She dabbled her fingertips across Nick's ultra-sensitive chest and stomach, making him flinch and squirm, the two of them giggling uncontrollably.

Eventually, slotted together like spoons, they drifted into sleep.

Though Nick felt relaxed as his conscious mind was pulled softly apart, he began dreaming almost instantly. He was strapped down in the dentist's chair again, with the suggestion of voices somewhere nearby. Although he did not have a light shining in his eyes on this occasion, his head felt as though it were held in a vice, and his limited vision offered him no more than a view of a dingy grey flat surface – a wall, or a ceiling.

Suddenly, no more than a few feet in front of him, he heard the familiar screaming whirr of the drill. Panic gripped him. His eyes flickered downwards, though for a few seconds he could see nothing. Then the sound of the drill began moving towards him, and all at once a shadowy figure edged into his field of vision. At first Nick thought that the figure had an abnormally small, flat-topped head, but as it moved forward into the meagre light of the dream-room, filling his vision, he suddenly realised what he was looking at.

It was Michael Mercy, his head missing from the nose upwards, like a boiled egg with the top sliced off. Blood bubbled over the ragged rim of flesh and bone and ran down what remained of the dead man's cheeks in rivulets. Mercy leaned over Nick, his cold blood pattering on Nick's face, his ruined, toothless mouth struggling to find a shape. Blood surged over the colourless lips and ran down Mercy's chin, accompanied by a voice, gurgling and oily, which uttered a single word: 'Genesis.'

Ten

In some ways Sasha was relieved that her dad wasn't in; it meant she would have time to compose herself. The fact that she had cried annoyed her. She was not a crying person, particularly not over shits like Dan had turned out to be. It wasn't so much the break-up of the relationship that had upset her; it was more the argument with Mum, that the shock of finding Dan in bed with someone else had exacerbated. Fuck him any way. He was a problem that she was well rid of. Tomorrow, when she was calm, she would make her peace with Mum and start to think seriously about moving out. She and Mum would probably get on much better once they weren't living in each other's pockets.

She liked her dad's flat; its homely clutter soothed her, made her feel safe. He'd left a couple of lamps on, as well as the kitchen light. Sasha wondered where he was – hobnobbing it with Jarvis Cocker or Brett Anderson or someone probably. She wandered over to his vast CD collection and perused it for a while before selecting Jamiroquai's *Travelling Without Moving*. As the music filled the room, she went through into the kitchen and opened the fridge. She grabbed herself a Grolsch, frosty with condensation, uncapped it and carried it back into the sitting room. For a while she sat on the settee with her feet up, gulping cold beer and staring blankly into space. Eventually, lulled by music and alcohol and her own inactivity, she began to feel sleepy.

She stretched and yawned; perhaps she should have a shower and then crash out on the settee with a duvet. She hoped she wasn't cramping her dad's style; if he came back with his new woman later on, her presence might take a bit of explaining. She swallowed the last of the beer, then stood up and made her way to the bathroom. It was small, and as pleasantly cluttered as the rest of the flat. A huge *MARS ATTACKS!* poster dominated one wall; dozens of framed photographs jostled for position on another. Behind the toilet was a deep shelf stuffed with required reading: – old copies of *Loaded* and *Q* and *Empire*, *A Handbook Of Body Piercing*, *The Guinness Book Of British Hit Singles*, *Rock' n' Roll Babylon*, and various *Viz* compilations, *Beano* annuals and *Tintin* books.

Sasha quickly undressed and draped her clothes over the wicker basket in the corner behind the door. Naked, she stepped towards the bath and reached out to the shower curtain, which was bright blue and emblazoned with a profusion of multi-coloured cartoon fish.

The shower curtain clattered back on its rail as she yanked it, folding up like a concertina. Standing in the bath was a man in black clothes, black gloves and black balaclava.

For a second Sasha and the man stood frozen, looking into each other's eyes. Then the man leaped forward and with terrifying speed and ferocity grabbed Sasha around the throat with his left hand and punched her several times in the face with his right.

His punches were like a series of explosions inside her head. Sasha was so startled that she didn't feel any pain at first. She was not even aware she had fallen down until she felt the rough surface of the carpet against her back. Though it seemed that swarms of black, buzzing flies were clouding her thoughts and senses, there was a part of her that was horribly aware of her nudity, terrified of what her attacker might do. Her only thought was that she had to remain conscious in order to fight him off. *Gottagetup, gottagetup*, her mind jabbered at her, but her limbs were useless. She tried rolling on to her side, curling up to protect herself, but before she could manage it the flies engulfed her completely and everything went black.

Eleven

When Nick had jerked awake from the nightmare, his body filmed with sweat, his heart pounding, Jenna hadn't stirred. Nick had woken to find himself lying on his back, his eyes springing open to stare at the ceiling. He continued to lie without moving for several minutes as the power of the dream dissipated, sank back into the sludge at the bottom of his mind, where it would lurk like a crab until the next time. After a while he slipped out of bed and went to the bathroom, where he urinated and splashed some water on his face before cupping his hands beneath the cold tap and drinking deeply. The water tasted sterile, leaving a bleachy aftertaste. The nightmare had chased away Nick's tiredness, but he went back to bed anyway, mainly because he hated the thought of Jenna waking up and thinking he regretted their love-making, had sneaked away to avoid facing her.

He lay on the sweat-damp bedclothes and closed his eyes, bracing himself against the dream images that he knew his waking mind would reconstruct whether he liked it or not. Sure enough, a picture of Michael Mercy's ruined head immediately snapped into sharp focus behind his eyelids. But Nick was grateful to find the image had lost much of its terrible potency. Instead he found himself mulling over the single word – *genesis* – that the dream version of Mercy had used. In the turmoil of the past twenty-four hours he had all but forgotten that the Gridlock version of Mercy had said something similar.

'*It's breaking through.*' Wasn't that more or less what he had said? But whatever could that mean? Apart from the band of the same name, the word 'genesis' made Nick think immediately of

63

the Biblical story – Adam and Eve – though really it meant 'beginning'. The beginning of something . . .

But of what, apart from the confusion that his life had become? Nick's mind began to drift, and his next conscious action was a jolt of surprise at discovering, when he woke up in the morning, that sleep had crept over him again.

Beside him Jenna was still sleeping, breathing deeply and evenly. In the morning light, augmented by the still-burning lamp, her skin looked flawless as silk. Nick leaned over and kissed her shoulder-blade; when she didn't respond he decided to make some coffee. He pulled on his boxer shorts and T-shirt, then went through to the kitchen, clattering about unnecessarily loudly as he familiarised himself with her domestic surroundings, still worried that if she woke up to lonely silence she would think he had run out on her. He filled the kettle and turned it on; found a tray, two mugs and a jar of Gold Blend. He opened the fridge and had actually taken out the bottle of milk before he realised it was covered in blood.

Startled, his red-smeared fingers jumped apart and the bottle dropped to the quarry-tiled floor. It smashed spectacularly, milk splashing over his bare feet and shins, shards of glass embedding themselves in his flesh, opening numerous tiny wounds.

Nick cried out and jumped back as the debris settled. Then, shaking, he examined the mess he had made. If the bottle *had* been liberally smeared with blood, as he'd momentarily thought, it had gone now, perhaps swamped by the greater volume of milk. He looked at his hands: there was not a trace of blood on either. Jesus Christ, what was *happening* to him?

He was mopping up the mess with kitchen roll, picking out the largest chunks of glass and putting them to one side, when Jenna sleepily appeared, wearing the same blue dressing-gown she had worn last night.

'What happened?' she asked, blinking confusedly down at the floor.

Nick made an instant decision not to tell her what he thought he had seen. If he kept on sharing his visions, how long would it be before she stopped blaming outside influences and began to suspect that his problems were largely, if not wholly, of his own making?

'I had an accident,' he said. 'The bottle slipped out of my fingers. Sorry.'

'You're cut,' she said, concerned.

Nick looked down at his legs, which were flecked with blood. 'Just a few scratches. They sting a bit, that's all.'

'You've got glass in your leg. I can see little slivers of it, glinting. Come on, I've got some tweezers in the bathroom – I'll get them out for you.'

Nick followed her into the bathroom, where she made him sit on the lid of the toilet and prop his feet up on the edge of the bath so that the shards of glass caught the light. Jenna spent the next five minutes plucking the glass out, her brow furrowed in concentration. Eventually she said, 'There. I think that's the lot.'

She put the tweezers aside and ran a flannel beneath the cold tap. 'You clean yourself up and I'll deal with the mess in the kitchen, then I'll make us some breakfast. Black coffee and croissants okay?'

Nick was about to say that that would be great, but before he could get the words out there was a noise from the hallway, like a large and angry wasp. Jenna glanced at him, forehead wrinkling, then left the bathroom. The buzzing stopped. 'Hello?' she said.

The voice was grainy with static. 'Miss Trenchard?'

'Yes.'

'Miss Trenchard, my name is Police Constable Sykes. With me is WPC Docherty. Would it be possible to come in and speak to you for a moment?'

Hearing this, Nick went into the hallway. Jenna raised her eyebrows at him, then spoke into the intercom. 'Er . . . what about?'

'It would be better if we spoke to you face to face, Miss Trenchard,' said a woman's voice.

Jenna glanced at Nick once again, as if for guidance. He shrugged.

'All right,' she said. 'Come on up.'

She pressed the button that would release the lock on the door downstairs and the two of them waited, Jenna drawing her dressing-gown tighter round her body. She looked anxious. 'I wonder what they want.'

'We'll find out soon enough,' said Nick. 'I'll just put some clothes on.' He ducked into the bedroom, tugged his jeans on quickly and was zipping them up with fumbling fingers when there was an authoritative and – it seemed to him – ominous double-rap on the door.

He scurried back out into the hallway, not wanting Jenna to be alone when she pulled the door open. He stood behind her as she twisted the latch and pushed down on the handle.

The male police constable standing on the threshold was uniformed, but he had removed his helmet and was holding it in the crook of his right arm. He was tall – at least six-three – and quite chubby, the flesh of his neck, mottled and raw-looking as if he had shaved too vigorously, lapping over the collar of his white shirt.

The WPC who stood beside him, her eyes on a level with his shoulder, had copper-coloured short hair and a pale, narrow face.

'Good morning, Miss Trenchard,' PC Sykes said, a sheen of sweat glistening on his upper lip. He looked at Nick. 'Morning, sir.'

Nick nodded. 'What can I do for you?' Jenna said.

'We're looking for a man we believe to be a friend of yours, miss,' WPC Docherty said. 'A Mr Nicholas Finch.'

Nick had half-expected this, though hearing his name gave him a jolt nonetheless. 'I'm Nick Finch,' he said, almost defiantly.

PC Sykes gave him a carefully neutral look. 'Ah, I wondered whether you might be, sir.' He glanced at his colleague, whose silence seemed to encourage him to go on. Then, lowering and softening his voice just a touch, he said, 'I'm afraid we've got some rather distressing news for you, Mr Finch.'

Twelve

Even before Nick knew that Sasha was in hospital, DI Baker had spoken to her. He had heard about the attack when he had arrived at the station at seven a.m. and had gone straight to the hospital, hoping that the girl would be willing and able to talk.

In fact, she had been *more* than willing. Though both her eyes had been swollen almost shut amid twin pouches of purple flesh, and her left cheekbone and nose were broken, she had remained calm and coherent, able to describe precisely what had happened. Baker had wondered whether the assault was connected with the Michael Mercy case, had even briefly entertained the notion that for some reason her father had carried out the attack; but from what Sasha had told him it appeared far more likely that she had simply disturbed a burglar.

Her voice had only faltered once during the telling, and that had been when she had recalled her fear, as she had slipped into unconsciousness, that she was about to be raped or murdered. However, the intruder had thankfully left her untouched, unviolated after knocking her out. He had simply made off, taking with him the video, the music system and as many CDs as he could carry.

The only slightly puzzling aspect of the case was how the man had gained entry to the flat; the front door had not been forced. Then again, there were only a finite number of lock combinations and a decent selection of keys could gain you entry to an alarming number of doors.

Before leaving, Baker had given Sasha a folded sheet of notepaper. 'I spoke to your father yesterday,' he told her, 'and I have to confess I'm a little concerned about him. If I may, I'd like

67

to give you my number at the station, just on the off-chance that you might need it.'

Though she had little mobility in her bruise-stiffened face, Sasha managed to look surprised. 'You spoke to Dad? What about?'

Baker brushed at a speck of imaginary dust on the sleeve of his jacket. 'I'm not really at liberty to say, Miss Finch.'

'It was drugs, wasn't it?' Sasha said immediately. 'Was that guy his dealer then?'

Baker leaned forward. He had checked out Finch's file, of course, and knew all about his unsavoury past. The fellow had been a very naughty boy indeed when he was younger, but his record had been clean for the past dozen or so years. 'I was under the impression that he had put those days behind him, Miss Finch.'

'So was I. I mean . . . yes, he has. As far as I know. It's just . . . I worry about him. He works in the music business, you see, and the temptation must be there for him all the time.'

Baker nodded understandingly. 'Well, rest assured, Miss Finch, there is no evidence that your father has either used or sold drugs since his release from prison in 1986. No, his name cropped up during the course of a separate investigation, in relation to an incident in which we know for certain that he had no active part.'

'Right,' said Sasha, wanting to be convinced but sounding doubtful despite her best efforts.

Abruptly, before she could enquire further, he stood up. 'Well, thank you very much, Miss Finch. As I say, don't hesitate to get in touch if you need anything. I hope you feel better very soon.'

From the hospital, Baker drove to a rather plush apartment block close to Chelsea Harbour, an area whose businesses consisted almost exclusively of antique shops selling outrageously priced goods and restaurants selling outrageously priced food. He parked in a spacious car park close to an elevated granite sculpture of what appeared to be an enormous Polo mint, then walked across to the apartment block: an edifice of clean grey stone, gleaming metal tubes (Baker supposed the tubes were meant to be aesthetically pleasing, though to him they looked like nothing more than hi-tech scaffolding) and an abundance of smoked glass.

The entrance lobby contained a large wooden desk, behind which perched a porter. The man acted like the snootiest butler in the world until Baker pressed his ID to the smoked-glass door, upon which he became so slimily obsequious that Baker felt like washing his hands after taking his leave of him.

Mark Cotto – another of the names that Michael Mercy had scribbled on his wall – lived on the ninth floor. He was a theatre designer, and a bloody successful one by all accounts. He had worked on a number of very prestigious productions in the West End, one or two of which Baker had even seen.

The lift was soundless, and smelled of new carpets and air-conditioning. Baker watched as the lights climbed smoothly to 9. Then, with barely a lurch, the doors slid open and he stepped out on to a landing that would have done credit to the most palatial of hotels. He was confronted with three doors, all unnumbered, though the names of the occupants had been printed on strips of card and inserted into slots beneath the gleaming, gold-coloured doorbell panels. The closest name tag to Baker read Ms L. Rawlinson-Jones. The second one read Mr M. Cotto.

Baker pressed his thumb to the cold golden nipple of the door-bell and heard a tastefully musical chine sound inside the flat. After Finch's odd about-face upon receiving his all-too-brief phone call last night (a call which Baker guessed had contained some kind of warning or threat), he had decided not to ring ahead but to arrive unannounced: the disadvantage, of course, being that the man he had come to see might very well be out.

He wasn't, however, though Baker was surprised when the door was tugged open. His friends and colleagues always claimed he had been blessed with a bat's hearing – a gift which had served him well on more than one occasion – yet this time he had heard nothing of Cotto's approach. Either the doors were extremely stout, the carpets extremely plush or Cotto extremely light-footed.

At least, Baker assumed it was Mark Cotto who stood before him. The man was no more than five-seven, stocky, round-faced, with dark receding hair scraped back into a ponytail and a neat goatee beard. He wore a well-cut, collarless, charcoal-grey suit and a collarless white shirt with no tie.

'Yes?' he said, his voice surprisingly soft, almost girlish.

'Mr Cotto?' said Baker.

'Yes.'

'Mr Cotto, I'm Detective Inspector Baker.' He flashed his ID. 'May I come in?'

69

'Of course,' said Cotto calmly, as if he had been expecting this. He turned and walked sedately down the corridor, leaving Baker to enter and close the door behind him.

He is light-footed, Baker thought, *and small-footed too*; his black suede shoes could be no more than size six or seven. Despite his physical stockiness, Cotto possessed an economy of movement, an almost balletic grace, that Baker found . . . the only word that sprang to mind was *creepy*. A little warily, Baker followed him down the corridor and into a sitting room with brick-red walls and a coral-coloured carpet. The surfaces were dominated by sculptures that were mostly abstract, disturbingly organic. They reminded Baker of strangely distorted human organs, sexually entwined sea creatures.

Above the ornate fireplace with its marble surround was a painting of a face rising from a mass of darkness; a well, perhaps, or a pit. The face was maggot-white, hairless, with black gashes for eyes and a larger gash for a mouth. Indeed, without ears, nose, lips, teeth or tongue, the face might have been a mask, a white pillowcase slashed with a knife, except that it seemed to possess a kind of instinctive idiot-life. The title of the painting, engraved on a plaque below, was 'Need'.

'Glenn's work,' Cotto said softly.

'I beg your pardon, sir?'

Cotto crossed the room and sat down, formal and straight-backed, on the edge of a busily patterned sofa. He looked up at Baker, his movements fastidious, precise. He blinked once, slowly, his dainty, beautifully manicured hands folded neatly in his lap. Those hands didn't move when he spoke, and neither did his head, nor his shoulders, nor his feet, which remained pressed to the floor.

'Glenn Coleman. My partner. Would you like some coffee, Inspector?'

'Er . . . yes, please,' said Baker, the offer catching him unawares.

Cotto stood without effort and padded soundlessly out of the room. Baker suppressed a shudder. He had met some strange people – some downright evil people – in his time, but he had never before encountered anyone so eerily still, so rigidly self-possessed.

He wandered around the room for a few minutes, telling

himself he was merely being curious, but subconsciously trying to find some evidence of human warmth, something to diminish the sinister, enigmatic aura that clung to Mark Cotto. The closest he came was a postcard of a seahorse propped against a clock on the mantelpiece, on the back of which was scrawled: *Dear M & G, Thanks for Wednesday. Wonderful evening. I love you both dearly. Tanya.*

Despite the dark walls, the sitting room was full of natural light, thanks to a pair of sliding glass doors which led out to a sizeable balcony. The balcony held some white wrought-iron garden furniture – a table and four chairs – and a large number of pot plants. Baker was standing at the doors, looking out at the view over Chelsea Harbour, when Cotto's soft voice intruded. 'Cream and sugar, Inspector?'

Baker jumped, turned round. Cotto had returned; he was sitting on the sofa again, a tray on the low table before him, pouring coffee from a cafetiere into two large blue-and-white checked cups.

'Not for me, thanks. I take it black,' Baker replied, a little too gruffly.

Cotto made no response. Expressionless, he handed Baker his cup and poured a generous allowance of cream into his own.

Baker decided to get down to business. He sat in an armchair facing Cotto, placed his cup on a small side table and reached into the inside pocket of his jacket. He withdrew the photograph of Michael Mercy. 'Mr Cotto, I'm here in connection with an incident that occurred yesterday morning, in Surbiton. Tell me – have you ever heard the name Michael Mercy before?'

Cotto regarded Baker steadily. 'No, I'm afraid I haven't.'

'Are you quite certain, Mr Cotto? Could Michael Mercy have been a business acquaintance, perhaps? Someone you had brief dealings with, whose name has temporarily slipped your mind?'

'I'm certain that I have never encountered either the name or the man before,' said Cotto, with such quiet conviction that Baker believed him.

The DI sighed. Feeling that he was doing no more than going through the motions, he held out the photograph. 'Would you mind just looking at this, sir, and telling me whether this man looks familiar at all?'

Cotto leaned forward and took the photograph with such a light touch that Baker hardly felt it leave his hand. *He'd make a great pickpock*—the DI began to think, and then the thought dissolved as his attention focused wholly on Mark Cotto. Something very strange appeared to be happening.

The instant the theatre designer held the photograph of Michael Mercy up to his face, he seemed to switch off. To glaze over. His eyes had grown as vacant as the eyes of the numerous corpses that Baker had seen during his career. The DI got the weird impression that if he were to go over and give Cotto a shove, the man would simply topple stiffly over like one of his unpleasant sculptures.

Baker had heard of a condition called catalepsy, in which the sufferer, often without warning, slipped into a trance-like state. He wondered whether it was catalepsy that was affecting Mark Cotto now. Perhaps it was this which accounted for his peculiar behaviour, his unnerving lizard-like stillness . . .

Baker licked his lips. 'Mr Cotto?' he said tentatively.

Cotto did not respond.

Baker spoke the man's name again, more urgently. This time Cotto *did* respond; he did not blink or jerk, like a sleepwalker awoken, but merely lowered his arm. He held the photograph out, making Baker stretch to reach it.

'I'm sorry, Inspector, the man is unknown to me,' he said in his soft, girlish voice.

Baker took the photograph and replaced it in his pocket, wondering whether to pass comment on Cotto's behaviour. In the end, he simply said, 'Are you – all right, Mr Cotto?'

Cotto looked at him steadily. For the first time Baker noticed how pale his eyes were, how large and dark his pupils. 'Perfectly, thank you.'

He's a druggie, thought Baker, reaching for his coffee cup. *He's high on something – that's why he's behaving like he is. Hell, he's so spaced out he isn't even asking who Michael Mercy is, what he's done, why his own name has cropped up in the investigation.*

And yet, even as these thoughts rattled through his mind, attempting to reassure, Baker knew that they didn't quite ring true. He had encountered many drug-users in his time and not a single one of them had behaved as Mark Cotto did. Drugs could make you soporific or crazy or friendly or insensible or any one of a hundred things, but one thing they did not do was give you a snake-like poise.

72

He decided to leave it for now. Explore other avenues, come back if needs be at a later date, when hopefully Cotto would be restored to normality. He picked up his cup, intending to gulp his coffee quickly and make his farewells, but as he brought the cup to his lips he focused on it for the first time, and instantly everything changed.

There was blood on the cup. Not much – just a thumbprint where in another second he would have placed his lips. Baker paused, then lowered the cup carefully back to the saucer. He looked at Cotto, at Cotto's hands. Sure enough, as the theatre designer raised his own cup and took a bird-like sip, Baker noticed that there were flecks of blood on the fingers of his right hand and faint reddish fingerprints on the handle of his cup, rather like the prints that a grubby child might leave.

Baker wondered why he hadn't noticed the blood when Cotto had taken the photograph or handed it back. Perhaps the theatre designer had held it in his left hand; or maybe he had actually cut his finger *on* the photo. After all, there wasn't a lot of blood – just about the same amount that might come from a paper cut.

All the same, it was odd for Cotto not to have noticed it, particularly considering how fastidious he seemed to be. Despite all that he had seen and heard and done during his twenty-one years on the force, Baker felt his mouth growing tacky; he had to swish his tongue around like a little mop to prevent it drying up altogether. He didn't understand what was going on; that was what was making him nervous. He would have felt better had Cotto suddenly produced a knife and lunged at him – at least then he would have known exactly where he stood, would have been able to react appropriately.

'Have you cut yourself, Mr Cotto?' he heard himself asking, his voice seeming to reverberate down a hollow tube.

'No,' said Cotto softly.

'You have blood on your hands,' Baker said, and now his voice was almost as soft as the theatre designer's.

Cotto looked at his hand with no surprise whatsoever. 'That isn't my blood. It's Glenn's,' he said.

Not just Baker's heart, but the whole world seemed to skip a beat. For a moment the DI felt certain he would be unable to speak. Then, with an effort, he blurted, 'What?'

'That isn't my blood, it's Glenn's,' Cotto repeated in exactly the same tone as before.

Baker swallowed, thinking furiously. He asked, with a calmness he didn't feel, 'Where *is* Glenn exactly?'

'In the kitchen,' Cotto said.

'Do you mind if I take a look?'

'Of course not.'

Baker left Cotto sitting primly on the settee and went out of the room into the hallway, pulling the sitting-room door closed behind him – he didn't want Cotto creeping up behind him on his dainty cat's-feet. His heart had begun to pump hard and fast, as if he had juddered to a halt at the end of a brisk three-mile run. He peeked round two doors – one opening on to a study full of sketches and scale models for stage sets, the other a walk-in cupboard containing a vacuum cleaner, an ironing board and a wooden shelf stacked with cleaning materials – before he found the kitchen.

He didn't know what he expected to find, but his first impression was that there was nothing wrong here. The room was spotlessly clean and full of bright sunshine flooding through the small window over the sink. There was a breakfast bar flanked by four tall three-legged stools; a large wine rack full of bottles; a dishwasher and washing machine; cooker and hob; microwave; fridge . . .

Fridge.

It wasn't until his gaze swept over it for the second time that Baker noticed the blood pooled on the floor beneath it. He crossed the room, his swimming senses giving him the impression that he was taking long, slow, loping strides. His hand reached out and gripped the fridge's chrome handle. There was a smear of blood to the right of it, shockingly red on the otherwise pristine white door. He tugged on the handle and the fridge came open with a wet sucking sound.

Baker's first impression was that there was something large and red and alive in there, something that oozed slowly like a slug. Then he saw that the movement was caused, not by anything living, but by the huge quantity of blood which the cold had reduced to the consistency of glue, dripping in thick candles through the grilles of the shelves. The blood was coming from the many severed body parts which had been stacked and rammed in

74

with the eggs and the milk, the butter and the tomatoes, the plastic tubs of hummus and taramasalata and mixed beans in vinaigrette.

Baker saw two hands and two feet (one of the feet had a black toenail as if something heavy had been dropped on it recently), chunks of hairy limb – it was difficult to differentiate between arms and legs – and slabs of what Baker could only assume were torso or buttock-flesh. In the perspex box at the bottom of the fridge which would normally contain salad was a human head, jammed in so that its distorted, blank-eyed, gaping-mouthed face was pressed against the perspex, gazing out.

Baker looked at the contents of Mark Cotto's fridge for a full minute before shutting the door. Contained in there was madness, pure and simple. Oddly, now that Baker had had Cotto's psychotic state of mind well and truly confirmed, he felt better equipped to deal with what was to come.

He stood up, his knees creaking. He turned and walked back out of the kitchen and down the corridor, keeping a wary eye out in case Cotto should leap at him from behind one of the doors along the landing. At the door of the sitting room, he paused a moment to listen, then braced himself and shoved the door open. He paused on the threshold, taking in the entire room at a glance. At first he thought that Cotto was hiding – or that he had fled. And then he caught a glimpse of dark movement, out on the balcony.

He's trying to climb down to the next floor, he thought. Then he realised what the theatre designer's real intentions were, and he broke into a run.

He was too late. His hand was still reaching for the handle of the double glass doors as Cotto stood on the railing, arms held out like a tightrope walker's. And by the time Baker had tugged the door open, Cotto was gone, his stout little body falling soundlessly through the air, arms outstretched as if to embrace the concrete below.

Thirteen

If it hadn't been for her hair, Nick would not have recognised her. As it was, he had to look twice at the girl with the swollen purple face to assure himself it was Sasha. The girl blinked at him through the bloodshot slits of her eyes and smiled a crooked, ghastly smile. 'Dad,' she said, the word wheezing out of her.

The instant he heard her voice, something took hold of Nick's innards and squeezed them hard. Like any parent, his worst nightmare had always been the thought of his child – his little girl – being hurt, be it physically or emotionally, it was impossible to describe the intensity and complexity of that protective urge. When Sasha spoke to him a whole plethora of emotions whipped though his mind like a sandstorm. Guilt and shame at not having been there to protect her; a sick, overwhelming desolation that she had had to undergo the pain and terror of such an awful ordeal; a sheer, burning rage directed at whoever had done this. At that moment, Nick would have gleefully tortured Sasha's assailant well beyond the point at which he screamed for mercy, would have rammed red-hot pokers into his eyes, hammered spikes of metal beneath his fingernails, removed his testicles with bolt-cutters.

He crossed to Sasha's hospital bed on watery legs, trying desperately not to show how upset he was. He planted a smile that really did not want to be there on his lips and said, 'Hi, How you doing?'

'Okay,' she said. 'Who told you? The police?'

He nodded. 'They came round to Jenna's this morning. That's where I was last night.' As he said this he felt his guilt and his shame grow even more acute; he had been merrily fucking a virtual stranger last night while, back at his flat, someone had been smashing their fists into his daughter's lovely face—

'Sorry for scaring you,' she said.

He felt tears rushing to the backs of his eyes then, and furiously tried to blink them away. 'Hey, *I'm* sorry for not being there,' he said, unable to prevent his voice from fading to a whisper. 'I should have been. I'm so sorry.'

Gently he reached out and they embraced one another. *My Sasha*, he thought. *My little girl. How could anyone do this to her?*

He knew *he* should have been the one comforting *her*; but all he could do was struggle to bite back his tears as she murmured, 'It's okay, Dad. It wasn't your fault.'

He heard a sound behind him, the scuff of feet on the tiled floor. He disengaged himself from his daughter and looked round. Linsey was standing there, holding a plastic cup of steaming tea. She looked thin, hollow-eyed.

'Hi, Linsey,' he said.

She gave the barest of nods. 'If I'd known you were coming, I'd have got you a cup.'

'It's okay,' he said, and gave a loud sniff in an effort to clear away the tears still brimming behind his eyes. 'Sit down,' he said, pulling up a metal-framed chair with an orange plastic seat for the woman who was the mother of his child. 'I'll go and get myself a chair from over there.' He indicated a stack beside the large double doors into the ward.

When he returned Sasha was sipping water through a straw from a plastic cup. She only sipped a little then put it aside. For a moment there was an uncomfortable silence. Nick felt inhibited in Linsey's presence; he and Linsey had always got on okay, but then they had always kept things light and relatively uninvolved between them. This, for them, was a whole new situation, a potentially emotionally-charged situation. It made him realise how little trouble Sasha had caused them both in her growing up. If there had been such a thing as a model child, then she was it.

'Well,' Sasha said finally in her effortful wheeze of a voice, 'isn't anyone going to ask me what happened?'

Nick looked at Linsey, but she refused to catch his eye. He shrugged. 'Well . . . if you want to tell us,' he said hesitantly. 'It's not that we're not interested – you know that. But I thought you might not want to talk about it.'

'I don't mind,' she said. 'In fact, it makes me feel better to talk about it. I mean, I think I'm handling it okay, but I still feel really shaky, really scared, when I think about it and talking makes it . . . makes it not seem so bad, somehow. Like I'm sharing my burden with others. Does that sound really dumb?'

'Of course not,' said Nick. Linsey shook her head, her lips tight.

'Right,' said Sasha. She settled back in her bed, her hands crossed over her stomach. Nick was gratified to see that she did not wince when she moved, suggesting that her injuries were purely facial: an observation which was borne out by her recounting of events.

'When I came to, the guy had gone,' she finished. 'I crawled to the phone and rang the police, and then – thank God – I managed to get myself dressed before they arrived. No way were they going to find me naked – that would have been *really* embarrassing.'

'And the police seemed pretty sure it was just a burglar?' asked Nick.

'As opposed to what?' said Linsey, a little frostily.

He felt flustered, but tried not to show it. 'Well . . . I don't know. A rapist, say.'

He saw Sasha wince and instantly felt a stab of regret. 'Oh, Sash, I'm sorry. That was pretty tactless.'

'No, it's okay. It's a natural thing to think.' She paused a moment, clearly preparing herself to voice something that would be difficult for her. Then she said, quietly, 'That was my fear. As I was lying there, all I could think was that I had to stay conscious because I was terrified of what he might do to me if I passed out. I couldn't, though.' For an instant a look of intense distress crossed her face; she seemed to gulp it down, nasty-tasting like medicine. Linsey took her hand as she continued. 'The policeman who came to see me this morning – Inspector Baker – said that he thought the guy was definitely a burglar.'

'Baker?' repeated Nick, startled.

'Oh, yeah – he mentioned he'd been to see you yesterday.'

Linsey's head jerked, bird-like, to look at him. 'Really? What about?'

'Oh . . . it was nothing.'

'It must have been something. What have you been up to, Nick?'

78

'I haven't been up to *anything*!' he exclaimed, aware that he sounded like a guilty schoolboy protesting his innocence.

Linsey jumped to the same conclusion that Sasha had jumped to that morning. 'You're not messing about with drugs again, are you?'

'Of course not,' he said, feeling like a criminal in spite of himself. Some of his misplaced guilt must have shown on his face, because Linsey scowled. 'You bloody are, aren't you?'

'No, I'm *not*,' said Nick undignantly, but Linsey was in full spate now, her words overlapping his.

'Well, I hope you're bloody satisfied. Thanks to your . . . your selfishness and stupidity, your daughter's been beaten to a pulp. You bloody bastard!'

'Mum,' urged Sasha, 'keep your voice down.'

Struggling to keep his own voice calm, Nick said, 'I haven't been taking drugs. I haven't bought drugs or sold drugs or even *seen* any drugs, not for years.'

This was not strictly true; in his line of work he saw plenty of drugs. Hell, he was even offered drugs on a regular basis – mostly blow, but also speed and even the big H on occasion. It would only make matters worse to tell Linsey this, however; she wouldn't believe he had never succumbed to temptation. She thought him weak-willed, undisciplined; though she had never come right out and said it, Nick suspected she regarded him as a terrible influence on her daughter.

'So why *did* Inspector Baker come to see you, Dad?' asked Sasha softly, giving him the opportunity to defend himself.

Nick sighed, and decided to tell part of it; just enough to get Linsey off his back. 'A casual work colleague – someone I've only met once or twice – committed suicide yesterday without leaving a note. My name was in his address book. I think the police are just following things up. Ruling out the possibility of foul play.'

He looked at Sasha, hoping she would not link this collection of semi-truths to his vision in the Gridlock. She didn't appear to, but she looked puzzled. 'Inspector Baker said he was worried about you. Why would he say that?'

Linsey was still regarding him suspiciously; Nick shrugged, trying to appear casual. 'I suppose because I got pretty upset when he broke the news to me.'

'I thought you said you hardly knew this man,' Linsey said.

'I didn't, but it was still a shock. Mortality angst, maybe.'

To Nick the explanation sounded weak, horribly implausible, but neither Sasha no Linsey commented on it.

'So how long are they keeping you in for, Sash?' he asked, deliberately changing the subject.

'Just overnight for observation. I know I look bad, but most of it's just bruising. He bust my nose and fractured my cheekbone, but I didn't lose any teeth, which is the main thing. I'll just have to put up with looking like Frankenstein's monster in a blonde wig for a few weeks.'

Nick grinned. 'So we still have a date for the day after tomorrow then? – The Portishead gig?' He decided to pretend he hadn't noticed Linsey's obvious disapproval.

'Just try and keep me away,' said Sasha.

Fourteen

Nick told Jenna – who had been waiting for him in the hospital car park – all about it on the drive back to his flat.

Jenna pursed her lips. 'Maybe this *is* all to do with drugs,' she said thoughtfully.

'Not you too,' said Nick in dismay, but Jenna responded quickly.

'No, no, I'm not accusing you of anything. What I mean is, perhaps the police have some reason to *think* you're dealing drugs – you know, because of your past. Maybe they're keeping tabs on you for that reason.'

Nick shrugged. 'It doesn't explain all the Michael Mercy stuff, does it?'

'No, but then again who's to say that everything is related?'

'Hmm,' said Nick obviously. 'I wish I just had some time and space to think all this through. I feel as though it's all whizzing around in my head and I'm not grasping any of it. This Inspector Baker, for instance – is he a real policeman, or what? If he isn't, then presumably it was the police who rang me up to warn me against him – but then who *is* Baker? What's his interest in all this? On the other hand, if he *is* a real policeman, then who the hell rang me up?'

'Quelle mysterioso,' murmured Jenna, grimacing in sympathy.

There was no grey van parked on the street when they pulled up in front of Nick's flat. Everything appeared quiet, normal. Yet despite this – and the fact that he had already spoken to the two police officers who had come to Jenna's flat that morning – Nick half-expected armed detectives to appear from nowhere and surround him the instant he stepped from the car, half-expected

81

panda cars to screech around the corner and slew across the road, cutting off his retreat.

He didn't see a soul, however, as he went through the gate and up the steps to unlock the front door, Jenna in tow. When he entered the building he expected it to feel different – *invaded*, somehow – but it felt the same as ever.

The two of them trudged silently up the stairs, almost holding their breath, Nick's hand trembling as he unlocked the door of his flat. Even here, apart from the gaps where his video, stereo and some of his CDs had been, nothing seemed out of place. He felt a morbid urge to check the bathroom, half-expecting – dreading it – to see Sasha's blood on the carpet. However, to his relief there were no spots or stains in evidence. He pulled the shower curtain back and looked down into the bath at the place where Sasha's assailant had stood. There were no dirty boot-prints, no scuffs or scrapes on the white plastic. Straightening up, he looked around for a moment, almost sniffing the air. It was not that he wanted to find evidence of what had occurred here; on the contrary. He wanted to ensure that there were no echoes of the ordeal his daughter had been through, no residue of her pain and fear.

'She'll be okay, you know.'

Nick jumped, then turned to see Jenna standing in the doorway, concern on her face. 'What?'

'Sasha. She'll be fine. I know it's a shock, but it wasn't as though she was badly injured.'

'I know,' said Nick. 'It's just . . . she's my little girl. I hate the thought of anything even remotely nasty happening to her.'

'She probably wants to protect you as much as you want to protect her.'

Nick smiled. 'Probably. Do you think I'm being silly?'

Jenna matched his smile with one of her own. 'Course not. Come on – let's go bug-hunting.'

For the next hour and a half the two of them searched the flat as thoroughly as they were able. They checked under carpets and items of furniture, between books and CDs, inside plant pots and on the tops of shelves. They even unscrewed light bulbs and Nick took the back off the TV to check inside. They found nothing.

'I don't even know what I'm looking for,' Nick admitted at last, feeling hot and frustrated. 'I've only ever seen bugs in James

82

Bond films. In real life they probably look nothing like they do in the movies.'

Jenna flopped on the sofa, her cheeks flushed. 'At least we tried.'

Nick fetched a couple of diet Cokes from the kitchen. He handed one to Jenna. 'Maybe the flat *was* bugged, but that guy last night came to remove them all. Maybe he was doing it when Sasha showed up, and when she found him in the bath he punched her out and took some stuff away with him to make it look like a burglary.' He crossed to the telephone and picked it up.

'What are you doing?' asked Jenna.

'I'm going to ring the police and find out if there really is a DI Baker. And if there is, I'm going to tell him everything I know.'

Fifteen

At the same time that Nick and Jenna were starting their bug-hunt, DI Baker was arriving back at the station, having stayed to oversee the clearing-up of the mess that Mark Cotto had become. He knew he had handled the Cotto situation badly, that he would have to face some tough questioning before the day was out. In leaving Cotto alone he had committed the cardinal sin: the man's strange behaviour, coupled with the blood on his fingers, should have been enough to ensure that Baker hadn't let him out of his sight for a moment.

It wouldn't have been *quite* so bad if this had been the first time that Baker – by entering Cotto's flat unaccompanied – had put himself in a delicate situation. In fact he was notorious for pursuing investigations alone, had been reprimanded for it on more than one occasion. Indeed, his colleagues often referred to him as 'Lone Wolf' (a nickname which Baker rolled his eyes at, but which secretly he rather liked). He knew, however, that it was a comment not only on his working methods, but also on the fact that he was unmarried, unattached, introverted: even – in their eyes – stand-offish and aloof.

It was not an image that Baker cultivated for effect; it was simply that he felt more comfortable on his own. People, he had found, cluttered up his physical and mental space, intruded on his thought-processes. He had tried explaining this to Dalby several times, but needless to say the Chief Inspector had never understood. Instead he had harped on in that annoyingly reasonable way of his about 'compromising situations' and 'unnecessary risks'.

The infuriating thing, of course, was that this time Dalby had been proved right. Baker had thought Cotto a safe bet. The theatre

84

designer had not been suspected of a crime or of being a witness to one; nor was he a known criminal. As he took the short, familiar walk to the Chief Inspector's office, Baker castigated himself for forgetting one of life's great truths: that the biggest blows always came when you were least expecting them. It was a lesson he had learned over and over again during his time on the force, yet on this occasion – perhaps caught unawares, disconcerted by Cotto's strange manner – he had allowed himself to become careless, complacent.

He double-rapped smartly on Dalby's door, not wanting to appear timid. When the summons came he entered Dalby's office. Like a reflection of the man himself, it was immaculately neat.

Dalby appeared to be engrossed in a sheaf of reports, head down, spectacles perched on the end of his nose, as if someone other than he had called 'Come' less than five seconds before. Baker was about to say that he'd come back later if Dalby was busy when the Chief Inspector glanced up. 'Ah, Mike! Come in, come in. Pull up a chair.'

A plush burgundy carpet rendered Baker's footfalls soundless as he crossed to a large desk whose surface looked as if it had been deliberately arranged to give the impression that a very busy but extraordinarily organised person worked there. Opposite the desk, standing proudly against the wall, was a glass-fronted display cabinet in which Dalby kept his gleaming golf trophies. On the walls were framed diplomas, a couple of tasteful but insipid land-scapes, and a large photograph of Dalby's perfect nuclear family – attractive wife, chip-off-the-old-block son, angelic daughter. Dalby himself, who was the only one standing up in the photo (right hand resting lightly on his wife's right shoulder, left hand on his son's left – the guardian, the protector, the solver of all ills), looked smug; but then, he *always* looked smug. He thought himself everybody's friend, everybody's confidant, everybody's agony uncle. Baker didn't think there was anybody in the station who actually *liked* him.

'You wanted to see me, sir,' Baker said, his voice neutral.

'Ah, yes. Yes, indeed I did.' Dalby leaned forward, resting on his elbows, and meshed the fingers of his hands together on his desk blotter. At forty-nine he was fit and tanned and looking forward to early retirement. He had a trim grey beard which made him look distinguished rather than old, and he was wearing his look of professional concern: 'social worker mode', his subordinates called it. 'There's no point beating around the bush, Mike,' he said. 'I'm afraid I'm going to have to take you off the Michael Mercy case.'

Baker flinched inwardly, but remained stone-faced. 'May I ask why, sir?'

'Of course you may, Mike. It's your prerogative.' At times like this, Baker was never sure whether the Chief Inspector was sincere or whether he was taking the piss. He remained silent, and after a brief pause Dalby went on. 'I'm simply acting on orders from the Commissioner.'

'The Commissioner? What's he got to do with it? Surely the Mark Cotto situation is an internal matter?'

'This has nothing to do with Mark Cotto, or so I understand – though I don't think you would have any cause to complain if it had, Mike, do you? I'm sure you are aware that the Cotto incident was appallingly badly handled—'

'Yes,' Baker said, 'I *am* aware as it happens, and I'm prepared to take full responsibility, but I don't see what—'

Dalby held up a hand, his brow creasing almost imperceptibly. 'Please, Mike,' he said mildly, 'if you will just allow me to finish? As I was saying, the Mark Cotto situation was badly handled, not least because you blatantly disobeyed my previous instructions not to act as a . . . er . . . lone wolf, as it were. I think from that viewpoint alone, the Commissioner would be more than entitled to remove you from the investigation pending further inquiry. You do realise there will have to *be* an inquiry about this incident, don't you, Mike?'

'I wouldn't expect anything else,' Baker said drily, and then added, as diffidently as he could, 'May I ask you something, sir?'

This approach, Baker knew, would appeal to Dalby's vanity: he liked to be thought of as the man with the answers, the man to whom subordinates deferred when they were confused or uncertain. And indeed, Dalby seemed almost to swell in his chair, to sit up straighter, his chest jutting. 'Of course you may, Mike,' he said generously.

'I was just wondering, sir . . . if the Commissioner didn't take me off the Michael Mercy case because of Mark Cotto, then why *did* he take me off it?'

Dalby pursed his lips, as if considering how much of his vast

86

store of information he should deign to impart. Finally he said, 'I understand that the Commissioner himself was acting upon orders received.'

'From whom, sir?'

Dalby looked momentarily uncertain. 'From a higher authority. I'm afraid I'm not at liberty to tell you any more than that.'

That's because you don't know any more, Baker thought, but nodded meekly. 'I see. So what am I supposed to do now, sir?'

'Your immediate task is to hand over your case file and computer records of the Mercy case over to me, and then to erase all information pertaining to the case from your hard disk.'

Baker blinked. 'Isn't that somewhat irregular, sir?'

'Irregular or not, Mike, it's what you are required to do.'

Baker looked at him hard for several seconds. 'And then what shall I do, sir?'

Dalby smiled, as if he were doing Baker a big favour. 'I suggest you take a week off, Mike. In fact, I insist upon it. It will give you time to collect your thoughts, recharge your batteries.'

'And what about the inquiry, sir?'

'The inquiry will still be there when you get back. These things take time, as you know. Now go home and relax.'

Not before printing out a list of the names that Mercy wrote on his wall, Baker thought. But he smiled. 'Yes, sir,' he said.

Sixteen

Nick spent that Friday afternoon working on the Thunderhead piece, finally completing and sending it just before seven a.m. For music he had to rely on his old JVC radio-cassette player and his stock of dust-gathering tapes, most of which he had replaced with their CD equivalents, but which he had felt loath to throw out. Good job: if it hadn't been for them he would have had to work in silence, which he hated. Especially at present. He would have forever been listening for footfalls on the stairs, for the surreptitious click of hidden cameras and microphones. Just because he and Jenna hadn't found anything didn't mean that the flat was clean, though Nick still believed that the man who had assaulted Sasha last night had been here to remove surveillance equipment. As to *why* he had come to remove it, Nick could only guess. He liked to think that whoever had planted the devices had no further interest in him, but thought it more likely that they had removed the stuff because they believed he and Jenna might be getting too close to the truth.

He yawned and stretched, leaning back in his typing chair. It was dark outside now, the flat lit only by the light from his screen and the umber wash of the street lamps, which adhered like oil to every surface.

Finishing the piece – which had captured his attention for the past five hours – only left a gap which the memory of that morning now rushed to occupy. A weight of frustration and anger filled his belly, and not just because of how he had felt when he had seen the results of what Sasha had had to endure. After the fruitless bug-hunt, he had called the police in search of DI Baker, only to be passed from pillar to post before finally being informed that Baker was on leave and unavailable.

'That's nice for him,' Nick had said caustically into the phone, 'but if he's on leave he's not the same man that I'm after. The DI Baker I want only spoke to my daughter this morning. He's dealing with the Michael Mercy case.'

'Would you mind holding the line, sir?' the very young-sounding constable on the other end said.

Nick sighed. 'Do I have a choice?'

'Sorry about the delay, sir,' the voice said blandly. 'I'll get back to you as soon as I can.'

Nick waited for several more minutes, listening to the hissing silence, wondering whether someone, somewhere, was listening in too, perhaps even recording the call. At one point he murmured, 'Lucky I'm not being murdered,' half-expecting a response, but none came. In truth he expected the young man to come back on the phone and say, 'I'm terribly sorry, sir, but *our* DI Baker has no connection with the Michael Mercy case. That's being handled by DI Bloggs.'

All at once, however, there was a different voice on the line – smooth, cultured, reassuring. 'This is Detective Chief Inspector Dalby,' the voice said. 'How may I help you?'

Nick repeated his desire to speak to DI Baker about the Michael Mercy case and was informed – very apologetically – that Baker was currently on a week's leave and would no longer be handling that particular inquiry.

'Well, who is then?' Nick asked.

'At the current time we don't have a senior officer *per se* attached to the inquiry,' Dalby said smoothly, 'but if you were to come into the station at your convenience, Mr ... ah ... Finch, then one of my officers would be only too happy to speak to you.'

'You've got no one attached to a major murder inquiry?' Nick said. 'You're kidding!'

'Please, Mr Finch – don't misinterpret my words. I said that we have no *senior* officer attached to the inquiry, which simply means that we are in a change-over period and that until a senior officer is assigned, then I myself will oversee the inquiry. Please be reassured, Mr Finch, that this change of personnel will have no detrimental effect on the speed and efficiency of the inquiry in question. I have a dedicated team working on it as we speak. And as I have already stated, there will be an officer ready and willing to hear your statement should you wish to come down to the station.'

Well, that's put me in my place, Nick thought. 'Okay. I'll come down to the station now, if I may.'

'Of course you may,' Dalby said. 'We'll be only too happy to see you.'

Jenna had offered to stick with him, call into work sick, but Nick had told her he thought he could manage alone. She had dropped him off outside, making him promise to get in touch later.

Inside the station Nick was introduced to DI Richards, a thin-faced man with swept-back blond hair who ushered him into an interview room. After switching on a tape recorder, Richards proceeded to listen to Nick's story with what appeared to be po-faced indifference. Indeed, although Richards' expression never changed (the man failed even to raise an eyebrow when Nick recounted his experience in the Gridlock, and the odd phone call that he had received during his conversation with Baker), as time wore on Nick fancied he could detect waves not merely of indifference but of open disbelief emanating from the man. This, in turn, undermined his confidence, causing his voice to falter and his head to drop, causing him in fact to begin to doubt the validity of his own story.

Finally, in desperation, he blurted, 'Look, I know how this sounds, Inspector, but it's all true. I promise you.'

There was a pulse of silence, during which the echo of Nick's bleating voice seemed to hang mockingly in the air. Then Richards said, evenly, 'I never suggested otherwise, sir.'

Nick looked down at the table, at his hands which he was struggling to keep from trembling. He felt so uncomfortable that he was finding it difficult to speak. His throat was thick as he mumbled, 'No, but . . . I know what you must be thinking.'

'Really, sir?'

'Yes. Well . . . I know what *I'd* think.'

He glanced up at Richards; the man's implacable face seemed to Nick like a mask, concealing the contempt that must be swarming behind it. Nick felt an urge to justify himself, to *make* the man believe in him, but he had neither the words nor – any longer – the conviction. His shoulders slumped; he felt weary, depressed. Suddenly he just wanted to be out of there.

'So what happens now?' he asked bleakly.

What happened was that, after being thanked for his time and assistance, Nick walked out of the police station and caught a tube

90

home. He had been treated with nothing less than a kind of deadpan courtesy by the DI, yet as he sat on the train and reflected on his experience he squirmed with embarrassment. He imagined Richards giving vent to his true feelings the instant he had left, dismissing him as a nutter, an attention-seeker, a time-waster. The fact that Richards had barely asked him any questions but had merely allowed him to stumble unchallenged to the end of his story was surely evidence enough that he had not taken Nick even the slightest bit seriously.

Nick sighed and rubbed at his face as if his humiliation clung to him like a layer of grime. He couldn't blame Richards for disbelieving him. Sitting in that quiet room, hearing the events of the last few days unfold from his own mouth, even *he* had to admit that it all sounded somewhat far-fetched.

The train rattled, jouncing slightly, the lights in the carriage flickering momentarily on and off. Remembering the smartly dressed couple who Nick believed had been following him the last time he had taken a tube ride, he glanced quickly up and down the carriage. There was no smartly dressed couple this time, but one of the passengers *did* catch his eye: a fat, bearded man reading a copy of the *Daily Express*. SLAUGHTER IN SUBURBIA, screamed the headline on the front page.

Nick glanced now at the coffee table in front of the settee on the far side of the room. That same headline was partly obliterated by the umber light shining in through the window. Upon leaving the tube, Nick had bought a copy of every newspaper that carried the Mercy story and had devoured the coverage with horrified fascination. The facts of the story didn't actually change that much from paper to paper; Nick learned little about the shootings that he didn't already know. Most of what he *did* learn was additional background information on the Mercy family, which seemed to focus on how normal, popular and successful they had been. The little girl, Hannah, had loved ballet and horses and was one of the brightest pupils in her school (weren't they always? thought Nick bitterly); the mother, Sara, had been a partner in a company that sold wedding dresses, and involved in numerous community projects, including the local children's hospice, for whom she worked tirelessly to raise funds; and Michael Mercy himself had been a member of the local rotary and golf clubs. He had even sung in his local choir.

91

The only blot on Mercy's copybook was the fact that he was also a member of a gun club, like other recent shotgun murderers such as Michael Ryan and Thomas Hamilton. Most newspapers, however, including the more lurid tabloids, seemed keen to stress that whereas Ryan and Hamilton had been social inadequates, Mercy had not.

It had been strange seeing it all in black and white, seeing the same photograph that Baker had shown him – Mercy grinning, standing in front of a stretch of water, his cheeks ruddy, hair tousled by the wind – staring out from each front page. It made it all seem ... not so much *real*, because it had been real enough before, but *official* somehow; it made Nick feel he was on the periphery of something big, and more out of his depth than ever.

Before immersing himself in the Thunderhead piece, he had called Jenna on her mobile – listening once again for tell-tale clicks on the line and hearing nothing – and spoken to her at length. She was by turns indignant and sympathetic when he told her how he had been treated in the police station; and yes, she had seen the papers; and yes, she would love to come and see Portishead with him and Sasha tomorrow night.

Now he stood up, intending to switch on some lights and close his curtains and make himself something to eat. He still felt anything but secure in his own flat, still checked to make sure the door was locked every time he went to the bathroom; but, with the perspective that daylight brings, last night's panic had abated somewhat. After all, what was the worst that could happen? If the police or some other official body were keeping tabs on him, then they couldn't do much more than arrest and question him, could they? And if they did that, eventually they would realise that they had made a mistake; they would be forced to let him go. He had nothing to hide, nothing to feel guilty about. It wasn't as if Britain was some banana republic or military dictatorship. He wasn't going to 'disappear'.

He crossed the room, turning on lamps as he went. As he leaned forward to drag the curtains closed he glanced down into the street below – and his heart gave a little jump. The grey van was back, parked across the street, opposite his house. Nick's first instinct was to shrink back from the window, but then a sudden and unexpected surge of anger rushed through him.

Hardly considering what he might be doing, Nick yanked the

curtains closed, stomped back across the room and down the hallway. He unlocked his front door and exited the flat. As though in an attempt to outrun his caution, he ran down the stairs, two, three at a time, feet slapping down, echoing in the stairwell. The cold air that swamped him as he stepped outside the building pulled him up short for a moment, but then he was jogging down the steps to the gate, only slowing to a walk as he crossed the road to where the van was parked beneath an overhanging tree.

It was odd being up close to it. He had previously only thought of it as one might think of a ghost: a vision glimpsed from afar, vanishing into thin air when one investigated too closely. Nick saw now how dirty the van was, how old and battered, the bodywork speckled and blotched with rust. The windows were of smoked glass. Nick cupped his hands and tried to peer through them, but could see nothing. Previously he had thought the van was unmarked, but in fact there *were* registration plates; it was simply dirt that had caused them to blend in with the rest of the vehicle. He bent and wiped a hand across the back plate, trying to memorise the number revealed beneath. Then he straightened up, walked round to the driver's door and banged on it with his fist.

There was no response. Nick banged on the door again, and then on the sides of the van. He banged so hard that the sound echoed clangingly up and down the street. He half-expected people to come to their windows to see what the commotion was about, and if this had been anywhere else but London they might have done. Finally, he placed both hands on the side of the van and shoved hard. The van rocked, creaking, from side to side and then came to rest.

Satisfied that the van was unoccupied, Nick turned to the house it was parked outside. The building was a little shabby, the garden overgrown, but there was a light burning upstairs. He pushed open a wooden gate that had seen better days and walked up the path to the front door. The doorbell sounded like the whine of a high-pitched drill as it vibrated beneath his finger, conjuring up other unwelcome memories. Thirty seconds after pressing it a second time, the door was slowly, cautiously, opened.

A young, bespectacled woman, probably Iraqi or Iranian, peered nervously through the six-inch gap she had created. Nick smiled encouragingly. 'I'm sorry to disturb you. I live across the road, and I was just wondering, is that your van parked on the kerb?'

He gestured behind him. The woman's eyes flickered to follow his finger, then returned to his face. Wordlessly she shook her head.

'Ah, right,' said Nick. 'I don't suppose you know who it belongs to?'

Again the woman shook her head, then pushed the door closed with a click.

'Well, thanks for your help,' Nick said to the closed door. He turned and trudged down the path, through the gate and up the path of the next house along. This house didn't have a doorbell, so he knocked. The door was answered almost immediately as if the occupant had been lurking on the other side.

Nick took a step back; the man confronting him looked as if he spent every spare moment of his time lifting weights. He was wearing a black vest which showed off his massive tattooed arms and shoulders and a good portion of his chest, armour-plated with muscle. His shaven head seemed small by comparison.

'Yeah?' he said, not exactly hostile but not exactly welcoming either,

'Hi,' said Nick. His voice sounded higher than he had intended it to, and he cleared his throat. 'I'm sorry to disturb you, but I was just wondering whether that grey van parked up the road there was yours by any chance?'

The man leaned forward as if there might be several grey vans to choose from; Nick caught a whiff of sour aftershave.

'No, mate,' the man said at last. 'Why, what's up with it?'

For a moment Nick's mind went blank: how could he explain his interest in the van? Then all at once inspiration struck him. 'It's just that I saw some kids hanging around it earlier. I wondered whether they might be trying to break in, thought I'd better warn the owner in case there was anything valuable inside.'

'Oh, right, I see,' the man said, and squared his shoulders. 'Well, sorry I can't help you, mate, but if I see any kids hanging around I'll see 'em off.'

I'm sure you will, Nick thought. 'I don't suppose you've got any idea who it belongs to?' he asked innocently.

The man shook his bullet-shaped head. 'No, mate. Sorry.'

'All right,' said Nick. 'Thanks anyway.'

94

'Yeah. See you, mate.'

Nick walked back to the van and prowled around it once more. He sighed, then looked up and all around him, as if the van's owner might be watching from some nearby window, might do something to give himself away. He briefly considered knocking on more doors, then decided against it; the head of steam he'd built up, powered by his indignation, was evaporating now. At least he'd confronted his fear, assured himself that the van was no phantom carriage. Indeed, it now seemed more likely that it was a low-grade passion wagon than anything else: there was probably a mattress in the back and packets of condoms in the glove compartment. Nick turned away, then paused a moment and went round to the back of the van. He extended a finger, and on the sticky layer of grime coating the dark windows at the back he wrote three words.

LEAVE ME ALONE.

Seventeen

Several hours later Nick opened his eyes and stared into the blackness above him. Until that moment he had been sleeping soundly; surprisingly, he had had no trouble at all falling asleep, and there had been no recurrence of his recent nightmares. Now, however, his head was so muggy, so . . . *clotted*, that he felt neither asleep nor awake but trapped in some limbo in between. Furthermore, without knowing why, he realised he was terrified. He had a distinct awareness that there was something in the room with him, something absolutely yet indefinably awful.

He tried to turn his head, certain that whatever it was was standing or crouching beside his bed. But he found that he couldn't move. He tried to lift his arms, his legs, tried to twitch a finger, but it was no use; his body was rigid, unresponsive. His terror became augmented by panic which screwed itself into him, rippling out along his useless limbs. He *had* to move, *had* to get out, away from the terrible presence that shared his room.

How long he lay there for he had no idea: it seemed like hours. Throughout that time his sense of dream-like terror never abated; in fact, it grew to such an extent that at last it seemed somehow to find a voice, to become a shrill and persistent ringing in his ears.

Then, like the blade of conscious thought pushed through the soft protective coating of sleep, Nick suddenly realised that the ringing was not *inside* but *outside*. It was the telephone, ringing in the darkness of his flat, a couple of rooms away. This link with the outside world seemed to be what he needed to break the paralysis; he suddenly jerked upright in his bed, his limbs spasming wildly. He looked frantically around him, but the presence – if it had ever been there – was gone. Feeling sick and dazed, he swung his legs

96

from the bed, stamped the pins and needles out of them, then staggered along the hallway to his sitting room.

A wash of umber light pressed against the closed curtains, trying to force its way in. In the darkness, the ringing of the telephone seemed appallingly loud, like the trilling of an alarm. Even now, Nick felt a little divorced from his body; he had to make a conscious effort to pick up the receiver and bring it to his ear.

'Hello?' he said, his voice little more than a whisper.

There was a series of clicks. Then he heard a strange, flat, mechanical voice. 'Endrant command,' it said.

Something blossomed inside Nick, something that felt like the unveiling of a memory he would rather not recall. His feeling of sickness and dizziness grew, and with it an increased sense of dislocation, as if his mind were trying to free itself from his body, to become independent of him. His mouth drained of all moisture and when he tried to respond he could barely pull his lips apart.

'Endrant command,' the voice said again. 'Endrant command. Endrant command.'

He had no idea why, but the words appeared to act like some kind of key, unlocking his soul, releasing something he had feared subconsciously for many years. He dropped the phone as if it had turned into a scorpion and jumped away from it, almost falling over. He was shaking uncontrollably, sickness coiling and cramping in his belly, unfocused terror almost overwhelming him, rushing to the surface of his skin, flooding from him like sweat.

Suddenly, shockingly, a pain opened in his head: a sharp, white-hot pain that felt like a knife slicing into the front of his skull, bissecting his brain.

I'm haemorrhaging, he thought, full of panic and yet at the same time oddly detached. *I'm going to die.*

He collapsed to the floor, but he didn't die. He just lay there, the pain sawing back and forth through his head. And then, just when it seemed that the pain was becoming so unbearable it would drive him mad, it began to fade.

Minutes later he was able to move, to push himself groggily into a sitting position. And seconds after that the pain had gone completely.

It had not left him unaffected though. It was as if it had scrambled his mind, leaving behind a legacy of random thoughts and intangible images, which swam in bright flashes through his skull like strange and exotic fish. His perceptions too were altered: each angle, each texture, each surface seemed to have acquired a significance he could not quite grasp, holding a promise of revelation, enlightenment, epiphany.

Nick looked down at his naked body. He saw with a sense of both wonder and horror that the sweat oozing from his pores was luminous. He wiped a hand across his stomach, leaving behind a smear of liquid light. All at once his stomach clenched as though reacting to the shock of what he was seeing; his mouth flooded with saliva as if he were about to be sick. He staggered to the kitchen and leaned over the sink, glowing hands clutching the stainless-steel sides. His mouth opened as he retched and a stream of saliva drooled out. As it pooled around the plughole, Nick saw that the saliva was luminous too.

He retched several more times without producing anything but strings of saliva that glowed with the intensity of molten metal. When he straightened up, trembling, it was to discover that one of the peculiarly unfocused thoughts in his head had coalesced into an urge, an uncontrollable impulse. It suddenly seemed vital to Nick to find out whether his blood was as luminous as the rest of his bodily fluids. It suddenly seemed the most important thing in the world.

Eagerly he yanked open a drawer, scrabbling until his hand emerged clutching a large bread knife with a serrated edge. He held out his left hand, palm upwards, and sliced the blade unhesitatingly across it. The sting of pain was exquisite as an orgasm. A line of blood followed the blade – at least, Nick assumed it was blood, for it was indeed as whitely luminous as his sweat and saliva. *Endrant command*, he thought, and seemed to hear that flat, mechanical, yet somehow compelling voice filling his head.

You are full of light, the voice told him. *You must let it all out. You have a duty to let it all out.*

'Yes,' Nick whispered. 'Yes.' But he needed a mirror: he had to *see* the light coming out of him.

The bathroom, he thought, and stumbled along the hallway towards it. The sting in his hand had dulled to a heartbeat-like throb; although Nick could still feel the light coming out of him, although it was a good feeling, it was also frustrating because the light was moving too sluggishly. He had to cut deeper, into a place where the light would not trickle, but gush – *fountain* – out of him.

Jugular vein, the mechanical voice in his head instructed him helpfully. *Open your jugular vein.*

'Yes,' he murmured. 'Jugular vein.' He went into the bathroom and looked at himself in the mirror. He was beautiful, made of trickles and sparks and beads of light, his eyes dark and unfathomable in the glowing stuff of his face. He brought up the knife and pressed the blade against his throat, cold metal against hot skin. He was about to make the incisive cut, the cut that would allow the light to gush out of him, when the face looking back at him from the mirror changed.

Though still constructed of clots of light, it was no longer his own face, but his daughter Sasha's. All at once Nick felt confused and guilty and ashamed. Sasha stared out at him, her luminescent features creased in concern. He saw her mouth open, her teeth and tongue bright with moisture. Then he heard her voice, soft, insistent.

'Dad, this is wrong. This is a trick to make you hurt yourself. Throw the knife away.'

He gasped as the pain opened in his head again, sharp but not as intense as before. Then the mechanical voice was back, persistent, cold and buzzing like a saw. *Open your jugular vein*, it said.

'No!' Nick shouted, and was shocked by the rawness of his own voice. The pain cut deep into his head again, and all at once Nick saw that the pain and the voice were all part of the same thing. It was a bad thing, he realised now, a terrible thing, whose intention was only to make him harm himself.

'No!' he shouted again, the word emerging this time as a defiant snarl.

Trying to ignore the pain in his head, he stomped to the Velux window set in the sloping roof above the bath, opened it and thrust out the hand holding the knife.

Despite feeling in control of his body and mind once more, Nick found that he could not immediately open his fingers to let the knife go. He felt as though an invisible hand were clamped around his own, squeezing it hard. His hand felt bruised where the handle was pushing into it. He gritted his teeth, his face creasing with physical and mental effort, and all at once his fingers sprang apart. He was not sure he had actually relinquished the knife until he heard it clatter on the roof tiles, slither away across the sloping roof and into the night.

Like a marathon runner who has reached the end of the course through sheer will-power, Nick's legs suddenly gave way. He sat down gracelessly, sick and shaking, the pain still lodged in his head. The mechanical voice seemed to speak inside him again. It was the voice of the pain, the voice of all that was bad in the world.

Endrant command, the voice said. *Endrant command.*

Nick pressed his face against the carpet. 'No,' he whispered.

There was a pause and then the voice said, *There are other ways.*

Almost immediately Nick heard a sound. A soft sound, like large drops of rain hitting a wooden surface. He didn't move, however, until he felt something falling on to his skin, something heavier, more solid, than liquid.

As he scrambled across the room to the light-pull, Nick realised that his sweat and blood and saliva were no longer luminous. He clenched the hand he had cut with the knife, which was aching intolerably, sticky with blood. Then something landed in his hair and wriggled for a moment, until Nick jerked up a hand and brushed it off. He reached the light-pull, stretched up and yanked it down. Whiteness flooded his senses, so harsh that merely screwing up his eyes was not enough; he had to clap a hand over them as well.

Long seconds passed as his eyes grew accustomed to the light. During this time he jerked and flinched as something continued to patter on his skin. Eventually the light bleeding through his fingers grew bearable, and finally he was able to open his eyes.

He looked at the section of white wall above the *MARS ATTACKS!* poster, and then at the ceiling. Initially he thought that he was witnessing nothing more than an effect of the light that had swarmed into his eyes. He frowned and blinked, trying to clear his vision, and at last realised that what he was seeing was no optical illusion. Fat white worms were oozing from the fabric of the ceiling and walls.

Nick looked up just as a worm dropped on to his shoulder, slithered down his arm and plumped to the floor. He cried out in disgust as another landed in his hair and lay thrashing from side to side until he swiped it away. The worms were landing in the sink and the bath, raining down on to the shelves where he kept his

100

books and toiletries, splashing into the toilet bowl like high divers. The carpet was a mass of wriggling white shapes. As Nick turned to the door of the bathroom and tried to pull it open, he felt them squirming and bursting beneath his bare feet.

The door wouldn't open; Nick couldn't work out why. He rattled the handle, desperate now, as the worms rained down on him. One fell on his face, sliding down his cheek and across his lips, its body moist as a brief kiss. He kicked the door, which shuddered but refused to splinter. Then, from the corner of his eye, he got the impression that something very odd indeed was happening to the mirror above the sink.

He whirled to confront it and saw a strange, smoky darkness curling beyond the glass, in place of his reflection. All at once a face – not his own – loomed from that darkness and swung towards him, distorted, swelling, changing shape as it came. It filled the mirror, its twisted mouth snarling, its eyes glaring. Then it swung away and another face, equally hideous, replaced it, followed by another, and another. The succession of faces seemed to him like personifications of different aspects of evil. They were filled with hatred, with the promise of depravity beyond imagining. They made Nick feel as if all his goodness and hope and love were being sapped from him; as if he were being overwhelmed by darkness.

Endrant command, the voice said coldly in his head. *Endrant command. Endrant command.*

There was a splash from the toilet bowl, as something broke the surface of the water. Then, before Nick's eyes, something began to rise up. It resembled a thick brown column of meat, charred in places, bloody in others. Inset into the meat were hundreds, perhaps thousands, of tiny black glittering eyes.

Nick squeezed his own eyes shut and pressed his hands to his ears. 'No,' he muttered. 'You don't exist. Go away. Go away.' Once again he sank to his knees, worms bursting beneath his weight, and then hunched over, foetus-like, until his forehead was almost touching his thighs. But despite his attempts to plug his senses, the voice was still there, like a cold knife carving through the soft meat of his mind, intoning its elusive yet deadly message: *Endrant command. Endrant command.*

To counter it, Nick did the only thing he could think of. He began to intone, to chant, to say the first words that came into his

101

head. He had never been a religious man, and so the words he heard himself speaking surprised him.

With worms pattering on his bare back, like rain made flesh, Nick muttered, 'Our Father, who art in Heaven, hallowed be Thy name . . .'

PART TWO:
BIG GUNS

Eighteen

Not for the first time Baker asked himself why he was doing it. Was it because this case was the most intriguing one he had come across for years – perhaps the most intriguing one he had *ever* come across? Was it because he felt a need to make amends for the way he had handled the Mark Cotto situation? Or was it simply his rather puerile way of getting back at Dalby – a safer and less confrontational alternative to pissing in the man's tea or punching him right in the centre of his infuriatingly smug face?

Well . . . yes, and no. There was an element of all these reasons behind Baker's actions, but there was something else too, another factor, and without this Baker believed he would quite happily have spent his week's enforced leave sinking ever deeper into what he knew many regarded as the torpid and rather sorry routine of his life.

Oh, he might have wondered once or twice about the names on Mercy's wall; might have briefly pondered the reasons why two apparently sane men had slaughtered their loved ones before destroying themselves. But he would not have let such concerns distract him for long from his solitudinous lunchtime pint, his microwaved suppers in front of the TV; nor from his daily stroll to buy groceries, his overlong perusal of the morning's paper, his garden-pottering, his car-cleaning, his house-tidying.

By nature Baker was a phlegmatic man, and though his colleagues referred to him as the Lone Wolf, he was happy enough with his meagre lot. He was not passionate or emotional or overly ambitious; he neither sought adventure nor embraced change.

All of which rendered his present behaviour uncharacteristic and – even to him – perplexing. He looked again at the name and address blu-tacked to the dashboard of his car – Julie Lean, 12 Fairmont Crescent, Sale, Cheshire – and as he pulled off the motorway and slowed for the roundabout at the top of the rise, reflected on that 'other factor'.

Perhaps more than anything it was his sense of justice – of fair play – that was urging him onward. If Baker did have a driving force, it was an instinctive desire to help maintain the staus quo; indeed, it was this which had prompted him to become a police-man in the first place. Yes, he thought, this was the crux: he did not like secrets, and abhorred – if such a passionless man as he *could* abhor – cover-ups. And the Michael Mercy case, he now believed, *was* a cover-up of one kind or another, and not a minor one either, involving as it did the violent deaths of at least five people.

Three murders; two suicides. What could possibly have prompted Mercy and Cotto to do what they had done? Desperation? Fear of discovery? Some form of psychosis brought on by . . . what?

And what was Nick Finch's connection to all this: and indeed, all the other people on Mercy's list? And from whom had Dalby received orders not only to take Baker off the case, but to remove him from the scene of operations? To be ordered not only to hand over his case file like a schoolboy handing over sweets for confis-cation, but also to remove all evidence of the case from his hard disk, was extremely irregular. The entire situation smelled very bad indeed to him, so bad that on this occasion he had been unable simply to turn the other cheek. If he had, he knew the bad smell would have lingered in his nostrils for a very long time, befouling his tidy little life, offending his sensibilities. Sometimes, he thought wearily, even the most insular of men have to stand up for what they believe in. The admission of this fact aroused no sense of nobility in him, but merely a heavy-hearted acceptance of what needed to be done.

He followed the signs towards Sale. Then he pulled off the main road into a garage forecourt and consulted his map for only the second time that day – and the first since he had left London. As usual, his sense of direction had not failed him and less than five minutes later he was pulling up in front of a pretty, pre-war, semi-detached house in a quiet and leafy suburban street.

106

He switched off the engine and looked at the house, hoping he hadn't had a wasted journey. This was the third choice of half a dozen Julie Leans on the list of possibles that the computer had thrown up. Baker had interviewed the first choice yesterday afternoon – a twenty-eight-year-old retail assistant who lived in Chiswick – and had concluded that she couldn't be connected with the case. The second choice, who had a Berkshire address, he discovered had emigrated to Nigeria some four months previously. Unable to contact Julie Lean number three by phone, he had decided on a whim to drive out here and speak to her personally. If this too proved to be a false trail, then perhaps he would move on to the next name on his list, come back to the Julie Leans later.

He got out of the car, pushed open the gate of number 12 and walked up the drive, his feet crunching on gravel. His eyes felt tired from concentrating on the road and his legs were stiff. In the little porch at the front of the house, he rang the doorbell. After a moment the inner door opened and an attractive woman in her mid-thirties with feathery auburn hair emerged to smile at him.

'Hello?' she said brightly.

Baker responded to her smile with a rather weary one of his own. 'Mrs Julie Lean?'

'*Miss,*' she corrected him, kindly but firmly.

'Miss,' repeated Baker, then introduced himself and showed her his ID. An elegant hand flew to her mouth.

'It's not Mum, is it? She hasn't had another fall?'

'No, no, it's nothing like that,' Baker reassured her. 'If you'll allow me to come in for a moment, Miss Lean, then I'll explain.'

She led him in, alternating between apologising for the mess in the hall (a muddy pair of hockey boots sitting on a sheet of newspaper; a stack of school exercise books on the bottom step of the staircase; a clutter of correspondence heaped on top of a narrow bookcase) and explaining about her mother, a frail seventy-four-year-old widow who was finding it difficult to recover from a broken ankle she had sustained in a fall at her home several months previously.

Baker kept nodding politely as she showed him into a small, untidy lounge with biscuit-coloured wallpaper and a chunky rust coloured three-piece suite. French windows looked out on an

107

unkempt but attractive garden with a pond and a cluster of wrought-iron furniture, a few apple trees forming a mini-orchard at the far end. As she spoke, Baker observed her, alert for even the merest sign of oddness in her behaviour. He had no idea what her usual disposition was, but her present loquaciousness certainly did not seem to contain any hint of agitation or intensity.

'Listen to me, rabbiting on,' she said, as if all at once becoming aware of his scrutiny. 'I'm sure you didn't come here to listen to my problems.'

Baker smiled stiffly but didn't contradict her. She waved him to a chair, then sat down herself on the settee.

Lightly, though with the merest hint of nervousness, she said, 'So what *does* bring you here, Inspector? I haven't done anything wrong, have I?'

'Not that I'm aware of,' Baker said. He looked around. 'Do you happen to have a daily newspaper delivered, Miss Lean?'

'No, I don't,' she replied. 'I used to, but I never got time to read it. Besides, they're always full of doom and gloom. Why do you ask?'

'Tell me, Miss Lean, have you seen or heard a news bulletin this morning?'

She frowned a little. 'No, I haven't. Why?'

'Because if you had, it would have made the question I'm about to ask you somewhat inconsequential . . . Miss Lean, have you ever heard of a man called Michael Mercy?'

She jumped, her brown eyes widening in shock. For a few moments she stared at Baker dumbly, seemingly incapable of speech.

'I can see that you have,' he remarked drily.

She blinked, sucking in a breath with a hiss. 'Yes,' she gasped. 'Yes, I have. But . . . how did you know?'

'Perhaps if you would explain to me how you and Mr Mercy became acquainted, it would make things a little clearer,' Baker said.

'Well . . . to be honest, we're not actually acquainted. Until just now I didn't know he actually existed. He was simply a name.' She saw Baker frowning and waved a hand in front of her face as though cleaning a chalkboard. 'Oh, dear – I'm not explaining this very well. You've caught me off-guard. It's perhaps better if I show you.'

108

She stood up, taking two steps towards the door. Remembering Mark Cotto, Baker asked quickly, 'Where are you going?'

Julie Lean was clearly taken aback. 'I'm just going to fetch something. I won't be a moment.' She gave a rather high-pitched laugh, clearly hoping to break the sudden tension. 'Don't worry – I'm not going to make a bid for freedom.'

'All right,' Baker said, half-settling back in his seat, 'but don't be long, Miss Lean.'

'I won't be,' she replied, and left the room.

Baker looked out at the garden again, vowing that if she was not back within a minute he would go after her. He noted that the grass needed cutting and some weeding needed to be done. The pond looked as though it could do with a clean and the fencing up by the little orchard had sagged and was obviously in need of repair. The interior of the house likewise appeared to be little more than a collection of half-finished jobs. On the floor by the settee were piled some cushions obviously in the midst of being re-covered; pictures in need of hanging were stacked against the dresser. Magazines opened and presumably half-read were scattered on the furniture and floor like broken-backed birds; bills waiting to be paid and forms waiting to be filled in sat neglected in a pile by the dusty TV.

To Baker, who was scrupulously tidy, the place was unsettling: he had to fight an urge to pick up the magazines and stack them in a neat pile. He looked up as Julie Lean re-entered the room, carrying a cardboard folder which she handed to him before sitting down.

'You'd better have a look at those,' she said.

Baker opened the folder and took out the topmost of several sheets of white typing paper. When he saw what was written on the paper he had to struggle to conceal his shock. In blue biro, in a neat measured hand, was a list of names, repeated over and over, covering every square inch of paper, some of the names foreshortened where they had lapped over the edge. It was the same list of names that Michael Mercy had written time and time again on the wall of his lounge before killing his family and himself. Except that, in place of Julie Lean's name, was Mercy's own.

Before Baker could say anything, Julie Lean asked in a carefully measured voice, 'Have you ever heard of automatic writing, Inspector?'

109

Baker looked up at her. 'Isn't it where someone writes without knowing they're doing it? Don't most of them claim to be influenced by the spirit of Dickens or Shakespeare or some such rubbish?'

A strained smile played around her lips. 'That's about the size of it.' She paused, then hesitantly said, 'This is very difficult for me, Inspector. As you said, it all sounds like such rubbish. But just recently I've found myself being . . . taken over periodically. By some form of presence. I feel it enter my mind almost like a grey cloud and I go into a sort of trance. When I come to – usually sitting at the kitchen table – I have a pen in my hand and this list of names in front of me. Only, the last time . . .' She faltered, looking troubled.

'The last time?' Baker prompted.

'It was different. When I came to it was like waking from a nightmare, and my wrist was hurting – *really* hurting – as if I'd sprained it. What I wrote was different too.'

She reached for the folder and Baker handed it to her. He saw her flick through pages and pages bearing the same list of names until she found what she was looking for. She extracted a number of sheets – perhaps two dozen in all – and handed them to him. 'The handwriting on the other pages is recognisably mine,' she said. 'This isn't.'

Baker looked at the top few sheets, then flicked through the rest to confirm that they were all the same. The writing on these sheets looked to have been done in a frenzied rage; the pen had even gone through the paper in places, leaving scratches and tears and holes. On every sheet, in huge, scrawling letters, were two words, repeated over and over: *Beware Genesis.*

'Have you any idea what this means?' asked Baker urgently, remembering Nick Finch's story about his vision in the nightclub toilet.

'No I don't,' Julie Lean replied, 'but it – frightens me. And part of me feels . . . oh, I don't know . . . as though I *should* know. Does that sound strange?'

'No stranger than a number of other things I've heard lately.' Baker shook his head pensively. 'How many of these . . . *episodes* have you had to date, Miss Lean?'

'Four,' she said without hesitation.

'And when did they start?'

110

'Eighteen days ago. September the twentieth. I remember it so clearly because it would have been Dad's seventy-fifth birthday – he died three years ago.'

'Hmm.'

'Is it significant?' she asked.

'What?'

'The date.'

'No, I don't think so,' Baker said distractedly. 'At least, not that I'm aware . . . Tell me, Miss Lean, have these episodes of yours always taken place at home?'

'Yes, thank goodness, though I live in constant fear that something will happen at school.' She must have mistaken his thoughtful look for incomprehension because she seemed to feel a need to add, 'I'm a primary school teacher. Goodness knows what would happen if I had one of my turns in front of the children.' She raised a trembling hand to pluck absentmindedly at the top button of her blouse.

'Have you consulted anyone about your . . . condition?' Baker asked.

'A psychic, you mean?'

He smiled thinly. 'I was thinking more of a doctor.'

'No, I haven't. I suppose I was hoping it was a temporary thing, that it would just go away. But after the last time . . . I don't know what to do.'

Her face seemed to clench then and Baker got the impression she was trying not to show him how worried she really was. He hoped she wouldn't become emotional; he wasn't very good at sympathy. He might *feel* sorry for the woman, but expressing it was another matter. Besides, it would only get in the way. He wanted to stay focused, remain in control.

'This may sound an unusual question, Miss Lean,' he said in a level voice, 'but have you recently had any murderous or suicidal tendencies?'

Her eyes widened. If nothing else, at least the question seemed to shock her from her own anxieties. 'Whatever do you mean?'

'Just that, Miss Lean,' replied Baker calmly. 'Have you ever felt the urge to kill yourself or anyone else?'

She laughed, but it was a shrill, splintery, humourless sound. 'Of course not. What a thing to ask!' Then she looked at him as

111

though something had dawned on her. 'You've got a reason for asking that question, haven't you?'

'Yes I have.'

'Tell me.'

Baker told her, his voice as calm and steady as ever, relating the facts and nothing else. He explained how Mercy had killed his wife and daughter and then himself, how he had written a list of two dozen names over and over again on the wall of his lounge before doing so; he told her how Mark Cotto had murdered and dismembered his partner before hurling himself to his death from the ninth floor of a block of flats.

Julie Lean listened, visibly stunned. When Baker had finished she whispered, 'My God, what's happening? What's going to happen to *me*?'

'Nothing, I hope,' said Baker firmly. 'I don't want you to worry, Miss Lean.'

'Not worry? How can I not worry?' She sounded desolate.

Baker looked at her without flinching, silent for a moment. He was not the kind of man to offer false platitudes. At last he said, 'I've spoken to another of the people mentioned on your list. Nick Finch. Like you, he has not reacted to whatever is happening to you all in the same way that Michael Mercy and Mark Cotto have reacted.'

'How *has* he reacted?' she asked.

'From what I can gather, he has seen . . . a vision.'

'A vision?'

'Of Michael Mercy's death. It appears he walked into a night-club toilet – of all places – and saw Mercy playing out his final actions before his eyes. Just as if it were real.'

'No,' Julie Lean said slowly.

Baker abruptly clapped his hands on to his knees, as if to denote an end to their meeting. He reached into his jacket for the notepad and pen he always kept there, found a clean sheet and jotted something down. Then he tore the page out and handed it to her. 'I want you to keep in touch with me, Miss Lean. If anything out of the ordinary occurs – if you feel odd or have any more of these episodes of automatic writing – please give me a call. My home number's there and also the number of my mobile. Will you promise to keep in touch?'

'Yes,' she said.

He bit back the urge to tell her not to lose the numbers amid the clutter. 'Incidentally, have you had any strange phone calls recently?' he asked instead.

'Strange in what way?'

'Wrong numbers. Bad connections.'

She thought for a moment, then shook her head. 'No.'

'Right. Well, I'd better be going.' He stood up quickly. 'Remember – call me. Any time of the day or night. I'll be here.' He tapped the breast pocket which contained his mobile.

'I will,' she said forlornly.

'And try not to worry,' he told her gruffly – the closest he could get to reassurance.

She tried to smile, but it was a feeble effort.

'Okay,' she said unconvincingly.

Nineteen

If the police computer was right, another of the people whose name was on both Michael Mercy's and Julie Lean's list – Ellie McKee – lived in a small village not far from Newcastle. Spurred on by his encounter with the schoolteacher, Baker decided to drive straight up there after leaving Sale. He would find and speak to Ellie McKee and then book himself into a Travelodge where he would spend the evening using the addresses of those on the list to plot out a quite literal route of enquiry.

He knew he should have done this in the first place; it was not like him to rush headlong into an investigation without thinking it through first. Outwardly he was his usual imperturbable self, but he found it hard to deny that the vagaries of the case – particularly the way in which it had culminated in his suspension – had affected him more even than he had first thought.

It was almost three fifteen in the afternoon when he set out from Sale. He had left London that morning in sunshine that seemed like a promise of an Indian summer, but now the sky was hazy, stained with cloud an even darker grey than his crumpled suit. The A1 was busy, but the junction that he pulled off at just before six seemed invisible to all other motorists, and he had the roundabout at the top of the rise all to himself.

He glanced at the signpost and took the first left, his road atlas open beside him on the passenger seat, though the route was pretty much established in his head. The village he was heading for was called Starkley; it was only a dozen or so miles from the A1 turn-off, but the roads leading to it were narrow and twisty, flanked by high hedges which bordered fields and woodland. They were roads on which you might be considered reckless if you found

114

yourself in fourth gear, though for the first couple of miles Baker didn't see another soul. Just as a dark glint of car registered in his rear-view mirror, it started to rain.

The drops were big as birds' eggs; the squall smothered his windscreen in seconds. Baker flicked on his wipers, which squeaked to rapid life, and touched the brake, slowing the car to under thirty. He glanced in his mirror once again, but rain had coated his back window like jelly, transforming the landscape into formless clots of mould – grey, black, green. He turned on the rear wiper, which hesitated a moment before swiping a fat arc through the coiling film of rain. At once he frowned and pursed his lips. The other car, a black Volvo, was considerably closer to him than it had been ten seconds ago and getting closer still, the driver paying no apparent heed to the poor driving conditions. Baker tutted, refusing to be intimidated, even when the car, less than twenty yards behind him now, began flashing its headlights.

Most cases of road rage, Baker knew, occurred on quiet country roads like this one. Yet, although he was irritated by the Volvo driver's behaviour, he was not prepared to rise to his bait. Instead he slowed right down, pulling over so that his wheels were virtually running in the gutter. He considered opening his window and cementing his intention by waving the Volvo past, but decided that the gesture might be construed as provocative by the other car's occupant, or occupants. There was always the possibility that the car behind was full of nutters who were hassling him just for the fun of it – in which case they had chosen the wrong man. Not that Baker would leap out waving his police ID and reading the Riot Act; but he would refuse to lose concentration, would continue to drive carefully, as he always did. Only if they actually forced him off the road or caused an accident would he react.

On this occasion, however, the driver behind him took the hint and, without indicating, pulled out to overtake. As the car sped past, Baker glanced surreptitiously to his right; through the Volvo's rain-stippled windows he thought he could distinguish the dark bulk of three, possibly four, people.

Then the Volvo was in front of him, its front wheel on the passenger side bouncing in a pothole, sending up a spray of filthy water. Not a man rushing his heavily pregnant wife to hospital then, thought Baker idly – just as the Volvo's brake lights flared

115

and it slewed round to cover both narrow lanes, blocking the road ahead.

'Shit,' Baker said, and stamped on his brakes. As his own car came to a halt, skidding slightly, he wondered whether what he had just seen had been an accident or a deliberate act.

He soon found out. All of the Volvo's doors except the driver's opened – Baker could see the driver sitting stoically in his seat, hands resting on the wheel, staring straight ahead – and three men got out. They all wore black sweaters and trousers, black gloves and black balaclavas. And all three were carrying handguns.

Baker rapidly changed gear and began to reverse, looking over his shoulder, hands steady on the wheel. His heart was beating a little quicker than usual, but he was still able to think clearly. He recalled a layby, perhaps quarter of a mile back; if he could reach that, he should have room to turn the car round and head back to the motorway. He tried not to think of the guns in the men's hands, tried not to think of them pointing those guns at him, pulling the triggers. All he could do was keep his head and . . .

He rounded a curve in the road. And saw another black Volvo, slewed across both lanes like a mirror image of the first, blocking his retreat.

He gritted his teeth, sighed, and brought his car to a halt. Through the rain-blurred side windows of the second Volvo he saw what looked like the black shapes of four more men: these men made no attempt to get out of their car. Knowing it was a futile gesture, Baker locked all of his doors, and then sat back and waited for the men who had got out of the first Volvo to appear around the corner, which they did approximately fifteen seconds later.

The man at the head of the trio approached his car unhurriedly, gun held loosely at his side; the other men trailed a little behind him, flanking him. Rain speckled Baker's windscreen, smearing his view, and then was swiped away. The man in the lead came around to Baker's window and tapped on it with his gun; Baker noticed the silencer screwed to the end of the barrel.

'Open up, please, Mr Baker,' the man called above the patter of rain. His voice, though muffled through the balaclava, was cultured, polite.

Baker had no choice. He reached out and wound down his window. A little flurry of rain came into the car, accompanied by a curl of chilly wind, as the man bent down to speak to him. He had blue eyes and blond eyebrows; Baker got the impression, despite the balaclava, that he was young – in his mid-twenties, perhaps.

'Hand over the list, Mr Baker,' he said.

Baker paused for just a second, then reached over to the dashboard, where the list reflected a white ghost of itself on to the windscreen. He picked it up and handed it over.

The man glanced at the list, then folded it and put it into the back pocket of what Baker now saw were black Levis. 'Thank you, Mr Baker,' he said. 'Now, I suggest you turn your car round, drive back to London, take a few days off as instructed and forget all about the Michael Mercy case.'

'May I ask why?' Baker said.

The man looked at him for a moment. Then he said, 'The Michael Mercy case is a matter of national security. It is being handled by the proper authorities.'

'Handled how?' asked Baker.

'Handled correctly,' said the man.

'I see,' said Baker. He took a breath. 'Tell me this. Are more innocent people going to die? Is that part of the plan?'

The young man stared at him for what seemed a long time; Baker returned his gaze unflinchingly. When the man next spoke, his voice was still calm, but Baker thought he detected a hard edge to it. 'Turn your car round and drive back to London. Enjoy your holiday, Mr Baker.'

Without waiting for a reply, the man turned and walked away.

Twenty

The visit from the policeman had caused the anxiety of the previous few weeks to escalate in Julie Lean's belly into a sickening fear. What was happening to her? What was *going* to happen to her?

At first, when she had started these . . . funny turns, she had thought there was something wrong with her brain, something physical, a tumour or . . . well, to be honest, she hadn't considered it might be anything *but* a tumour. The automatic writing, the list of names, had seemed almost incidental to that possibility. People, she knew, did all sorts of odd things when their brains were affected; all kinds of peculiar activities were sparked off. Some people – the kindest, mildest people – came out with streams of obscenities, that was one thing she had heard. Was picking up a pen and writing down the same two dozen names over and over again any more peculiar than that?

She had assumed, at first, that the names were *just* names, randomly chosen by her mutinous brain. Then it had occurred to her that the names were perhaps those of real people she had once known but forgotten – past pupils, old workmates, school friends, casual acquaintances.

It was only recently that she had started to come round to the idea that perhaps there wasn't anything actually *wrong* with her, not physically at least. She had begun to wonder whether what was happening was perhaps the awakening of some kind of psychic gift. She had got some books on the paranormal out of the library and certainly her own case had seemed to mirror many of those she read about in the books. Perhaps, then, she was not sick, but somehow – whether by accident or design –

had tapped into an unexplored realm of her own subconscious mind.

All the same, her 'gift' – if that was what it was – had still worried her, particularly after that last time when she had regained consciousness to find that weird and somehow frightening message scrawled with manic ferocity on sheet after sheet of paper. For the last two or three days she had been toying with the idea of going to see someone; a psychic or a medium, someone who had experience of such things. Now, though, after Inspector Baker's visit, she was thrown into turmoil once more.

In fact, she had been *so* thrown by his visit that she hadn't yet been able to get her head around what he had been suggesting; it was only now, half an hour later, that she felt calm enough to think about it. Could there really be a group of people – the people whose names were on her list – to whom odd things were happening? People just like her? But what did it mean? Were they being manipulated in some way? But why and how and by whom? It all seemed so outlandish, so unbelievable; but if what Inspector Baker had said was true, there was evidently *something* very strange going on.

'Why me?' she said out loud in a small voice, raising her head as if whoever was doing this to her might be watching, listening. 'Why me? I'm no one.'

She jumped as the telephone started to ring, and hugged the cushion she had been clutching tighter to her belly. She had been in this position since Baker had left, curled up foetally on the settee, her body still and the house still around her, but her mind whirling, raging.

It's them! she thought, but almost immediately her mind began to reassure her. *No, it isn't; it's Mum or Janice, or perhaps even Inspector Baker, ringing to see if I'm all right.* Nevertheless, her legs were shaky as she crossed the room and went into the hallway. She picked up the telephone and held it to her ear. 'Hello,' she said.

There was a series of clicks, like someone fiddling with light switches, and then a buzzing sound. Then Julie heard a dry, flat, mechanical voice. It spoke two words, and repeated them over and over again: 'Endrant command. Endrant command. Endrant command. Endrant command . . .'

They were the most extraordinary and terrifying words Julie

119

had ever heard, not least because they seem to fly from the phone like hooks directly into her brain, tearing through the soft tissue and embedding themselves deep. Yet although the words were accompanied by the most terrible, sickening pain she had ever experienced, Julie found them compelling, mesmerising. She could not put down the phone.

She began to repeat the words, whisper them; after a while the pain seemed to ebb and the words became not frightening but soothing. They seemed to swirl around her brain like a cleansing liquid, erasing her anxieties. The sensation was so exquisite that when they also began to erase her thoughts and memories and will she found that she had no objection whatsoever.

At last she put the phone down. She felt happier than she had ever felt before; and for the first time in her life she knew without hesitating exactly what she had to do. She walked down the hallway of her house, opened the door and went outside. Closing the door carefully behind her, she moved down the gravel drive to the gate.

And there it was, idling on the kerb outside her house, just as she had known it would be, just as she had been *told* it would be. As she approached the grey van, the back doors were pushed open by unseen hands. Julie climbed in and the doors closed behind her. The van idled for a few seconds longer, and then, with a gout of blue-grey fumes, it dragged itself from the kerb and rattled away up the road.

Twenty-One

Nick woke up with a faint but persistent buzzing in his head and a metallic taste in his mouth. As he sat up nausea climbed from his stomach to his throat and he was forced to take deep breaths to combat it. While he did so, memories crept timidly back into his mind: the phone call; the luminous bodily fluids; the worms; the faces in the mirror; the thing that had risen from the toilet bowl . . .

Sensory attack, he thought: the phone call had unlocked some dormant part of his brain, encouraged it to create hallucinations so intense they had seemed real. For what reason he could only guess. To drive him insane? Or merely to break down his defences, make him compliant?

But who would do such a thing? Why were they picking on him? Because of his vision, or because his name had been on Michael Mercy's list? Could Michael Mercy have received the same treatment? Had he succumbed to such an extent that he had been driven to commit murder and then suicide?

The thought so frightened Nick that, when he got up, he couldn't stop trembling. The sky was hazy, deadening the light inside the flat. *How many more of us are there?* Nick thought. Dozens? Hundreds? Thousands? Perhaps the whole population of the country was at risk; perhaps he was simply among the most vulnerable. In that case, who were the enemy? A foreign power? Aliens? The idea of aliens subjugating the population with mind-control rays almost made him smile. Almost – but not quite. Because although it was a ludicrous notion, he knew now *he* was under attack. Somewhere out there, someone was out to get him. He had almost cracked last night, didn't know whether he would be able to withstand another onslaught.

121

He had recited the Lord's Prayer, concentrating desperately on every word, until he was hoarse. Finally he had managed to find the strength to crawl to the bathroom door, overcome the mental block, or whatever it was, that had prevented him from opening it before, and to shuffle on hands and knees back to his bedroom. He had crawled under the duvet, continuing to recite the Lord's Prayer until he fell asleep. Now he was awake again, his head clear but for that faint, irritating buzzing.

He walked unsteadily along the hallway. He hesitated a moment outside the bathroom door, his stomach rolling over. Then he pushed it open and went in. As he had thought, there was no sign of the worms that had fallen like a tropical storm last night; no sign of the thing from the toilet bowl. The mirror was just a mirror, reflecting his pale, haggard face.

Keith Richards after a night on the tiles, he thought before bending over the sink and splashing cold water on his face. He gasped at the shock of it, and at the pain in his palm where he had cut himself, but at least it made him feel alive again. He emptied his hugely inflated bladder, shaved, brushed his teeth, took a hot shower and put a plaster on his slashed and still-stinging hand. Afterwards he felt cleansed, purified; even the buzzing in his head had gone.

Seeing the clock in his lounge disorientated him again; it read 6:08, which couldn't be right. Surely he'd been trapped in the bathroom with his nightmares until close to that time? What was more, he felt certain he had been asleep for a good while after crawling back into bed. He picked up the clock, thinking it must have stopped, but it was still ticking merrily away.

His watch, he found after plodding through to the bedroom to retrieve it, showed the same time as the clock, but was that a.m. or p.m.? To find out, he turned on the TV, where Captain Mainwaring was giving Pike a withering look. *Dad's Army*. That would make it ten past six in the *evening*. Had he really been asleep for twelve hours? He rubbed his forehead distractedly. God, he was due to meet Sasha and Jenna at seven thirty in the Rising Star on Grape Street, prior to the Portishead gig at the Academy. He didn't feel much like going out; but on the other hand he'd be grateful for the company. Also, it would give him a chance to talk through last night's experiences with Jenna, ask her advice about what he should do. After yesterday he was reluctant to go back to the police; this new, even more bizarre addition to his story would only consolidate their belief that he was a nutter. So what *could* he do? There was only one thing he was certain of: he couldn't fight what was happening to him alone.

He crossed the room and looked out of the window, down into the street below. The grey van was not there. He went into the kitchen and made himself a tuna-fish sandwich and a coffee. As he ate his sandwich in the sitting room, he stared at the telephone, half-afraid it might ambush him in some way if he took his eyes off it.

After finishing his sandwich, he switched off the TV and crossed back to the telephone; it seemed to be drawing him like a magnet. After a moment he put his hand on it, perhaps expecting to feel a vibration, or the tingle of an electric shock, but he felt only cold plastic. He picked up the receiver and held it a foot or so from his face, ready to smash it back into its cradle if that odd mechanical voice tried again to insinuate itself into his mind. Satisfied for now that no more than the dialling tone was humming at him, he put the receiver to his ear and dialled Linsey's number.

It was Linsey herself who picked up the phone; she sounded tired, but then she always did.

'Hi, Linsey – it's me,' Nick said. 'Is Sasha there? Did she get back from the hospital okay?'

'Yes, she did,' Linsey said, and now she sounded not only tired but hostile.

'Do you think I could speak to her?'

'I don't think she should come out tonight, if that's what you're after,' Linsey said, making Nick feel like a boyfriend trying to sidestep the barrier of a strict and disapproving mother. 'Her face is badly bruised and swollen, she's on medication and she's exhausted. I think it would be best for her to stay in and rest.'

'What does Sasha think?' Nick asked.

Linsey gave an exasperated sigh. 'Well, of course *she* wants to go out with you. But I don't think she's up to it, Nick. Try to explain that to her, will you?'

'Look – let me just speak to her.'

Another short silence. 'All right. But try to be a responsible parent for once in your life.' Linsey put down the phone with a loud clunk before Nick could respond.

He waited for perhaps thirty seconds, sipping his coffee to allay his nervousness; after last night, the hissing silence on the line seemed ominous, a void waiting to be filled.

Then there was a softer clunk, and Sasha's slightly breathless voice: 'Dad! Hi.'

'Hi,' he said. 'How are you feeling?'

'Sore.'

'Your mum thinks you should stay home tonight.'

He heard her sigh, imagined her rolling her eyes. 'I'm *fine*. I may look like crap, but I feel okay, honest. And I've been really looking forward to this gig. Don't tell me I can't come, Dad.'

'I'm not telling you anything,' he said. 'You're old enough to make up your own mind. You do realise that everyone will be gawping at you, though, don't you? For different reasons than usual, I mean.'

'That's their problem,' she said defiantly. 'Actually it'll make a nice change not to have blokes sliming up to me every five minutes.'

'They'll probably slime up to you anyway and offer to kick my head in for knocking you about.'

'Oh, I *see*,' she said, teasingly. 'So it's just yourself you're worried about? You're not bothered about me at all.'

He laughed; it felt liberating to do so. 'You know me,' he said. 'Selfish to the core.'

She gave a mock sigh. 'As your daughter, it's a cross I have to bear.' Then she lowered her voice, presumably so that Linsey wouldn't hear. 'Anyway, there's no way I can miss out tonight. I want to meet your new woman.'

He smiled. 'All right – but do us a favour, will you? Tell your mum that at least I *tried* to get you to take her advice.'

'No problem. See you later, Dad.'

'Yeah. See you.'

Though his flat was certainly no haven, leaving it made Nick realise how much last night's sensory attack had undermined his sense of security. He had never suffered from agoraphobia, or been particularly paranoid, but the instant he stepped outside, he felt vulnerable, oppressed, as if he were being watched from a hundred different vantage points.

Sitting on the tube was not much better; the air was so stifling that it took all of his willpower not to hurl himself out of the doors at each station and rush to the surface to drink in lungfuls of cool and relatively fresh air. His peripheral vision seemed abnormal too, he saw sights that he knew had no basis in reality, but which momentarily seemed as tangible as the rest of his surroundings. On the platform at Camden Town he saw what appeared to be a being made of light, beckoning him, its movements slow as seaweed fronds in a deep-water tide; at Goodge Street he glimpsed a grey-skinned man with no features, stepping out of the next carriage. He craned his neck to look again, but the faceless man, if he had ever been there, had vanished into the crowd.

He hurried off the train at Tottenham Court Road, glancing behind him to ensure that he wasn't being followed. He didn't appear to have any specific pursuers, though he couldn't shake off the feeling that a great many people were regarding him surreptitiously, turning aside to murmur to their companions, who would then glance at him in turn.

Classic paranoid point-of-view shot, he thought to himself ironically, even as his eyes darted from side to side. Faces seemed to loom grotesquely into his field of vision as if filmed through a distorted lens, just like in the movies. Of course, he wasn't so far gone that he didn't realise there couldn't really be this many people involved in the conspiracy against him. Although he felt fidgety, nervous, he was also pretty sure he wasn't attracting undue attention due to his appearance or his manner. Which meant that most of what he was feeling was self-induced: though knowing that still didn't provide him with any comfort to speak of. His anxiety was like a fever that he couldn't shake, deep-rooted and virulent.

He stepped on to the escalator, which began to lurch him towards the promise of fume-filled but moving air. On the opposite side, coming down, was a Chinese girl in a blue satin dress, with a wart-hog's tusk curling from each cheek. Nick squeezed his eyes shut. He didn't open them again until he sensed he was near the top. He stepped off the escalator without glancing behind him, a pulse jumping in his throat.

The Dominion on the corner of Tottenham Court Road, where *Grease* had given way to *Beauty And The Beast*, was a palace of light, milling with foreign tourists and pensioners' coach parties. Nick tried not to look too closely; he was fearful of how his skittish imagination might transform faces, physiques. He was afraid that his subconscious might overwhelm him if he allowed it any leeway. For that reason he kept his eyes lowered to his feet, only peripherally aware of the crowds streaming past him. As he walked he caught snippets of conversation:

'. . . hot rod cow, but the best one's David Ginola. His name's an anagram of vagina dildo . . .'

'. . . didn't want him to keep gawping at my nipples all day, so I decided to wear . . .'

'. . . told him if he didn't stop fucking me about, I'd fill his fish tank with petrol and drop a fucking match in . . .'

The tide of broken conversations carried him to the Rising Sun, whose clientele was a combination of Armani and Prada-wearing city types, young Europeans so smart in their casualness they looked as though they'd stepped straight off a catalogue shoot, and finely toned backpackers with genuine tans and sunbleached hair, their rucksacks perched by their chairs like pets.

Neither Sasha nor Jenna were there when Nick arrived. He found a seat, ordered a Grolsch and tried hard not to look like Johnny No-Friends. Despite having slept for twelve hours he felt tired, though his fatigue was more mental than physical. As he swigged his beer, he noticed two men: their build and their no-nonsense haircuts made him think immediately that they were plain-clothes policemen. They were sitting at a table ten yards away, sipping pints of Guinness and staring at him. Nick moved his chair, trying not to make the movement look obvious, and casually turned his back on them. He looked down at a wet ring of beer on the table, shifting his head to different angles until it caught the light and shone like gold. He took the concert tickets and back-stage passes out of his jacket pocket and examined them. From the general hubbub of conversation around him, he heard a woman say, 'Endrant command.'

He looked up quickly, but there was no indication of who had spoken. He told himself he must have misheard, or imagined it. He gulped at his Grolsch, wishing that either Jenna or Sasha would arrive.

When he felt the hand on his shoulder a few minutes later, his instant thought was that it was one of the Guinness-drinking men. He twisted in his chair, almost knocking his beer over – and saw Jenna smiling down at him, in a filmy blue top with white flowers on it, dark boot-cut trousers and black, high-heeled boots.

126

'Hi,' she said brightly, draping the jacket she had been carrying over the chair next to his. Then her features narrowed with concern. 'Are you okay?'

He made himself smile. 'Fine. I was miles away, that's all. You look great. What are you drinking?'

She told him she'd have what he was having and he went to the bar, waiting his turn to be served behind a tall German with a neatly trimmed beard as blond as the sun, who appeared to be ordering a complicated round for at least forty people. Behind the bar, beneath the row of optics, was a long mirror with the pub's name engraved on it. Nick glanced idly into the mirror – and froze.

The mirror reflected the back of the head of the barman who was serving the German. From where he was standing, looking over the German's shoulder, Nick could see that the barman's skull had been crushed as though he had been hit with a sledge-hammer. From the oozing mess of splintered bone, blood, hair and brain tissue, was emerging a number of fat white worms, identical to the ones that had rained down on him last night.

'No,' he murmured, loud enough for the German to glance curiously over his shoulder at him. When the German turned back to continue detailing his massive order, Nick squeezed his eyes shut and promised himself silently but fiercely that he would not submit to the hallucination.

'Sank you,' he heard the German say, and opened his eyes to see the barman giving him his change. He looked fearfully into the mirror again. The barman's head was intact. As the German squeezed past, carrying the first of the many drinks which were clustered on the bar, Nick took his place.

'Yes, mate?' the barman asked.

'Six bottles of Grolsch, please,' Nick heard himself saying, and immediately wondered why he had ordered so many. He told himself he could handle whatever his errant brain threw at him without getting plastered, that he would be safe now that Jenna was here, but he didn't change his order. He walked back to the table with two in each hand and one in each pocket of his jacket. Jenna raised her eyebrows as the bottles chinked down on to the table.

'How many friends have you got coming tonight?'

'There's only the three of us,' Nick said, 'but I just thought . . .

127

if I got two bottles each, it'll save us from having to go to the bar again.' It sounded pretty lame.

Jenna looked sceptical. 'What if I only want one? And what if Sasha can't drink alcohol because of her medication?'

'I hadn't thought of that,' Nick said, not entirely truthfully, and made himself laugh. 'I suppose I'd have to get rat-arsed! Mind you, that won't be hard. Working in the rock'n'roll business, it's practically a job requirement.'

She adopted an expression of mild rebuke; Nick wasn't sure whether or not she meant it. It made him realise how little he really knew Jenna, despite the intense few days they had spent together. She had seen him *in extremis*, stripped bare in more ways than one, but he was aware that the only way to get to know someone properly was to spend time with them doing normal things, living normal lives, having normal conversations . . .

'That was a joke,' he said. 'A pretty poor one considering my background, I'll admit.' He wanted to steer the conversation around to what had happened to him last night, but he wasn't sure how to go about it. Although eager to get her perspective on events, Nick couldn't help thinking that even if she didn't start regarding him as a paranoid basket-case, sooner or later she was bound to find his constant whinging becoming tiresome.

'So what have you been doing today?' he asked her, making a stab at normality.

'I had a lie-in this morning. Then I had lunch with a friend and we went shopping. How about you?'

'I've been asleep all day,' he wanted to say, thinking that it could lead to a slow unveiling of the reasons why. But then he pictured her eyes glazing over, her face trying to hide an expression of contemptuous disbelief, and so he said, 'I haven't done anything much. Just worked, mostly.'

'And nothing's happened to you?'

He found himself shaking his head. 'No.'

'No more visions? No funny phone calls?'

This time he hesitated and she frowned.

'Nick?'

'What?'

'Something else *has* happened, hasn't it?'

He shrugged miserably. 'Look, don't worry about it—'

'No, tell me. I want to know. I want to help you.'

128

He took a sip of beer and stretched his face in a grin. 'You make me sound like a mental patient.'

She looked distressed. 'I'm sorry, I didn't mean to.'

'No, *I'm* sorry,' he said. 'It's just . . . I don't want to be seen as a burden. I don't want you to start regretting that you ever got involved with me. I mean, I keep telling you all this stuff, but you haven't got much proof that it's true, have you? I mean, *I* know I saw a vision of a guy blowing away his family and then himself, and that came true, and I know the guy had written my name on the walls inside his house, but how do *you* know all the other stuff I'm telling you isn't just in here?' He jabbed at the side of his head with a finger.

'If you tell me it's happening, then I believe you,' she said. 'I know you're not crazy.'

'Yeah, but *how* do you know? You hardly know me.'

'I think I know you well enough to trust you,' she said.

'That's so naive it's unbelievable.' The words were barely out of his mouth when he was raising a hand in apology. 'That was a really twatty thing to say. It's just . . . it's this situation I'm angry at, not you.'

'It's okay,' she said, and paused to take a drink from her bottle before taking his right hand in both of hers. 'Look, Nick, I'm not wet behind the ears, and the whole Michael Mercy thing notwithstanding, it *has* crossed my mind once or twice that, understandably, you might be a bit more paranoid about stuff than you need to be. But that doesn't mean I don't like you and that I don't want us to be friends – or more than friends. Whether most of what's happening is real or not, I want to be there for you. It's as simple as that.'

He felt touched; sad, even. 'I wish all this shit wasn't happening,' he said. 'Why can't we just have a normal relationship, like everyone else?'

She squeezed his hand. 'We *will*. We'll get all this sorted out, you'll see.'

'I don't see how. I mean, where do we start?'

'*You* can start by telling me what happened last night.'

'You really *will* think I'm crazy then.'

'Nick,' she said warningly.

'Hi. Is one of these beers for me?'

Nick turned to look at Sasha as she touched him affectionately

129

on the back and lowered herself into the seat next to him. Despite having seen her in the hospital, he was shocked by her appearance, and though he tried not to show it his greeting turned to a choking lump in his throat. If anything, she looked worse now than she had yesterday. Her face, incongruously framed by her beautiful blonde hair, was like a Halloween mask, the swollen flesh a riot of yellows and purples and greens, her eyes little more than bloodshot slits in blue-black pouches.

'Well,' she said, her swollen lips muffling her voice a little, 'if you're not going to answer my question, aren't you at least going to tell me I look gorgeous?'

Nick rallied quickly and said, deadpan, 'I've never seen you looking more beautiful.'

'Thank you, Dad,' she said, and held out her hand. 'You must be Jenna.'

Jenna took her hand. 'Hi, Sasha. Good to meet you. How are you feeling?'

'Physically, not too bad though I'm buzzing with paracetamols at the moment. Mentally I'm still a bit shaky, but I'm determined not to let this thing get me down.'

'You're very brave,' Jenna said. 'If it had been me, I'm pretty sure I wouldn't have wanted to come out so soon.'

Sasha shrugged. 'I'm not bothered about people staring at me, if that's what you mean. But . . . I dunno . . . when something like this happens, you suddenly feel really vulnerable, as if you've had the rug pulled out from under your feet. I don't want to let that feeling get the better of me.'

Jenna nodded. 'A friend of mine got mugged a few years back, and he wouldn't leave his house for weeks afterwards. He ended up getting very depressed. A lot of people – his girlfriend included – got really fed up with him, thought he was milking the situation. I don't think people realise how much an act of violence can affect you unless they've actually been on the receiving end. I mean, he wasn't badly hurt or anything, this friend of mine. He was just punched in the face and his wallet was stolen. But it was simply that it was so . . .'

'Unexpected,' supplied Sasha. 'Yes, I think it's the fact that it can come from anywhere, at any time. We go round with this belief that we can avoid violence if we want to, but sometimes we can't, and the world suddenly becomes a much scarier place.

Also, there's, like, a personal element involved. You think: why me? Why did *I* get attacked? Why was *I* chosen? In my case, of course, it was because I was in the wrong place at the wrong time, but it's still a real shock to find that you can became a victim so easily, that to some people you're nothing but some object that's stopping them doing what they want.' She reached for a Grolsch. 'Is this your personal supply, Dad, or what?'

'Help yourself,' said Nick, wafting a hand. 'But should you be drinking if you've been popping pills all day?'

'Probably not,' she said, 'but I think there are extenuating circumstances.'

He smiled wryly. 'Yeah, I wouldn't disagree with that.'

For the next half-hour Nick pushed his own anxieties to the back of his mind and concentrated on helping Jenna and Sasha get to know each other. It was important to him that they get on and each time a connection was made between them – each time they found themselves in sympathy – his heart gave a little leap.

When all the Grolsch was gone he went to the bar to get another round, which Jenna insisted on paying for. This time the back of the barman's head in the mirror looked perfectly normal, and Nick saw nothing else to alarm him; even the two Guinness drinkers had gone. As the barman scooped his change from the cash register, Nick sneaked a look at Jenna and Sasha, and was pleased to see them chatting away, Sasha gesturing animatedly, Jenna nodding, laughing.

Fifteen minutes later, after his fourth Grolsch, Nick's head was buzzing pleasantly. Despite everything, he felt relaxed, almost happy; sitting here with his two favourite women made him feel that no problem was insurmountable. He looked at his watch and saw that it was almost nine; the doors of the Academy had opened at seven thirty.

'We'd better make a move,' he said, slurring his words slightly, 'or we'll miss the band.'

Jenna picked up her half-full bottle and chugged it down impressively. When they went outside it was drizzling, the shiny streets blotched with the reflections of street lamps. Jenna and Sasha linked arms with Nick and they hurried along, all three of them suddenly in a silly mood as if the cold, fresh air had combined with the alcohol in their systems to produce an alto-gether more potent brew.

'Oh, don't go so fast, you're jogging my face,' Sasha gasped, which made them all laugh uproariously. 'Ow,' Sasha protested between hoots of laughter. 'Ow – that hurts.'

The Academy was only five minutes' walk from the pub. People were still trickling in, handing their tickets to a black guy with a beard and a leather beret. Outside the entrance doors a couple of big guys, wearing blue sweatshirts with SECURITY emblazoned across their fronts, moved from foot to foot, hands clasped in front of them. As Nick, Jenna and Sasha unlinked arms and moved towards them, Nick reaching into his pockets for the tickets, one of the bouncers stepped forward. 'Tell us who did that, love, and I'll kick the shit out of him for you.'

Sasha raised her eyebrows. 'Actually, it was my girlfriend,' she said loudly. 'She caught me in bed with another woman.'

The bouncer grinned and winked at his mate. 'I don't suppose you'd sell me a video, would you?'

'Of course,' said Sasha. 'I've got a copy of *Dumb and Dumber* I don't want any more. It would suit you and your mate down to the ground.'

Jenna was laughing as they went inside. 'That was excellent. Did you see his face?'

'Yes – it was the ugly thing on the front of his head,' said Nick. 'Right, who's for drinks?'

Jenna asked for an orange juice and Sasha a Coke. They arranged to meet up by the emergency-exit door to the right of the stage, then Nick pushed his way to the bar.

The Academy was a long, featureless, high-ceilinged room with the stage at one end and the bar at the other. It had mauve walls, a railed podium about ten feet in front of the bar which at present housed two guys and a mixing desk, and a couple of alcoves in the wall opposite the entrance; one for merchandise, the other for 'Refreshments' – burgers, hot dogs, chips, tea, coffee.

Nick had been to see many bands here; despite the Spartan surroundings, he liked the Academy as a venue. The stage was large, the acoustics good, and the bottled beer – although expensive – always ice-cold.

There was a capacity turn-out for Portishead, who, though not prolific, were extremely popular, and always put on a mesmerising live show. The bar area was packed and Nick knew that it was going to take him a while to get served. As he waited he glanced around, on the lookout for people he knew. All at once, out of the corner of his eye, he caught a glimpse of someone, standing motionless in the crowd, staring straight at him. Turning his head, Nick saw a large, well-built man moving away, and felt a slight contraction in his stomach. He wasn't certain, but he thought it was one of the Guinness drinkers from the Rising Sun.

His sense of unease persisted as he negotiated his way back across the room with the drinks. He glanced around constantly as he moved slowly towards the girls, but the minimal lighting and the pressing crowd meant that making anything other than a cursory inspection of the vast room was impossible.

'At last,' Sasha said above Bowie's *Diamond Dogs*, playing over the speakers. 'We thought you'd run out on us.'

'It was a trifle busy,' he said, handing them their drinks. Then he turned once more, on edge now, to try and study the crowd.

For the next ten minutes the three of them stood and did little more than drink: they spoke only intermittently because it was too much effort to raise their voices above the music. As he drank, Nick's bladder began to prickle and then to ache. He glanced at the stage, saw that the roadies were almost done setting up the equipment. Perhaps he could suppress the urge until after the gig. He knew from past experience that if he did that, though, he'd only end up wanting the gig to be over so that he could go for a piss. He sighed and shouted, 'I'm just going to the loo.'

'They'll be on any minute, Dad,' Sasha said, gesturing at the stage.

'I know. I won't be long.'

He squeezed his way through the crowd, which was beginning to surge forward, sensing the imminent arrival of the band. The toilets were through a set of double doors in the far corner of the room and down a flight of stone steps. As he descended, the odour of sour piss rising to meet him, he couldn't help but think that the last time he had entered a club toilet his entire world had turned upside down. What would be waiting for him this time? he wondered, and then immediately reprimanded himself. *Nothing.* There would be nothing waiting for him. Last time it hadn't been the location that had been significant, but the experience itself. What had happened in the Gridlock toilet could just as easily have happened in his flat, or in a restaurant, or on the tube.

All the same he couldn't help feeling nervous as he entered the smelly, dimly lit toilet. Now that the band were due on any minute the room was deserted; all he could hear was the burble of pipes, sounding like indigestion, and the dull thump of music playing upstairs. He walked across to one of several urinals, swimming with piss-soaked fag ends, on the wall to the right of the door, and unzipped himself. He had just started to pee when he heard the clack of footsteps descending the stone steps outside. Instantly his bladder stuttered and clenched. Nick half-closed his eyes and did what he always did to make himself relax, which was to make a mental list of things fitting whatever category happened to pop into his head. Beatles songs; Hammer films; types of fruit; footballers whose surnames began with the letter S . . .

British sitcoms, he thought now, and began mentally to reel off titles. *Dad's Army, Citizen Smith, Only Fools And Horses, One Foot In The Grave, Some Mothers Do Have 'Em . . .*

Someone entered the room and came to stand beside Nick, on his left. Nick didn't turn to look at the man, but he got the impression that he was a pretty big guy.

Steptoe And Son. The Likely Lads. Red Dwarf . . .

Someone else came in. He moved to Nick's right, his shoulder almost brushing Nick's. This time Nick did glance up – and found himself face to face with one of the Guinness drinkers from the Rising Sun.

He had no doubt that the man on his left would be the other Guinness drinker. This time Nick's bladder did not just clench, it seemed to freeze, painfully sealing in what remained of his piss. Still clinging to the hope, unfounded he knew, that nothing sinister was going on, he stared straight at the wall and recited desperately: *Butterflies, Drop The Dead Donkey, Father Ted, 'Allo, 'Allo . . .*

'We want you to come with us, Mr Finch,' the man on his left said.

Nick's head jerked round. The man had a square face and close-cropped hair. His expression was neither friendly nor hostile.

'Why?' Nick asked, his own voice sounding as though it had been put through a strainer. He was six feet tall, but both men were two or three inches taller than he was and considerably broader.

'We're not at liberty to answer any of your questions, Mr Finch,' the same man said in a mild, factual tone.

134

'Are you the police?' Nick asked, tucking his cock back into his trousers and zipping himself up. 'Are you arresting me?'

'No questions, Mr Finch,' the man repeated.

'But you can't expect me to come with you if I don't know who you are,' Nick protested, wishing he could control the shrillness, the wobbling of emotion in his voice.

'Don't make us use force, Mr Finch,' the man on his right said. He was an inch shorter but a little broader than his companion, with black hair and a dark-stubbled face. He spoke in a Geordie accent.

Nick didn't know what to do. He couldn't make a break for it. Nor could he refuse to accompany the men; he was in no doubt that then they would only hurt him before making him do what they wanted. On the other hand the thought of meekly obeying their orders made him feel sick.

'Can't you at least tell me where you want to take me?' he asked desperately.

'Sorry, Mr Finch,' the man on his left said, and reached out as if to take Nick's arm. 'Let's go, shall we?'

Instinctively Nick jerked away, half-raising his arm, and with lightning reflexes the man on his right grabbed him and twisted the arm he had raised painfully behind his back. Nick cried out, feeling a little of the piss he had been unable to release earlier squirt down the leg of his jeans. 'Let go,' he shouted, adrenaline causing anger as well as fear to surge through him. 'Fucking let *go* of me, you bastard.'

To his surprise the other man gave a nod and the dark-haired man released his grip. 'There's no need for any unpleasantness, Mr Finch,' the square-faced man said.

Though he was badly scared, Nick tried to use the anger inside him to give him strength 'Why don't you just leave me alone?' he snapped. 'I don't know who you think I am, but whoever it is, you're making a mistake. I haven't done anything.'

'There's no need for any unpleasantness, Mr Finch,' the square-faced man repeated calmly, like a robot. 'All you have to do is come with us.'

'Oh, yeah – and what will you do to me if I do? Take me somewhere quiet and beat the shit out of me, or worse?'

'If we wanted to do that we coulda done it here,' the Geordie muttered.

135

Nick looked at him, unconvinced by his argument. 'I've got people waiting for me upstairs,' he said, trying his best to make it sound like a warning. 'They'll wonder where I've got to.'

'That's not our concern, Mr Finch. Now, please come with us.' The square-faced man turned to lead the way out, effectively ending the conversation. The dark-haired man put a fist into Nick's back and pushed, not too violently but enough to make Nick stagger forward a few paces as his spine flared with pain.

He walked between the two men, stomach fluttering with fear, bladder aching intolerably. He had a vague hope that once the men got him upstairs he could shout for help, or somehow lose himself in the crowd. However, outside the toilet, the square-jawed man turned not left, towards the stairs, but right, leading them further down the corridor. At the end of the corridor was an emergency-exit door; the square-jawed man took hold of the release bar and forced it down with a grinding clunk. The door swung open.

Cold air grappled with Nick as he stepped forward; his face was pummelled by a flurry of icy pinpricks. Dread leaped in his stomach. The narrow alleyway they had emerged into was at the side of the building, only twenty yards from the main entrance and a busy main road, but to Nick it might as well have been the middle of the Australian outback. As the man at his back shoved him forward, litter slithered beneath his feet; around him, the walls glistened. The promise of light from beyond the buildings stuttered with raindrops, as if the air were full of orange static. Beside two large metal bins on castors, around which piles of cardboard boxes were slowly deflating to brown mush in the rain, was parked the grey van that had plagued Nick for the past few weeks. Even now it was so anonymous that, viewed from the main road, it would have appeared almost invisible, shapeless as the shadows around it.

The square-faced man walked up to the van and opened the rear doors. 'Get in,' he said.

Before Nick could respond, there was the roar of an engine and a shriek of brakes which made him cower and throw his arms up as if a bomb had gone off. Next moment he was blinded by head-lights from the car that had turned into the alleyway.

Nick heard a wild shouting emanating from the two men who had been attempting to kidnap him, though he could not make out any words because of the simultaneous sound of slamming car doors and the frenzied pounding of blood in his head. Acting instinctively, he turned and sought the dubious protection of the two big metal bins, plunging into the sodden tower of cardboard boxes beside them, sending some unidentified animal – a mouse, perhaps, or a rat – scurrying in panic. He had no idea whether he could be seen either by his would-be abductors or the new arrivals, but he crouched down in the narrow space between the bins and the slimy wall, frantically dragging wet cardboard over him. From this vantage point he had a limited view of what was happening. He could see the car now, big and dark, expensive-looking, orange light sliding on its wet surface. He could see the men who had got out of the car and were advancing remorselessly on the grey van.

If anything, these men were even more terrifying than the two who had ambushed Nick. There were four of them, for one thing, all dressed in long black overcoats with the collars turned up. As they walked past his hiding-place, Nick saw that one was a fat skinhead with a goatee beard: another was a black guy with dread-locks and shades. What made the whole scene seem unreal as a movie – and yet at the same time so scary that his body seemed to be melting in shuddering spasms from the inside – was the fact that all four men were carrying very large handguns.

There was a weirdly silent pause after the men passed out of his range of vision. And then the shooting began. Informed by the cops and robbers movies he'd watched all his life, Nick knew instantly that the high-pitched, sneeze-cough sound of the mens' guns meant that they were using silencers. Part of his mind still refused to accept what was happening. *I'm listening to a bloody gun battle*, he thought with a kind of wonder. And then a second voice, a more knowing voice, kicked in. *No. You're listening to an execution.*

It was this thought – the cold, hard brutality of it – that got Nick moving. His first instinct had been to seek shelter, to make himself as inconspicuous as possible, but now he simply wanted to put as much distance as he could between himself and the men with the guns. All the same it was hard making himself stand up and sidle around the bins, wet cardboard falling away from him, leaving him exposed. He clung to one of the bins for a moment, staring into the headlights of the big black car, wondering if there were any more men in there and whether, if he began to run, someone would step out and shoot him too.

His body felt as though it were made of the rain which was coming down a little harder now, but he had to risk it; he couldn't stay here. He broke from cover and began to run, and though he lurched and stumbled, he was amazed at how well his legs supported him. He squeezed through the narrow gap between the open doors of the car and the slippery side wall of the Academy and made for the light.

His breathing was so ragged, his heartbeat so thunderous, that behind him he could hear nothing – no shouts, no sounds of bullets tearing into human flesh. The two men who had been drinking Guinness in the Rising Sun were probably dead now, he realised. Only five minutes ago he had been speaking to them – and now they were dead. His back felt as broad as a house-wall: every second he expected to feel the punch of a bullet between his shoulder-blades, the brief but incredible pain as his spine was severed.

But five minutes later, on the teeming streets of Central London, he was still alive. Still running.

Twenty-Two

During Portishead's second song Sasha turned to Jenna. 'Dad's taking a long time,' she shouted.

Jenna cupped her hand to her head, then put her mouth close to Sasha's ear. 'Perhaps he's gone to the bar.'

'Pardon?' Sasha shrieked, the effort making her face hurt.

Jenna mimed drinking and pointed to the back of the room.

Sasha shrugged. She knew Dad wasn't the sort to queue for a drink when a band he really liked was onstage, but she couldn't think of a way of telling Jenna this without making it sound like point-scoring. Two songs later she turned to Jenna again. 'I'm going to have a quick look for him.'

'I'll come with you.'

'No – it's okay. You wait here in case he turns up. He's probably met up with some music-biz mates of his. I won't be long.'

Sasha turned and wormed her way through the crowd, which was easy to do despite its density. That put paid to her theory that Dad hadn't been able to fight his way back to them through the crush of people. She made her way to the bar, but there were only a few dedicated drinkers hovering around there now and her dad was not one of them.

She wasn't exactly *worried* about him – but it was unlike him not to return. And a couple of things about his behaviour, and about what had happened over these past few days, had been niggling her, the disparate components attempting to form themselves into some kind of cohesive conclusion in her head.

There had been their odd conversation two days earlier over lunch, for example. Dad had confessed to having had some kind of hallucination in the Gridlock – which seemed to be a

139

culmination of several weeks of bad dreams and paranoid thoughts. Then there had been the intruder in Dad's flat; both Dad and DI Baker had seemed unwittingly to indicate that he had been more than a mere burglar. And finally there had been the Detective Inspector's comment that he was worried about Dad – which seemed increasingly peculiar the more Sasha thought about it – and Dad's rather unsatisfactory explanation of the policeman's concern.

Taken individually, these events were little more than snippets of oddness, quickly forgotten; but taken as a whole, could these oddities be construed as constituting the surface of something deeper? If she had known her better, Sasha might have confided in Jenna, but she had no desire to discuss her half-formed anxieties for her father with a virtual stranger, even though she knew Jenna had been there in the Gridlock when Dad had had his . . . *experience*.

She made her way to the corner of the auditorium, through the double doors that led to the toilets and down the stone steps. What with the bad smells and the dull beat of music coming from above, it was like being in the belly of something alive. The door of the Gents, painted a turquoise so hideous that the designer must have been either mad or colour-blind, was closed. Sasha pushed it open a few inches. 'Dad? It's me. Are you in there?'

There was no reply. Sasha pushed the door open a little further and peered round it, half-expecting to find Dad passed out on the floor in a drunken stupor (yet, although he'd been quite pissed, he'd been nowhere near paralytic) and half-fearing she would stumble across something altogether more serious. He could have been beaten up; or his years of drug abuse might have caught up with him and he could have collapsed (was this possible? She wasn't sure), or maybe she had been right the other day and these odd thoughts and visions of his had been symptomatic of some kind of brain malfunction, some serious disease.

The toilet, however, was empty and there was no indication that anything untoward had taken place there. Sasha checked the cubicles, but they were empty too. She sighed, and was about to head back upstairs again when she heard a bang.

She jumped, then recognised the sound for what it was: a door thumping against its frame. She hurried out of the Gents and peered in the direction of the sound. At the end of the dingy corridor she could see an emergency-exit door wafting to and fro in the breeze that was blowing through it. It was the kind of door with a release bar, the kind that could only be opened from the inside. Could Dad have opened it? The wind shoved at the door, making it bang against its frame again, as she made her way towards it.

Cautiously she pushed the door open and went outside. She found herself in a narrow, poorly lit alleyway, strewn with rubbish. The drizzle was cool, almost refreshing, but the sudden flurries of wind which accompanied it bit into the bruises on her face, making them ache anew.

The place was quiet; there appeared to be nobody here, though there was a grey van with dark windows parked a few yards away. Sasha walked up to it, remembering how Dad had mentioned a grey van when they had had lunch, wondering how much of a coincidence this was. She touched it, as if to ensure it was real, then tried the doors, which were locked, before cupping her hands and attempting to peer through the windows, which were too heavily tinted to see through. She walked round the van several times, at a loss for what to do. She peered up the length of the alleyway, towards the golden light of the main road, then down towards the wall that linked the Academy and the building beside it, making the alleyway a dead end.

She saw the blood.

She froze, her innards clamping then releasing slowly, allowing her heart to flutter. In the fragile, drizzle-etched light, the blood on the wall and ground was dark, almost black, yet never for a moment did Sasha doubt that it *was* blood. There was something about its texture, about the spattered patterns it formed, that somehow made it incapable of being anything else. On hollow legs she walked towards it.

Someone or something had died or been badly injured here; there was too much blood for it to have been otherwise. 'Oh, Dad,' Sasha whispered, and suddenly pictured the lugubrious DI Baker at her hospital bedside, telling her that he was worried about her father. *Call me*, he had said, *if anything happens*. Anything – what word had he used? Strange? Unusual?

She ran back into the Academy, pain jolting in her face with each step. She ran along the corridor and up the steps into the heat and the noise, the crush of people, the swoop of coloured lights

141

like the onset of migraine. She wanted to shout at the band to shut the fuck up, wanted all the noise and the people to go away so she could think and function. She rushed up to the bar, shouldering aside a swaying man with dead-drunk eyes, and thrust her swollen, bruised face towards a barman with bleached blond hair and an eyebrow stud. The barman's eyes widened at the sight of her.

'Have you got a phone?' she yelled.

He looked relieved that she didn't seem to want to involve him in anything more complicated. 'No, sorry,' he replied, shaking his head.

'This is an emergency!' Sasha shouted back at him, her voice raw above the music. 'There must be a phone somewhere in the building.'

He looked at her as if anguished by indecision, then nodded resignedly. Lifting the flap at the side of the bar for her to pass through, he said, 'Come with me.'

Twenty-Three

The TV was on. But though Linsey was staring at the screen, lying on the settee with her feet up, she wasn't really watching it. She was so angry that the only way she had been able to force herself to unclench her teeth was by making something to eat. Not that she was hungry – her anger was screwed up tightly inside her, turning her stomach into a hard, tight pain. Her teeth tore at brie-smeared French bread with such ferocity that it was as if she was punishing it rather than eating it. Occasionally she would pick up a cocktail stick from the small table in front of her (one of a 'nest' she had bought back in the seventies when such things were vaguely fashionable) and viciously spear a stuffed olive from a bowl, popping it into her mouth along with the bread and the cheese. She would have opened a bottle of wine if her stomach hadn't felt so tender, and if she thought she could have got even half-drunk without losing control of her emotions.

The worst thing was that she was not even sure *why* she was so angry. All right, so she and Sasha had not been hitting it off recently; and she had not been happy about Sasha going out tonight, so soon after coming out of hospital; and Nick's failure to dissuade Sasha from going out – yet another example of his irre-sponsibility – irritated her no end. And yet . . . and yet . . . Even all this should not have made her feel as enraged as she felt now.

She honestly believed that only a tissue-thin membrane of . . . what? Decorum? Convention? Sanity? was preventing her from screaming and crying and running around the flat like a madwoman. There was a part of her that wanted to smash every-thing, destroy the home she had carefully built up over many years, tear down her life.

143

Her life. That was a joke for starters. She didn't *live*; she merely existed. She got up, went to work, came home: an endlessly repeating cycle, every day the same. She was halfway to seventy and had bugger all to show for it. She had never had what she would call a meaningful relationship with a man, was at loggerheads with her daughter, didn't even have any proper friends to speak of. Now that she and Sasha were growing apart, there was no one she could turn to.

Not that being alone, aloof, had ever bothered her before. She had always had a tendency to keep people at arm's length; with men particularly she had always indulged her instinctive urge to maintain the status quo, to not rock the boat. She didn't know why. Maybe it was because she had been let down in the past, because her dreams had been shattered one by one.

But if all this – this general dissatisfaction with the non-event of her life – was the cause of her fury, then why was it only coming out now, and why all at once, in a great whoosh? She had had years to get used to her setbacks, had even thought she had come to accept them, to absorb them, bury them deep. Now though, suddenly, it was as if the ground were giving up its dead. All at once, in her mid-thirties, she wanted to fight her way out of the hole she had dug for herself, but she had been in it for so long that she didn't know how to go about it, where to start.

Sasha, she supposed, was the catalyst. In spite of the hardships and the sacrifices Linsey had made, she had always had Sasha to care for, to cherish, to be proud of. Sasha had been her focus; everything she had ever done since her daughter's birth had been with Sasha in mind, and had therefore been worthwhile, had given her life purpose.

Now, though, finally – inevitably – Sasha was beginning to assert her independence. She didn't need her mother any more. And it really felt to Linsey as though the only thing she had ever really cared for was tearing itself from her, leaving a wound that would never stop bleeding. It had been bound to happen one day, she knew, but it had always seemed too distant to worry about. But such things had a habit of creeping up on you unawares, hitting you between the eyes when you were least expecting them.

She picked up the cocktail stick and was in the process of jabbing at another stuffed olive when the doorbell rang upstairs.

144

Linsey paused, put down the stick and glanced at the green numerals of the clock on the video. It was after half-ten. Who could be calling at this time of night? It couldn't be Sasha; she had a key. Most probably someone who wanted one of the residents upstairs. Sighing, she pushed herself up from the settee, crossed the lounge into the kitchen and went from there along the hallway and up the stairs that led to ground level. The door to her flat was on the latch, but there was no chain on it. She thought about calling 'Who is it?' but didn't want to sound like a frightened old woman, so she twisted the latch and pulled the door open.

Two men in suits were standing on her doorstep. They looked like bouncers, or policemen. One was thick-set with dark, oily hair, Italian-looking; the other was boyish with sandy hair. He smiled at her warmly.

'Mrs Finch?' he asked.

Linsey bridled. 'No.' The man looked at her quizzically and she felt compelled to explain. 'Nick and I never married. He's the father of my daughter, that's all.'

'Of course,' the man said, shaking his head and rolling his eyes self-deprecatingly. 'I do apologise.'

'That's all right,' Linsey said, and glanced at the dark-haired man, who stared back at her, expressionless. 'Er . . . what can I do for you?'

The sandy-haired man smiled again and gave her a brief flash of an ID card in a wallet which she had no time to focus upon. 'I'm Detective Inspector Salmon; this is Sergeant Briggs. We'd like to ask you a few questions about Mr Nicholas Finch if we may, Miss . . .?'

'Greene,' said Linsey. 'What's he done?'

Salmon glanced to his right, at the staircase which led to the upper-floor flats. 'If we could come in for a few minutes, Miss Greene? It is rather a . . . delicate matter.'

Linsey hesitated for a moment, then held the door wide enough for the two men to enter. The dark-haired man smelt of an after-shave that stung her nostrils; Linsey stepped back as he lumbered past her, shivering without knowing why.

She closed the door and followed the men down the stairs. 'The lounge is left at the bottom, along the hallway and through the kitchen,' she said, and then, almost in the same breath, 'My daughter, she's not involved in whatever Nick's done, is she?'

'I think you need have no worries on that score, Miss Greene,' Salmon said. 'What a lovely home you have here.'

'Thank you,' said Linsey distractedly. She followed the men into the lounge. Salmon sat down on the settee; Briggs stood in the corner by Sid the budgie's cage, a dark, brooding presence.

Not wishing to sit with her back to Briggs, Linsey sat on the armchair to the right of the TV. 'So what *has* Nick done?' she asked.

Salmon made a steeple out of his fingers, then rubbed his hands slowly together; they made a dry sound. 'To be honest with you, Miss Greene, he hasn't exactly *done* anything. He's simply . . . disappeared.'

'Disappeared?' repeated Linsey blankly.

Salmon smiled. 'Perhaps I'm being a trifle melodramatic. It might be more accurate to say that he has temporarily – slipped from our clutches, as it were.'

'Do you mean you're going to arrest him?' Linsey asked.

'Oh no,' said Salmon. 'We simply wish to speak to him. He's helping us with our enquiries.'

'We want to know where he is,' Briggs said, speaking for the first time, his voice a rumble.

Linsey glanced at him; she didn't care for the accusatory way he was staring at her. A little indignantly, she said, 'Well, I can tell you *exactly* where he is. He's with my daughter. They've gone to a concert, at the . . . er . . . the Academy, I think it's called. It's a club near Oxford Street.'

Briggs shook his head and bared his teeth like an ape. 'Not good enough.'

'What my colleague means, Miss Greene,' said Salmon mildly, 'is that we were already in receipt of that particular snippet of information. A couple of my men approached Mr Finch at the Academy this evening. It was there that he managed to elude them.'

'But he went with our daughter,' said Linsey. 'So where's *she* now, may I ask?'

'We don't give a fuck about your daughter,' Briggs growled.

Linsey's eyes widened, shocked by the man's sudden vehemence. Fear jumped inside her, then was swamped by the old, familiar anger. '*You* may not, but I do! Who the hell do you think you are, talking to me like that in my own home?'

146

'Shut up,' said Briggs.

Linsey jumped to her feet, trembling now with a fear-spurred rage. 'Get out of my house now!'

Briggs sniggered.

'I mean it. If you don't get out, I'll . . .'

'What?' Briggs said mockingly. 'Call the police?'

'Please sit down, Miss Greene,' said Salmon. His voice was still mild, but Linsey could detect the steely undertone to that had crept into it.

She looked from Salmon to Briggs, then back to Salmon again. She remained standing, but folded her arms across her chest: a flimsy gesture of protection. 'What do you want?' she asked, her voice splintery, the momentum of her anger stymied by Salmon's lack of confrontation.

'We just want to know where Mr Finch is,' Salmon said reasonably.

'Well, if he's not with my daughter, then I don't know.'

'She's lying,' said Briggs.

Salmon looked at his companion. 'Do you think so?'

'Definitely.'

'I am not *lying!*' snapped Linsey, glad to feel the anger building again.

'You're a lying bitch,' said Briggs. 'Finch has been in touch with you.'

'No, he bloody hasn't. Why should he?'

'Just tell us where he is, Miss Greene,' said Salmon wearily.

'I don't *know* where he is,' said Linsey. 'If I did know, I'd tell you. Why are you giving me such a hard time? Hey, what are you *doing?*'

Briggs had half-turned and was opening Sid's cage with his meaty fingers. He reached in and grabbed the blue budgerigar, enclosing it in his fist so that only its head was visible. Sid gave a little nervous chirrup, but he was a mild-mannered bird and made no attempt to peck at the man's hand.

'Put him back,' Linsey said as Briggs drew his fist from the cage.

'Tell us where Nicholas Finch is,' Salmon said.

'Look, I've told you – I don't *know* where he is, and I don't particularly care. I'm not the one he'd turn to if he was in trouble.'

Briggs took Sid's head between the thumb and forefinger of his free hand and gave it a sharp twist. The bird's head came off easily. There was a spurt of blood and a snapping thread of gristle – and that was it.

'*Nooo*!' Linsey screamed, a sick, fizzing disbelief rushing through her body. She ran at the man but he shoved her back with such savage ease that she crashed into the armchair, her legs folding beneath her. Briggs turned to the peach-coloured wall behind him, held out his arm and squeezed the tiny bird's headless body as if it were a tube of tomato puree. A jet of blood and a crimson slop of guts squirted from Briggs' fist and on to the wall. Linsey began to shake and sob, her hand going to her mouth. She thought she was going to vomit.

'Tell us where Nicholas Finch is,' Salmon said, his voice now a monotone, lacking any pretence of warmth whatsoever.

'I don't *know*, I don't *know*,' Linsey whimpered, tears running down her face.

Briggs dropped the crushed bundle of blue feathers on the floor, then crossed the room, causing Linsey to moan and flinch, drawing in her knees. But the dark-haired man walked past her without so much as a glance. With the bloody hand that had held the bird's body he picked up the cocktail stick Linsey had been using to spear olives and jammed Sid's head down on to it. The budgie's tiny beak was open as if in surprise; his black bead eyes still appeared to be alive and aware. Briggs stuck the cocktail stick, topped with the head, into the cheese like a grotesque garnish. A trickle of blood from the neck cavity ran down the stick and formed a dark red bead on the chalky rind of the brie.

Salmon smiled and stood up. 'Do you know, Miss Greene, I think I believe you,' he said. 'So sorry to have troubled you. We'll see ourselves out.'

He sauntered to the arch that led to the kitchen and passed through it. Briggs lingered for a moment, looking down at Linsey with undisguised contempt.

She stared back at him, trying to regain control, not wanting him to have the satisfaction of seeing how terrified and distressed she was. As he took a neatly folded white handkerchief from his pocket and began to wipe the blood from his hands, she hissed, 'You're not a real policeman!'

Briggs laughed and put the handkerchief back in his pocket. Then he followed Salmon from the room.

Twenty-Four

'What took you so long?' Sasha snapped, hurrying forward as Baker, looking somewhat rumpled, flashed his ID at the bouncers and entered the foyer of the Academy.

Baker gave a small, resigned sigh, as if used to this sort of disrespect. 'I came as soon as you called, Miss Finch. Actually I should have been spending the night in Newcastle, so you're lucky I was able to come at all.'

'She's in a bit of a state,' Jenna said by way of apology, and placed what was presumably intended to be a calming hand in the small of Sasha's back.

Sasha flinched from her touch and rounded on her. 'I am *not* in a state!' She immediately checked herself, raising both hands in apology. 'All right – I admit I am a bit wound up. I'm sorry.'

'Nothing to be sorry about,' Jenna said.

'Do you think we could have a look at this alleyway you mentioned on the phone, Miss Finch?' Baker asked.

Sasha nodded and led the way out into the drizzle, the dull heartbeat-thud of music from the main hall fading behind them.

Approached from the well-lit street, the alleyway seemed full of a blackness so thick it was like tar. Shapes and details were not immediately apparent, and they had ventured a good ten yards before Sasha realised what was missing.

'Oh,' she said, coming to an abrupt halt.

'What's the matter?' asked Jenna.

'The van's gone.'

Sasha walked up to where the van had been parked, but there was no indication that it had ever been there; this area of litter-strewn concrete was as slick with drizzle as the rest of the ground.

149

'Perhaps its owners came back for it,' Jenna said.

'When I spoke to you on the phone, Miss Finch, you mentioned that you'd noticed some blood,' said Baker.

'That was further back, at the end of the alleyway.' Sasha led them to where she had seen the blood stains earlier. She was finding it harder to adjust her eyes to the darkness this time; it was as if the shadows had drawn together, solidified, jealously guarding their secrets. The shards of orange light seeping in from the main road, reflected off the dips and ruts in the wet concrete, broke and changed beneath her feet. She reached the wall at the end of the alleyway. Then she looked around in confusion. She squatted and touched the ground. Finally she straightened up and turned to Jenna and Baker, standing expectantly behind her.

'It's gone.'

'Perhaps the rain washed it away,' suggested Jenna.

Sasha shook her head. 'There was too much of it. There'd be some trace.'

Baker came to stand beside her. He was casual, hands in pockets. 'It appears that someone has been tidying up.'

'It *was* here!' Sasha said vehemently as if he had accused her of lying.

'I believe you,' said Baker.

'So what happens now?' Jenna asked.

Baker pushed his lips out as if in contemplation. 'Anyone fancy a cup of tea?'

Sasha stared at him. If her eyes had not been swollen almost shut they would have widened in disbelief. 'You've got to be kidding! My dad's disappeared. Anything could have happened to him. We've got to . . .'

'Got to what, Miss Finch?' asked Baker gently. 'Run around like headless chickens?'

'Don't patronise me,' Sasha said caustically. 'We've got to – I don't know – tell the police!'

'I *am* the police.'

'Well, you should be doing something then. Organising a search, questioning people—'

Baker shook his head. 'I believe our time would be better spent sitting down, comparing notes and developing a strategy. There's a great deal you don't know about this situation, Miss Finch.'

'Like what?' asked Jenna.

'I know an all-night café not far from here. A quiet place. Let's go there and I promise I'll explain everything.'

Sasha looked around as if she had missed something vital. A little desperately she said, 'I don't know. I feel as though we should be *doing* something.'

'Half an hour – that's all I ask,' said Baker. 'If, after that time, you still think we should let the force handle this, then we will.'

Sasha sighed, her shoulders slumping a little. 'All right.' She turned and began to walk dejectedly out of the alleyway, back towards the main road.

It took less than five minutes to reach the café. It was tucked down a side street as if hiding from the public, a narrow place which spilled its glow out on to the wet pavement through windows grimed with pollution. White letters on a green-painted sign announced it as Mik's Coffee Lounge. As Baker pushed open the door, a bell jangled insipidly, causing a thin, balding Greek man collecting crockery at a nearby table to look round.

'Ah, Mr Baker,' the man said enthusiastically, 'how are you?'

'Can't complain,' said Baker laconically. 'Yourself?'

'Ah, you know. Overworked and underpaid, my beautiful wife nagging me to an early grave, my children running riot, getting up to God knows what.' He grinned. 'Life is good.'

Baker smiled along with him and looked around. Apart from the three of them and Mik the café was empty.

'If you can find a free table, it's yours,' Mik joked. 'What can I get you?'

Baker raised his eyebrows questioningly at the women. 'Coffee for me, please,' said Jenna. 'Decaff.'

'Tea,' mumbled Sasha reluctantly; she felt she had been forced here against her will.

Baker ordered coffee for himself and the three of them sat down. Sasha didn't give them time to draw breath. 'So what don't I know?'

Baker laced his hands together on the table and took them slowly and methodically through the events of the past few days. Their drinks arrived as Baker was halfway through his account of his meeting with Mark Cotto. Finally he told them about being taken off the case, and his encounter with the balaclava-clad men that afternoon.

'Jesus,' said Sasha, sitting back. 'Who do you think they were?'

151

Baker shrugged 'A government faction, perhaps, though they may have military connections.'

'Like M15, you mean?' said Jenna.

'Oh, far more covert and ruthless.'

Jenna half-smiled. 'You mean, these secret government groups actually exist? I thought all this kind of stuff was made up by conspiracy theorists and UFO spotters.'

'You'd be surprised,' said Baker, 'how many of these so-called conspiracy theories have more than a grain of truth in them.'

'How do you know all this?' asked Sasha.

'As a police officer you hear things over the years. Rumours mostly, but when something like this happens it sets you thinking. You start to put two and two together.'

Sasha thought for a moment. So you think these same people who stopped you on the road . . .' she hesitated a moment, '. . . took my dad?'

Baker looked at her steadily; knew she was thinking of the blood she had seen. 'It's possible.'

'But why? I mean, Dad can't be important to them. He's only a music journalist.'

'Maybe it's a case of mistaken identity,' said Jenna.

Baker shook his head. 'I doubt it. From the evidence, I'd say that this group – whoever they are – have been keeping tabs on him for some time.'

'It must have something to do with this vision of his. This Michael Mercy thing.'

'Yes, but remember that only happened a couple of days ago.' He looked thoughtful. 'It may have been that which finally gave them the impetus to act, I suppose.'

Sasha pressed her fingers to her temples. 'This is so bloody *unbelievable* . . . Okay, accepting that what you've said is true, what can we do? How can we find out what's happened to Dad?'

Baker sipped his coffee. Even in the face of extraordinary events he seemed as imperturbable as ever, thinking things through calmly, methodical. 'My only suggestion is to blow the thing wide open.'

'How do we do that?' asked Jenna.

'By going to the newspapers. I've got a number of contacts within the media: good ones. I'll phone around and try to fix something up for tomorrow. In the meantime I think it would be a good idea to keep our heads down. In fact, to be on the safe side, it might be best to find somewhere safe to stay for tonight.'

'You honestly think we're in that much danger?' said Jenna.

'It's possible. After all, you both know more than you should.'

Sasha shook her head. 'I can't afford a hotel. I haven't got that sort of money, and I'm certainly not asking Mum.'

'I can,' said Jenna. 'I'll pay for both of us, don't worry.' Sasha opened her mouth to protest. 'If you want to pay me back at a later date, you can.'

'Thanks,' said Sasha, looking relieved. She poured herself more tea from the metal pot that Mik had brought. 'I just wish we didn't have to wait until tomorrow. Anything could be happening to Dad. You do think he's okay, don't you?'

'I'm sure he is,' Jenna said quickly. But Baker remained silent.

'I'd better ring Mum,' Sasha said miserably. 'I'll tell her I'm staying at a friend's.' She got up and went over to a payphone on the wall by the counter. Mik, drying crockery, smiled sympathetically at her, presumably because of her battered face. As she punched in her home number, Sasha wondered whether the man who had assaulted her in Dad's flat had been a member of this government group. If so – and if they were capable of doing this to her – what might they have done to Dad, their real target? She tried to put her anxieties out of her mind as the pips went, tried to sound carefree as she said, 'Hi, Mum, it's me.'

She was ready for the bad mood her mum might be in – Mum was in a bad mood pretty much all the time these days – but she did not expect to hear the hysterical sobbing on the other end of the line, the shrill, scared voice bleating, 'Sasha, where *are* you?'

Several minutes later Sasha stumbled back to the table. Even through the purple bruising and the swelling, her face looked ashen; bad enough for Jenna to rise from her seat and exclaim, 'Sasha! What's wrong?'

Sasha plumped down heavily in her seat. 'Those bastards,' she whispered.

'What's wrong, Sasha?' Jenna said again, reaching out and grasping her hands. 'What's happened?'

Sasha looked up. A tear trickled from her purple-fleshed eye and rolled down her cheek. 'Those bastards have been to see Mum. They killed Sid.'

'Who's Sid?'

'Our budgie. Mum said one of them –' she hitched in a breath, trying to swallow her sobs – 'one of them took Sid out of his cage and twisted his head off. I mean, who would do . . .' Her voice cracked and her head slumped forward. Tears began to drip on to the table top, wet coins that grew and blended together.

Jenna's chair screeched on the floor as she shuffled closer to Sasha. She put an arm around the younger girl's shoulders and looked at Baker. He was regarding Sasha too, stony-faced. After a few moments he spoke, quietly. 'Miss Finch.'

Sasha didn't respond. Baker cleared his throat. 'Sasha?' he said, awkwardly.

Sasha looked up, carefully wiping her eyes. Baker looked a little embarrassed to be intruding on her misery. 'I know you're upset, Sasha, but I think we need to get your mother out of there. But I'll need your help. Do you feel up to it?'

Sasha nodded, sniffed. 'Yes. It was just a bit of a shock on top of everything else. Sorry to be so wet.'

Baker made a vague flapping gesture, dismissing the apology. 'I'd like you to ring your mother again – your voice is probably the only one she'll trust at the moment. Tell her to throw a few things into an overnight bag and wait for a cab to come and pick her up.'

'Okay,' Sasha said, and with Jenna's help she rose to her feet. Baker rose too and as the girls headed for the phone he walked up to the counter to pay Mik.

As Mik handed him his change, he leaned forward conspira-tionally. 'What happened to the girl?' he hissed. 'Her boyfriend beat her up?'

'Something like that,' said Baker.

Mik shook his head. 'Nice girl like that. Why do people do such things?'

Baker shrugged. 'Search me.'

154

Twenty-Five

It began to rain harder as if taunting him, scuttling in the leaves above his head like an army of rats. Nick pulled his jacket even tighter around him and pressed himself against the trunk of the tree beneath which he had taken shelter. He couldn't stop shaking; he felt sick and his head was pounding, as if the images and thoughts that filled it were too terrible to contain. He kept trying to make himself calm down, take deep breaths, but it was impossible. His breath ratcheted through his chattering teeth as if he'd run a race.

He hadn't felt like this since he was at school, running and hiding from the big kids. At the time the bullying he had endured at the age of twelve had seemed like the worst thing that could ever happen to anybody, but at least then he had had his parents – both now dead – to run home to. Now he simply had nowhere to turn.

After fleeing the alley, he had run like a madman through the streets until he reached the tube station at Tottenham Court Road. He had plunged down the stairs into the darkness like a rabbit disappearing into its burrow, and was sitting on a train for home, gasping and sweating and wild-eyed, attracting nervous covert glances from everyone around him, before he realised what he was doing.

Of course he couldn't go home: his flat would be the first place they would look for him. Neither could he go to Jenna's or Linsey's – they would be sure to find him there too. He thought of Sasha and Jenna at the Academy, wondering where the hell he'd got to. He hoped that the men with guns didn't know that he'd been with the two women, didn't go looking for them in the hope

155

of finding out where he was, or to take some sort of revenge on them. If anything happened to either of them he'd never forgive himself. Linsey, too: what if they burst into her flat with their guns, looking for him? What were they capable of doing to her?

He pressed the heels of his trembling hands hard into his eyes in an attempt to squeeze the thoughts out. The tube carriage, rattling through the tunnels, suddenly seemed hot and oppressive. At the next stop he leaped to the door and jumped off, the stale air and the panic that he was trying to suppress making him feel ill, feverish. For a while he wandered the streets, dodging from shadow to shadow, not knowing what to do. The buildings made him nervous: too many observation points, too many places to hide. In the end he had made his way to Regent's Park. And here he still was, pressed against a tree, doing his best to melt into the darkness, the rain dripping through the leaves and soaking him, but giving him a modicum of security too, making him feel at least partially screened from the outside world.

If he had not been so disturbed by what had happened he would have found it almost peaceful here, despite – perhaps because of – the rain. As a kid he had loved to sit in the steamy shower, just out of range of the water battering down into the plastic bath, pretending he was in a jungle, sheltering beneath a tree during a tropical downpour. Fantasies had been easy to conjure back then: later, he had had to use drugs to push himself into anything like a similar state. It was funny, but he hadn't thought of the shower fantasy in years; maybe it had suddenly come into his mind because tonight's events had reduced him to a scared kid all over again.

At the moment, despite the rain, he simply didn't fancy moving from here. He didn't exactly feel safe huddled beneath this tree (he didn't think he would feel safe ever again), but neither did he feel in any immediate danger, and that seemed to be the best he could hope for. He was pretty sure he hadn't been followed; if he had, his pursuers would surely have made their move by now.

He wondered about checking into a hotel, but knew he would feel too vulnerable, too easy to trace. The same was true of hostels and refuges – and besides, it wasn't as though he needed some-where to sleep, was it? He was far too wound up for that. No, the best thing would be to wait here until daylight, out in the open where he could run if he had to, and then make his way to the nearest police station and put himself in the hands of the law. He didn't now believe that it was the police who were after him, not after seeing those men with their guns.

He closed his eyes briefly and pictured the black guy with the shades and dreadlocks, the fat skinhead with the goatee. He shuddered and opened his eyes again. The lights of London, twinkling and blurring through the rain, seemed far away. The rain eased a little and Nick shifted position slightly. Now, pattering gently through the leaves above his head, the rain seemed to be whispering to him, lulling him to sleep.

Twenty-Six

'How are you feeling now, Mum?' Sasha asked, sitting on the bed.

Linsey, propped up by pillows, looked dumbly at her daughter's bruised and battered face and tried to concentrate on formulating an answer to her question. She felt odd more than anything, felt as though she were looking at Sasha through the wrong end of a telescope, as though her daughter's voice was echoing down a long, narrow tunnel. It was as if she had been sedated; but she hadn't been, she was sure of that.

She forced a smile. 'Not too bad, thanks. A bit tired.' Her own voice sounded hollow and muffled in her ears. She opened her mouth wide to try to make her ears pop and saw Sasha looking at her curiously. Closing her mouth she said, 'I didn't – *take* anything last night, did I, Sasha?'

'Like what?'

'A pill. Did anyone give me anything to calm me down?'

'No, Mum. You were quite calm when you got to the hotel. Upset, but . . . okay.'

'Oh,' said Linsey and lay her head back on the pillow. She felt woozy, almost drunk. The patterns in the wallpaper seemed to ripple and bulge. She closed her eyes.

She was vaguely aware of Sasha's warm hand closing over her own (it seemed so far away), and then Sasha's voice coming to her from the top of the well at the bottom of which Linsey felt as though she was lying. 'It's just a reaction to last night. You're tired and upset and you probably need something to eat. Come on, I'll help you get dressed, then we'll go down to breakfast. We're due to meet Jenna and Inspector Baker in twenty minutes.'

Linsey could quite happily have stayed in bed all day – all week, all year – and simply drifted, allowing her mind, light and empty as a balloon, to float and bob aimlessly, going wherever it wished. However, she allowed her daughter to drag her out of bed and direct her towards the bathroom. She showered and dressed in a daze, sat on the edge of the bed and closed her eyes while Sasha brushed her hair.

The next thing she was aware of was Sasha asking, 'Are you *sure* you're all right, Mum? You look a bit strange.'

Linsey opened her eyes again. 'I'm fine,' she heard herself saying. And she *was* fine, at least in the sense that whatever was clouding her mind had also dulled her emotions to such an extent that she no longer felt scared, or angry. Even the horror of Sid's death could not penetrate the fug. She could remember what had happened, but it seemed somehow unimportant. A small part of her realised that she should not be feeling like this, that something was wrong, but the greater part welcomed the feeling, revelled in it, wanted it to go on and on.

They went down to breakfast, Linsey feeling as though she were floating through the red-carpeted corridors. She wondered vaguely if she looked strange as well as feeling it, but no one seemed to glance at her twice, not the other residents, nor the hotel staff, nor even Nick's latest, nor the policeman who had come in the taxi to meet her last night. Both the policeman, Baker, and the woman, whose name Linsey could not remember, were already sitting at a table for four in the restaurant, their breakfast spread out in front of them.

The woman was sipping coffee and toying with a bowl of muesli; Baker was working his way stolidly through a full English breakfast. As Linsey and Sasha approached with laden trays from the self-service counter, the woman looked up and gave a tight, tense smile. 'Hi.'

'Hi,' replied Sasha. 'How did you sleep?'

'Not too well. You?'

'Oh, okay. I'm sorry you were on your own.'

'No problem. I kept my door locked and hid under the covers.'

Linsey sat down and started taking items off her tray, unable to shake off the peculiar impression that her own actions were unconnected to her. Baker gulped egg, leaving a trace of yolk at the corner of his mouth, and said a curt good morning. Linsey said good morning back. No one else seemed to think as she did that her voice sounded like a dull echo in an empty room.

She was neither hungry nor thirsty, but she ate and drank automatically, only half-listening to the conversation ricocheting around her. Her mind was too slow, too somnolent, to grasp the details, but she got the gist of it. Baker was telling them about some meeting he had fixed up with a journalist friend of his at another hotel across the city. When the woman asked why the journalist couldn't come to them, the policeman replied that it would be best if they kept moving, that they didn't want to stay in one place for too long.

The more she listened, the more thick and muzzy Linsey's head became and the more detached she felt. Sasha had said that having something to eat would make her feel better, but in fact it was having the opposite effect. After a while, her wooziness ceased to be a mildly pleasant feeling. As the four of them sat there, eating and drinking and talking, her temples began to prickle and then to ache. It was not until her head felt as though it were splitting in two that she drew attention to herself. Unable to stand the pain any longer, she suddenly slumped forward, her hands coming up to support the nodding weight of her head. Through the ringing in her ears she heard Sasha's voice, distorted but full of concern. 'Mum, what's the matter?'

'Headache,' Linsey gasped. The effort of speaking sent blinding flashes of agony through her head, which reduced any response from Sasha to a wordless buzz.

She felt her shoulders being grasped, felt herself being forced gently back in her chair. Then something was being pressed against her lips. Pills. She opened her mouth and felt them slip inside, felt the cold shock of liquid against her teeth and tongue. It had a sharp taste. Orange juice. She wanted to gag but she made herself swallow until she was sure the gritty pills were gone, washed into her system.

People spoke to her. She couldn't hear what they were saying, couldn't see anything except harsh lights and distorted shapes. She felt herself being hauled to her feet, made to walk. Now she was no longer floating, but was a solid weight of pain that erupted into fresh bursts with each jolt, each step. She wanted to cry out, to protest, and maybe she did, but it didn't make them leave her alone. Just when she thought she could stand it no longer, that she

160

was going to pass out or throw up, she felt herself being lowered slowly, tenderly, into a sitting position, arms wrapped around her back, supporting her.

The cessation of movement had an extraordinary effect, or perhaps it was the fresh air blowing into her face. All at once her vision cleared and the distorting static in her head faded away. Then, abruptly, like a dark cloud passing from the sun, the pain was gone. She looked quickly around her, taking in her surroundings.

She was sitting with Sasha on one side and Nick's girlfriend (Jenna, she remembered now) on the other, on the wide base of a marble pillar just outside the hotel foyer. Baker was standing with his hands in his pockets on the kerb of the service road in front of the hotel, watching the traffic passing by beyond the stone gateposts of the hotel entrance as if deliberately isolating himself from the stricken woman in his company.

Linsey licked her lips. 'Um . . . I feel a bit better now,' she mumbled sheepishly.

Sasha blinked at her in surprise, then her face broke into a delighted grin. 'Mum! You're back with us!'

Jenna's reaction was more cautious. 'You virtually passed out in there, you know.'

'Did I? Well, I'm okay now. A bit woozy, that's all.'

'What brought it on?' asked Sasha.

'I don't know. All at once I just got this terrible headache. I couldn't see or hear anything.'

'It must have been the heat,' said Jenna, snaking her supporting arm out from behind Linsey's back. 'Hotels are always too hot and stuffy.'

Baker turned. 'Here's our cab,' he announced, as one pulled in through the entrance gates. He glanced at Linsey. 'How's the – er . . . the invalid?'

Linsey didn't care for being referred to in such terms. She stood up smartly. 'Much better, thank you.' The cab cruised to a halt. 'Where are we going?' she asked Sasha.

'To see the Inspector's press contact.'

They climbed into the cab and Baker gave the driver instructions that Linsey couldn't catch, keeping his voice low. Clearly he wanted to keep their destination a secret.

'I only hope this helps us find Dad,' Sasha murmured as the cab pulled out into the traffic.

161

'We're doing the only thing we can,' said Jenna, sitting opposite Sasha with her back to the driver. Linsey, sitting beside her daughter, took her hand and squeezed it; the pressure was reciprocated. Perversely, despite the situation, she felt a little glow of warmth inside her. It was unfortunate that it had taken something as drastic as Nick's disappearance to bring her and Sasha closer together than they'd been in months, but she tried to allay her guilt by telling herself that Nick was not yet lost to them, that they were doing all they could to get him back.

It was a bright, cold day after last night's rain and the streets, lined with shops, were busy with both people and traffic. Linsey tried to spot some reference point, to work out exactly where they were. Last night she had been in too much of a state to observe their route, had seen nothing but Sid's head jammed on to the end of the cocktail stick like a war trophy, the contents of Sid's body squirting from Briggs' fist on to the wall. The memory provoked a shudder, a wave of dismay and disgust. And when she looked out of the cab window and saw something bloody approaching along the pavement, moving in and out of the crowds, she thought for a confused moment that what had happened last night had been so terrible, so vivid that her subconscious had somehow superimposed it on to the present.

But as the bloody object got closer Linsey realised what she was really looking at. She sat bolt upright in her seat. It was a young girl, perhaps fifteen years old, naked and covered not only in blood but in bruises. She looked as though she had been slashed, beaten and stripped before being discarded, or perhaps escaping on to the streets. But the most shocking thing of all was not the mere fact of the girl's presence, but that nobody was paying her the slightest attention. She was staggering along, hands held out in supplication, her face stark with pain and distress. Yet people simply walked past, ignoring her completely. Linsey was appalled. She felt physically sick. How could people be so callous? Then they were past the girl, Linsey twisting her head to look out of the back window, trying to spot her in the crowd.

'What's the matter, Mum?' Sasha asked.

Linsey turned, wild-eyed. 'Did you see that girl?'

'What girl?'

'Just now, walking along the pavement. She was naked and covered in blood. People were just ignoring her!'

162

'Where?' said Sasha, shocked, leaning across Linsey to peer out of the window.

'I can't see her now.'

Baker looked at Linsey, his face giving nothing away. 'I was looking out of the same window and I didn't see anything.'

'But you *must* have done,' Linsey insisted. When there was no immediate response she said angrily, 'So what are you saying? That I'm making it up?'

'Of course not, Mum. No one's saying that.'

'Maybe you were just mistaken,' Jenna suggested.

'I know what I saw.'

There was silence for a moment, and then Jenna said, her voice giving nothing away, 'Well, even if she was there, I'm sure someone will have helped her by now.'

The four of them lapsed into silence, Sasha casting anxious glances at her mother, Linsey thinking about what she had seen. Only now, with the incident past, did she begin to doubt the evidence of her own eyes. Perhaps the girl *had* been an hallucination, brought on by stress and exhaustion. But was it possible to hallucinate something so vivid? Presumably so, otherwise one would always recognise hallucinations for what they were. She thought about how oddly detached she had felt when she had woken up that morning; her migraine-like headache which had passed so suddenly it seemed like a dream. She couldn't deny that she still felt a little woozy, a little detached from reality.

She looked out of the window again. On the opposite pavement, four boys, each no more than ten years old, were beating a dog to a bloody, twitching pulp with baseball bats.

As Linsey adjusted her vision in an attempt to determine whether the scene was indeed real, a lorry passed by in the opposite direction, blotting the boys and their hapless victim from view. By the time the lorry had passed by the boys – if, indeed, they had ever been there – had, like the girl, been obscured by the crowd. Linsey half-turned to her fellow passengers, then thought better of it; she didn't want to endure their loaded questions, their sceptical, patronising looks for a second time.

She licked her dry lips, heart thumping, muddled thoughts racing. Was she going mad? Had last night's incident unbalanced her mind? She recalled how she had felt yesterday before the men arrived. She had had to fight an urge to rampage through the flat, smashing the place up. Would a sane person have wanted to do such a thing? If what she was witnessing out on the streets was simply a figment of her imagination, how much of last night's incident might she also have imagined? Perhaps the bogus policemen had not existed at all. Perhaps Sid was still alive. Or perhaps – she felt horror jolt through her – she had killed the budgie herself.

No, she couldn't believe that. She might be having problems, but she wasn't that far gone. She shifted in her seat and glanced at Sasha, who was looking anxiously out of the window, face tense beneath her bruises, swollen eyes blinking rapidly in the sunlight.

On the opposite pavement another figure snagged Linsey's attention, a man to whom her eyes felt drawn. He was tall and rangy, wearing a thin, grubby, ill-fitting shirt. He had wild, dirty hair, a scrubby beard, mad eyes. He was striding along the pavement, cutting through the people, going against the flow. He reminded Linsey of a shark, swimming among shoals of less dangerous fish.

A woman was walking towards the man, pushing a baby in a pushchair. A split-second before the man and the woman met, Linsey just knew that something terrible was going to happen. She felt her stomach lurch, felt herself half-rise from her seat, as the man suddenly lunged forward and grabbed the baby. In the next instant he was holding it aloft by one leg, his bony hand wrapped around its chubby ankle. The baby, upside down, was struggling feebly, waving its arms. The mother was screaming, pleading with the man, begging him to let go.

The man grinned. His teeth were long and yellow, like ancient piano keys. As the woman reached up for her baby, the man's free hand – long and bony, almost skeletal – clamped over her face and he shoved.

The woman took several rapid steps backwards and fell, banging her head on the pavement; even above the growl of traffic, Linsey fancied she heard the crack. A couple of passers-by stepped out of the woman's way as she sprawled on the concrete, but no one did anything to intervene. Linsey felt her world closing in, felt herself gripped by panic and horror, as the man laughed and began to swing the baby round and round his head like a lasso. And then he let go, and the baby flew out across the road and fell amid the traffic. Linsey instinctively reached out, desperate to catch the falling infant. '*No!*' she screamed at the top of her voice.

Everyone in the cab jumped and looked at her, their eyes wide and shocked. The cab lurched to a halt as the driver automatically stamped on his brake, causing Linsey to sprawl forwards on top of Jenna, her head thumping the glass partition.

'What the *hell's* going on?' the driver said, his voice deep and throaty, like the snarl of an animal. As Linsey, with Jenna's help, struggled to her feet, she glanced into the driver's cab and saw something that made the fine, blonde hairs on her arms prickle and stand upright.

The steering wheel beneath the driver's hands was no longer a steering wheel at all. It was a coiling black serpent.

Linsey opened her mouth to cry a warning, but no sound came out. She watched as the black snake slithered through the man's hands, curling back on itself to form a circle. And now the driver's hands were changing too, the fingers lengthening, nails stretching into talons, the skin darkening and cracking, becoming scaly like the snake's.

In Linsey's world, there was now only herself, and the driver. The others in the cab; the busy street outside; the dreadful things that she had witnessed: they were all bleeding away, becoming negligible. The driver started to turn towards her, twisting his head slowly, mockingly. Linsey wanted to cower away, to escape from him, but her body felt locked.

The driver turned all the way round and Linsey found herself staring into his face.

It was a human face. Linsey felt a moment's relief washing through her. Then the driver opened his mouth, and suddenly he wasn't human any more.

His mouth was full of jagged fangs; his tongue, lolling between them, was black and glistening. The tongue flopped from the driver's mouth like a giant leech and began to undulate towards her, its tip twitching as if it were sniffing the air. All at once Linsey found that her paralysis was gone. She threw herself at the cab door. '*Let me out! Let me out!*' she screamed.

The door opened and suddenly Linsey was sprawling in the road, pain tearing into her knee, the blare of a car horn filling her head. As she scrambled to her feet, the fading echoes of the horn were drowned by a slobbering roar from the cab behind her and she ran, dodging between cars and lorries, to the pavement on the opposite side of the road. Now she was among people – though not the same people she had viewed through the cab window. These were shuffling parodies of mankind, their heads lumpy, misshapen, like melting waxworks, their features a hideous jumble of eyes and teeth and hair.

Stumbling away from one of these creatures, she barged into another, and felt its body give like rotting fruit beneath its clothes. The creature made no protest; instead it reached up and touched her face, blindly, exploratively. Its flesh was cold and wet and it left a sticky smear of itself behind. Linsey let out a cry of disgust and pulled away, swiping at her face with her sleeve. She saw an opening between a greengrocers and an electrical shop and plunged towards it.

Finding herself in an open-ended alleyway she began to run, though within seconds she felt exhausted, stress draining the strength from her limbs, making her wheeze and rasp, causing a cold, drenching sweat to burst from her skin. Sick and light-headed, she looked around for somewhere she could rest for a few minutes, some hidey-hole she could crawl into like an injured animal. Outside the delivery entrance of the greengrocers were several piles of fruit boxes, leaning one against another, waiting to be broken up and taken away. Unwittingly aping Nick's actions of the previous evening, she staggered towards them. Seeing that there was a narrow gap between the boxes and the wall, she ducked behind them, out of sight.

She crouched there, her head spinning, body trembling with cold and terror. She wrapped her arms around herself, squeezed her eyes tight shut in an effort to make herself as small as possible, so small that she might even disappear. For a few seconds, huddled in the darkness behind her eyelids, she felt secure. Then she heard slow, measured footsteps, approaching her hiding place. She pressed herself back against the wall, praying they would walk on past, but the footsteps stopped in front of her. Yet, even when she heard the scuff and scrape of fruit boxes being pulled aside, she kept her eyes shut, clinging desperately to the childish belief that if *she* couldn't see then she couldn't, she *wouldn't*, be seen.

There was a short pause, a hovering moment of expectation, during which she honestly believed that she had not been discovered. Then whoever, whatever, was standing above her, looking down on her, spoke, and the voice was unlike anything she had ever heard before, thin and trilling and totally inhuman.

'Face me, Linsey Greene,' it said. 'Without me, you are lost.'

Linsey knew she had no choice but to look into its face. She found it physically difficult to open her eyes, had to use her fingers to prise the lids apart. Instantly light flooded into her sockets, making them grind and throb like toothache, turning her world white. The glare faded quickly, enabling Linsey to see the figure standing above her: at first in silhouette and then in terrible, terrible detail.

The creature had the body of a man, and was dressed like an undertaker: in a sombre suit, white shirt, black tie. But its head, albeit in proportion to its body, was that of a budgerigar. It should have been a ludicrous sight but it wasn't; it was her purest nightmare made manifest. The creature's black, bulging, expressionless eyes twitched as it regarded her; its plumage – identical in colour to poor Sid's – ruffled each time a faint breeze blew down the alleyway. As it opened its beak to speak, small white maggots spilled out and pattered to the ground like rain.

'You have become possessed by a spirit,' the creature told her in its trilling voice. 'It is sitting astride your mind, controlling your thoughts. You are its horse.'

Linsey knew there was something wrong with the logic of this, but she couldn't work out what it was. All she wanted was to be well again, normal again. If there was a spirit, then she wanted to know how to be rid of it. Nothing else mattered.

The creature tilted its head to one side as if listening to her thoughts. More maggots spilled from its half-open beak. When it leaned forward, Linsey felt the maggots falling on to her skin, into her lap. 'A spirit has no use for a blind horse,' the creature said.

Twenty-Seven

Sasha walked down the crowded street for the third time, her battered face attracting curious glances. Mum had not been moving quickly – indeed, she had been weaving and staggering as though drunk – yet somehow she had managed to disappear in the time it had taken Sasha to get the name and address of the hotel they were heading towards from Baker, and then negotiate the slow-moving traffic that Mum had hurtled recklessly through, seemingly oblivious to the screech of brakes and the blare of car horns. Mum had been behaving strangely all morning, but just before becoming hysterical, losing it for no apparent reason, she had seemed okay, despite her odd outburst a few minutes earlier about the naked girl she claimed to have seen stumbling along the pavement.

Sasha's head was spinning with all that had happened in the past thirty-six hours. In that short time her world had been turned incomprehensibly upside down. Was her mother mad? she wondered. Or was she being got at in some way, like her father, her mind perhaps manipulated by the same government group? But if so, how? By the use of drugs? And, more importantly, why? Mum and Dad weren't anything special – so why had they become targets? It didn't make sense.

Sasha was about to walk past the greengrocers and the electrical shop yet again when she noticed the dark thread of alleyway between them. It was worth a look; though if Mum had run down there she could be anywhere by now. As she strode down the alleyway Sasha felt full of nervous energy, felt as if she were running out of time. She had to find Mum, and then rejoin Baker and Jenna at the hotel, hopefully in time to speak to this journalist friend of Baker's and give her side of the story. She was worried that Baker and Jenna wouldn't emphasise strongly enough how *serious* the situation was, how important it was to expose these people, whoever they were, and find Dad. Because, after all, no one else but her really had an emotional stake in the outcome, did they? Not even Jenna: she and Dad had met only a few days ago.

Sasha had walked no more than a hundred yards when she heard a sound that sent prickles of dread across her shoulders and down her back. It was a quiet whimpering, like an animal in distress. It was coming from behind several haphazard stacks of fruit boxes to her left. Sasha's legs seemed to grow heavier as she approached. She reached out to move a couple of boxes aside – and there was Mum, sitting with her back against the wall, head bowed, straw-like blonde hair obscuring her face, fists clenched in her lap.

'Mum,' Sasha said softly, but her initial flood of relief was swept away when she saw blood drip from under her mother's overhanging curtain of hair and join the previously unnoticed puddle between her knees.

'Mum!' Sasha said, more sharply.

Slowly, slowly, Linsey raised her head.

Sasha stepped back, sucking in a jolt of air; that was the only thing that prevented her from screaming. Her mother's eyes were gone, gouged from sockets which shed tears of blood. Only strips of tendon were left, dangling over Linsey's lids like thin, dead worms.

Sasha felt as though she were falling. She closed her own eyes and breathed hard to prevent herself passing out. When she opened them again, she saw the bloody tears running down her mother's cheeks, and fell to her knees. Feeling sick and faint, she whispered, 'Mum. Who did this to you?'

In response Linsey raised her hands from her lap and opened them. In each was an eyeball, dangling bloody roots; one was punctured, leaking jelly. Sasha clamped a hand to her mouth and tried to stop the hysteria leaping inside her from bursting forth. Linsey's lips began to move; Sasha forced herself to lean closer to her mother's ruined face. She heard Linsey whisper, with a kind of joy, 'The spirit has left me now. I felt it go.'

Twenty-Eight

Nick didn't realise he'd dozed off until he jerked awake with a start.

He was slumped on his haunches, his back against a tree trunk spongy with last night's rain, shivering from the damp chill that had seeped through his clothes and coated his skin. He moved his right leg to push himself into a standing position; immediately a cramp seized it, twisting and crushing the muscles inside. Nick's head snapped back and he gave a choking cry. He could do nothing but knead the leg with his fingers and wait for the pain to subside.

It was morning and the rain had stopped. Indeed the sun was out, its light catching in the jewels of moisture scattered in the still-lush grass. The air was brisk and cold, a stiff breeze busily shuffling the few clumps of early autumn leaves from one location to another. There were a few strollers out, walking alone or hand in hand or in chattering groups, but no one paid Nick the slightest attention, not even when he pushed himself from the shadowy shelter of the dripping tree and into the sunlight. He stood swaying for a moment, feeling and no doubt looking like shit, unable to stop shivering. Then, stiff-legged and stooped as an old man, he began to walk.

His plan had not changed since last night: he would make his way to the nearest police station and tell them everything. First, though, he needed a hot shower and – despite the fear that still churned in his gut – something to eat, otherwise he would keel over. He squelched his way to the Outer Circle and from there to Euston Station, where he used his cashpoint card to withdraw fifty pounds. If he remembered rightly, there was a leisure centre just

170

off Gower Street where he could grab himself a shower for a £2 entrance fee.

Twenty minutes later hot water was jetting into his hair and on to his upturned face, thawing the cold out of his skin. It was an exquisite feeling, but he couldn't enjoy it to the full. He felt too vulnerable standing there, naked, his vision blurred and his ears filled with the drumming of water. After only a couple of minutes, reluctantly, he switched the water off and padded through to the changing room to dry himself on the big, green, fluffy towel he had been able to hire for a pound. His damp clothes steamed on a chunky radiator between a long wooden bench and a set of grey lockers. The only other people in the changing room were a fat, hairy man whose handlebar moustache made him look like a walrus, and two boys of around ten with stick-thin legs, whispering and giggling as they got dressed, their wet hair sticking up in spiky clumps.

Once dry, Nick sat and wrapped the towel around him, glancing up nervously each time someone new entered the changing room, wary even of those who came in dripping from the pool. Shrieks and laughter echoed from the pool area itself, the sounds made shrill as the cries of bats by the high ceiling and tiled walls. At last he peeled his clothes from the radiator and put them on, shuddering as the warmth faded quickly from them to reveal that they were still damp. Out in the fresh air again he walked briskly, swinging his arms, the wind ruffling his hair. He was soon dry.

He ate breakfast in a café in Great Russell Street, chewing Danish pastries and drinking strong coffee as he watched the world go by. It was odd, but last night's events now seemed simultaneously dream-like and as stark and real as anything that had ever happened to him. He wondered whether he should call Sasha or Jenna, but decided against it; his would-be kidnappers, whoever they were, might well be monitoring the phones of anyone he'd be likely to try and ring in an attempt to pinpoint his location.

There was a police station on Tottenham Court Road, Nick remembered vaguely, a grey-stoned place with steps leading up to large wooden doors. He paid for his breakfast and left, and ten minutes later was pleased to find that his memory had served him well. Now that he was close to his goal he felt more nervous than ever, perhaps partly in anticipation of what might be awaiting him. He leaped up the steps two at a time as if he were being pursued and shoved at the wooden doors. After the brightness of the day the interior of the building was so dark that, for a few seconds, he couldn't see the details of the desk sergeant's face.

The place was quiet as a church as he walked to the desk, but he had taken no more than two steps when telephones began to ring, which made him feel as if the place had been waiting for him to enter before bursting into activity. The desk sergeant's sleeked-back hair and pug nose made him look like an East End gangster masquerading as a policeman. He didn't look up from his paper-work until Nick had placed his hands on the desk and was leaning towards him.

'Morning, sir,' the sergeant said then. 'What can I do for you?'

Nick had already worked out what he was going to say, but his lips were dry as he said it. 'I need to speak to someone about a murder that I witnessed last night.'

Twenty-Nine

The Majestic Hotel in Hammersmith seemed to have been built solely to give old colonialists a taste of former glories. Though luxuriant, it was, in essence, only one rung above a theme pub. The bejewelled elephants flanking the expansive staircase – and the Asian art adorning the walls – were like a defiant declaration that the spirit of the Raj was still flourishing, in theory if not in practise. Baker and Jenna made their way across the reception area – the carpet so plush and yielding that it was like trudging through a snowdrift – to a door in the corner, which proclaimed it led to the Calcutta Bar.

Baxter Mead – Baker's contact – was living up to the stereotype of his profession, sitting on a bar stool and downing whiskies though it was barely ten in the morning. He was a bloated, red-faced man with lumpy features and straight brown hair that flowed over the shoulders of his dark checked jacket, leaving crumbs of dandruff.

'Mikey, hi!' he exclaimed, before downing his drink in one and clumping across the bar in a pair of tan-coloured cowboy boots, into which were tucked the legs of jeans so tight they seemed in danger of bursting beneath the weight of his paunch. He grabbed Baker's reluctantly proferred hand and pumped it vigorously. 'How you keeping? Well, I hope. You *look* well. And who the hell's this gorgeous creature?'

Before Baker could reply, Jenna stepped forward and thrust out her hand. 'Jenna Trenchard.'

The force of her handshake evidently took Mead by surprise. Raising his eyebrows, he said, 'Well, Jenna, if you always grip that hard you can come out with me any time.'

Jenna smiled tightly. 'I've booked us a room,' Baker said. 'Shall we go?'

Without waiting for a reply, he turned and trudged towards the reception desk. Mead put a sweaty hand around Jenna's upper arm as she went to follow and spoke through a whisky-smelling grin. 'Let's hope there's a mini-bar so we can have a little party. Hey, I thought there were supposed to be four of you?'

'The others got detained,' said Jenna. 'They should be joining us soon.'

Mead nodded, jowls quivering like a Saint Bernard's.

The room Baker had booked was on the fifth floor. Aside from the mock-Indian fabric designs used for the curtains and bedsheets, it was like every other hotel room Baker had been in: plush but soulless. Mead leaped backwards on to the bed, causing the springs to groan in protest, then made himself comfortable, back against the headboard, legs stretched out, cowboy boots crossed one over the other. He took a dictaphone from his jacket pocket and dropped it casually beside him. 'Ready when you are. Just shoot from the hip. I'll ask incredibly insightful and thought-provoking questions as we go.'

'Miss Trenchard, if you'd like to give your version of events first,' Baker said, and turned away to the tray beside the bed to make tea. Jenna nodded, pulled up a chair and began to relate the circumstances of her unorthodox meeting with Nick in the Gridlock on Thursday night.

Mead put his hands behind his head and watched Jenna's mouth as she spoke. He was not silent for long. As soon as she began to describe Nick's recounting of his vision in the club toilet, the journalist grinned. 'Numero uno chat-up technique,' he muttered. 'I must try it sometime.'

Jenna scowled at Mead, then looked to Baker for guidance as he handed out tea. Baker gave a curt nod. 'Go on.'

Jenna doggedly continued, telling Mead about Nick's later insistence that he had foreseen the death of Michael Mercy and his family, and about his fear that he was being watched and followed, that his phone was being tapped.

'Sounds like major-league paranoia,' Mead commented. 'You sure this boyfriend of yours wasn't a couple of Crunchie Bars short of a selection box?'

'No, he wasn't. *Isn't*,' Jenna snapped. 'If you're not going to

174

take this seriously, I really don't see the point of carrying on.' She glared not only at Mead but also at Baker, as if to let him know that by remaining silent he was letting her down.

Baker sighed. 'There's a great deal more to tell yet, Baxter. I'd advise you not to jump to premature conclusions.'

Mead spread his hands. 'Hey, everyone be cool! My mind is an open book.'

'Sure,' muttered Jenna.

'It *is*. Truly. Look, I'm really interested in what you're telling me. These little jokes of mine are just my way of lightening the mood.'

'Well, they're not lightening mine,' Jenna said curtly.

'Right, okay – I can live with that. Mikey told me about this Finch guy doing a disappearing act last night and I understand that you're worried about him. I respect that.'

'I doubt it,' said Jenna.

'Hey, come on! Beneath this rugged exterior beats a heart of pure schmaltz.'

'Could we just get on with it?' Baker said wearily.

'Sure. Whenever you're ready. But let's jettison this tea thing, okay? This is a stressful situation we've got here. What we need is a proper drink to chill us all out.'

'No thanks,' Jenna said through gritted teeth. 'I'm fine with tea.'

'As am I,' added Baker.

'Well, if you guys don't want to relax that's your prerogative.' Mead rolled gracelessly from the bed, crossed the room and opened the mini-bar, dropping to his knees before it like an acolyte seeking absolution at the shrine of his deity. As he selected several miniature bottles of spirits he gestured vaguely at the dictaphone. 'Don't mind me – just carry on. Tape's still running.'

Jenna sighed, then recommenced her story. When she had finished she moved aside and Baker took up the mantle.

Mead – draining the miniature bottles with one swallow and lining them up like skittles on the bedside cabinet – showed his first real spark of interest when Baker mentioned the list of names that Mercy had written on the wall of his sitting room – information which the police had previously withheld. The journalist raised his eyebrows then; but he sat bolt upright when Baker quietly revealed that Nick Finch's name had been on the list.

175

'You're kidding,' he said. 'So what's the connection between Mercy and Finch? Did they know each other?'

Baker shook his head. 'I don't believe so. At present I'm still trying to establish the connection between all these people. That there is one must be undeniable, and that it is . . .' he hesitated, '. . . beyond our normal understanding is undeniable also.'

'Beyond our understanding? What do you mean?'

'He means something really weird is going on,' Jenna said.

'You mean weird as in . . . what? Some sort of cover-up?'

'Could be,' Jenna said, 'and on a big scale. We're talking government involvement here.'

Baker grimaced; he preferred caution. 'I must stress that at present our evidence is largely circumstantial, our theories the result of informed guesswork more than anything else.'

Mead's eyes were pink with alcohol, but suddenly he seemed sober, serious. 'Tell me more,' he said.

Baker told it all: Cotto's suicide; being relieved of his duties; speaking to Julie Lean; being confronted by the armed men yesterday afternoon. The more he told the more excited Mead became, the more questions he asked. Finally the journalist grinned a grin that threatened to split his red, sweaty face in half. 'This is fantastic. Just fantastic,' he said.

'Glad you're pleased,' Jenna said drily.

'Well, so you should be! This'll be front-page news by tomorrow. It's the scandal to end all scandals. You mark my words, some very important heads will roll for this one. The public'll love it. By this time tomorrow the whole country will be talking about Nick Finch.' Mead's pink eyes turned misty. 'Yeah, I can see it now. They'll probably make a film of it. You ought to think about writing a book – you could sell the rights for a bomb.'

Jenna turned to Baker and said, with evident distaste, 'Is he for real?'

Before Baker could reply, Mead swung his legs from the bed and stood up. He swayed slightly, then reached for his dictaphone and pocketed it. 'I've got to get moving on this right now,' he said. 'This is big, big, big.'

'What about Sasha and Linsey?' asked Jenna. 'Aren't you going to wait for them?'

'Get 'em to call me,' Mead said. 'Mike's got my number.' Suddenly he frowned, looking worried. 'Hey, this is an exclusive,

176

right? You're not gonna cut anybody else in on this?'

'All we ask is that you provide us with the coverage we need,' said Baker.

Mead grinned. 'You got it. Well, see you around, guys.' He waddled to the door, fat, denim-clad buttocks bouncing, and exited after flipping his finger in a farewell salute.

There was an odd, silent moment. Then Baker said, hesitantly, 'Well, that seemed to go quite well.'

Jenna shook her head dismissively. 'What a moron.'

'He's a good journalist, though.' Baker collected up the tea cups and as many of the miniature spirit bottles as he could carry and took them over to the dressing table. The cups he put on a tray, the bottles he dropped into the wastebin with a shrill clatter. When he turned around he thought Jenna was reaching out her hand to him until he realised that she was holding a small, black handgun.

'You received two warnings to leave this case alone,' she said, 'but you ignored them both. I'm very sorry, Inspector Baker, but you've become something of a liability.'

She shot him twice in the chest. There was virtually no sound as she pulled the trigger. Baker felt little pain, but the darkness rushed over him surprisingly quickly. He fell down, his thoughts dissolving, and when Jenna calmly walked forward and shot him twice more in the head, he was already gone.

177

Thirty

Kevin Costner? No – too bland. It needed to be someone with character, someone who could carry a witty line, someone with originality. Someone a little left of centre, not so mainstream. Someone like . . . Jeff Goldblum! He'd be ideal. Okay, so their physiques didn't exactly correlate, but he had the same kind of energy and mystique as Baxter, that *je-ne-sais-quoi* quality that pulled in the chicks.

That Jenna whatsherface, for example. Okay, so she hadn't really been up for his humour, but that was understandable; the chick had a lot on her mind. But deep down Baxter could feel that little spark of attraction, that little fire that, given time, would almost certainly have blossomed into a raging inferno.

Right, so Jeff Goldblum would play him in the film of the Baxter Mead story (okay, so it wasn't exactly *his* story, but he was going to be the one to bring it to the attention of the world, and as such he would therefore be the pivotal character in the whole thing) and Jenna could be played by . . . someone feisty, someone a little neurotic maybe, but still sexy as hell.

Mead clicked his fingers as a face swam into his mind, attracting the attention of a number of people standing close to him on the tube platform. That dark-haired skinny chick who was in *Scream*: what was her name? Courtney Cox! Yeah, she'd be ideal.

It was all falling into place now. Maybe Costner could play this Nick Finch guy, and Mike Baker could be played by . . . who? Tommy Lee Jones? No, too enigmatic; you needed someone a little more down to earth. How about . . . Mead grinned. John Goodman! Okay, so physically Baker and Goodman couldn't

178

have been more different, but hey, what did that matter? This was the movies, right? And as long as Goodman played the role really deadpan, really low-key, he'd be ideal. Of course, you'd have to relocate the whole thing to New York or LA, but that shouldn't be a problem. This story would be big with a capital B wherever it took place.

Mead glanced up at the digitalised information display: two minutes to his train. The station was pretty busy. There was a school party a little further along, a bunch of kids shouting, making a lot of noise for the sake of it, their voices bouncing back from the curved walls. Closer to him were some Chinese tourists, maybe a dozen of them, looking a bit perplexed. One of them was squinting through thick glasses at an ad for Madame Tussaud's, face creased in concentration.

My story will affect all these people, Mead thought, and felt a little tingle in his belly. *Pretty soon no one will think of the government the way they do now. Their whole perception of how things work, how things are run, will change. The conspiracy theorists, dismissed for years as kooks and crazies, will be able to hold their heads up high, to nod and say, 'We told you so. We knew all along that this was how things were.'*

His thoughts turned reluctantly from fame and film deals to more immediate matters. He needed a headline – a great headline, the best he'd ever come up with. What was that phrase he had used back at the hotel? The scandal to end all scandals? Well, okay, that was a starting point. Something along those lines . . .

There was a rumble from deep down the tunnel, a rush of air. Mead stepped forward in anticipation, looked down the tunnel and saw the white flare of sparks in the darkness. As the train's headlights glared out of the tunnel, he was aware of somebody stepping up smartly beside him. He looked round and was surprised, and pleased, to see Jenna smiling warmly at him. Clearly she'd felt too inhibited by Baker's presence to show her true feelings in the hotel room. Baxter had been right about that spark of attraction. A brief flash, a scene from the as-yet untitled and unwritten film passed through his mind: Jeff Goldblum turning to see Courtney Cox standing at his shoulder. 'Hi,' he would say in that soft, strange way of his, his eyes dark and expressive, puzzled yet knowing. 'Hi,' she would reply, blushing a little. 'You know, I just had to get out of there. I thought maybe we could go for a drink somewhere, talk some more . . . about the story, I mean?'

'Sure,' Jeff Goldblum was saying in his head when Jenna reached up with both hands and gave him a sharp shove in the back. Caught off-balance, Mead fell forward, horribly aware in an instant of what was about to happen to him but too startled to make any sound. He put out his hands instinctively, but there was nothing to grab hold of. For a split-second before it struck he was aware of the train bearing down on him, people starting to scream. Underpinning this was an infinitesimal but nevertheless intense moment of dark, bitter, terrible regret. And then the train smashed the life from him, reducing him to nothing more than a half-column on page four of tomorrow's paper.

Thirty-One

The two officers interviewing Nick – DI Osgood and DS Summers – were sympathetic and courteous. More importantly they seemed to take his story very seriously. Bolstered by cups of syrupy coffee, Nick told them everything. They in turn asked him a great many questions, at intervals excusing themselves and leaving the room for ten, fifteen minutes at a time – presumably, thought Nick, to check out certain aspects of his story and set lines of enquiry in motion.

Eventually Nick was fixed up with a special day pass and told to make use of the canteen and other facilities. DI Osgood, a tall man with tight, curly hair and a chubby face, told him that although he was free to come and go as he pleased, it would be useful if he could stick around for as long as possible – if that was convenient. Just so that he was available for 'immediate reference.'

Sitting in the canteen by himself, eating a chicken salad roll and drinking tea, Nick finally began to feel secure for the first time in what felt like weeks, finally began to feel that before much longer his life would be back on track. It felt almost like being a little boy again, when seemingly insurmountable problems would be solved quickly and easily by his parents. Sometimes life got too hard to bear alone and it was good to shift the burden to somebody else: somebody qualified and capable, somebody who knew what they were doing.

After lunch he answered more questions. Sometimes he even answered the same questions he had answered before – 'Just to get things absolutely clear,' Osgood reassured him. As they had done previously, the two officers came and went. Occasionally Nick would go for a stroll, to stretch his legs, but mostly he would remain in the interview room, warm and relaxed, elbows on the table, happy to sit and feel safe, to be in a place where there were people with the power to act, people who believed in his story. A place where he was beyond reach.

After a longer absence than usual, Osgood and Summers re-entered the room and Summers – an attractive woman with reddish-blonde hair – smiled at him. 'Sorry about that, Nick,' she said. 'We really appreciate your patience in sticking with us today.'

Nick shrugged. 'No problem. If it helps to get all this lot sorted out, then I'll stay for as long as it takes.'

'Well, actually,' Osgood said, 'the Commissioner has been on the phone. The good news is that he's eager to assign some of his top men to this case, to make it an A1 priority. What you've told us today, Nick, might very well give us the information we need to push forward in a number of very important inquiries. I can't say too much, but they involve a pretty major crime syndicate that we've been chasing for some time.'

'However,' said Summers, 'the bad news is that the Commissioner would like you to speak to his men immediately. We've had instructions to drive you there.'

'I know it's been a long day,' Osgood said, 'and if you don't feel up to it I'm sure we can persuade them to put if off until the morning.'

'No, that's okay,' said Nick, thinking that if the previous few days were anything to go by a great deal could happen between now and the morning, 'I feel fine.'

'In that case,' said Osgood, 'we might as well set off.'

The two officers led Nick through the back of the building and into a small car park. Osgood pressed a button on his key-ring and a maroon Cavalier unlocked itself. Summers held the door open for Nick, who climbed into the back, then she got into the front passenger seat, next to Osgood. The car smelled strongly of the lavender air freshener that dangled from the rear-view mirror. Nick put on his seatbelt and the car moved off.

They drove in silence, Nick happy to have a rest from talking, to look out of the window at the bustling streets. It was late afternoon, almost the rush hour, and traffic was slow-moving. The pearly sky was a thinning membrane against which darkness was

182

pressing. While he had been in the police station it had rained again; pavements and roofs shimmered with water. He thought of last night, spent huddled beneath a tree, icy rainwater dripping down on him. He shivered at the memory of how cold and afraid he had been. Here in the car he felt cosy and protected, the heater breathing out warmth, the engine snoring softly as if encouraging him to sleep. Suddenly his eyelids felt heavy; he closed them, and almost immediately a delicious somnolence stole over him. He gave in to it, began drifting down a long, dark corridor, deep into himself.

His aching neck woke him up; instantly he felt disorientated. He wondered what he was doing sitting on a train, where he was going. He looked around, and his memory came flooding back. They were on a dual carriageway, lined with shops and businesses, swarming with traffic. It was darker than it had been when he had closed his eyes, dark enough for headlights. He looked at his watch – 5 : 45. He had been asleep for just over an hour. In that time, with this traffic, they may well have travelled only a dozen or so miles. He looked around for landmarks, and saw none. He realised, with a pang of anxiety, that not only did he not know where he was, but neither did he know where he was being taken; he had not even thought to ask. As the car cruised to a stop at a row of glaring red eyes that were traffic lights he leaned forward to speak, but before he could open his mouth there was the screech of brakes from behind them.

Nick braced himself for the crunch of impact, though he knew that the car behind could not have been travelling at more than ten or fifteen miles an hour. However, the impact never came. Nick was half-turning to confirm his assumption that the car behind them had managed to stop in time when, suddenly, the front passenger door was yanked open.

Before Nick or either of the detectives could react, a man wearing a balaclava and shades leaned into the car and pointed a large handgun at Summers' head. An instant later there was the gravelly shattering of safety-glass and an arm whipped through the driver's window. Even as Osgood was raising his arms to protect himself from the glittering fragments that were showering down on him, the owner of the arm – another man dressed and armed as the first – turned off the engine and ripped the key out of the ignition. He then pointed *his* gun at Osgood.

183

'Get out of the car,' he said calmly. 'Both of you.'

Nick expected the detectives to refuse, or at least to make some kind of protest, but they obeyed without question, unsnapping their seatbelts and climbing slowly out of the car.

'Now turn round and walk away and don't look back,' the man who had smashed Osgood's window said. Neither Osgood nor Summers even hesitated. Without a word they began to walk away from the car.

Nick watched them go, feeling betrayed and abandoned, knowing at the same time that they had had no alternative, that in their position he would have done the same thing. The lights had changed to green and cars were driving past him, many of the drivers looking over to see what was going on, their faces mildly curious as if they were watching a scene from a movie. No one intervened as Nick's door was pulled open and he was ordered to get out.

He wondered what the people who were driving by made of all this. Most of them probably thought that the gun-carriers were some kind of SWAT team and that Nick was the bad guy – a drug pusher, perhaps.

'Walk to the black BMW parked directly behind your car and get in the back,' one of the men said. Nick thought his legs were going to give way, wondered whether the men would shoot him in cold blood if he stumbled. Somehow he managed to remain upright, and slid into the back of the BMW to find another armed, balaclava-clad man already there, idly pointing his gun in Nick's direction. The man who had ordered him into the car climbed in beside him, the two men squashing him between them. 'Lean forward,' the man said, 'and place your forehead against the seat in front.'

They're going to execute me, Nick thought, panic clawing at him. He began to shake, wanted to plead for his life, but was afraid of inciting the men to violence. He hesitated, choking back a sob.

'Place your forehead against the seat,' the man repeated.

Nick did so, shaking badly, his stomach beginning to cramp. The man who had broken Osgood's window got into the front passenger seat and the BMW pulled smoothly away from the kerb. Several interminable seconds passed and then Nick felt something being wrapped around the lower half of his face, hands bumping against his neck as they pulled the gag tight. Next

184

moment his vision was obscured, the blindfold similarly tightened and tied.

'Now,' the man said, 'just hold still and this won't hurt a bit.'

Nick barely had time to register the words before he felt a stabbing pain in his arm. He flinched, made a strangled sound beneath his gag, imagining a knife, imagining the two men stabbing him and laughing, spilling his blood, torturing him for kicks.

His head began to swim; although Nick fought against it, terrified of passing out, of losing all control for the second time in an hour he felt himself beginning to drift down a long, black corridor. He struggled pathetically, to no avail. In his last second of consciousness he wondered whether he would ever see daylight again.

PART THREE:
THE CHICKEN HOUSE

Thirty-Two

It was over three hours after Linsey had leaped out of the cab when Sasha finally arrived at the Majestic Hotel. She had left her mother lying in a hospital bed, eyes bandaged, body twitching and restless despite the heavy sedation she was under.

Sasha felt utterly numbed by what had happened. For the moment she was working on automatic pilot. After leaving Linsey – feeling guilty for doing so but knowing that there was nothing more she could do for her right now – she had rung Baker's mobile number. Receiving no reply, she had decided to take a cab to the Majestic.

Now, as she walked up the fancy steps and between the huge marble pillars carved in the shape of rearing elephants into the reception area, she wondered what she would do if Baker and Jenna had already left without leaving her a message. She daren't go back home, nor to her father's; she could go to her friend Ceiron's and keep trying Baker's mobile number from there, but she was reluctant even to do that. If she *was* in any sort of danger, she didn't want other people dragged in unnecessarily. Being mixed up in this sort of trouble was like having a contagious disease; you made a hermit of yourself so you didn't pass it on.

It was only when Jenna stood up sharply, smoke coiling from the cigarette in her hand, that Sasha noticed her. Her dad's girl-friend had been sitting well concealed in the shadow of a tall, exotic plant, on a chair fussy with beads and gold braiding. Jenna's thin face looked drawn, her lips pursed.

'Hi,' Sasha said, suddenly feeling the weight of explanations bearing down on her, 'how did it go?'

189

'Oh, really well. The guy seemed to think it would definitely be front-page news tomorrow.'

Sasha nodded, trying in vain to drum up a little enthusiasm. 'That's great. You did tell him everything, didn't you? You did tell him what I'd seen in the alleyway? The blood and the van and all that?'

'We told him everything. Don't worry – we did you proud. But how did you get on? Did you catch up with your mum?'

Sasha suddenly began to cry, great hitching sobs that contained more than a hint of hysteria. All at once her protective layer had dissolved; she felt scraped raw, physically and emotionally. She stumbled to the chair in which Jenna had been sitting moments earlier and slumped into it. Jenna crouched before her, stroking her arm, shielding her from prying eyes.

'Hey, hey,' she said softly, 'whatever's the matter?'

'Mum's blind. Something . . . something . . .' Sasha made an attempt to swallow the sobs that were threatening to overwhelm her. All at once her words came in a tearful rush. 'Something made her tear her own eyes out.'

'Oh my God.' Jenna's hand went to her mouth. Her eyes were wide. 'Look, just . . . just sit here for a minute. I'll—' She rushed off, leaving her half-smoked cigarette crushed in an ashtray. Sasha stared at it, her hand half-concealing her face from public view, until Jenna came back.

'Drink this.' A fat-bellied glass with a thin stem was thrust under Sasha's nose. The reddish-brown liquid in the glass had a sharp smell.

'What is it?'

'Brandy. It'll calm you down. Warm you up. Whatever.'

Sasha tentatively sipped the brandy. It burned all the way down her gullet and into her belly where it glowed like a hot coal. She gulped it down until she had finished it, numbing her lips and tongue. 'Thanks,' she whispered.

'Better?'

Sasha nodded.

There was a brief but heavy silence between the two women. Then Jenna said awkwardly, 'Look, obviously I do want to know what happened with you and Linsey, but don't feel obliged to tell me if you're not up to it. Just – tell me in your own time, okay?'

'Okay,' Sasha said. Carefully, using the end of her sleeve, she wiped the tears from her swollen eyes. 'I didn't know you smoked,' she said.

'I don't. That is . . . I gave up a couple of months ago. This is the first time I've lapsed.'

'Right,' Sasha said softly, and then, as if it were a natural progression, 'So where's Inspector Baker?'

'He went on ahead. He gave me an address that he said was a safe house. He said that when you and . . . that when you arrived, we were to get a cab and meet him there.'

'Okay,' said Sasha, pushing herself to her feet, 'we might as well go now.'

'Are you sure you're all right?'

'Not really, but sitting here weeping won't make things better, will it?'

Jenna gave her a tight smile and went over to the reception desk to call a cab. While they waited, Jenna told Sasha the details of her and Baker's meeting with Baxter Mead. Sasha only half-listened, sensing a tension between them: the tension of her own untold story. She wondered when she would feel up to telling all of it, wondered too whether she and Jenna would ever become good friends, whether life would ever return to normal. She tried to imagine herself, Jenna and Dad sitting down to a meal together, chatting and laughing, all of this long behind them. But she couldn't. She didn't dare wonder whether she would ever actually see Dad again; she had to believe that that was a question, not of *if*, but *when*.

Sasha had not seen the receptionist approach, but suddenly he was leaning over them, a tall, slim, rather beautiful young man with dyed blond hair. 'Your cab has arrived, Miss Trenchard,' he said, his voice softly confidential as if imparting a secret.

Jenna thanked him and the two women made their way out of the hotel to where a black cab was idling on the forecourt. 'Could you take us to this address, please?' Jenna said, handing the driver a piece of paper. The man glanced at the paper, nodded and set off. He eventually eased his cab to a halt in one of the many shabby, quiet streets between Tottenham and Walthamstow. The terraced houses – a good third of which looked derelict – were tall and narrow, the kerbs bumper-to-bumper with cars. Jenna leaned forward, paid the driver, waving away Sasha's offer to share the fare, and the two women got out. As the cab drove away, Jenna turned, pointing. 'I think it must be – this one.'

The house she was indicating had an overgrown garden and paint peeling from the windowsills and front door. One of the upper-floor windows was boarded up; the roof had apparently been marked out for target practise by defecating birds. Beside an iron gate scabbed with rust, a For Sale sign leaned askew, like an executioner's axe about to fall. Jenna walked to the gate and held it open. 'After you.'

Sasha, a little perplexed, preceded her up the path to the house. At the front door she hesitated. 'Should we knock, or did the Inspector give you a key?'

'He said the door would be open,' Jenna said, and shrugged. 'Try it.'

Sasha did so. Sure enough, the door opened. Facing them was a drab hallway, the wallpaper and carpet long bled of colour, grey with age and neglect.

'Smells a bit musty,' said Sasha dubiously. She'd imagined a safe house would be devoid of character but antiseptically clean – not like this.

'Try the door there, to your left. It looks as though it should lead into the sitting room.'

Sasha stepped forward, opened the door and walked in. Two men dressed in charcoal-grey suits were standing in the gloom, pointing guns at her head.

For a moment nobody moved, as Sasha stared at the two men in disbelief. Then she half-turned to warn Jenna – and saw that Jenna too was pointing a gun at her head.

'I think it's time to nail our colours to the mast,' Jenna said.

192

Thirty-Three

Waking up was an interminable process. It felt to Nick like trudging through one cobweb-strewn room after another. He was aware that he was no longer asleep, no longer dreaming, for minutes before he could open his eyes. And then, just as he was beginning to think he would never make the breakthrough that would bring him fully conscious, he opened the door of one more dim, dusty room and light flooded in.

At once he was forced to close the eyes he had momentarily opened: the light was too harsh, too painful. For a few moments he relied on his other senses to gather information. He was lying on a yielding surface – a mattress, he presumed – firm but not uncomfortable. He could feel an odd but not unpleasant pulse in his head; at first he assumed it was an echo of his own beating heart, but he quickly realised it was too rhythmic to be anything other than an electronically generated signal. What the hell were they *doing* to him? He felt strange, confused, opposing emotions twining together in his mind. Whatever the true purpose of the pulse was, he could feel it soothing and relaxing those parts of his brain which generated anxiety; and yet the fact that his brain was being tampered with at all was enough to alarm him.

He moved his head slightly, smelled fresh bed linen, underlaid with the merest hint of cigarette smoke. He was cocooned in silence; he was quite certain that he was alone. Anxious to view his surroundings, he opened his eyes once more, and immediately light hit him like a punch, then sank back to a more manageable level. Nick looked around.

The first thing he saw was the machine on the table by the side of his bed. It was square, compact, inset with a number of switches and dials, and a small readout screen. Nick guessed it must be monitoring his brain activity. A number of leads trailed from the back of the machine to what Nick assumed, from the feeling of tightness around his temples, were sensor pads attached to his head. He tried to raise a hand to touch one of the pads – and realised with a shock that he couldn't move. Raising his head as much as he was able and looking down the length of his body he saw that he had leather restraints around his wrists and ankles.

Immediately, despite the soothing pulse in his mind, his heart began to beat a little faster. He had always hated the notion of being tied up or trapped or shut in; the mere thought of it made him feel breathless and panicky. What if no one came to release him? What if they left him here, strapped to the bed for days or even weeks, his muscles cramping and withering, his mattress and himself growing sodden and stinking with his own piss and shit? Or, worst of all, what if they – whoever *they* were – were planning to torture him? He was all too aware that if they decided to remove his testicles with a pair of pliers or ram a screwdriver up his nose and into his brain he wouldn't be able to do a thing to stop then.

His breath was coming too fast now for him to control; his heart was pumping uncomfortably hard in his chest. He closed his eyes and tried to concentrate on the placating effect of the electronic pulse.

He managed, just about. The pulse did seem to prevent the panic from engulfing him. Telling himself that for his own good he must calm down, remain positive, gain as much information as he could about his situation, he opened his eyes once more.

This time he looked beyond the bed and the machine and the restraints, and saw that he was in a small, poky room, sparsely furnished, the walls painted a dull green. There were cardboard boxes piled against the wall to his left. On the other side of the room, behind the machine on its battered, wooden side-table, were a refrigerator, a drinks cabinet with a glass door containing bottles of spirits, and a TV and video recorder inset into a black lacquered cabinet. A cheap lampshade above his head provided little protection from the glare of the hundred-watt bulb hanging from the centre of the ceiling. On the opposite wall, facing the foot of the bed, was a door, which – as if Nick had willed it – suddenly opened.

He braced himself, his innards pulling up tight into his stomach, but the figure who entered looked anything but threatening. He was a young, willowy man with straight blond hair and round-lensed spectacles, wearing a cream sweater and jeans. When he saw that Nick was awake he gave him what seemed to be a genuinely friendly smile, then closed the door behind him and walked over to the bed.

'Hi,' he said brightly. 'How are you feeling?'

'Okay,' replied Nick warily, and then, gambling on the fact that this man looked unlikely to punish him for the question, asked, 'Where am I? What's going on?'

The young man leaned forward to peer at the monitor on the machine. Apparently satisfied, he said airily, 'Oh, don't worry about that. You'll find out in due course. How's your head?'

'Okay, thanks,' said Nick. He glanced at the machine. 'What does that *do* exactly?'

'That pulse you can feel in your mind is a form of reversion therapy, and this thing,' said the young man, patting the machine as if it were a pet, 'is a kind of mental vacuum cleaner. It's sucking out all the junk you've had implanted into your mind, all that "endrant command" bollocks.'

Nick's stomach gave a lurch. 'What do you know about that?'

'Only what Mr Hallett's told me.'

'Who's Mr Hallett?'

'You'll meet him soon.'

Nick sighed. The young man might be pleasant enough, but he was giving little away. 'Aren't you going to tell me *anything*?' he asked, feeling bolder now.

The young man laughed. 'Look, if I stole Mr Hallett's thunder he'd have my guts for garters. But ask your questions. If I can answer them, I will.'

'Right,' said Nick, 'how long do I have to be linked to this machine? And why am I strapped down? And why—'

The young man held up his hand to stop the flow of interrogation. He sat on the edge of the bed. 'I can unhook you from the machine now if you're sure you feel okay. And you're only strapped down for your own safety. Sometimes, when the programming's deeply ingrained, the brain is apt to resist and people tend to throw themselves around a bit. You weren't too bad, though – you twitched and shouted out once or twice, but

195

most of the time you were good as gold. Your willpower must be pretty strong.'

'I wouldn't say that,' said Nick, thinking of the many times he had abandoned himself to drugs or booze. He opened his hands, drawing attention to his restraints. 'Could you untie me now? I've never really been into bondage.'

'Sure,' said the young man, grinning. He peeled off the sensor pads – Nick wincing as they tugged at the fine hairs on his temples – and then unbuckled the straps around his ankles and wrists. He did it with no qualms, no caution, whatsoever, even though someone in Nick's position might have been expected to feel justified in punching the young man in the throat and making a bid for freedom.

Nick sat up, rubbing his wrists, bending and stretching his legs, painfully easing his muscles back to life. 'Why was I kidnapped?' he asked bluntly.

'You weren't *kidnapped*,' said the young man is a tone of mild admonition. 'You were rescued.'

'*Rescued?*' said Nick, surprised. 'What do you mean?'

The young man pulled an apologetic face. Gathering the leads into a manageable bunch in his hand he began wheeling the little table and its machine towards the door. 'That's Mr Hallett's territory, I'm afraid. I'll tell him you're up and about, and when he's ready to see you he'll answer all your questions.'

'That's big of him,' said Nick drily. 'So until then I'm a prisoner?'

'You're not a prisoner – you're a guest. Okay, so I'm going to have to lock the door behind me – security reasons and all that – but believe me, Nick, you are among friends here. Pour yourself a drink, watch a video – those boxes there are full of them – and before you know it, someone'll come back to help you. Okay?'

Nick sighed. 'Do I have a choice?'

'Not really. So you might as well relax and enjoy yourself.'

Thirty-Four

Despite the guns, Sasha felt furious rather than scared. She had always hated violence but given the opportunity, she honestly believed she was capable of killing Jenna for what she had done. The bitch had inveigled herself into her father's affections, been party to their fear and confusion and despair, and all the time she had been one of the bad guys. As soon as Sasha had turned to find Jenna holding a gun to her head, the components had clicked quickly and somehow inevitably into place. And so, instead of looking confused and asking what was going on, Sasha had hissed venomously, '*Where's my dad?*'

'We don't know,' Jenna had replied calmly. 'He got away from us last night. That's why we need you.'

'As bait, you mean, to lure him out of hiding?' Jenna responded to this with no more than a casual shrug. 'Who are you really – apart from an evil bitch?' Sasha snapped.

Jenna half-smiled, and Sasha realised how childish the insult sounded. It was the best she could do, however; her mind was too full of hate and fury to allow her to be cool and articulate. What she really wanted to do was fly at this woman, tear her eyes out, hurt her more than she had ever hurt anyone in her life.

'I'm no one important. I'm just doing my job,' Jenna said with infuriating smugness.

'Just like the Nazi death-camp guards,' retorted Sasha.

Jenna smiled again. 'What's so bloody funny?' Sasha said.

Jenna was clearly unwilling to be drawn into a slanging match. She ignored the question. Glancing over Sasha's shoulder at the two silent, besuited men, she ordered, 'Bring her to the car.' Then she turned and walked out.

197

Sasha was escorted out of the house and down the garden path at gunpoint. She briefly considered making a run for it, but almost immediately decided she probably wasn't *that* indispensable. Besides she didn't particularly want to know what being hit by a bullet felt like. If she had seen a passer-by she might have tried to signal to them, cry for help even, but the street was deserted. At the garden gate one of the men behind her took her arm whilst the other went ahead. There was a car waiting at the kerb, a dark blue Mitsubishi Lancer. Jenna eased herself gracefully into the passenger seat, next to a man wearing spectacles and the obligatory dark suit, whose hands were clutching the steering wheel like a selfish child refusing to part with his favourite toy.

Sasha was ordered to get into the back between the two men and put her seatbelt on. There then followed a long and silent journey out of London, during which Sasha sat and smouldered, her mind racing with thoughts and emotions. She could have given Jenna a hard time, could have peppered the back of her hateful head with demands and insults, but she decided that it wasn't worth it. Insulting the woman would only result in Sasha getting even more enraged because of Jenna's lack of response; demanding to know where she was being taken would only emphasise the vulnerable and disadvantageous position she was in.

Sasha wondered what had *really* happened when Jenna and the Inspector had met Baker's journalist friend that morning. It seemed unlikely that Jenna and her colleagues would allow the story to appear in the newspapers the following day, but to what lengths might they have gone to keep Baker and the journalist quiet? Thinking of this almost caused Sasha to break her silence, but in the end the thought of Jenna's self-satisfied voice explaining exactly how she and her colleagues had remained one step ahead of Sasha and Nick all the way overcame her need to know. In an attempt to stifle her curiosity she looked out of the window and tried to concentrate on where they might be going. It had taken them well over an hour to meander out of London and stop-start their way down the southbound lane of the M25. They followed that motorway for half a dozen junctions before pulling off on to the M20, in the direction of Maidstone, and eventually – if they followed the road all the way to the coast – Folkestone.

Were they going abroad? she wondered. Perhaps Jenna was a

Russian spy. But as soon as the thought formed she dismissed it; it sounded so ludicrous. Besides, the Russians were no longer our enemies, were they? At least, not overtly. God, what on *earth* had Dad dragged her into? She wondered if he knew what was going on. If he did, it was going to be hard to forgive him for a lot of things, not least for what had happened to Mum, if . . . no, *when* she next saw him.

A few miles from Folkestone, the driver surprised Sasha by pulling off the M20 and heading north. It was late afternoon by this time; the dark clouds that had accompanied them out of London had become thicker, more permanent. Now and then, flurries of rain coated the windows, distorting the view, then retreated, sulking. They headed into the countryside, eventually pulling off the B-road they had been driving along and slowing down as they negotiated country lanes flanked by thick, old trees and dark green hedges. They saw very few people; though they did pass the occasional guest-house and cluster of cottages, which, roughly constructed from the materials of the local terrain, seemed merely a less disordered part of the natural landscape.

At last, approaching a gap in the high hedge, the car slowed to a crawl, the driver turning the vehicle tightly on to a narrow, unmarked track. The track curved through a scrubby field and disappeared behind a thick wedge of trees. It occurred briefly to Sasha that she might have been brought out here to be disposed of, then buried so deeply that her remains would never be found, but immediately she reproached herself for the illogicality of the thought. A moment later the real purpose of their journey became apparent.

Tucked behind the trees, hidden from view, was a barn-sized building made of white metal. In front of the building was a small airstrip, stretching out darkly into the field like a line of scorched earth. Parked at the hangar end of the airstrip, nose pointing at the sky as if eager to be up among the clouds, was an aeroplane.

It was not a big aeroplane, certainly no three-hundred-seater passenger jet, but neither was it a two-man job. White, stubby and compact, giving the impression it was built for speed, it looked as if it could seat at least two dozen people in relative comfort. Its short wings, equipped with powerful-looking engines, were speckled with fat, transparent coins of rain. A man in blue overalls was standing in the doorway of the hangar smoking a cigarette.

When he saw the car jolting across the field towards him, he flicked the cigarette away and stood up straight, like a soldier coming to attention.

The driver stopped the car and Jenna got out and walked over to the man. The two of them talked for a while, the man gesticulating at the plane, nodding. Eventually the man went back into the hangar and Jenna picked her way back across the field to the car. With childish spite, Sasha willed her to slip in a cow-pat and fall flat on her face.

'Ready for take-off in five minutes,' Jenna said, reaching the car unscathed, much to Sasha's disappointment. She sat back down in the passenger seat, but left her door open, allowing a cool breeze into the stuffy interior.

Sasha had a sick, nervous fluttering in her stomach. It came from the knowledge that she was no longer in control of her life, that she was entirely at the mercy of these people. In an attempt to allay the feeling, she said acidly, 'Going on holiday, are we?'

Jenna turned and smiled. 'Not exactly.'

'Well, wherever *you're* going, you do realise that I can't come with you? I don't have my passport.'

Jenna's smile didn't falter. 'I like you, Sasha, but this acerbic humour of yours is a bit tiresome. If you haven't got anything more constructive to say, then I suggest you be quiet.'

Sasha felt outrage surging inside her, bitter as bile. 'I'll say what I fucking like! What right have you got to kidnap me like this and make me get on a plane to God knows where? I haven't done anything wrong and neither has my dad. We just want to be left alone.'

'Look, I really do understand your feelings—' Jenna began coolly.

'Well, bully for you!'

Jenna sighed. 'It's really not worth talking to you while you're in this mood. Perhaps we can have a proper chat when you've calmed down.'

'You'll be waiting a bloody long time,' Sasha said.

'That's no problem. We have all the time in the world.'

The casual ominousness of Jenna's words was like a body-blow. Sasha's mouth and throat went so dry that for some minutes she couldn't speak. She liked her life and at that moment she wanted it back so badly the feeling was like a sharp pain in the pit

200

of her stomach. The thought of being unable to move freely – of being told what to do, where to go – was so unbearable that she had to fight an almost overwhelming urge to scream and kick and flail, to plead for her freedom. Somehow she managed to clamp herself in, concentrated on generating some saliva in her mouth. Finally, her voice rasping a little, she glared at Jenna. 'If I get just one chance to hurt you, I will.'

The woman seemed entirely unperturbed. Holding Sasha's gaze, Jenna said quietly, almost soothingly, 'Believe me, you won't get the chance.'

Three minutes later they were inside the plane, which smelled of new carpets. They certainly weren't travelling economy; the seats were so big and comfortable they were almost like armchairs, and the aisle was wider than on a normal passenger aircraft. Sasha, Jenna and the two gunmen were met by a smart, efficient woman in her forties who assigned them all seats and instructed them to put on their seatbelts. Several minutes later the plane trundled down the runway, picked up speed and launched itself smoothly into the air.

They had been airborne for perhaps ten minutes when the woman unclipped herself from her seat on the front row, where she had been perched like a tour guide, and approached Sasha. 'If you would care to freshen up before dinner, Miss Finch, I'll show you where your changing room is.'

Sasha was a little wary, but knew that she would relish some time away from Jenna's presence. 'Thanks.'

The woman led Sasha along the aisle to the back of the plane and through a door into a short, narrow corridor, inset with several other doors. She opened the second on the right and ushered Sasha into a small changing room containing a toilet, a sink, a shower unit and a built-in wardrobe. She told Sasha to make herself at home, to feel free to come and go as she pleased whilst the plane was in flight, to ask without hesitating for anything she might need. Sasha was taken aback, but thanked the woman. 'My plea-sure,' the woman said, and went out, closing the door behind her.

Sasha felt grubby and small and alone, full of despair and confusion. She sank down on to the toilet seat and, unable to help herself, began to weep. It was only when it occurred to her that there might be hidden cameras in here, filming her every move, that she stopped, angrily swiping the tears from her bruised face.

She slowly peeled off the clothes she had been wearing for the past twenty-four hours and dropped them in a heap on the floor. If there were hidden cameras then whoever was monitoring them was getting a real eyeful – but so what? If voyeurism was where their sick little minds were at then she felt sorry for them. As long as they didn't get the satisfaction of seeing how upset and scared she was underneath she couldn't care less.

The shower was hot and fierce; she rubbed vigorously at her grimy skin with lemon-scented soap, wishing she could scrub away the last twenty-four hours as easily. It seemed inconceivable that so much had happened since she got ready to go out with Dad and Jenna last night. This time yesterday she hadn't even *met* Jenna, but in a very short time the woman had become her ally, her comforter, her partial confidante, and was now the most bitter enemy she had.

Sasha stayed in the shower until her skin was red and tingling, the pads of her fingers wrinkled as walnuts. Then she wrapped a huge, fluffy white towel around herself and sat for a while longer, the water cooling on her blonde hair and trickling icily down her back, the beat of the engines thrumming through the floor, the vibration like a tiny electrical current on the soles of her bare feet.

At last she dried those parts of her that hadn't dried naturally and ruefully eyed the pile of grubby clothes on the floor. Idly she wandered across to the built-in wardrobe and opened the door. It took a moment for what she was seeing to fully register in her mind.

The clothes in the wardrobe were all her own; even down to her socks and underwear. Tentatively she reached out and touched a neatly folded stack of T-shirts to allay her suspicion that the whole thing was some kind of illusion. After her initial surprise, the real-isation of the truth filled her with cold fury. People – the two gunmen perhaps – must have gone to her home, the house she shared with Mum, broken in and sorted methodically through her things, taking what they had been instructed she would need. She wondered what else they had brought with them, wondered what they had deemed important to her welfare. Had they brought her Snoopy toothbrush; her CD collection; the Pat Barker paperback she'd been reading; the threadbare rabbit – Flop – that she had had since she was a baby? It was her perception of the calculated arro-gance of their decisions, as much as the knowledge that they had

202

delved without care or permission into the most intimate nooks of her life, that made her feel so furious. She thought about putting her grubby clothes back on just to spite them, of refusing to wear anything they'd touched, but in the end decided that such an action would harm no one but herself. And so she selected fresh underwear and socks, green leggings, a black T-shirt and a baggy, rust-coloured sweater, and as she dressed she tried to dispel the image of blank-faced men with grey suits and big, sweaty hands.

She didn't want to give Jenna the opportunity to smirk at her outrage, and so she said nothing when she rejoined the others in the main body of the plane. She had promised Jenna that she would hurt her if she got the chance, and she supposed that she could have done it here, could have flown at her with her fists flailing if she had been quick about it, but the victory would have been brief and hollow, the damage to Jenna no more than superficial.

No, she would bide her time, wait for the right opportunity. When she hurt Jenna she wanted to do it properly. She supposed she should have been ashamed of her feelings, but she wasn't. She felt nothing but a cold desire to make the woman suffer for what she had done to her and her loved ones.

As soon as she sat down, the woman who Sasha thought of as the stewardess came over and gave her a sheet of laminated card, explaining that it was the dinner menu. Jenna and the two men had evidently made their choices; they were sitting back in their seats now, relaxing, sipping aperitifs. One of the men was sucking on a Panatella, his head wreathed with pungent smoke.

As with the clothes, Sasha's first instinct was to refuse the menu, but again she realised that there was nothing to be gained from denying herself. All the same, she half-hoped that no vegetarian option had been provided so that she could hand the menu back, curtly stating that she didn't eat dead animals, but in fact there was not just one vegetarian meal on offer but several. She deliberately took a long time making up her mind; she didn't want Jenna to see her as easily pleased. Eventually, though, she selected aubergines stuffed with continental lentils and mushrooms, buttered rice and a yoghurt and cucumber salad.

She felt ashamed of herself for being even the remotest bit hungry, but hungry she was. When the woman asked her politely if she would like a drink, Sasha requested a cold bottle of Rolling

203

Rock, hoping to catch her hosts out – again, with no success. A minute later the bottle was in her hand, ice-cold, frosty with condensation.

The food was delicious and Sasha devoured it all, then followed it up with tiramisu and coffee. Afterwards she put on the headphones suspended over her seat and watched the in-flight movie: *Twelve Monkeys*.

She was all too aware that she was falling into the trap of compliance, going with the flow – but what else could she do? Kicking up a fuss right now would only leave her kidnappers unmoved and weaken her own position by letting them know how upset she was. In a strange way she would have felt more comfortable if her captors had treated her as the prisoner she undoubtedly was; all this kindness and courtesy was merely disorientating. She simply didn't know how to react to it. She was constantly having to remind herself that she was here against her will.

The movie was good, but Sasha found she couldn't concentrate on it properly and somewhere towards the end, exhausted by the thoughts whirling in her head, she fell asleep. She dreamed of blundering semi-naked through a big, empty place, full of confusing signs, unattended counters, long queues of silent, blank-eyed people. There were many doors in this place, but apparently none of them were exits. She was desperately, hopelessly lost, not to say acutely embarrassed to find herself in nothing but her underwear. She was circling a series of tables for what seemed the hundredth time in an effort to reach a glass door that remained frustratingly distant, when a hand touched her shoulder and she woke up.

The first thing she was aware of was the sun blazing through the window, shining on her face. Then she sensed someone standing in front of her, and focused on Jenna, who was straightening up, and who said, before Sasha could react, 'We're here.'

Thirty-Five

The departure of the young man was followed by the longest two hours of Nick's life. Too hyped-up to settle to anything, he spent most of the time pacing restlessly around the room, channel-hopping on the big black TV, rooting aimlessly through the cardboard boxes full of videos, which weren't to his taste, judging by their sleeves, most of which depicted semi-naked Oriental girls engaged in martial arts. At one point he grabbed himself a bottle of Beck's from the fridge, but after two swallows he put it aside; the alcohol only exacerbated the apprehension souring his stomach. He was sitting on the bed, staring unfocused at MTV, when he heard a sound in the corridor outside. His stomach clenched with anticipation as the door was unlocked and opened.

It was not the young man who stood there, but someone taller, older, wearing a well-cut dark suit and a grey silk tie. The man's hair was cropped short; his face was composed of such sharp angles that the hollows of his cheeks appeared to contain perfect inverted triangles of shadow. He spoke in a gruff, East London accent, though his words were polite enough.

'Good evening, Mr Finch. If you're ready, Mr Hallett will see you now.'

Nick bit back a rejoinder, deciding it was perhaps unwise to be antagonistic. Instead he forced a smile. 'Thank you.'

'After you, Mr Finch,' the man said, pushing the door wider and indicating that Nick should take the lead. Nick nodded, switched off the TV and crossed the room. Despite the man's courtesy, Nick felt a little nervous as he approached him. Perhaps it was simply his imagination, but he couldn't help feeling that the man was swathed in an aura of repressed menace, potential violence.

He stepped into a narrow, dimly lit corridor, the walls and carpet unremittingly brown, the hanging light bulbs – set at regular intervals along the ceiling – suffocated by thick red shades. Very faintly he was aware of something that had not been apparent in the room – the thump of music, coming from somewhere beneath his feet.

'What is this place – a nightclub?' he asked, turning to the man.

The man's expression didn't change, and neither did his voice, which remained polite but flat. 'I'm sorry, Mr Finch, but I'm not at liberty to answer any of your questions.'

'Fine,' said Nick, and turning back he pulled a face which the man didn't see and continued along the corridor. He was almost at the end of it when the man spoke again. 'This is it, Mr Finch.'

Nick's throat grew tight. The man's voice had been so emotionless that his words had sounded almost like a threat. He turned, half-expecting to see the man holding a gun on him, but in fact he was merely gesturing with his hand to a door on Nick's right.

'In here?' Nick said stupidly.

The man nodded. 'Just walk in, Mr Finch.'

Nick licked his lips, then opened the door and stepped over the threshold into the room beyond.

What struck him first was the blue fug of cigarette smoke, so thick it stung his eyes. This room was even more ill-lit than the corridor, a couple of small lamps throwing meagre illumination on to a large round table around which sat perhaps a dozen men, smoking, drinking and talking. Among the men, Nick recognised the black guy with the beret and shades and the fat skinhead with the goatee, both of whom had emerged from the car in the alleyway, guns drawn, the previous night. All the men were dressed in suits and ties, though some had taken their jackets off and draped them over their chairs.

Another thing that the men had in common was that they all looked extremely tough; despite the fact that he himself was over six feet tall, Nick couldn't help feeling like a small child who had stepped into a room full of adults. Fear sent his mind into a strange kind of overdrive, and he found himself – not for the first time – making lists in his head, this time of movies which resembled the scene in front of him: *The Long Good Friday, Get Carter, The Krays, The Godfather, Reservoir Dogs* . . .

'Nick, old son,' said the man at the farthest side of the table, cutting into his thoughts, 'good of you to join us.'

The men around the table all turned to look at Nick, their faces as implacable as that of the man who had led him here. Under their combined gaze, Nick felt as though he were shrivelling. Again he forced a smile and managed to restrain himself from raising his hand in a nervous half-wave, before muttering, 'That's okay' – as if he had actually had a choice in the matter.

The man at the head of the table gestured to a chair beside him. 'Come and sit down. Have a drink.'

'Thanks,' Nick said, and walked across the room on legs that he hoped weren't shaking visibly. He tried not to cough as smoke fingered its way spikily down his throat and into his lungs. As soon as he sat down a generous measure of Scotch was poured into a tumbler and thrust in front of him.

The man who had spoken – Nick assumed this was Mr Hallett – was thick-set, hirsute, his heavy features smothered in what appeared to be a permanent five-o'-clock shadow. Dark wiry hair smothered the backs of his huge hands; stuffed into a light grey suit, he would have appeared ape-like, if it hadn't been for his keen, watchful eyes. Behind him, framing him, was a large, glass-fronted cabinet full of boxing trophies.

'I know exactly what you're thinking, Nick,' he said, leaning forward.

'Do you?' Nick replied, trying not to let his apprehension tremble in his voice.

'You're thinking: Where the hell am I? What are these fucking goons going to *do* to me? Am I right?'

Nick smiled and shrugged, trying to appear nonchalant. Hallett – if that was indeed who he was – looked at him expectantly, making Nick feel that a more fulsome response was called for. Hesitantly he admitted, 'Well, I do have a few questions.'

The man guffawed loudly. '*A few questions*! You hear that, Mad Dog?'

'Yes, Mr Hallett,' said the black guy.

'I'll bet you've got so many questions they're squirting out of your arse!'

Nick made himself grin to accompany the chuckles of the men around the table.

'I'm Jack Hallett,' the man confirmed, sticking out a hand, 'and these men you see around you are my own personal Knights of the Round Table. They may be a fucking ugly set of bastards – but take it from me, you're a lot better off with us than you would have been with the law. Am I right, Mad Dog?'

'Spot on, Mr Hallett,' said the black guy.

'Why's that?' Nick ventured.

Hallett nodded in approval. 'Curiosity. I like that. And I'll tell you *exactly* why that is, old son. The boys in blue were about to sell you down the fucking river. If we hadn't come along, you'd be a fucking laboratory monkey by now.'

Nick looked at Hallett, who was nodding wisely, as if what he had said made everything crystal-clear. When Hallett lifted his glass to his lips, appearing to indicate that no further explanation was forthcoming, Nick shook his head. 'I'm sorry, I don't understand.'

Hallett swallowed half his Scotch in one gulp and then banged the glass down on the table. Nick had already come to the conclusion that he was not a man with a delicate touch. Everything he did, he did loudly, boldly, with total assurance.

'Of course you don't, son,' he said. 'None of them do, not at first. The people we're dealing with may be evil cunts, but they're fucking professionals – you've got to give 'em that.'

'And who is it exactly we're dealing with?' Nick asked.

'All in good time, son. It's too much to take in all in one go. And I'm not a man who's good with words. I prefer to show first, talk later.'

Nick sighed. 'The young guy, the one who took the machine away, said you'd answer all my questions.'

'And so I will, son. So I will. But like I said, all in good time.'

'But can't you tell me *anything* now?' Nick asked, his frustration overcoming his nervousness. 'I mean, I don't know how you know about me, or why you should have bothered to rescue me – or why I even needed rescuing. And I don't know anything about you, apart from your name.'

Hallett grinned slyly. 'Course you don't, son. But don't worry, you will. But we've got to do this my way or not at all. Sorry, son – but that's the way it is. All right?'

Nick shrugged. 'I suppose it'll have to be, won't it?'

'Too right, son,' said Hallett.

'Okay. So what happens now?'

'I want you to go on a little job with a couple of my men. You don't have to do anything – I just want you to watch, see how things are done. Once you understand what's what, then we'll talk again. How does that sound?'

To Nick it sounded ominous, made him feel not only that he was horribly out of his depth, but that he was floating further and further away from the shore. He nodded slowly, hoping to convey the impression of someone considering a reasonable business proposition. As casually as he could, he replied, 'Yeah. Fine.'

Thirty-Six

'Welcome to the Chicken House,' Jenna said.

Sasha stood outside the door of the plane, at the top of the set of metal steps leading down, and looked around. Below her were Jenna and one of the besuited men. Behind her was the other man, the one who had been smoking Panatellas. The 'stewardess', it seemed, was staying put, presumably for the return journey. Maybe she lived on the plane and never got off. Nothing would surprise Sasha now. There had been no sign of a pilot or any other crew; for all Sasha knew, the plane had flown here on automatic pilot.

They had arrived at some kind of military installation set in the midst of a barren landscape surrounded by mountains. A fierce sun had scorched the colour from the sky and enveloped everything in a dry, baking heat that made Sasha regret having put a sweater on. Looking around, she could see clusters of bunker-like buildings, a couple of aircraft hangars around which several jets and light aircraft were gathered like insects, perhaps two dozen army vehicles – some stationary, some moving slowly between the buildings – and a large number of soldiers, all of whom were carrying guns. Around the installation were two high chain-link fences topped with barbed wire, with a deep ditch in between. Confronted with these sights, these sounds, Sasha felt her stomach curdling with dread. More than ever before, she felt an awfully long way from home.

She was led on foot across the baking concrete to the largest of the bunker-like buildings. No one paid them the slightest attention, even though they seemed to be the only civilians here. It took a good five minutes to reach the bunker, by which time Sasha had taken off her sweater and tied it around her waist. Her battered face pulsed with pain in the heat and her scalp itched with sweat. She despised Jenna more than ever for managing to look so cool.

The front of the bunker, a pale block of a building, was dominated by a pair of steel doors, twenty feet square. Inset into the doors was a smaller one, attached to which was a red opaque panel and a push-button keyboard. From the inside pocket of her jacket Jenna produced a keycard which she pushed into the slot. Deliberately positioning her body so that Sasha could not see the keyboard, she tapped in a combination. After a few seconds the red panel lit up; Jenna placed her left hand on it and silently, with an action so smooth it was almost graceful, the door slid open.

Jenna led the way into a brightly lit, air-conditioned, pristine-clean vestibule, devoid of everything but the craning eyes of surveillance cameras. Two pairs of lift doors were set into the opposite wall. Like the main doors, they were made of highly polished steel. The group's reflection swelled and wavered, their features blurring, as they approached the doors. Jenna went through the same process with the card and keyboard and print sensor and, when the lift doors opened, she stepped smartly inside and pressed a button before Sasha could even move.

Sasha was ushered into the lift by the two men. The buttons on the panel inside the door were numbered from one to thirty-six, though there were several unmarked buttons above and below these. The doors closed and Sasha felt the lift begin to descend. Suddenly she was alarmed despite the fact that she knew the bunker had been too small to contain any floors above ground level. She felt an urge, so strong that it surprised her, to lurch forward and jab at the topmost button on the panel; the instinctive fear of descending into the earth was almost primeval.

She breathed deeply and clenched her fists, hoping that Jenna would not notice her distress. When the lift stopped and the doors opened, Jenna led the way along a white-walled corridor, the ceiling inset with starkly fluorescent strip lighting, the floors carpeted in grey. No one had said a word since Jenna had first welcomed her to this place she had referred to as the 'Chicken House' (the comment had invited a question, which was precisely why Sasha had not asked one), but now Jenna stopped outside one of several white doors set at exact intervals along the landing. 'Here we are,' she said.

'What's this then?' said Sasha, as Jenna went through the rigmarole with the security panel yet again. 'The torture chamber?'

'Hardly,' said Jenna drily. There was a buzz and she opened the door. 'This is where you'll be staying.'

The room they entered was not unlike a clinical hotel suite. Leading off from the main room were two others: a kitchen to the right, a bathroom to the left, both small but extremely well-equipped. Sasha saw with a pang of hatred towards Jenna that many of her personal effects had indeed been transferred from home, including Flop, who was lying on the bed, and her entire CD collection, which was arranged in alphabetical order on several shelves next to a brand-new music system.

'You do think of everything, don't you?' she muttered, unable to keep the bitterness from her voice.

Jenna gave a relaxed little shrug. 'We do our best. There's nothing to be gained from making this an unpleasant experience, is there?'

Sasha ignored the dig and nodded instead at the ceiling, where surveillance cameras covered all areas of the room. 'Not exactly going to get much privacy, am I?'

'Necessary, I'm afraid,' Jenna said briskly. 'You'll soon get used to it.'

'I suppose there are cameras in the bathroom too?'

'Of course.'

'Oh, great. So all your grubby little operatives get to watch me taking a crap. They'll be swapping videos of me in the shower before the week's out.'

Jenna smirked. 'Don't flatter yourself.'

Sasha didn't know whether it was Jenna's words or her expression that caused her to crack. But suddenly she was shouting so loudly it was making her face hurt.

'You've got no fucking right to *keep* me here! I haven't done anything wrong! I want to go home *now*!'

The two men tensed at her outburst, their hands going instinctively to their jackets, but Jenna remained as unruffled as ever.

'This is your home for the foreseeable future. And no matter how much you scream and shout, I'm afraid you'll have to get used to that fact pretty quickly.'

'All you need are some jackboots and a little moustache and you'd make the perfect Hitler,' said Sasha venomously.

Jenna smiled. 'You won't wind me up. I know I'm doing the right thing. I'm doing what's right for my country, and whether you believe it or not, I'm even doing what's right for you.'

Thirty-Seven

Mad Dog drove, wearing his shades despite the darkness. The fat, goateed skinhead, whose name was Sherman, sat in the passenger seat, and Nick sat in the back. He wanted to ask whether he could remove the blindfold he had been obliged to wear for the walk through the building to the car, and for the beginning of the journey, but the silent presence of Hallett's gun-toting henchmen was intimidating and he couldn't force the words out.

The descent through the building had involved several stair-cases and a number of carpeted corridors before the three of them had emerged into what Nick guessed – from the echoey quality of the sounds, the sudden chill of the air and the hard surface beneath his feet – was an underground car park. Now, sitting in the car, he could still feel the meaty grip of Sherman's guiding hand on his arm. He knew that Sherman had held on to him to prevent him falling downstairs and tripping on uneven surfaces, but he had still felt like a prisoner, despite Hallett's insistence that he was 'an honoured guest'. When he had asked why he had to wear the blindfold, Hallett had said, 'It's just a precaution, son. What you don't know now can't hurt you or us later.' Nick had taken that to mean that, should he at some stage fall into 'enemy' hands, he would not be able to lead his captors back to Hallett.

As if reading his thoughts, Mad Dog said, 'You can take your blindfold off now, Mr Finch.'

Nick did so, blinking at the glare from the street lamps and the headlights of other cars, which for a few seconds seemed to jab at his eyeballs like blunt fingers. If he *was* ever questioned about Hallett's whereabouts, all he would be able to reveal was that, judging by the thump of music that had grown louder as they

214

headed downwards and then faded altogether as they descended further still, the man's base did indeed seem to be situated above a pub or a club.

Sherman twisted in his seat, moving in the awkward, effortful way peculiar to very large people, and stared at Nick. He had a piercing, unsettling stare, and Nick's mouth went dry as he was subjected to it. He felt pinned by the stare, like a butterfly on a board, until Sherman unexpectedly grinned – which was almost as disconcerting.

'Do you want to know the truth, Mr Finch?' he said in a surprisingly gentle voice.

Before Nick could respond, Mad Dog groaned. 'Oh, fucking hell, Sherman – not again! How many times I have to tell you, no one wants to hear your fucked-up theories?'

Sherman seemed unoffended by Mad Dog's outburst; indeed, he regarded him with something close to compassion. 'They aren't just theories, Mad Dog, and deep down you know that. But like everyone else, you've been conditioned to accept things the way they are, to reject the real truth.'

'Yeah, yeah, man. Whatever you say,' Mad Dog muttered.

Sherman turned back to Nick. 'Is your mind as closed as Mad Dog's, Mr Finch?'

'Um . . . I don't know,' Nick said lamely.

Sherman nodded earnestly. 'Uncertainty. That's good.' He paused as though rallying his thoughts, and then spoke confidentially. 'Tell me, Mr Finch, are you prepared to hear something that will change the way you think forever?'

'That will make him realise what a fucking *fruit-cake* you are, you mean,' snorted Mad Dog.

Sherman shook his head sadly. 'Can't you see, Mad Dog, that's not really you speaking? It's your conditioning. You've been programmed to respond like this.'

'Bullshit,' said Mad Dog. 'I ain't been programmed by nobody.'

'You only *think* you haven't, but you have. Free will is a myth.'

'Yeah, right,' sneered Mad Dog; evidently he had heard it all before.

Sherman turned again to Nick. 'What about you, Mr Finch? Do you ever get the feeling that your thoughts are being controlled?'

Nick thought of the phone call (*endrant command*) and the

subsequent hallucinatory bombardment he had suffered. 'I don't know,' he said slowly.

'I think you do, Mr Finch,' Sherman said, and a zealous light seemed to spring into his eyes. 'I think you know very well. And I know what's behind it all.'

'Jesus, here we go,' murmured Mad Dog.

Sherman was undeterred. 'What would you say, Mr Finch, if I were to tell you that the elected government of this and every other country was nothing more than a bunch of puppets?'

Nick was not sure how to respond, but he felt some sort of answer was expected of him. 'Puppets of who?'

'Aw, man, don't encourage him,' Mad Dog moaned, but Sherman was getting into his stride now. Beads of sweat glittered on his forehead as if he were literally warming to his subject.

'Puppets of an occult group called the Old Ones,' he said. 'They control everything, Mr Finch. They're behind every drugs cartel, every arms deal. Even the men actually doing the deals don't know this – they've been programmed too. But with the blessing and co-operation of our royal family and every other royal family in the world, the Old Ones have accumulated – and continue to accumulate – a massive amount of money which is known as the Black Budget.'

'That's racist, man,' said Mad Dog with the resigned air of someone who knows that his pitiful attempt to build a dam will not stop the flow of a great river.

'The Black Budget is used to fund top-secret projects such as mind-control rays which subdue the population,' Sherman continued. 'Also the Old Ones have been in contact with aliens for a long, long time, long before Roswell – which, as a matter of fact, was nothing but a smokescreen – and some of the money is being used to develop technology that the aliens have given to them.

'Another thing the Old Ones do is saturate the planet with occult symbols hidden in advertising hoardings, TV programmes, newspapers, company logos, pop music, computer games – you name it. These symbols are slowly but surely working their way into the fabric of society. They're gaining power all the time.'

'This is the best bit,' said Mad Dog contemptuously. 'Tell Mr Finch what these symbols are for, Sherman.'

Sherman flashed Mad Dog another indulgent, pitying look, and then said grimly, 'When the symbols are strong enough, the Old

Ones will use them to call up the Anti-Christ, whose power they'll use to establish a new world order.' He licked his lips. Nick could smell his sweat, sharp beneath a weakening layer of aftershave and deodorant. 'It won't be long now, Mr Finch. Another few years, maybe less. Already, if you look closely enough, you can see the evil seeping in between the cracks. Soon it'll be too late to stop it. We've got to act now. If we don't, we're finished.'

His fat face, sweat pouring down it, was almost bestial in its intensity. Nick, who had subconsciously pressed himself back against the seat as he stared at Sherman with round, alarmed eyes, wondered whether the skinhead meant that the two of them alone should 'act now', or whether he was referring to mankind in general. He didn't know what to say, and fortunately was saved from commenting by Mad Dog, who hooted with laughter.

'You see what I mean, man? Ain't that the craziest load of bull-shit you ever heard?'

Nick had to agree that it was, but with Sherman still staring at him fixedly he didn't like to say so. Instead he was diplomatic. 'Who – er – told you all this stuff?'

The fervour was dying from Sherman's eyes now like a smouldering fire. It was as if his mad theory had brought with it a peculiar rush of energy; now it was expounded, and his story told, he was sinking into a strange kind of torpor. 'Nobody told me,' he muttered petulantly. 'I just *know*.'

Mad Dog glanced at his partner. 'Tell the man about Romania, Sherman.'

Sherman scowled, his earlier insouciance abruptly darkening into a growling sullenness. 'Romania isn't important.'

'Yes it is. Tell him.'

'*You* tell him.'

'Okay then.'

Mad Dog glanced into the rear-view mirror, his shaded eyes making his face unsettlingly blank. Nick looked back at him, feeling at a distinct disadvantage.

'A few years ago, Sherman was in prison in Romania,' Mad Dog said. 'He escaped by getting himself into hospital, where the security was not too good, if you know what I'm saying. But – and this is the crucial thing, man – the way he got himself in there was by covering a fucking big rusty nail in his own shit and banging it

217

into his brain with a metal tea cup. Since then his thinking ain't been too hot – and that's putting it fucking mildly.'

'Christ,' Nick murmured, horrified, but also wondering whether Mad Dog and Sherman had some sort of double-act going here, whether in fact they were simply making fun of him. Something of his disbelief must have shown on his face because Mad Dog turned to his colleague. 'Go on, Sherman – show the man your fucking scar.'

Nick expected Sherman to protest, but the big man simply sighed and lowered his head like a bull. Sure enough, on his crown Nick could see a circle of white shiny scar-tissue where the stubble would not grow.

Raising his head again, Sherman said, sulkily, 'Actually my thinking was not impaired. I aimed very carefully.'

'Was there . . . *any* damage?' Nick ventured.

'Minimal,' Sherman said. 'I have no sense of smell.'

'Which means the guy's great for cleaning up shit, if you know what I mean,' Mad Dog said, and cackled.

Nick laughed dutifully, which seemed to be a sign for the two men in front to lapse into silence. Little more was said for the rest of the journey, which Nick passed by staring at the back of Sherman's head, wondering uneasily what other crazy thoughts were percolating in there.

At one point they passed a large hoarding advertising Obsession perfume: despite himself, Nick found himself examining it closely, looking in vain for anything that might be construed as an occult symbol. He wondered how dangerous Sherman could be, how unpredictable. Nick only hoped that the skinhead didn't suddenly get it into his twisted mind that he was some sort of threat – a spy for the Old Ones, or something. He wondered whether, in such a circumstance, Mad Dog would be able to keep his partner under control; whether he would even try.

They were cruising through a run-down estate by now, a place of crumbling concrete and boarded-up windows, of graffiti-daubed bus shelters squatting in drifts of broken safety-glass. The only patches of grass Nick could see were choked with weeds and rubbish and the burnt-out remains of cars. Between decaying tower blocks were swathes of wasteland strewn with rubble and scrap metal. The only people in evidence were gangs of kids in dark, baggy clothes and baseball caps. They watched the car as it cruised past, their faces blankly hostile.

'Home, sweet home,' Mad Dog said. 'I grew up around here.'

No one responded and Mad Dog did not elaborate. Three minutes later he brought the car to a halt at the base of an evil-looking tower block.

He and Sherman got out. Nick hesitated, wondering whether he should get out too. His question was answered by Sherman, who, after closing his own door, pulled Nick's open. It was a cold night, a foretaste of winter. In front of the main doors of the tower block, whose reinforced glass panels resembled a mass of spiders' webs, litter cavorted in a mad whirlwind dance, scraping the concrete. Mad Dog led the way, moving with a smooth arrogance, Sherman ambling along behind him. Nick brought up the rear, wondering what they were doing here, what Hallett wanted him to see. He had a feeling it wouldn't be pleasant.

The main doors were ajar, moving slightly in the wind, the place where the lock had once been nothing more than a splinter-edged hole, as if something had taken a bite out of the wood. Mad Dog pushed the door open with his foot and led the way inside. The interior of the building smelled of bad drains and dirty washing. In front of the lift doors lay a rat, dead and decaying. Its eyes were gone and its lips had shrivelled back over its bared teeth.

Mad Dog pressed the button to summon the lift and the doors opened with a groan, like the mouth of a dying old man releasing the stench of disease. The smell was so bad that Nick stepped back, his eyes close to watering. It was obvious that the lift had been used as a toilet – for some considerable time.

'I think we'll use the stairs,' Mad Dog said.

The staircase smelled almost as bad, and Nick ascended with his hand clamped over his nose and mouth, taking shallow breaths only when he absolutely had to. On the third floor, Mad Dog shoved open a door and led the way on to a dingy landing. He stopped outside the fourth of six doors and pointed at it silently, questioningly. Sherman nodded.

'Okay,' Mad Dog whispered, 'here's the deal. I go in first, you come in behind Sherman, Mr Finch. And keep well back. You got that?'

'What's going to happen?' Nick whispered nervously.

219

'Just a bit of business – that's all.'

'Is there going to be trouble?'

Mad Dog turned his black-shaded gaze on Nick once more, his face unreadable. 'Hey, I'm not a violent man. I just do what I have to do. You ready, Sherman?'

Sherman nodded. All at once he looked bright, alert.

'Let's go,' Mad Dog said.

The two men raised their right legs and brought the soles of their boots crashing against the door. It flew open and they rushed inside. His heart in his mouth, Nick went in after them. He found himself on a short, narrow landing with wallpaper hanging soggily off the walls, and doors leading off on both sides. Mad Dog and Sherman were already disappearing through the second door on the right. Immediately Nick heard shouting and he faltered for a second, a thought flashing through his head: *I could do a runner*. Then he thought of the maze of streets outside – the gangs of feral kids roaming the area – and, sick with fear, he went into the room after them.

The place was a hovel, the filthy carpet and equally filthy furniture strewn with old newspapers, mouse droppings, empty beer cans and cigarette butts. In one corner a stack of foil takeaway containers resembled some weird silver sculpture coated in black, furry mould. In front of a greasy, grimy TV showing a video of a woman masturbating in a bath, a man and what looked to Nick like an underage girl were having sex. The girl was on her hands and knees, her head resting on the seat of an armchair; she was so soundless and compliant she looked as though she were asleep. The man, by contrast, was grunting and whooping, pumping savagely into her from behind, his white, skinny, pimply body lathered in sweat. Either they were totally engrossed in what they were doing, or they were completely out of it on drugs; they seemed blissfully unaware of the fact that Mad Dog was standing over them, shouting.

Mad Dog shook his head and stepped back; as if on cue, Sherman waded forward, grabbed the skinny man by his straggly hair and lifted him up. Nick saw the skinny man's thin white penis plop out of the girl and stand to attention on his stomach. Then Sherman shoved him across the room, causing him to pinwheel backwards for a moment before crashing into a chair.

Mad Dog stepped forward again, grabbed a handful of the girl's

220

long, reddish hair and lifted her head off the seat. For a terrible moment Nick thought she was dead; her eyes were closed, the sockets dark and sunken, and her mouth was gaping.

Then her eyes opened a crack. 'Wha?' she said.

'Get dressed and get out,' Mad Dog said, pulling the girl upright.

Pain jumped across the girl's face and she scrambled shakily to her feet to prevent her hair being pulled out at the roots. Nick guessed that she must be no more than thirteen or fourteen years old. He felt sick and shaken, wanted to jump in and tell Mad Dog to leave her alone, but the man's sudden cold ruthlessness seemed to present too dangerous a bridge to cross. Nick always felt paralysed by violence, despite its having been an everyday occurrence in prison; always felt too shocked and scared by the raw, bestial instincts it roused in the aggressors to intervene. He was grateful when Mad Dog let go of the girl, having first shoved her in the direction of a pile of clothes on the settee.

In something of a daze the girl got dressed, pulling on knickers and jeans, trying and failing to do up her bra with trembling fingers before abandoning it and shoving it into her pocket. She finally covered her small breasts with a grubby yellow Spice Girls T-shirt. As she sat on the floor to pull on her trainers, Mad Dog picked up a black puffer jacket and threw it at her.

'Now get out,' he repeated.

The girl looked up and said something in a voice so small it was barely audible.

'What?' Mad Dog said dangerously.

'He hasn't given me my stuff. I need my stuff,' she whimpered.

Mad Dog turned to the naked man cringing in the armchair. 'Where is it?' he said.

The man was like a craven hound which expected a beating. In a whining voice he said, 'I don't know what she's talking about.'

'Don't fuck me about,' Mad Dog snapped, 'or I'll chop off that little pencil dick of yours and make you eat it. Where's the fucking stuff?'

The man cringed. He had bad skin and a skull-like face; a beard straggled half-heartedly from his pointy chin. 'It's under the cushions on the settee. But she ain't finished paying for it yet.'

'Shut the fuck up,' Mad Dog said, picking up the cushion and hurling it at the tower of takeaway containers. The tower collapsed, causing a large number of small dark things to scurry for cover. Beneath the cushion was a square plastic bag containing some white powder. Mad Dog picked it up and tossed it to the girl. 'Early Christmas present. Now fuck off.'

The girl grabbed the bag and bolted. The naked man drew up his knees and wrapped his arms around himself as Mad Dog and Sherman turned their attention to him. In a high, wheedling voice, he said, 'What do you want? I ain't done nothing.'

'You been dealing on Mr Hallett's patch again, Jacobs.'

'No, I haven't!'

'We've just seen the fucking *evidence*, you dumb cunt!'

Jacobs cringed at Mad Dog's raised voice. 'Just a few regulars,' he said. 'Nothing major. Come on, Mad Dog – you know I wouldn't cross Mr Hallett. I'd be stupid to, wouldn't I?'

'You would be and you have been,' Sherman said. His voice was not merely soft now, it was silky; terrifyingly so.

'Look, fair's fair. I'm just trying to get by, that's all. Everybody's got to make a living, haven't they?'

'Not necessarily,' Mad Dog said, words which sent a chill through Nick and caused Jacobs' mouth and eyes to widen in horror.

Jacobs' Adam's apple jerked in his scrawny throat as he spoke, his voice tremulous. 'Hey, come on, Mad Dog. We've known each other a long time. I'll tell you what – I'll cut Mr Hallett in on my profits. Ten per cent, what do you say? I mean, it's money for nothing, isn't it? You can't go wrong with that.'

Mad Dog shook his head almost sadly. 'You don't get it, do you, Jacobs? How many times have we warned you about this very same thing? How many times, Sherman?'

'Five,' said Sherman gravely.

'Five,' repeated Mad Dog. 'Now, in my opinion, that's five times too many, but Mr Hallett's a very forgiving man, you know what I'm saying?'

'Oh yes,' Jacobs said, nodding eagerly. 'Mr Hallett's a fine man. One of the best.'

'That's right. Now he's given you five chances to stop treading on his toes, and what do you do? You keep putting those fucking hobnailed boots right back on again! Now what do you think about that? You think we're a bunch of fucking suckers who you can keep on running rings round?'

222

'No, of course not, it's just . . . I need to make a living.'

'So get a fucking job!' Mad Dog snarled.

'Yes I will,' Jacobs said, evidently seeing this as a way out. 'I'll get a job. You tell Mr Hallett I'll take his advice and I'll start looking for a job straight away.'

Mad Dog shook his head. 'I was speaking hypothetically. It's too late for all of that now. Mr Hallett has decided to make an example out of you.'

What little colour there was in Jacobs' face drained from it; Nick had never seen anyone look so terrified. Jacobs repulsed him, but what was happening here repulsed him even more. He wanted to rush forward, to say that this had gone far enough, but he couldn't make himself do it. He knew he would hate himself for it later, but he couldn't do anything except stand still and watch.

Jacobs was pleading now, babbling: 'Don't hurt me, Mad Dog. Please don't hurt me. I'll be good, I promise. I'll never deal again. I'll move out of the area. Look, I've learned my lesson. Please, just leave me alone.'

'I'm not gonna lay a finger on you,' Mad Dog said, 'and neither's Sherman here.' He nodded to Sherman and the big man lumbered back. Jacobs watched him retreat with a stricken, hunted expression, wondering what was going on, what trick they were pulling.

Mad Dog removed his shades.

For a moment there was a kind of stand-off in the room, everyone silent and motionless. Mad Dog was staring intently at Jacobs, whose gaze was flitting between the black guy and the big skinhead, wondering from which direction the attack would come.

Then Jacobs coughed, his hands going to his stomach. A bemused, quizzical expression came over his face. He coughed again, then flopped back in his chair with a groan as if uncomfortable after an enormous meal. When he coughed a third time, Nick saw something that made him blink in disbelief. Just for an instant a flicker of blue fire had seemed to come from the man's mouth, to play around his lips before dissipating.

Nick had barely managed to convince himself that he had imagined it when there was a whoosh, followed by a crackling sound. He gave a strangled cry and took an involuntary step backward as blue flames began to gush from Jacobs' stomach and mouth. Nick saw the man's white flesh darkening, burning, smoking. Jacobs' eyes rolled up into his head and he slumped even further in his seat, his now-flaccid penis draped across his skinny thigh like a bloodless worm.

The blue fire began to consume him, running down his arms and legs, crisping his pubic hair. His skin began to bubble and split, turning first bright red and then brown, like an overcooked sausage. Fat oozed from his skin and pooled on the chair beneath him; it dripped from the soles of his feet on to the floor. A smell which overrode all others – which was far worse than any of them – began to fill the flat. It was the smell of rancid, charred pork. Nick pinched his nose hard with his fingers, certain he was going to vomit.

He should have got out, should have torn his eyes away from the absolute, awful horror of the thing, but he couldn't; he could only stand there, rooted to the spot, and watch. Jacobs didn't struggle, didn't cry out, and his passive acceptance was perhaps most horrible of all. He simply sat there, his arms waving feebly, as the blue fire reduced him to a shrivelled, blackened mass, more like a lump of charred and twisted wood than a human being.

A part of Nick's mind was wondering why only Jacobs was burning, why the things around him remained unscathed, even the chair on which he was sitting. Then he felt something tighten around his arm. He shifted his gaze and realised that Mad Dog, now wearing his shades once more, was tugging at him.

'Time to go, Mr Finch,' he said.

Thirty-Eight

By the time they got back, the numb, disbelieving horror that Nick had felt while watching Jacobs die had mutated into a sickened, restless fury. No one spoke in the car, though Nick couldn't believe that Mad Dog and Sherman were silent for the same reasons as he was. Maybe it was considered crass to talk about the executions they carried out, or maybe they simply regarded them as no more than a minor piece of business, barely worth comment. Or maybe the two of them – considerate, sensitive guys that they were – were simply giving Nick time to reflect on what he had seen.

They had been driving for twenty minutes when Sherman, without turning, said quietly, 'Would you mind putting the blindfold back on, Mr Finch?'

The anger was filtering through now, burning in him, and Nick suddenly wanted to scream at them, to demand how they could concern themselves with something so banal, so unimportant, after what they had done. However he forced himself to remain silent, to conserve his anger, and he snatched up the blindfold and put it on, then sat ramrod-straight, lips tight, until they reached their destination. He got out of the car, tensing beneath Sherman's helping hand, and walked stiff-legged between the two men, saying nothing, until they came to a halt at the top of a flight of stairs and Mad Dog said, 'You can take it off again now, Mr Finch.'

Nick snatched the blindfold from his eyes and threw it on the floor. He found himself standing outside the door leading to Hallett's inner sanctum. 'Would you let go of my arm please?' he said curtly to Sherman. Sherman did so, and without waiting for an order or an invitation, Nick shoved open the door and strode inside.

This time only Hallett was there. He was sitting, as before, at the round table, like a father who has sent his children out to play and was stealing ten precious minutes for himself. He appeared to be deep in thought, puffing meditatively at a large cigar, a drink by his elbow, though he looked up when Nick entered and nodded a greeting. Clearly he had been expecting him.

'Come in, son,' he said, and waved expansively at the array of seats before him. 'Grab a pew.'

Nick came in but he didn't sit down; sitting with the man would have seemed too much like condoning what had happened. Instead he walked up and stood over him, his anger finally giving him the courage to speak his mind.

'What were you trying to prove,' he said tersely, 'sending me to watch two of your men commit murder? If you were trying to impress me or frighten me, it didn't work. I just found it sick. Disgusting.'

Hallett regarded Nick without expression for a moment. Then he asked calmly, 'Tell me, son – what did you actually see?'

'What?' snapped Nick.

'What did you actually *see*? When you were with Mad Dog and Sherman. Tell me what happened.'

Nick scowled. 'Are you taking the piss or what?'

'No, son – I'm asking a simple question. Think about what you actually saw, then describe it to me.'

Nick was still scowling. 'I saw two of your men kill somebody.'

'How?'

'Are you trying to pretend you don't know?'

Hallett's voice hardened just a touch. 'How did they do it?'

Nick took a deep breath. 'They burned him to death.'

Hallett nodded slowly. 'I see. Are you sure about that?'

'What do you mean, *am I sure*? Of course I'm fucking sure! I saw it happen.'

'You mean they doused him in petrol? They set him alight?'

Nick hesitated. For the first time he thought about what he really *had* seen. He had been so horrified by the man's terrible death that, unbelievably, his mind had pushed out the most extraordinary detail of the whole affair.

226

'No,' he said, then shook his head, confused and irritated. 'I don't know.'

'Once he was in the chair, did you see either of my men lay a finger on Mr Jacobs?'

'No,' said Nick again, thinking: *Once he was in the chair?* How did Hallett know that Sherman had shoved Jacobs into a chair?

Before he had time to think about it, Hallett asked, 'How do you think Mr Jacobs died, son?'

Nick was floundering now, losing the impetus of his anger. 'I don't know.'

'I'll tell you, shall I?' Hallett said, and tapped the side of his temple with one stubby finger. 'It was the power of the mind, son. The power of the mind.'

Nick stared at him. 'What do you mean?'

Hallett raised his glass to the light and scrutinised the contents, as though searching for impurities. Then he took a sip and set it down again. 'People can be made to believe all kinds of things if you know how to do it,' he said quietly.

'You mean, you made Jacobs *think* he was going to burst into flames and so he did?' Nick asked.

Hallett smiled. 'What do *you* think?'

Nick was silent for a moment. Then he said, 'I think either you're all mad here, or I am. First Sherman spouts on about Old Ones and mind-control rays and aliens and God knows what else —'

'Oh, Sherman,' Hallett murmured with a smile, 'you don't want to listen to what *he* says.'

'— and now you're telling me that Mad Dog burned a guy to death just by using his mind.'

'No, son. I'm not telling you that.'

'What?'

'Mad Dog didn't kill anyone.'

'But you just said —'

'Hear me out. Mad Dog didn't kill Jacobs.' He paused, for effect. 'I did.'

'*You?* But you weren't even there!'

'Maybe not in body – but in mind. I was looking out through Mad Dog's eyes, chanelling my thoughts through him.' He shrugged. 'It's an arrangement he's comfortable with. We trust each other.'

Nick looked at him for a long moment, dumbfounded. Then, quietly, he spoke. 'You *are* mad.'

'Oh, for God's sake, son,' Hallett retorted with a sudden flare of anger, 'wake up and smell the fucking coffee! I know for a fact that plenty of crazy stuff has been happening to you over the past few days. Don't try to deny it.'

Nick thought about his vision in the Gridlock, the subsequent revelation about Michael Mercy; his overly vivid nightmares; the hallucinatory attack following the 'endrant command' telephone call . . .

'All of that can be explained,' he said weakly.

Hallett shook his head, his anger replaced by weary amusement. 'Oh, yeah? Explained how?'

'I took a lot of drugs when I was younger. People who do that can have flashbacks, get paranoid . . .'

Hallett was still shaking his head. 'Listen to you, son. Listen to how desperate you sound. You *know* there's more to it than that, don't you?'

Nick fell silent again. He didn't speak for maybe half a minute. At last he said, 'Okay. But even if what you're telling me is true, then you're still admitting to murder, aren't you? You still *killed* Jacobs, whether you touched him or not.'

Hallett sighed, closed his eyes briefly. 'Forget fucking Jacobs,' he muttered. 'The man was scum. He was a drug dealer and a paedophile – he wrecked lives. I've done the world a big favour by getting rid of him.'

Nick couldn't deny that he had some sympathy with Hallett's position. He had come across men like Jacobs in prison – morally bereft parasites who bullied those weaker than themselves but became spineless when challenged – and had always thought the world would be a far better place if they could be put down, taken out of circulation for good. But harbouring thoughts of summary justice and actually watching that justice put into practise were two entirely different things. If he had learned anything from the experience, it was that two wrongs did not make a right.

'We're talking about a human life here,' he said feebly. 'How can you be so callous?'

Hallett squinted at Nick through a drifting question-mark of cigar smoke. 'Let me ask you something, Nick. If that had been *your* daughter Jacobs had been fucking tonight – your daughter

228

at the age of thirteen – would you still have been so pious about it?'

'I'm not being *pious*, I'm just . . . Look, I know what it's like being addicted to drugs. I know how desperate you can get. I know how prepared you are to do absolutely anything to get a fix.'

'Yeah, and Jacobs is a sewer rat. He takes advantage of that. At least, he used to – he won't be taking advantage of any more little girls. Because that's what he did, son. He'd target little girls, knowing that if he got them hooked he'd be able to fuck them. And we're not just talking teenagers here. We're talking girls as young as eight or nine. Have you ever seen an eight-year-old girl with needle-tracks in her arms, offering you a blow job in return for drug money?'

Nick pursed his lips. He knew that Hallett was not exaggerating. During his own addiction he had seen and done some terrible things. Finally, quietly, he said, 'You still haven't explained to me exactly why you wanted me to go along tonight.'

'I wanted to prepare you for the truth,' Hallett said.

'What truth?'

'The truth of what we are.'

As with Sherman earlier in the evening, Nick was not sure whether the 'we' included him, or whether Hallett was simply referring to himself and his cronies. 'And what are you? I mean, I know you've told me about Jacobs, but . . . what made you like that?'

'Time for a few explanations, I think,' Hallett said. 'Mad Dog, bring Ray here, would you?'

Nick turned, surprised to see Mad Dog standing by the door with his arms folded. He hadn't realised the man had followed him in; he must have remained a silent presence during his exchange with Hallett.

'Yes, boss,' Mad Dog said now, and exited.

'Can I pour you a drink, Nick?' Hallett asked.

Nick hesitated, again feeling that drinking with the man, accepting his hospitality, was tantamount to condoning his activities.

But Hallett gave a small, bitter smile as if he understood Nick's reasoning and pushed the decanter across the table top with his fingertips.

'Tell you what, son – I'll just leave it there. You help yourself if you feel like it.'

Hallett stubbed his cigar out in an ashtray already crammed with butts and sat back in his chair. 'While we're waiting, son, I'd like to show you something.'

He put his arms down by his sides, then all at once his chair was sliding backwards. Nick blinked; for one ludicrous moment he thought that the table was going to sink into the floor like in some sixties spy movie. Then Hallett manoeuvred himself out from behind the table and Nick realised that he was sitting, not in a chair, but a wheelchair. Hallett's upper body was well-developed, his shoulders broad, but his legs ended in stumps at the knees.

Hallett looked down at himself with an expression of cool appraisal, like a man checking a dinner suit for stains.

'What happened?' asked Nick, thinking: *Gangland warfare. A bomb. Retribution. The Long Good Friday with Bob Hoskins as invalid.*

Again Hallett smiled as if he could read Nick's mind. 'Nothing dramatic. A childhood accident,' he said. 'It happened when I was eight years old. Me and a bunch of mates went down to the local railway line to play chicken. Of course, I wanted to prove that I was the toughest by being the last one off the line.' He chuckled throatily. 'Unfortunately my timing was slightly out. Bloody ironic, really – I wanted to show that I was the one with the most guts, but I didn't plan on having the bloody things spread all over the tracks.'

His chuckle became a laugh, but Nick winced. 'That's awful.'

'Best bloody thing that ever happened to me,' Hallett said, and then laughed even louder at Nick's astonished expression. 'Oh, I don't mean at first – it wasn't one of the best days of my life, though I was unconscious for most of it, and pretty heavily drugged for the next couple of weeks.

'The worst thing, though, early on, wasn't the pain or even knowing I was going to be a cripple for the rest of my life, it was the nightmares I was having. Terrible they were. I'd wake up screaming and crying and shaking. Funny thing is, I can't for the life of me remember what they were about. When I try I just come up against a blank wall.'

'Maybe your mind blocked them out because they were so traumatic,' Nick said.

Hallett nodded. 'Maybe. I know the doctor at the time put them down to the trauma of the accident. He said it was my mind's way of coping with what had happened, flushing out all the bad memories.'

Nick sensed movement behind him and turned to see Mad Dog re-enter the room, accompanied by the slim, blond-haired man Nick had first met here. The blond-haired man smiled at Nick. Hallett acknowledged the two new arrivals with a nod.

'That wasn't just it, though,' Hallett continued, 'because pretty soon I realised that I could tell what people were thinking. I thought I was imagining it at first. I thought all that sitting and lying around recovering from my accident was sending me a bit doolally. So I started testing people. I didn't tell them outright that I knew what they were thinking, but I'd make innocent little comments or ask questions that would surprise them so much it would make them *tell* me. For example, I remember once my old mum came in and she was wondering about what to make for pudding that night. Should she use up the rhubarb and make a crumble, or should she make a spotted dick? Anyway, I said something like, "You know what I really fancy, Mum? I really fancy some rhubarb crumble for tea tonight." Well, you should have seen her face. "You must be psychic," she said. "That's just what I was thinking about."'

'Well, that sort of thing happened again and again, and I kept practising and practising, until eventually I wasn't just reading minds, I was doing other things as well.'

'Like what?' Nick asked, feeling nervous enough to try stifling his own thoughts.

'I started having premonitions. I knew things were going to happen before they actually did. Then I realised that not only could I read people's minds but I could control them as well; I could make them *do* things.

'At first, when I found this out, I was like a kid in a sweet shop. The best-looking women would find me irresistible without knowing why. I'd make people buy me presents and drinks, give me money.

'This ability, this gift – whatever you want to call it – has made me invulnerable. I know that I can trust my employees a hundred per cent. If any one of them has so much as the glimmer of a bad thought about me, then I know it straight away. And if someone got in here wanting to hurt me, they wouldn't be able to do it. If you, son, were standing here now, pointing a gun at me, I'd be

231

able to make you turn that gun on yourself, just by thinking about it.'

'What if you were asleep?' said Nick. 'Or what if someone . . . I don't know . . . planted a bomb in the basement?'

'I'd still know about it. I've got an instinct for these things: a sixth sense. Something in my head tells me when there's danger around. Funny that you should mention bombs though, son. A couple of years ago I had a premonition that one of my business rivals had planted a bomb in a restaurant where I was planning to eat. So I gave the cops an anonymous tip-off, used my gift not only to save my own life but to save the lives of dozens of innocent people.'

Nick wondered whether Hallett was telling him this to make Jacobs' death seem inconsequential by comparison, and then embarrassedly tried to quash the idea. It was disturbing to think that he could have no secrets from this man; but in an odd way it was liberating too, for it meant that he might as well speak his mind. Astonished to find that he was actually beginning to believe Hallett – even though he'd seen nothing to support his story except Jacobs bursting into flames – Nick said, 'Do you mind if I ask you something?'

Hallett poured himself another drink. 'In your mind you've already asked it, son, so go ahead.'

'Why haven't you made more of yourself? I mean, if you can do what you say you can . . .'

Hallett laughed. 'What are you saying, son? That I'm some kind of loser?'

'No, I just mean . . . well, if you can make people do whatever you want, why aren't you . . . I don't know . . . living in a villa in the south of France, or on a yacht in the Caribbean?'

Hallett evidently found the question amusing. 'What makes you think I *haven't* got a yacht in the Caribbean?' He took a sip of his drink and then gestured expansively around him. 'I've got all I want here, son. I'm not a greedy man. I'm happy with my little empire.'

'But what I mean is, with your gift, why do you have to even bother with men like Jacobs? Why do you have to get involved in crime at all?'

Abruptly Hallett's face darkened. Quietly he said, 'Crime is a dirty word, son. I'm a businessman. Don't you forget that.'

Feeling reckless and scared, Nick blurted out what was in his mind. 'Businessmen don't murder their rivals.'

Hallett's body was still, his face like stone. Despite his physical handicap, his was an imposing, intimidating presence. In the same gravelly murmur he said, 'I've never in my life punished anyone who didn't deserve it. And I've brought a hell of a lot more happiness to people than pain. Isn't that right, Mad Dog?'

'That's right, boss,' Mad Dog said dutifully.

'Okay,' said Nick as if conceding the point. He sighed and finally sat down, feeling physically and emotionally drained. 'I still don't understand why you wanted me to go along tonight. And why you're telling me all this now.'

'That's because you're confused, son. And I don't blame you; it's a lot to take in. But if you were thinking straight, you'd realise that everything you've learned tonight is the reason you're being hunted.'

'What do you mean?'

'Isn't it obvious, son? You're like me. You've got the power too.'

Nick's head snapped up. He was wide awake now. Hallett was sucking on yet another cigar, squinting at him through a writhing mask of blue smoke.

'Don't be daft. I've never been able to do any of the things that you can do! In fact, until the last few days I'd never had any kind of psychic insight whatsoever.'

'You've never had your legs chopped off by an express train either,' said Hallett.

For a moment Nick was silent as he struggled to cope with this new information. 'So what are you saying? Some people have this power lying dormant in them, and now they're being hunted down by . . . who? The authorities?'

Hallett nodded. 'A government faction. A bunch of so-called scientists and para-military operatives.'

'They call themselves the Illuminati,' said Ray, and laughed as if he found this amusing.

'Only your power isn't dormant? The trauma of the accident brought it out?'

Hallett tapped cigar ash into an ashtray. 'Bang on.'

'So . . . how do you *know* I've got this power in me as well? And how do the people who are after me know?'

233

'They know because they made you.'

Nick stared at him. 'What do you mean?'

Hallett poured himself and Nick a drink; this time Nick picked up his glass and took a sip without comment or hesitation. He felt he needed it.

'It's taken a while, but with the help of one or two contacts I've finally managed to piece most of the story together. It started back in the mid-sixties. In some of the remoter parts of the Soviet Union there was a famine, which went on for months and which the Russians, not surprisingly, kept stumm about. Unknown to the rest of the world, whole communities were starving to death, hundreds of people dying every day. Anyway, one of Russia's big criminal organisations – and there are a fuck of a lot of them out there, always have been, however much the Kremlin try to play it down – decided to take advantage of the situation and started sending agents round all the villages, offering to buy the kids. The villagers weren't told who these people really were. They claimed they were representatives of some Western relief organisation, and that the kids would get sent over to Europe or America and be adopted by childless couples over there. Now a lot of these Russian peasants were poor and uneducated, and so they let their kids go, thinking that it was their only chance, that they'd have a better life somewhere else. Course, they were wrong, weren't they? The kids were just sold on like cattle to whoever would pay the highest price. Some were sold into slavery and prostitution, some were sent to Central and South America where they were used for organ transplant research, and some were used by the military of various countries to clear minefields, by which I mean—'

'I know,' said Nick, shocked. 'I've been having dreams about it.'

Hallett nodded, as if he understood. 'One bunch of kids,' he continued, 'were bought by an Anglo-American research group: the Illuminati. The group had, and still have, a base somewhere in Europe – I haven't found out where yet – nicknamed the Chicken House, where they carried out a series of experiments on the kids to . . . what was it again, Ray?'

'Their purpose was to artificially promote and enhance human capability and evolution,' Ray recited.

'That's right,' Hallett agreed. 'One series of these experiments was known as the Genesis Project. The Illuminati wanted to create a group of people with psychic powers so strong that they could be used as military and political weapons. Basically, they wanted this group – who were known as psi-humans, or post-humans – to be able to read the minds of their enemies; more than that, to influence their enemies' thinking.'

'And you're saying that you and I are both . . . psi-humans?' said Nick, incredulous. 'That we come from Russian peasant stock and when we were kids the Russian Mafia sold us to a research organisation who performed experiments on us?'

Hallett nodded. 'I know it's hard to believe, son,' he said, almost gently.

'*Hard?*' Nick's voice was shrill, his laughter splintery. 'It's not hard – it's impossible! You're either mad or joking. I certainly wasn't born in bloody Russia. I was born in Chelmsford and I lived there till I was eighteen with my mum and dad. I even remember standing up in my cot, being pushed along in my pram. My parents have photographs of me when I was a baby, ones of me as a toddler, playing in the garden, digging on the beach. I can show them to you if you like.'

From behind him, Ray said, 'I'm afraid that won't prove anything, Nick.'

Nick twisted round in his seat. 'Won't *prove* anything? What are you bloody talking about? Of *course* it'll prove something! It'll prove that you're all living in cloud-bloody-cuckoo land.'

'You're getting awfully aggressive, Nick,' Ray pointed out calmly.

'No, I'm not. I just don't like people making a twat of me, that's all.'

'It's a defence mechanism, Nick. You're programmed to act violently if anyone threatens to expose your false memories with the truth.'

'*False memories*? What the fuck are you on about?'

'Your childhood memories are false. They've been constructed by the Illuminati. Your real memories have been repressed—'

'I don't have to listen to this shit,' Nick snarled, and jumped to his feet.

'Yes you do, son,' Nick heard Hallett say mildly, and all at once he found that he couldn't move. There was a pressure in his mind; his limbs felt locked. It seemed as though dozens of invisible

235

hands were holding him, pushing him down, forcing him back into his seat—

Then the pressure was released, and for a second he felt light and dazed. He looked at Hallett with something like wonder. 'You did that?'

'Sorry, son,' said Hallett, matter-of-fact. 'I had to. It's important you listen to what we say.'

'I know it's hard to accept,' said Ray, 'but believe me, Nick, your parents aren't your real parents. They adopted you, probably when you were five or six years old.'

'So you're saying that my parents were government agents or something?' Nick scoffed.

Ray smiled. 'I doubt it. It's more likely that they were simply desperate for a child but couldn't have one themselves, and for whatever reason had been unsuccessful in their attempts to adopt or foster. There has always been a limited number of children available to couples in Britain – never enough to go round.'

'We reckon the Illuminati vetted various couples across the country, then contacted them and let them know they could get them a child – but only if they kept their traps shut,' said Hallett. 'Permanently that is.'

Ray nodded in confirmation. 'It's likely that your parents were told you were one of several children smuggled illegally into the country from a Soviet orphanage, and that if the truth were ever to be discovered and your origins revealed, the Soviet authorities would demand you back.'

'But my parents would never have gone along with anything like that,' Nick said. 'They were honest, law-abiding people. It broke their hearts when I got sent down.'

'They might have been law-abiding, but they would also have been extremely desperate,' said Ray. 'Believe me, Nick, the Illuminati would have been scrupulously careful in their selection of guardians for the Genesis children. It may even have been the case that those selected who did say no were subsequently eliminated.'

'Killed, you mean?' said Nick, appalled.

Ray shrugged. 'I'm only guessing, but it's not beyond the bounds of possibility.'

'It's what I'd do if I was in the Illuminati's position,' said Hallett.

Nick shook his head, confused. 'But why didn't my parents ever *tell* me that I was adopted – when I was older, I mean?' Immediately he raised a dismissive hand. 'No, you don't have to answer that. It's obvious, isn't it? The Illuminati must have put the fear of God into them. It wouldn't have done for us to start digging around in our pasts, would it?'

He released a weary sigh; for a moment he seemed to slump, as if the weight of all that he was discovering today were physically wearing him down. Ray and Hallett watched him in silence, giving him space and time to assimilate the information. At length Nick raised his head and plaintively repeated a point he had made earlier. 'But I've got loads of photographs from when I was a baby—'

'Tell me this,' said Ray, 'do any of the photographs of you from being a toddler up to the age of, say, six include your parents?'

Nick looked at him, and an expression of dawning realisation appeared on his face. 'No,' he said slowly. 'Now that you mention it, they don't. But the baby photos do. Oh! I suppose that baby wasn't me.'

Ray's only response was a shrug and a sympathetic raising of the eyebrows.

There was a brief silence as Nick struggled to come to grips with all he had been told. Finally he said, 'But if I was adopted at such a late age, wouldn't my parents' friends and neighbours have known about it? Surely they'd have let something slip as I got older.'

Ray's shake of the head was patient. 'The Illuminati would have dealt with all eventualities. I suspect one of the provisos of your adoption would have been that your parents immediately relocate to where nobody would suspect the truth about your origins. Additionally I would guess that your parents were a very insular couple and that you had very few relatives. Am I right?'

Nick nodded. 'My dad was an only child and my mum's only sister lived abroad. She never had children, which meant I didn't even have any cousins.' Almost reluctantly he added, 'And my grandparents died before I was born.'

'You see, son,' Hallett said, his voice a quiet rumble, 'it all fits.'

Nick had to agree, though there were still many aspects of the situation he didn't understand. 'What about the dreams I've been having?' he said. 'If what you're telling me is true, then how come

237

I've been dreaming about what happened to some of the other children who was sold? Those weren't my experiences.'

Hallett shrugged. 'We still don't know the *full* story, son – what we've got we've put together piece by piece, like a jigsaw puzzle. It's possible that we were all earmarked for minefield clearing and that the Illuminati bought us from whoever had purchased us from the Russians. Then again, maybe it was just something – like the bogeyman – the Illuminati used to threaten us with if we didn't co-operate. Maybe they filled our heads with fears and nightmares so we'd do whatever they told us.'

Nick shuddered as he thought of how vivid his recurring dream was, as he recalled the horribly maimed children strewn in the minefield, in too much agony to do anything but lie shaking and keening like dying animals. He thought of the soldier raising his rifle, of his colleagues casually telling him not to waste his ammunition. The memory left a bitterness inside him, a sense of despair, desolation, at the callous cruelty of human nature. He tried to swamp it with another question.

'If all of this happened thirty years ago, how come the Illuminati are coming after me now?'

'We don't know for certain,' said Ray, 'but what we believe is that initially the results of the Genesis Project were inconclusive, and thus the whole series of experiments was deemed a failure and therefore abandoned. You and Mr Hallett and the other twenty-two psi-humans were brainwashed into believing that the families you were placed with were your real parents, and you were more or less left alone to get on with your lives. However, it now seems apparent that the Illuminati didn't cut the apron strings entirely, but kept you all under casual observation. What's sparked off this latest wave of activity is the fact that just recently the programming of some of the subjects has been breaking down. Over the last nine months, six of the twenty-four have committed suicide, two of them having first become psychotic and performed murderous acts.'

'Topped a few people, he means,' interrupted Hallett. 'But that's Ray for you. He'll never use a simple word when a posh one will do.'

Ray acknowledged Hallett with a wry smile and continued. 'The Illuminati therefore seem to have decided to reel in the remaining subjects and run them through the mill one more time.

238

In my opinion, I think they want to determine whether the subjects' psychic powers have developed with physical maturity; and if they *have* developed, have they done so sufficiently to be quantified? Most importantly, have they done so sufficiently to be exploited? If the answer to these questions is yes, then I believe the project will be resumed. However, if it's no . . .' He shrugged, '. . . then in my humble opinion I suspect the project will be terminated once and for all.'

'The project – or us?' said Nick.

Ray grimaced apologetically. 'You *are* the project.'

Nick put a hand to his head. 'I don't believe this is happening to me.' He attempted to stabilise his reeling thoughts. 'So . . . how were we turned into psi-humans in the first place?'

'Have you heard of biological determinism, Nick?' Ray asked.

'Er . . . I'm not sure.'

'It's the basis of eugenics. The belief that all we are and all we can become is solely determined by our genes.'

'Right,' Nick said. 'So they fucked about with our genes in other words?'

Ray nodded again. 'The technical term for it is somatic intervention. Basically what happened is that thirty years ago the Illuminati managed to isolate and enhance the gene or set of genes determining psychic ability. Unfortunately, by doing so they also appear to have set little mental time-bombs ticking in the heads of an alarmingly high proportion of their subjects.'

'Great,' said Nick. 'So any minute now I could turn into a raving psycho?'

'I think it might take a little longer than that,' said Ray seriously, 'but . . . well, frankly, yes.'

'So where does that leave us?' Nick asked, looking at Hallett, hoping for reassurance. But Hallett shrugged nonchalantly.

'In my case, son, it leaves me precisely where I was before. I'm just going to go on living my life, and if one day the Illuminati decide to come for me . . . well, they'll find themselves with a war on their hands.' He knocked back the last of his drink. 'Not that they will,' he added.

'What makes you so sure?' asked Nick.

'I've got insurance, son. If they find out about *me*, then they'll find out *that* pretty quickly. All the evidence I've collected on the Genesis Project – and I'm talking hard evidence, none of your

239

circumstantial bollocks – is secured in a bank vault, and if I should – shall we say – die anything other than a natural death or disappear in strange circumstances, that evidence will be made public.'

'What if you die in an accident?'

'I avoid accidents.' He grinned. 'But if I did, well, that'd be their tough shit, wouldn't it?'

'Okay,' said Nick, 'and where does all this leave me? Am I a prisoner here?'

'Course not, son. You're a guest. You and me, we're practically brothers. That's why I sent my boys to rescue you. I'm offering you a chance. If you want, I can set you up with a new life, a new identity – I've done it before. You'd have to cut all your old ties – ex-wife, daughter, girlfriend, flat, job, everything – there'd be no going back. But it could be your only way to stay free.'

Nick looked at Hallett, puffed out his cheeks and blew a deep breath. 'Shit,' he said finally, 'is that really the only way?'

Hallett nodded slowly. 'I know it's tough, son.'

'*Tough?*' repeated Nick, and laughed. 'That's an understatement. I'd be throwing my whole life away, abandoning everything that means anything to me.'

'If the Illuminati get you, son, you'll be doing that anyway. And if you refuse my offer they *will* get you, believe me. At least my way, you've got a chance of escaping.'

Nick felt sick and hollow, directionless. He didn't know what to do, which way to turn.

'I'd have to think about it,' he said eventually. 'But if I did decide to take you up on your offer, would there be any chance of seeing my daughter and maybe my girlfriend again first? Or at least getting some word to them that I'm safe?'

Hallett looked at him, considering for a long time. Finally, he spoke in a low gruff rumble that sounded almost tender. 'We'll see what we can do, son,' he said.

Thirty-Nine

They left her until the morning before coming back. Sasha spent a great deal of that time lying on the bed, feeling like nothing more than a vessel for her constantly buzzing thoughts. She had hoped that giving the thoughts free rein might release some of them, relieve the pressure, but they circled angrily and ceaselessly like a swarm of wasps trapped in a confined space.

It anguished her to imagine her mum, blinded and sedated in a hospital bed, thinking herself abandoned. She wondered where Dad was and what he was doing, how long it would be before Jenna found him and lured him into the trap. She tried to work out what, aside from his vision in the Gridlock, Dad could possibly have done to draw the attentions of the people who had casually plundered and torn apart their lives. He seemed like an innocent victim; but was it possible he had been leading a secret existence, telling her lies for months, perhaps years? What link could he possibly have with the other people DI Baker had told her about? And how much involvement – if any – did Jenna and her ilk have in the violent deaths of these people and their families?

Eventually, exhausted by the churning of her own mind, she switched on the TV and used the remote to flick through the channels, giving up when she reached seventy-two and the stream of foreign-language porn, shopping, news and sport showed no sign of abating.

She played some music (Oasis, loud, hoping it would piss them off), and briefly considered using some of the food in the ridiculously well-stocked kitchen to cook herself a meal, then decided against it. Since the plane had touched down, the grinding, empty feeling in her stomach had intensified to such an extent that she

241

couldn't imagine ever feeling hungry again. All the same, wanting to maintain her energy levels, keep herself strong, she took an apple from the fruit bowl that her captors had thoughtfully provided and munched it without enthusiasm. She noted that it was a Braeburn – her favourite variety. It made her hate them all the more.

Across the room, opposite the foot of her king-sized and (she had to admit) extremely comfortable double bed were two window bays, side by side, complete with curtains. Instead of glass, however, were two halves of one divided mural, depicting fields and trees, sunshine and blue skies.

All at once, staring at the deliberately cheerful, wholly artificial depictions of normality, Sasha was overwhelmed by a wave of despair which almost immediately turned to bitter anger. She hurled the remains of her apple across the room where it hit the right-hand mural with a wet splat and rebounded on to the plushly carpeted floor, shedding lumps of white pulp.

The tears came then, sudden and fierce, and Sasha rolled on to her stomach and buried her bruised face in the pillow, tried to stop her body from shaking, so they would not see. Later, lying on the bed fully clothed, she slept fitfully and fretfully, waking up disorientated some time later. She had no sense of time or place; for several long and frightening seconds her mind remained blank. When her memories did begin to filter back, it only made her feel worse. The thought that she might never again see the sun, never feel fresh wind on her face, filled her with a desperation so acute it was close to panic. She made herself coffee, though she still didn't feel like eating. She was sitting listlessly in her armchair, the cup at her side, when the door gave an insectile buzz, then opened.

A man came in, square-set, good-looking in a bland, clean-cut, American-college-boy kind of way. Sasha almost smiled when he spoke with an American accent, a hint of a Southern drawl that she gained the impression he was constantly trying to repress.

'Good morning, Miss Finch. Would you mind coming with me, please?'

Just for an instant Sasha considered throwing hot coffee in his face and making a run for it. Then she rejected the idea; they would know what she'd done straight away, and no doubt recapture her within seconds. And then what? She had no doubt they

242

had the capacity to make her life very uncomfortable indeed. Deep down she knew that if they so desired they could break her spirit. She was tough – but not indestructible.

'Where to?' she asked sullenly.

'We need to carry out a number of routine preliminary procedures, that's all,' he replied, and smiled.

'What kind of procedures?'

'Upon entering the facility, it is required that the physical and mental health of each of our visitors be fully assessed.'

'A visitor?' Sasha repeated, and gave a humourless snort of laughter. 'So that's what I am, is it?'

The man's smile remained fixed but friendly. 'That is your official status, yes.'

'So I'm not an inmate, then? A prisoner? A hostage? Because as far as I'm concerned, a visitor is someone who is passing through, someone who goes somewhere of their own free will, stays for a while and then leaves. Or am I wrong? Because if I'm not I'd like to leave *now*, please.'

The man's smile never wavered. 'I'm afraid accession to your request exceeds my jurisdiction at this present time.'

'You mean you're not going to let me go?'

'I'm not authorised to do so.'

'So if you *were* authorised you *would* let me go?'

'The request is irrelevant.'

Sasha gave a sigh, half of amusement, half annoyance. 'I bet you're great fun at parties.'

The man ignored the jibe. 'Miss Finch, I must repeat my request that you accompany me immediately.'

'All right, all right. Doesn't a girl even get the chance to finish her coffee or brush her teeth around here?'

'If you wish for more time to prepare yourself I'm sure that can be arranged.'

'You make it sound like an execution,' Sasha said, then sighed. 'It's okay, I'll come as I am – bad breath and all.'

She abandoned her coffee and, prompted by a gesture from the man, preceded him out of the room. He pulled the door shut and told her to wait by the lift. As she walked the short distance across the corridor, she glanced up and down, looking from some weakness, something she might be able to exploit later. At the end of the corridor was a double door marked EMERGENCY STAIRS;

243

like the lift it was made of metal and had a security panel on the wall beside it. Her chaperon did as Jenna had done with all the other doors Sasha had seen here: keycard, combination, hand-print. As they waited silently for the lift, Sasha wondered whether it would ever be possible to escape from a place like this. To do so you'd have to disable the surveillance cameras without making the security staff suspicious – which seemed an insurmountable task in itself. Then you'd have to steal a keycard, overpower someone and force them to use their hand-print. And somehow get them to reveal their combination. The only way Sasha could imagine that might be achieved was by torturing them – not really an option for her – or somehow getting them on your side. No, she had to face it: she was stuck here until they decided to let her go.

The lift arrived and she and her chaperon stepped inside and ascended several floors. It stopped with barely a jolt and the doors opened smoothly and soundlessly. They stepped out into a corridor which was wider and longer than the one outside Sasha's room. It reminded her of a hospital corridor, though it was much more featureless: there were no coffee-machines, no pot-plants, no helpful signs pointing the way. Though the corridor ended in a blank wall twenty yards down on the right, to the left it stretched perhaps three times the length of Sasha's corridor before branching into two. There were a series of metal double doors along the wall opposite the lift, like the doors to laboratories or operating theatres.

Sasha was wondering how close she was to the surface when the man gently took her arm.

'If you'll just step across the corridor with me, Sasha,' he said, 'we'll be going into room three.'

'This is where I have the electric-shock treatment, is it?' she said, joking to hide her nervousness.

He smiled. 'Nothing like that. It'll be quite painless, I promise you.'

They crossed the corridor, his hand light on her arm, and stopped outside a set of doors with the number 3 inscribed on a small white plaque above them. More security – keycard, combination, hand-print; Sasha tried surreptitiously to work out what combination he tapped in, but like Jenna he leaned forward a little, effectively shielding himself.

The red panel lit up and the door buzzed. Her chaperon let go of

244

her arm to push the door open. Again, here was a split-second that Sasha could have taken advantage of – but what was the point? Personal security was only lax because there was no chance of escape.

Politely the man held the door open for her as she entered. The room was large and pristine-white, full of complicated-looking electronic equipment whose function she could only guess at. Most of the equipment appeared to be connected to various computer terminals, some of which were manned by men and women wearing long white coats. Sasha was not sure whether the people were medical personnel or research assistants; the room could have been used for either function, dominated as it was by a large, white, pod-like structure. The pod – to which much of the surrounding equipment appeared to be linked – was hollow; a black bench like a doctor's examination table jutted from a circular orifice at its base. Looking at it, Sasha could not help but think of a vast white head, featureless but for a gaping mouth and a black, lolling tongue. The image made her shudder slightly.

A number of white-coated personnel turned to look curiously at her as she entered, and though most went back to their work, one came over, a small-boned, ginger-haired woman with a smiling, pretty face.

'Hi,' the woman said, extending a hand which boasted a ring on every finger. 'I'm Jo Swanwick. You must be Sasha.'

'Yes,' Sasha said gruffly. 'What is this place?'

'Oh, it's nowhere special. Just one small research project among many.'

'What kind of research do you do here?'

'Medical. Jaws here is the most advanced body-scanner ever invented. He's designed to give the patient an exhaustive physical examination – he can detect any ailment or physical problem, no matter how minor. If you've got a pimple or a sore throat or a pain in your big toe he can tell us what's caused it. Similarly, he can pinpoint any chemical imbalances in the body, so if a patient is suffering from a psychological illness – is unable to sleep, or is unaccountably nervous, say – then Jaws can draw our attention to the physical causes behind that.'

'Sounds brilliant,' Sasha said. 'So pretty soon there'll be no need for any more doctors.'

Jo Swanwick's smile widened. 'Oh, I don't think we're quite at

245

that stage yet. Jaws can diagnose, but he can't treat. Also, his bedside manner leaves something to be desired.'

'He *is* like most doctors then,' Sasha said, making Jo Swanwick laugh.

Sasha smiled along with her, but though the woman was pleasant enough, she couldn't help feeling that this whole encounter was strangely surreal. Here she was, a prisoner for some reason unknown to her, being given a guided tour as if she were some visiting dignitary.

'Why are you telling me all this?' she asked bluntly.

Jo Swanwick looked a little surprised. 'Just to put you at your ease. We're not ogres here, Sasha, whatever you may think.'

'To *put me at my ease*? What do you – oh, I get it. You want to use me as a guinea pig for your machine.'

Jo Swanwick shook her head. 'It's not a case of being a guinea pig, Sasha. There's no risk factor involved here at all – Jaws is perfectly safe. Using Jaws is simply the quickest and most efficient way to collect all the data that we need about you.'

'So if your machine's so perfect, why isn't it being used around the world? Do you want to keep it all to yourself?'

'Believe me, we're working for the good of humankind here. But look around you,' said Jo, waving an arm. 'At the moment, Jaws takes up an enormous amount of space – not to mention the fact that the equipment in this room, which comprises a single system, costs millions upon millions of pounds. While the system itself is perfect, for most medical facilities it would be an impossibility. We need to find ways to streamline it before releasing it on the open market.'

Sasha eyed the scanner dubiously. 'What if I don't want to go in there?'

'I'm afraid you don't have a choice,' her chaperon, who had been standing behind her, said.

'You mean, you'll *force* me?'

'You'll be sedated as you sleep and then brought here.' He shrugged. 'But we don't really like to do that. We prefer everything to be upfront, out in the open. Our visitors are human beings, after all.'

'Thank you for noticing,' said Sasha acidly; then she sighed. 'Okay, I'll do it. As long as you can promise me that it won't give me cancer. What do I do? Just lie on the bench?'

Jo Swanwick crossed the room and opened the drawer of a desk beneath a computer terminal, taking out a white cellophane-wrapped package. Pulling the cellophane off, she shook out what Sasha realised after a few moments was a white garment – a shapeless, knee-length, short-sleeved dress, made of what appeared to be waterproof fabric.

'You'll have to undress first,' she said, 'and put this on.'

'What – in front of all these people?'

'You can go behind the computer terminal there. It'll provide you with pretty good cover.'

Three minutes later Sasha emerged, feeling self-conscious, rustling as she walked. Jo Swanwick handed her a pair of black goggles and told her to put them on, then instructed her to lie face-up on the bench, hands by her sides, feet uncrossed.

'Just relax,' she said. 'This won't take long. Are you ready?'

'As I'll ever be,' said Sasha.

After a few moments there was a humming sound and the bench started to retract into the scanner. Sasha swallowed, trying not to think of coffins disappearing through red curtains into crematoria ovens. It was very bright inside the scanner, a harsh, intimidating brightness that made her screw up her eyes despite the goggles. Sasha had never suffered from claustrophobia, but all at once she was uncomfortably aware that she could neither sit up nor get out of the belly of this thing without help.

Light played over her for what felt like an hour or more. Sasha tried to empty her mind, to think of other things – pleasant things – but all that did was remind her of what she had been forced to leave behind, and what she might never recapture.

Eventually the bench slid out of the pod of light and into what, until her eyes adjusted behind her dark goggles, seemed like the pitch blackness of the laboratory. Sasha sucked in air, though there had been no lessening of oxygen inside the scanner, and sat up gratefully. As she took the goggles off, screwing up her eyes, she was aware that her entire body, from her scalp to her toes, was tingling.

'How do you feel?' Jo Swanwick asked.

'Like I've just taken a very cold shower in a very hot country. Or vice versa.'

'Don't worry – that'll pass.'

Sasha crossed to a black typing chair over which her clothes had been draped. 'Can I get dressed now, or is there something else you want to test out on me?'

Jo Swanwick smiled. 'Well, there is our new bowel irrigation system – it's all done with lasers . . . No, I'm joking. You can get dressed.' A few minutes later, when Sasha and her American chaperon were ready to leave, the red-haired woman briefly took her hand. 'Bye for now, Sasha. See you around.'

'Not for long, I hope,' Sasha replied, and felt uncomfortable at the look that she received in response. It was sympathetic and knowing, the look of a relative who knows a loved one is dying and is finding it hard to keep the truth from them.

Then the red-haired woman turned quickly away, and Sasha had to resist an urge to grab her, to demand to know what Jo Swanwick had been told about her. Her chaperon seemed to read the situation, and moved swiftly to defuse it. 'Let's go, Sasha,' he said firmly.

Once they were back out in the corridor, Sasha said, with a brightness she didn't feel, 'What shall we go on now? The log flume? The ghost train?'

The man smiled his bland, indulgent smile. 'Now you have an appointment with Dr Starkey.'

'Who's Dr Starkey?'

'You'll see.'

He led her away from the scanner room and the lifts to the end of the corridor, turning left where it branched. Sasha wondered what she would see around the corner – some sort of hi-tech nerve centre perhaps, like something out of a James Bond movie. However, the reality was far more mundane. Around the corner was merely a slightly narrower corridor, double doors replaced by single ones, like in the corridor where her room was located, deeper in the complex.

This corridor also branched into two. Coming to the end of it her chaperon led her to the right, halting outside a white unmarked door.

'How do you find your way around down here?' Sasha asked. 'A trial of breadcrumbs.'

'It's a maze, I admit, but you get the hang of it after a while.' He performed the usual security routine and opened the door.

The area they entered was small and poky; more of a viewing gallery than a room. It contained a portable EEG machine sitting atop a trolley on castors; the machine was little more than a metal box inset with a few dials and a small screen. Four leads tipped by suction pads trailed from a single jack plug in the back of the machine.

The opposite wall was composed almost entirely of tinted glass. It overlooked a larger, brighter room, where a chimpanzee squatted forlornly in a small, square cage. In front of the chimpanzee, out of its reach, was a table on which sat three large tupperware containers, each full of chopped-up fruit. The containers were identical aside from the colour-coded labels affixed to them – one blue, one red, one yellow.

'Take a seat,' her chaperon said. 'Dr Starkey will be along in a minute.'

Sasha sat. Miserably she watched the chimpanzee, which was staring at the bowls of fruit. For the most part the creature was patient, though now and then it threw its arms above its head in apparent frustration and uttered a shrill, chittering cry.

They had been waiting for the best part of ten minutes when the door buzzed and opened and a white-coated man entered. He was thin, with a balding head, pinched features and small, round spectacles. He had a crusty stain that looked suspiciously like baked-bean juice on his lapel; his breast pocket bristled with different coloured biros, reminding Sasha of geeky Mr Rhodes, Head of Physics at her secondary school.

'Good morning, good morning,' he said, his voice a nasal whine. 'And how are we today?'

The question was so dismissive that Sasha didn't even bother answering it. The man who Sasha assumed was Dr Starkey spent a few minutes checking the machine, then abruptly clapped his hands together.

'Right. Today we're going to play a little game!'

'Whoopee,' said Sasha drily.

'It's a brain-power game,' he went on, undeterred. 'I'm going to set you a little task and monitor the readings on this screen here. Just to make sure that the old noddle is in good working order.' He gave a small, tight smile.

'And afterwards, if I'm a very good girl, can I have jelly and ice cream?' Sasha said.

Starkey smiled vaguely, seemingly unaware of the sarcasm fuelling her riposte. He wheeled the trolley over. 'I'm going to have to wet these little suckers and stick them to your head. Don't worry – it won't hurt.'

Starkey wet the suckers with a scrap of sponge which had been sitting in a small tray of water. He attached two to Sasha's forehead and two to the sides of her temples.

'Now,' he said, 'what I want you to do is to try to assert your will over the monkey.'

'Why?'

'I've told you – it's a game.' It was the first time he had responded to her questions and comments directly.

Sasha was silent for a moment, then she sighed. 'All right – if it'll make you happy. What exactly do you want me to do?'

'In three minutes' time the door of the cage will open and the monkey will be released. Before that happens, using the power of your mind, I want you to try to convince it to eat only out of the blue bowl. Try to make the creature believe that the contents of the other two bowls are tainted in some way – poisoned, perhaps.'

Sasha flashed the bespectacled man a condescending look. 'I bet you don't get out much, do you?'

He ignored her. 'We're wasting time. You have approximately two minutes and forty seconds left.'

'All right, all right. Keep your hair on.'

Starkey frowned and his hand jerked instinctively upwards. Recognising that she had finally hit a raw nerve, Sasha felt a little surge of victory, which increased when she glanced at her American chaperon and saw that he was trying hard to conceal a smile.

She placed her elbows on the table and stared at the chimpanzee, thinking: *Blue bowl – eat only out of the blue bowl*, imagining the others full of maggots and rot. It occurred to her to wonder why she was co-operating, but in spite of herself she found she was actually interested in the experiment; she wanted to know if, given enough time and concentration, it *was* possible to telepathically influence the behaviour of another creature. The supernatural, psychic powers – all that stuff – was an area in which, like many people, she had a passing interest – certainly she was open-minded enough not to dismiss such things out of hand. What was perhaps more interesting in this case, however, was that the authorities here seemed prepared to take the subject seriously

– unless of course they had some hidden agenda, and all this was merely a smoke-screen for something more sinister.

She tried to put her doubts and speculations out of her head and to concentrate solely on the matter in hand. *Blue bowl*, she thought, *blue bowl, blue bowl, blue bowl, blue bowl . . .*

Abruptly, with the harsh sound of steel sliding on steel, the cage door sprang upwards into a slot in the ceiling.

The chimp flinched back for a moment; then, evidently realising there was no immediate threat, it leaned forwards, sniffing the air. Apparently satisfied, it bunched its hands into bony-knuckled fists and placed them on the floor, shifted its weight on to its long arms and moved slowly out of the cage, looking around.

Sasha, observing its tentative progress, was surprised at how tense she was. Silently, completely oblivious to the two men behind her, she was still mentally jabbering the same two words, like an incantation. She watched the monkey move over to the table and then agilely clamber up on to it. The creature regarded the contents of the three bowls, as if deliberately letting the tension build. Then it thrust its hand into the yellow-marked bowl, selected a chunk of melon and began to eat.

'Bugger,' said Sasha. She sat back, genuinely disappointed. She watched the chimp eating for a moment, delving into all three of the bowls, selecting choice morsels from each. Then she turned to Dr Starkey.

'I failed,' she said, and shrugged. 'But what did you expect? You can't make someone do something just by thinking about it, can you?'

Starkey was too busy examining results on the readout screen to answer her, but her chaperon smiled blandly.

'No,' he said, his voice as unconvincing as the expression on his face, 'you can't.'

251

Forty

The building was derelict. Perhaps it had once been a warehouse, or a factory. There was rubble and debris everywhere, fallen spars and twisted girders, rain running down the black walls and drooling through holes in the roof, making the place slippery, slimy, mossy as a forest. Nick's stomach was cramped with fear; he moved in a crouch, dodging from one piece of flimsy cover to another. Something was pursuing him, though he wasn't sure what until he ducked down behind something – a box or an old workbench – and looked back the way he had come.

On the far side of the factory floor was an arch, like the entrance to a castle or cathedral, black dripping chains dangling from its apex, twisting and chinking in the wind. An icy bluish light was pouring through the arch, accompanied by slashing rain, like a ceaseless volley of tiny silver arrows.

As Nick watched, a shadow appeared, sliding across the uneven carpet of light like a dark stain. His breath froze in his throat as, padding in the wake of its own shadow, came a dog. The dog was large and vicious-looking, its thick fur matted and filthy; but it was none of these things that caused terror to curl like a foetus in Nick's belly. In a way he couldn't define, but with an intensity both raw and dream-like, the dog seemed to radiate evil.

Nick shrank down, the moisture draining from his mouth, the strength seeping from his limbs. Perhaps it was this tiny move-ment that alerted the dog, for it moved its head slowly, almost robotically, in his direction. Its eyes were small and black as pebbles and should not even have been visible in this light and at this distance, but they seemed to burn into him, through him. It stretched its jaws wide, baring its teeth, and then it roared like a

252

lion, fire gouting from its mouth. As the fire curled into the air and disappeared with a hiss, the dog began to gallop across the factory floor towards him.

Seized by panic, Nick turned to scramble away, but for some reason he could not get to his feet. He simply lost balance and fell down again, his hands splatting on the cold, slimy ground. He could hear the dog behind him, its galloping feet, its panting breath.

And then he felt its jaws clamp around his upper arm and he screamed and woke up.

The first thing he saw when he opened his eyes was someone lunging towards him. He threw up his arms and flinched before realising that the figure was not jumping towards him but away from him, presumably in surprise when he had cried out. As recent memory muscled its way back into his head, attempting to oust the vivid panic of his dream, he recognised the figure as the blond-haired man, Ray, his eyes so wide they seemed magnified.

'Christ! Are you all right?' Ray gasped.

Nick's body relaxed slowly; he let out a long sigh. 'Yes – yes, I'm fine. You gave me a shock, that's all. I was . . . was dreaming.'

'Must have been a doozy,' Ray said. 'And as for *me* giving *you* a shock . . .'

Nick sat up and rubbed his face as if the memory of the dream still adhered to his skin like grime. 'What time is it?'

'Almost eleven.'

'In the morning?'

'Unless I'm much mistaken.'

Nick blew out another sigh and tried to get his head together. Lately he had been sleeping at such weird times and in such weird places that, physically, he felt almost as though he were jet-lagged. However, it was not his physical condition that concerned him so much as his mental one. His sense of his own identity was like a wild horse that his rodeo-rider of a mind was trying desperately to cling on to. Not only was the present confusing and his future uncertain, but he was now being asked to accept a past that he had no recollection of, that seemed to make a mockery out of his whole existence up to this point. He felt rootless; betrayed; cast adrift from all that he knew. Last night he had lain awake for so long with thoughts whirling through his head that it had felt like his skull was ready to explode.

In the end he had got up and turned on the light, and had only resisted the almost overwhelming temptation of the drinks cabinet because he knew if he started drinking he would never stop. Instead he had switched on the TV, flicking through the stations until he found a twenty-four-hour sports channel showing a football match between Brazil and Peru. That at least had distracted him enough to enable him to clear his mind and, eventually, fall asleep. But now he was awake, and already he could feel the confusion, the bewilderment starting to crowd in on him once again.

One thing at a time, he told himself firmly, and asked, 'Is there somewhere I can get a shower? I could also do with a change of clothes – though I don't suppose there's any chance of that.'

'A shower I can help you with. As for the clothes, I'm afraid you'll have to make do for the time being. Give us a list and we'll send someone to get you what you want.'

Nick gathered up his clothes and followed Ray out of the room. Directly across the landing was a door which the young man opened to reveal a cramped space containing a wash-basin and a shower cubicle. There was soap and shampoo and fresh towels, shaving equipment, a tube of toothpaste and a toothbrush still in its cellophane wrapper.

'Guest bathroom,' Ray said, and added with a smile, 'I don't want to rush you, but Mr Hallett would like to see you as soon as you're ready.'

'What about?'

'I believe he has some news for you.'

'What sort of news?'

'I'm not sure.'

'I'll be out in ten minutes.'

In fact he was out in seven, steam billowing around him as he opened the door, his face flushed with heat.

'After you,' Ray said, and the two of them made their way to what Nick was beginning to think of as Hallett's inner sanctum. Hallett was sitting in his accustomed place before the trophy cabinet, eating his breakfast from a silver service laid out on a spotless white cloth that had been draped over the round table. There were scrambled eggs, toast and preserves, a jug of what looked like grapefruit juice and a steaming cafetiere from which rose the rich aroma of fresh coffee. Hallett's clothes were protected by a large white napkin, tucked flamboyantly into his shirt collar at the throat. It looked comical but Nick would never have dared laugh. He wondered whether Hallett ever moved from this room, or indeed from his current position in front of the trophy cabinet. An image played in his mind of Mad Dog coming in to give his boss a sponge bath in his wheelchair, of Hallett sleeping with his head on the table. Then Nick remembered that Hallett would be able to read all these less than flattering thoughts in his mind if he so wished, and tried desperately to stifle them. To cover his embarrassment, he said, 'You wanted to see me?'

Hallett swallowed a mouthful of egg, then belched quietly. He waved to a place on his right that Nick presumed had been set for him. 'Yes, Nick, old son. Sit down. Have some breakfast.'

'Thanks,' Nick said, realising how hungry he was, 'I will.'

He sat and Hallett told him to help himself. As Nick began to eat, Hallett asked, 'Sleep well?'

'Not particularly,' Nick replied. 'Bad dreams.'

'Had a lot on your mind, I expect. Not that I was peeking.'

Nick smiled a little guiltily and glanced around to bring Ray in on the conversation, but the blond-haired man had made a quiet exit. Turning back to Hallett he said, 'Ray said you had some news for me.'

'Yes – I've heard one or two little titbits on the grapevine.'

'Such as?'

'Why don't you finish your breakfast first? Then we'll talk.'

Nick frowned at Hallett. Though neither the man's manner nor his voice had changed, all at once he felt his appetite fading. 'I'd rather know now.'

Hallett sighed, but pushed his plate away, as if to indicate that he respected Nick's wishes. 'The news isn't good,' he said gruffly. 'Apparently there was some sort of incident yesterday, the upshot of which is that your daughter's mother is in hospital and your daughter and girlfriend have disappeared.'

'*Disappeared*?' said Nick. 'What do you mean?'

'What I say. Nobody knows where they are.'

'Well, they're probably just . . . lying low. Hiding somewhere.' Nick was trying to convince himself as much as Hallett.

'It's a possibility, but I doubt it. My boys are pretty good. If the women were holed up somewhere they'd know.'

'So what are you saying? That they've been kidnapped?'

255

'Looks that way.'

'But *why*?'

'At a rough guess I'd say to get to you.'

'Shit,' said Nick desperately. Feeling like a child – and all too aware that he sounded like one he said, 'What should I do?'

Hallett sipped coffee from a china cup that looked like a toy in his large, stub-fingered hand. Clearly this was all in a day's work to him. 'I can get a couple of my boys to run you to the hospital to speak to your ex.' He looked thoughtful for a moment, weighing up the risks of such a venture. 'We've already given the place a careful shufti. Should be safe enough.'

All at once Nick felt guilty. He had automatically prioritised the news of Sasha's and Jenna's disappearance and all but disregarded the fact that Linsey was in hospital.

'What happened to Linsey?' he asked.

Hallett, for once, looked almost sorrowful. 'We don't know exactly. But word is that she's blind.'

'*Blind?* How the hell did that happen?'

Hallett shook his head. 'Details are a bit hazy – but it seems like she might have done it to herself. Put her own eyes out.' He tutted, as if in disapproval.

Nick gaped in shock. '*Why?* Why would she do that?'

'Maybe she saw something that was too much for her to take. Or maybe she couldn't help herself.'

'What do you mean?'

Hallett gave Nick a look that was almost pitying. '*I* could make someone do that, Nick, if I wanted to. Think about it. The Illuminati have already rounded up some of us – maybe about half of us. They could be using those of us they do have as weapons.'

'Forcing them to attack people mentally, you mean?'

Hallett nodded.

Nick blew out air that felt as though it was hardening in his throat and wiped a palm back and forth across his forehead, trying to massage away the beginnings of a headache. 'But why attack Linsey? She's no threat to them.'

'Maybe she got in their way. Maybe they took it out on her because they couldn't get to you. Maybe they're letting you know they mean business. Or maybe they just wanted a bit of fun.'

'Fun?' repeated Nick, sickened.

'They're only possibilities. Even I don't know everything.'

'So I mean . . . is she blind as in . . . permanently?'

Hallett did not pull any punches. 'Sounds like a guide-dog and white-stick job.'

'Shit,' Nick breathed again. He had a cold, fluttery feeling in his stomach. 'This is all my fault.'

'How do you work that one out?'

'Well, if it wasn't for me, Linsey and Sasha and Jenna would all be fine. Getting on with their lives.'

'True, but you can't blame yourself for that, son. You didn't volunteer to be a guinea pig for those bastards. Everything that's happened is down to them. None of this is your doing. Don't let those fuckers make you feel guilty.'

Nick might have been touched by Hallett's words if he hadn't been so preoccupied with his concern for the three women.

'Is there any chance I could go and see Linsey now?' he asked hesitantly.

Hallett nodded. 'Of course, son.' He pulled a mobile phone out of his pocket. 'Mad Dog, could you step into my office, please?' He put the phone away. 'I'll send you out with Mad Dog and Sherman again – seeing as how you know them.' He made it sound as if Nick had built up a cosy and unbreakable rapport with the two men, as if they were capable of providing Nick with the emotional support he would need in the difficult times ahead.

Five minutes later Nick was sitting in what he guessed was the same car as yesterday. He couldn't be certain because he was once again wearing his blindfold. When Sherman had put the blindfold on him, Nick had said, a little tetchily, 'I'm not going to lead them to you if I get caught, you know. Whatever they do.'

'You might not have a choice, son,' Hallett replied. 'None of the others will be as good as me, but there're bound to be one or two who'll be able to take information out of your head as easily as if you'd handed them a written statement.'

Now, sitting in the car, Nick asked, 'Which hospital is Linsey in?'

'Stoke Newington,' replied Mad Dog.

'They *do* things in hospitals,' Sherman piped up ominously. 'Experiments.'

'Aw, man, don't start with that fucking shit again,' Mad Dog groaned.

Apart from Nick asking – and being granted – permission to take his blindfold off a few minutes later, the rest of the journey thankfully passed in silence. Sherman chose not to inflict any more of his thoeries on his passenger; perhaps even he sensed Nick's pain.

The hospital was modern and featureless, its pale walls greyed by a quarter-century of pollution. Mad Dog parked at the back and the three of them walked round to the entrance, Nick in the middle, feeling like a celebrity flanked by bodyguards.

Judging by the looks they received in the waiting room, his perception of this image was not misplaced. Self-consciously – wishing that Mad Dog would at least take off his shades – he walked up to the reception desk and asked a girl with blonde dreadlocks and a ring through her bottom lip which ward Linsey was in.

She directed him to the third floor; they took the lift. 'I don't trust lifts,' Sherman announced as they watched the lights climb slowly from one to three.

Mad Dog tutted. 'You don't trust nothing.'

'I trust the trees,' Sherman said sombrely.

Mad Dog looked at him. 'You're fucking crazy, man, you know that?'

They found the ward easily enough, Mad Dog and Sherman looking around constantly as if they expected trouble, their hands never far from their breast pockets. As they reached the double doors that led into the ward, Mad Dog peered around them. 'Me and Sherman'll wait out here,' he said, with surprising tact. 'Give you and your lady a chance to be alone.'

Nick was touched by Mad Dog's thoughtfulness, though his immediate reaction was a desire to tell Hallett's henchman that Linsey was not in fact his 'lady'. However, he left the words unsaid, feeling that they were uncharitable somehow, that empha-sising his lack of involvement with Linsey was denigrating her in some way. So he simply muttered, 'Thanks,' and walked into the ward, his stomach rolling with nerves.

If he didn't known that Linsey was blind he might not have recognised her; his gaze was only drawn to the woman in the sixth bed on the right because of the thick white pads taped over her eyes. But this couldn't possibly be Linsey, he thought. This woman – on her back with her mouth partly open as she slept, her

258

thin arms lying on top of the sheets that were pulled up to her chest – was far too old and frail.

Then he saw her blonde hair, dead and straw-like, straggling over the pillow, framing her face, and the truth hit him hard enough to make him stumble. Halfway up the ward's wide central aisle was a desk at which a plump nurse with black curls and skin so white it looked almost translucent was sitting drinking tea and making notes on a clipboard.

'Excuse me,' Nick said, keeping his voice low; the ward seemed to possess a hushed, reverential quality, like a church.

The nurse looked up and smiled helpfully. 'Yes?'

'Would it be possible to speak to Linsey Greene? The – er . . . lady in the bed there?'

'Are you from the police?' the nurse asked warily.

'No, I'm her . . . um . . . ex-husband,' Nick said, for the sake of convenience. 'Why do you ask?'

'I assumed you'd come to see if she was able to speak yet about the attack.'

'So she *was* attacked?' Nick said, his voice rising enough to earn a sharp look from a hatchet-faced woman in the bed opposite Linsey's, knitting what seemed destined to become a hideously bright-pink baby's cardigan.

The nurse frowned. 'Have you spoken to Mrs Greene's daughter?'

'Her name's Sasha and she's my daughter too. And no, I haven't – nobody seems to know where she is. That was one of the things I wanted to ask Linsey.'

The nurse grimaced apologetically. 'I hope you weren't relying on it. I don't think you'll get much out of her at the moment. She's under sedation, she has been ever since she got here. I'm not sure she even knows she's in hospital.'

'Well, would it be possible just to sit with her for a bit? I don't know when I'll be able to come again.'

The nurse smiled in approval. 'Of course.'

'Thanks,' said Nick. He hesitated. 'Have you any idea who attacked her?'

'No. To be honest we don't even know whether she *was* attacked, or whether her injuries were self-inflicted. Your daughter didn't seem to know either.'

'Was it you who spoke to Sasha?'

259

'Yes, but only briefly. She was in a bit of a state – as you can imagine.'

'What did she say happened?'

The nurse hesitated. 'How much do you already know?'

'All I've been told is that Linsey's blind and it might be permanent.'

'That's right. It seems that your ex-wife and daughter were together in a taxi when your ex-wife got out and ran off for no apparent reason. It took your daughter a while to find her; when she finally did so either she'd inflicted considerable damage to her own eyes – or somebody else had.'

Nick winced. He wanted to ask how the injuries had been inflicted, but couldn't think of a way of phrasing it without the question sounding ghoulish. Instead he asked, 'When was she brought in?'

'Yesterday. Late morning. Your daughter stayed with her for about an hour, then she left. She said she'd come back later, but she never did.' The nurse sounded a little reproachful.

'Okay,' said Nick. 'Thanks for your help. I'll go and sit with her now.'

He crossed to the bed, unable to prevent his mind filling with sickening images of sharp objects being rammed savagely into eyeballs – knives, sticks, fingers. He couldn't imagine having to survive without his sight. He thought he'd rather die than go blind.

He sat in the chair next to the bed, hesitated for a moment, then took Linsey's hand. It was limp and cold, bony and light, making him think of a chicken's foot. He felt a thickening in his throat and swallowed to clear it. In the bed Linsey was breathing shallowly, her chest barely moving. Nick tried to remember a time when they'd liked each other enough to sleep together, and couldn't. To his shame he couldn't even remember the night that Sasha had been conceived. He had probably been out of his head at the time.

Eventually he managed to clear his throat enough to murmur her name. She didn't respond, so he spoke it louder, squeezing her hand. She closed her mouth, moved her head slightly, then settled again. Nick leaned closer, smelling the faintly antiseptic odour of the gauzy pads over her eyes.

'Linsey? It's me, Nick. Can you hear me?'

No response.

He sat back, thinking that perhaps it might be best to go away

260

and leave her alone, let her sleep peacefully. After all, she would probably be in a lot of pain when she woke up, and she would certainly be in distress, so what right did he have to deny her a few more hours of blissful oblivion? But then again, if she had been fully aware of the situation, wouldn't she have wanted to help? He pictured himself sitting here at a later date, Linsey propped up by pillows, saying angrily, 'You should have woken me, Nick. You should have realised I'd always put Sasha above myself.' He leaned forward again; this time he spoke directly into her ear. 'Linsey, where's Sasha?'

This time she moved her head from side to side, a groaning sound coming from deep in her throat. Her mouth opened and she murmured a few words. Nick leaned further forward, but all he could hear were words which sounded like 'spirit' and 'horse'. He resisted the urge to shake her; instead he muttered with even more urgency, 'Sasha, Linsey. Where's Sasha?'

Linsey merely sighed, then settled back into sleep. Nick sighed too, in frustration, and stood up. He looked down at her frail, sleeping form, then bent forward and kissed her gently on the forehead. 'Tell her I was here, would you, when she wakes up?' he said to the nurse. She nodded and he walked out of the ward.

When he got back he asked if he could see Hallett and was led once again into the inner sanctum. He was not surprised to see the man sitting in his usual place. There was a laptop computer on the desk in front of him, to the left of which a mobile phone sat like a paperweight on top of a sheaf of paperwork. Classical music was playing softly in the background.

'Berlioz,' Hallett said. 'Helps me to concentrate. I don't suppose you're much of a classical man, are you, Nick?'

'Not really,' said Nick curtly.

Hallett nodded slowly. 'I don't need to read your mind to tell that you want to get down to business. Well, sit down, son, sit down. I was just catching up on the accounts, but they can wait.'

Nick sat. 'I went to see Linsey – but you know that.'

Hallett nodded.

'You said you thought she might have been attacked mentally, forced to do what she did.'

'That's right.'

'Well, why didn't they attack *me* like that? If it's me they're after, why go for her?'

261

'For a start, they wouldn't want you to damage yourself like Linsey did,' Hallett said. 'They'd want you intact. But I don't think that's the real reason. What I reckon is that those of us they do have up at the Chicken House are still pretty rough and ready. The Illuminati'll be training them up, but at the moment our boys and girls'll only be using a fraction of their real power. Their abilities'll be rusty because they haven't been properly used for years. Chances are the Illuminati can't yet get through the barriers you've got built into your brain, barriers which they originally put there. That's what they were trying to do the other night when you got that phone call – unlock the barriers. Only they fucked up, didn't they? Some of us they got through to, some of us they sent fucking mad – like that bloke who killed his wife and little kid and then blew his own head off. And some of us – like you – managed to resist.'

'And what about you?' said Nick.

'Ah, well, I went off too early, didn't I? Thanks to this lot –' he banged the arm of his wheelchair – 'everything they'd put into my head to stop me finding out about myself just fell apart. Since then I've managed to use their fucking barriers and build new ones of my own around them. They can't get to me now. I'm too strong for the fuckers.'

'And in the meantime, while they've been trying to get to us, innocent people like Linsey and Michael Mercy's family have been caught in the crossfire.'

Hallett nodded. 'That's the way I see it. They're scum, Nick. Men without honour.'

Nick took a deep breath. 'I want you to do me a favour. I want you to help me get Sasha and Jenna back.'

Hallett was silent for a moment. Then he said, 'How?'

'Well ... you've got men, resources, knowledge ...' Nick tailed off. Hallett was shaking his head.

'Sorry, son. I can't do it.'

'Why not?'

'Because it's not worth my while. I don't mind sticking my neck out for you, getting you away and setting you up somewhere beyond their reach – I've done it before and I'll probably do it again. But I'm not going to start a war against these people.'

Nick sighed. 'I suppose I knew you were going to say that. Which means that if I'm going to have any chance of getting

262

Sasha and Jenna back, there's only one thing I can do. Isn't there?'

'Is there?'

'Like you said before, they've only been taken to get to me. They're the bait and I'm the big fish.' He gave a hollow laugh. 'The way I see it, I'd never be able to live with myself if I didn't take the bait.'

Forty-One

'More coffee, Mr Finch?'

Nick had been looking out at the clouds, clumped like bubble-bath foam on the watery sky below him, and thinking about the first time he had been on a plane. He must have been five or six years old – which now made him wonder, briefly, whether the flight had ever actually taken place. He supposed, if he chose to accept Hallett's version of the truth, it would always be like this from now on: trying to work out which of his earliest memories were based on actual events and which were mere mental poly-filla, fabrications to block up the section of his mind from which his real memories had been gouged.

But no – he *had* been on that flight, he was sure of it. He and his parents had gone on a once-in-a-lifetime trip to see his mother's sister in Hong Kong. Aunt Dilys had stayed there until her death in 1986 – the year that Nick had been released from prison. Uncle Len, her husband – who Nick remembered as a fat, jolly man with thick-lensed spectacles and a permanently sweaty face – had moved back to England so quickly after the funeral that Nick had wondered whether he'd been hankering after the old country for years. He now lived in Sidcup, though he and Nick only commu-nicated via annual Christmas cards. Nick wondered whether Uncle Len knew anything about the circumstances surrounding his adoption. As he had been abroad at the time, probably not.

The young stewardess was still waiting patiently, cafetiere poised.

'Oh . . . yes, please,' said Nick. 'Sorry – I was miles away. I've had a lot to think about these past few days.'

'That's quite all right, sir,' the girl said, flashing a generous smile that displayed the requisite number of perfect teeth and just a hint of healthy pink gums. She was tall and willowy and beautiful, her hair glossy and vibrant as a shampoo ad.

The girl poured his coffee, smiled at him again and moved on. As he sipped, Nick tried to compose himself mentally; events had moved so quickly since that morning, when he had decided to turn his back on the protection offered by Hallett, that his thoughts felt like ball-bearings pinging around the pinball machine of his skull.

Had Hallett been telling him the whole truth? The evidence he had offered had been strong, yet now he was away from the man's influence Nick found that he didn't want to believe his story, and not only because he had been treated so courteously since giving himself up. Accepting that what Hallett had told him was true was like having the rug pulled out from under his feet. Even through the tough times, Nick had always retained a strong sense of identity, of who he was and where he came from, but now Hallett was asking him to accept that his whole life had been a lie. Nick didn't *want* to be the offspring of some unknown Russian peasant; he didn't *want* his parents to have adopted him; he didn't *want* to be part of a system which experimented on children and treated people like laboratory rats.

Mad Dog had taken Nick – blindfolded naturally – to the centre of London and had dropped him off in Tottenham Court Road, even calling out, 'Good luck, man,' before speeding away. Nick had gone straight back to the police station before he could have second thoughts and had asked to speak to DI Osgood. Osgood had been astonished to see him, and politely, even sympathetically, he and DS Summers had encouraged Nick to give them as much information about his kidnappers as he could. But Nick had stuck faithfully to the story he had agreed with Hallett. He told them he had spent the past twenty-four hours lying on a bed, bound and blindfolded, that occasionally people had come into the room but no one had spoken to him. Eventually he had been carried some distance, down what he thought were several flights of stairs, to a car. He had been put into the boot and then his kidnappers had driven away with him. The journey had lasted what felt like an hour or more, but may have been less than that. At last the car had stopped and his kidnappers had taken him out of the boot and placed him on the ground. They had loosened his bonds, then got back into their car and driven away. By the time Nick had managed to untie himself completely and remove his blindfold they were gone. He had found himself on a deserted building site in Tooting Bec, whereupon he had made his way back to Tottenham Court Road.

He didn't know whether Osgood and Summers believed his story. He told it as simply as he could, resisting the urge to embellish it. They asked him many questions; some questions they asked several times. When Osgood asked repeatedly, whether he was *certain* he hadn't heard his kidnappers speak even so much as a word, Nick had looked him in the eye, surprised at how easy he found it, and had shaken his head. 'No.'

At last they seemed to accept his story. They asked if he wouldn't mind waiting for a few minutes and then went away, presumably to confer in private. Nick sat alone, thinking about the last words he and Hallett had spoken to one another. 'Are you going to let me go, even though I know your names?' he had asked boldly.

Hallett had smiled. 'You don't know our names, son. You don't know anything about us. We don't exist.'

Nick wondered exactly what Hallett had meant by that. If he meant he could somehow block the information in Nick's mind from anyone who might want to access it, then why couldn't he also have blocked Nick's knowledge of the location of his head-quarters? Perhaps he simply meant that he did not exist *officially*, that he and his men operated so far below (or above) the law, under assumed names or a variety of them, that they would prove impossible to track down.

Osgood and Summers were gone for twenty minutes. When they returned, Osgood placed a sealed pack of ham and tomato sandwiches, a Snickers bar and a Styrofoam cup of coffee in front of him like an offering.

'Here you go, Nick. Thought you might be hungry. Sorry to have kept you so long.'

'Thanks,' said Nick, but he left the food untouched.

'How are you feeling?' Summers asked.

'Fine.'

'Not hungry?'

'Not really. Thirsty, though,' he said, and peeled the lid off the coffee cup.

Osgood sat opposite him and leaned forward, placing his elbows on the table, meshing his fingers together.

Cosy-chat mode, thought Nick, sipping his coffee, which tasted not unlike creosote.

'You remember when you were here yesterday? You remember where we were going when you were taken?'

Nick nodded.

'Well, if you feel up to it we'd like to try again. I know you've been through a terrible ordeal, but it's partly because of that that we're rushing on this. It's important that we catch these men as quickly as possible.'

How much do they know? Nick thought. *And how much do they think I know?* A part of him wanted to call their bluff, to say, 'Look, I'm not stupid, I know you're planning to lead me into a trap, but I'm going to go along with you anyway because I want to see my daughter again.'

Instead he nodded. 'Okay,' he said wearily.

'The thing is,' Summers said, flashing a glance at Osgood, 'it's not just us – the police, I mean – who are dealing with this situation now. There are other . . . agencies involved. International agencies.'

She doesn't like this, Nick thought suddenly. *She's been ordered to hand me over, told what to say, but she doesn't like what's going on. It smells bad to her, offends her moral sensibilities. You can see it in her eyes, hear it in her voice.*

He said nothing, however, waiting for her to continue. It was Osgood who took up the reins.

'I know this is a lot to ask, Nick, but . . . do you think you can take some time off work?'

Nick shrugged. 'Suppose so.'

'You see, the thing is, we'd like you to work with us on this one if you can. We'd like to fly you out to meet some people, tell them what you know. We'll pay all your expenses, of course, and reimburse you for any loss of earnings during the period that you're away.'

'Okay.'

Osgood looked surprised, and relieved, at Nick's easy acceptance of the suggestion.

Summers, however, looked wary. 'Are you sure you don't want more time to think about it, Nick? I mean, considering what you've been through . . .'

Nick wondered whether perhaps he wasn't being just a little *too*

267

willing here. He said, 'I just want this nightmare over with. I'll do whatever I can to end it. But . . . can I ask a few questions?'

'Of course you can,' said Summers, back on track now, as if by refusing to be a totally passive victim, by showing at least a modicum of interest in his fate, Nick was somehow salving her conscience.

'How long will I be away for?'

'Not too long, hopefully,' said Osgood neutrally.

'Days? Weeks?'

'It's hard to say. Not too long,' he repeated.

'What I'd also like to know is, who are these "international agencies" you mentioned?'

This time Osgood paused before replying. Eventually he said, 'I'm afraid we can't tell you that. I'm sorry to be so vague, but what you've got to understand, Nick, is that this is a very delicate operation.'

'Don't worry,' said Nick blandly, 'I understand that very well.' He looked up and smiled. 'So where am I being flown to – or are you not allowed to tell me that either?'

Osgood smiled back at him; Summers stood uneasily by the door, looking embarrassed. Nick decided that, despite the situation, he quite liked her.

'There's a . . . I suppose you'd call it an installation. In Eastern Europe,' Osgood said. 'That's where the operation is being engineered from. Once you're safely there, you'll find out more about what's going on, I promise.'

I bet I will, thought Nick, but he merely shrugged. His instinct was to play dumb for as long as possible, to pretend to accept whatever half-baked bullshit they served him. 'Okay. So when can we go?'

'No time like the present,' said Summers. Though her tone seemed light, Nick didn't think that the bitterness he could detect beneath the surface of her words was merely in his imagination.

That conversation had taken place over five hours ago. Osgood and Summers had then driven Nick to a small private airfield in Kent, where he had been greeted by several young, well-spoken, tough-looking men in suits.

'Mr Finch,' their apparent spokesman had said, striding over and offering a hand for Nick to shake, 'thanks very much for coming. Your co-operation in this matter is much appreciated.'

268

'That's okay,' said Nick, wondering whether the men were members of the group that Hallett and Ray had told him about. The Illuminati.

The man – whose name was Reynolds – introduced his colleagues, then said, 'I'm told our plane will be ready in fifteen minutes. Can I get you anything in the meantime? The facilities aren't up to much here, I'm afraid, but I think we can run to tea and coffee.'

Osgood and Summers slipped quietly away, leaving Nick alone with the men. Less than half an hour later they were airborne. During the flight Nick was plied with food and drink and told not to hesitate to ask for anything that he required. There was even an in-flight movie, *Twelve Monkeys*, though he passed on this because he had already seen it. So well was he treated, in fact, that eventually he felt the hard edges of his doubt and cynicism being eroded away, felt uncertainty creeping in. By the time the plane began to descend prior to landing, he no longer knew who or what to believe.

Could Hallett have been lying to him after all? But if so, for what purpose? Certainly *some* aspects of his story were true: Nick had no doubt that the man possessed an awesome mental ability to influence others – he had felt the power himself. It was also true that there were no pictures of Nick and his parents together before he was five or six years old. How had Hallett known this? It couldn't have been by reading his mind; Nick hadn't realised it himself until Hallett and Ray had pointed it out. And if all the stuff about the Illuminati *was* a fabrication, then how had Hallett come by his powers? Was he some kind of genetic mutation, a premature jump forward to the next stage of man's evolutionary cycle?

Reject Hallett's story, outlandish though it was, and nothing else seemed to make sense. For instance, why had Hallett gone to the trouble of having Nick kidnapped only to let him go the next day? Perhaps he had heard of Nick's vision and, seeing him as a threat, had tried to recruit him to his cause. Perhaps he had subsequently let him go because, having met Nick, he realised he was not the danger he had envisaged.

So many ifs and buts; so many whose and whats and whys. Who, most importantly, had bugged his flat, beaten Sasha up, blinded Linsey, been responsible for the phone call that had nearly

269

driven him insane? Could it really have been his present courteous travelling companions or their superiors? Had it been Hallett? Or was it some third agency he was not yet aware of?

Another thing: he had gone along with this in the hope of finding Sasha and Jenna, or even of offering himself as a captive in exchange for their freedom; but what if they weren't waiting for him at the other end of the line? He had tried to ask the men if they knew of the women's whereabouts before getting on the plane, but Reynolds had held up his hands and smiled a friendly warning. 'Hey, Nick, no questions now if you don't mind, okay? It really is best if we leave all the talking until we get there.'

Because it distracted him from the confused jumble of his own thoughts, Nick was relieved, albeit apprehensive, when the plane sliced through the clouds and began to descend towards the earth. Swallowing to relieve the painful pressure in his ears, he looked out of the window. The sun was shining on what appeared to be endless miles of grey and craggy mountain ranges which jutted from sand that seemed to glow like copper. Where the hell were they – the Sahara Desert? Somewhere in Eastern Europe, Osgood had said. If so, then the barren landscape was an unsettling sight for the simple reason that it made Nick realise how little he knew about this part of the world. To him, Eastern Europe conjured up no doubt steretyped notions of drab buildings and a downtrodden workforce, food queues and secret police. He supposed he had imagined the 'installation' to be situated in the midst of a concrete urban sprawl – though with hindsight that would have been foolish, wouldn't it?

He didn't actually see the installation itself until they were almost down, and then not properly until the plane doors opened and he stepped out on to a set of clanking metal steps. Though he had been half-expecting it, the trappings of the place – the armed soldiers, the military hardware, the barbed-wire topped fences with the ditch in between – made him wonder what he had got himself into. If Hallett *had* been telling him the truth, how could he possibly hope to battle against all of this? Back in the police station in London, with a cup of coffee in front of him and life bustling along outside, Nick had perceived himself to be one step ahead of the opposition. Here, though, all that optimism and, yes, arrogance suddenly seemed to count for nothing. There would be no one to tell, nowhere to run to, if things suddenly turned bad.

And Hallett – if Hallett was his ally – was thousands of miles away.

Reynolds appeared behind him, casual and relaxed. 'Welcome to the Chicken House!'

'The Chicken House?' repeated Nick, remembering Hallett's story and thinking uncomfortably that another part of it at least was true.

'Just our pet name for it. On account of the fact that a lot of the people here are cooped up for weeks, even months, at a time. But don't let me put you off,' he said with a friendly grin. 'It's quite comfortable really. Come on, I'll take you over to the main complex.'

They descended the steps and began to walk across the sun-baked concrete towards a large, featureless, bunker-like structure which Nick estimated to be a good quarter-mile away. Reynolds took a pair of sunglasses from his pocket and put them on.

Reservoir Dogs, thought Nick, playing his mental movie game again. *Men In Black*. To stop the game becoming something more fundamental – a protective mantra which he didn't want to feel he needed – he resorted to chit-chat. 'I feel like a tourist who's arrived in the middle of nowhere without any luggage.'

Reynolds grinned. 'You'll be provided with all you could possibly need in the complex. In fact, with your permission, we could even fetch some of your own things from home and fly them out here for you.'

'There's no point doing that, is there?' said Nick quickly. 'I mean, it's not as though I'm going to be here for long, is it?'

With his shades on it was impossible to tell what Reynolds was thinking. But he avoided Nick's questions, and thus failed to provide him with the reassurance he craved. 'Just a suggestion, Nick. It would be no trouble.'

They walked across to the main complex, Nick feeling the heat of the sun on the back of his neck, its thick warmth weighing down his now very grubby clothes. But at least he was still moving freely, and at least Reynolds was still being warm and courteous – which had to be a good sign. After all, the people here presumably had no one looking over their shoulders. If Nick *was* to be treated as a prisoner – or, worse, a human guinea pig – they could just as easily have abandoned the charade and clapped him in irons the instant the plane touched down.

271

The huge steel doors fronting the main complex threw hard, bright, distorted reflections back at them as they approached. It wasn't until they were close that Nick noticed a smaller door with some kind of access panel and push-button keyboard attached to it.

'Where exactly is this place?' he asked. 'What country are we in?'

Reynolds turned, his manner still easy, nonchalant. 'Sorry, Nick, but I'm not allowed to tell you that. Security reasons. If too many people know too much about the complex, then our vulnerability to enemy attack increases. You do understand?'

'Oh, yeah, sure,' said Nick, nodding sagely.

'One thing I can tell you, though: there's good climbing in those mountains.' Reynolds pointed and instinctively Nick turned to look. When he turned back, Reynolds was placing the palm of his hand on the opaque panel, now glowing with a red light.

The door slid open and they walked through into an unfurnished ante-chamber with a pair of lift doors at the far end. There was a similar access panel here. Nick saw Reynolds take a keycard from his pocket and push it into a slot in the panel, then tap in an access code. When the plate lit up he placed his hand on it and the lift doors opened.

Moments later they were descending into the earth. Looking at the buttons numbered one to thirty-six, together with additional ones both above and below, making some fifty in all, Nick said wonderingly, 'This place must be enormous.'

'It is,' said Reynolds, taking off his sunglasses and putting them back in his jacket pocket. 'It descends three-quarters of a mile into the earth and there are forty miles of corridors – or so I'm told. It's an easy place to get lost in.'

Nick wondered whether his words were intended as a warning. 'I'll bet,' he said.

The lift buttons did not light up, nor was there any other display to indicate how far they had descended, though they seemed to sink for a long time. At last, however, the lift stopped and the doors opened. With a wave of his hand, Reynolds invited Nick to step into an utterly featureless corridor, the white walls punctuated only by evenly spaced closed doors.

'Very nice,' said Nick dubiously.

Reynolds looked apologetic. 'It's functional, I know, but there are so many projects going on here that the complex gobbles enough funds as it is. No point charging the taxpayer more just to make the place look pretty.'

'I suppose not,' said Nick as Reynolds turned left and began to lead the way down the corridor. For the next five minutes they walked along so many identical corridors, turning sometimes right, sometimes left, that Nick began to wonder whether he wasn't being deliberately led round in circles just to disorientate him. Finally, however, Reynolds stopped and indicated a door to his right. 'Here we are.'

As he attended to the security panel Nick said, a little apprehensively, 'So where's here?'

Reynolds placed his hand on the glowing panel; the door buzzed and he pushed it open. He held it wide. 'Nowhere special. Just a place to wait.'

Nick stepped in and looked around. The room had armchairs, a couple of small sofas made of squishy brown leather, and a large coffee table made of pale pine and strewn with magazines: *Time*, *Country Life*, *National Geographic*, *New Scientist*. It was like being at the dentist's, albeit an expensive one.

'What am I waiting for?' Nick asked.

' "Who" is more to the point,' said Reynolds. He flashed a sudden smile. 'If I tell you, it'll spoil the surprise. Just make yourself comfortable – I don't think you'll have too long to wait. If I don't see you again, have a pleasant stay.'

'You're not going?' said Nick, surprised.

'I have to. Things to do. I have to be back in England by this evening.'

Nick found he was a little dismayed. He had not exactly built up a rapport with Reynolds, but the man *was* his only link with home, which surely counted for something. 'Right. Well . . . thanks.'

'My pleasure,' said Reynolds, and left the room, the door buzzing as it closed behind him.

Nick left it for thirty seconds, then tried the door; predictably, it was locked. There was another door on the other side of the room and he tried that too, with the same result. In each corner of the ceiling a small security camera peered down at him. Nick gave one of them a self-conscious grin and sat down in an armchair. He sat in silence for a minute or so, his hands folded in his lap, then began to leaf through a copy of *Time*. He wished that something would happen.

Although he had specifically been waiting for it, when the door on the far side of the room buzzed several minutes later it made him jump. He put down his magazine and looked up as the door opened. When Sasha walked in, with Jenna behind her, his heart leaped.

Sasha looked at him and stopped dead, her bloodshot eyes widening as much as her still swollen lids would allow. Then she was rushing towards him and he was rising from the sofa, holding out his arms to embrace her. Sasha threw her own arms around him with such force that it almost knocked him down again.

Nick held her tightly for several seconds, his face buried in her blonde corkscrew curls, her face pressed against his chest. He stroked her hair and then, tenderly, her face, his fingers coming away wet from her bruised cheeks. He tried to speak her name, to tell her not to cry, but his throat felt as though there were a rock stuffed in it. He looked up at Jenna and gave her a smile to let her know he hadn't forgotten her, that he was delighted to see her too. But Jenna didn't reciprocate. Nick noticed that, oddly, she was dressed more formally than usual, in a blue jacket and skirt and white blouse. She seemed to appraise the reunion of father and daughter almost coolly, as if it were something to be tolerated, even endured. Nick wondered whether she was jealous of the closeness between him and Sasha; or perhaps she was simply angry at him for getting her into this mess.

It was Sasha who spoke first. 'Oh, Dad,' she moaned, 'they got you too.'

He cleared his throat and disengaged himself from her so that he could look into her face. 'No one *got* me, Sash,' he said. 'I came out of choice, hoping you and Jenna would be here, and you are. How did you two get here?'

Sasha twisted away from him, and for a moment Nick wondered what he had said to make her angry before realising that her anger was directed at Jenna. '*She* made me come.'

'*Made* you? I don't understand.'

'She's one of them, Dad. She was stringing you along all the time. She took me to a house where she said we were supposed to be meeting DI Baker, but when we got there, two of her thugs were waiting for me, pointing guns at my head. When I turned

274

round, *she* was pointing a gun at me too. She made me get into a car and we drove to this airfield in the middle of nowhere where there was a plane waiting to fly us out here. They've been keeping me a prisoner, Dad. And now that you're here, you'll be one too.'

For a moment Nick was so stunned that he could think of nothing to say. It was Jenna herself who, with a half-amused expression, confirmed Sasha's accusation. 'You're hardly a prisoner, Sasha.'

'Oh, and what would you call it?' Sasha retorted. 'You lock me in a room all day, and only let me out so you can do experiments on me.'

'*Experiments*?' exclaimed Nick.

'She's exaggerating,' said Jenna drily. 'She has an extremely comfortable suite; naturally we have to lock the doors because security is of the utmost importance here. As for experiments, we have asked Sasha to take part in several harmless mental tests, and she has complied.'

'Is this true?' asked Nick.

Sasha looked momentarily nonplussed. 'Well, yes – but I've only complied because I'm scared of what they'll do to me if I don't.'

'Oh, really?' said Jenna, smiling.

'Yes, *really*,' snapped Sasha. 'Don't tell me you wouldn't have shot me if I'd tried to escape back at the house?'

'Of course we wouldn't have shot you. We used the method we did simply because it was the quickest and most efficient way of getting you here.'

'That's bollocks and you know it,' Sasha said. 'Besides, it doesn't alter the fact that you betrayed us. You lied to Dad, pretended to like him – when all you were really doing was drawing him into your web like a fucking black widow spider.'

It was the first time Nick had heard Sasha use the word 'fuck'; even in these circumstances, it startled him a little. It was silly; anyone else and he wouldn't have batted an eyelid. But this was his daughter. However, he let it go. He had a bigger hurt to face.

'How could you do it?' he said to Jenna. He was unable to keep his voice from sounding plaintive. 'I really liked you.'

'I liked you too. I *do* like you,' Jenna said, though there was no warmth in the words.

'You *slept* with me,' said Nick.

275

'So?'

'What do you mean, *so*? I suppose you're going to tell me it was just part of your job, that it meant no more to you than filing a report.'

Jenna raised her eyebrows. Perhaps, cold as she was, she honestly didn't know why he was making a fuss. 'Well, yes, it *was* part of my job. But I'm not saying it wasn't pleasant.'

'Oh, thanks a lot.'

'There's no point talking to her, Dad. She's got no feelings,' said Sasha passionately.

Jenna shook her head. 'Why do you keep insisting on seeing me as the enemy?'

'Because you *are* the enemy,' Sasha snapped back. 'Maybe it's just me being picky, but I never seem to get on with people who point guns at me and lock me up.'

'I've already explained that we had a very delicate situation to deal with, that extreme measures were called for.'

'Measures like doing something to my mum's brain so that she gouged her own eyes out, you mean?'

Jenna sighed as if she found the subject tiresome. 'As I have already explained to you, Sasha, that was nothing to do with us.'

'Bollocks!'

'Believe what you like, but there is another faction involved here, one whose methods are more ruthless than ours. That's why we couldn't waste time, indulge in long-drawn-out explanations, try to persuade you of the necessity of our actions. To ensure your safety, we needed to get you here as quickly as we could.'

'And what about DI Baker? And the journalist that you were supposed to have met? What about *their* safety?'

'I have no knowledge of their present whereabouts,' said Jenna, deadpan. '*My* priority was to ensure the safety of you and your father.'

Sasha shook her head fiercely. 'You're lying! We don't even know *why* we should be in danger, or why you've brought us all the way out here—'

'I think I know,' Nick interrupted.

Sasha looked at him. 'Do you?'

'Yes,' said Nick, and turned to Jenna. 'Are you a member of the Illuminati, or do you just work for them?'

There was an instant of shock on Jenna's face, then it was gone. 'I don't know what you mean.'

'Yes you do. Oh, I know you can't have been in there right at the beginning, but you know all about the Genesis Project, don't you? Well, I've got news for you, Jenna – so do I.'

'I wish *I* did,' said Sasha indignantly.

'What would you say,' Nick said to his daughter, 'if I were to tell you that you were half-Russian?'

Jenna's face was set like stone.

'I'd say, what the hell are you talking about, Dad?'

Quickly Nick told her the story that Hallett had told him, though naturally he omitted the part about Hallett himself. Throughout the account, Sasha's expression gradually became more incredulous.

'Is this for real, Dad?' she said finally.

He raised his hands. 'I know how you feel, believe me. I felt the same as you at first. But I've . . . seen stuff. I've had enough evidence to believe that what I'm telling you is true.'

'So you're . . . what . . . some sort of psychic?'

'Some sort. Apparently,' said Nick, and shrugged a little sheepishly. 'It's all repressed, though. At the moment I feel just like everybody else.'

'I need to sit down,' Sasha said weakly and plumped heavily on to one of the sofas. She put a hand on either side of her skull as if her brain could hardly contain the incredible information that it was being asked to accept. 'I can't get my head round this. I feel like I'm stuck in an *X-Files* episode.'

'I'm sorry,' Nick said, and moved forward to place a hand on her shoulder; she covered it with her own hand. 'And I'm sorry you and Linsey got dragged into this because of me. I went to see Linsey in hospital, but she was asleep. Sedated. I didn't get the chance to talk to her.'

Sasha was silent for a few moments. Then she said, 'It's not your fault, Dad. You're as much a victim as me and Mum. It's that bitch and whoever she works for that's to blame.'

Nick looked at Jenna; the woman rolled her eyes briefly, as if she found Sasha's continual hostility tedious in the extreme. 'You haven't said anything for a while,' Nick said angrily. 'Aren't you going to tell me that the story I've just told Sasha is the biggest load of crap you've ever heard?'

277

Jenna shook her head coolly. 'No, Nick, I'm not. Now that I've accomplished my mission and got you here safely, there's no reason why I should lie to you. I'd be very interested to know where you got your information from, though.'

'You forget,' Nick said, grinning, 'I'm psychic.'

'He shoots, he scores,' said Sasha with admiration. 'So let me get this straight. The reason we're all here is because something's starting to go wrong with this Genesis experiment which took place years ago, and that's why these Illuminati people are reeling you all in like fish?'

'Why don't you ask Jenna?'

Sasha looked at Jenna. 'Well?'

Jenna remained calm. 'Yes, it's true – the bare facts at any rate. Though you do have a rather interesting slant on events, Nick.'

'Do I? In what way?'

Jenna gestured at the sofas and chairs. 'Why don't we both sit down? All this standing up is rather confrontational, don't you think?'

Nick shrugged. 'Whatever you want.' He sat next to Sasha on the sofa. She wrapped both her hands tightly around his left arm, as if afraid he might disappear. Jenna sat in the armchair that Nick had previously occupied and crossed her legs gracefully.

'You were saying?' Sasha said pointedly.

'What you both seem to have overlooked,' Jenna said, 'is that if it hadn't been for the intervention of several allied governments back in the nineteen-sixties, neither of you would have been here today. As a child, Nick, if you hadn't remained in your village and starved to death, you would have been taken to South America or the Far East where you would have been sold into slavery or prostitution. Or worse.

'What the British government and its allies did, in effect, was to rescue you from a fate worse than death. Believe me, the ethics of this situation were discussed at great length before any action was taken. There was some concern over the issue of human beings – and more especially children – being purchased like so much merchandise, but it was ultimately decided that the end would justify the means.'

'Decided by who?' Sasha butted in.

'By representatives of the governments involved.'

'By yourselves, you mean? By power-mad egomaniacs with no scruples who just wanted to get one over on the enemy.'

'That's rather a hysterical reaction, Sasha. I would have expected more subtlety from someone with your intelligence.'

'Don't patronise me,' Sasha retorted. 'I can see right through you. If you were such philanthropists, why didn't you just buy *all* the children being offered for sale and give them new lives in the West? Or, better still, why didn't you let the general public know what was happening and, together with your so-called allies, rally your forces to do something to stop what was going on?'

'It wasn't practical,' said Jenna.

'Oh, why not? No profit in it?'

For the first time Jenna showed a flash of anger. 'What would you have had us do? Get together with the Americans and go storming into Soviet territory just to put a stop to the unpleasant but relatively minor operations of Russia's criminal underworld? In the political climate of the time, such an action would have caused World War Three, you silly little girl.'

'Fuck you!' snarled Sasha, her body tensing as if she were about to leap at Jenna. Nick grabbed her arm before she could.

'Hey, let's calm down,' he said. After a moment of simmering silence he nodded to Jenna. 'Go on.'

'The children we took were treated well,' she continued. 'They were not harmed, they were not distressed in any way by the research processes we subjected them to. In fact, they were extremely happy. They had never known such luxury, had never received such attention. They played together, and they developed warm and loving relationships with many of the staff, whom they viewed as surrogate mothers and fathers. We explained to them exactly what we were trying to do and they were willing participants.'

'And in return for being rescued you messed up their brains,' said Sasha coldly. 'No offence, Dad.'

'Not intentionally,' said Jenna. 'At the time of the Genesis Project the long-term effects of somatic intervention coupled with psychological modification were not known. It was estimated that, given the delicate and painstaking approach employed by the research team, there would *be* no long-term effects. Sadly, however, this has not turned out to be the case.'

279

'So what are you saying?' said Nick. 'That the Genesis subjects are beginning to self-destruct?'

'Some of them, certainly.'

'And I suppose that has nothing to do with all that "endrant command" stuff?'

Jenna gave a small, almost wistful smile and blinked slowly. 'I'm afraid that was another miscalculation. The problem with the Genesis Project you see, Nick, was that it was too far ahead of its time. I'm not saying it wasn't an admirable – perhaps even an *incredible* – achievement, but with hindsight it becomes apparent that the project's originators, though many of them were leaders in their chosen fields, were, in certain areas, fumbling in the dark. Now, the "endrant command stuff", as you call it, was implanted as a safety valve. If the Genesis subjects suffered any unforeseen mental distress as a result of the modifications made to their minds, then the endrant command would be employed, the theory being that it would placate the subjects, make them calm and compliant.'

'Only it's had the opposite effect, hasn't it?' said Nick. 'It's turned some of them into raving psychopaths.'

'That's hardly fair,' Jenna said. 'The endrant command was only employed because some of the subjects were already beginning to show a worrying tendency towards irrational and unpredictable behaviour. It was hoped that the endrant command would act as a calming influence. Unfortunately in some cases it's had rather a different effect.'

'So now,' said Nick, 'you've brought back those of us who are still in one piece to . . . what? Repair the damage? Or terminate the experiment?'

Jenna gave a half-smile. 'We've not brought you back simply to wipe you out, if that's what you mean. At the time, despite the eugenic breakthrough, the Genesis Project was considered not exactly a failure but only a relatively minor success. It was decided, after much deliberation, that the tiny steps forward that had been made did not justify continuation of the project, so it was abandoned. The children were implanted with false memories and found homes with carefully vetted childless couples in the British Isles, all of whom were given documentation "proving" the child to be their natural offspring, together with a generous financial allowance which would continue to be paid annually as long as the child was never given any inkling as to his or her true origins. We kept tabs on the children from a distance, but none of the abilities we had been trying to draw out of them seemed to be showing signs of manifesting themselves. And then this year, all at once, the dam burst. After thirty years, memory barriers began to break down and abilities to show themselves in all sorts of unpredictable ways. We don't know why. It could be the effect of the ageing process on the brain cells. As I've already said, unfortunately, in some cases, this period of "breaking out" has been accompanied by various other psychological – anomalies. Naturally, therefore, our priority was to bring the surviving subjects in again before more damage could be done. Hopefully now we can find out what's going wrong and put it right.'

'And then what?' said Nick. 'Will you use us as psychic weapons, as you originally intended – or will you let us go?'

'That's rather up to you,' said Jenna coolly.

'Really?' Nick was sceptical.

'Of course. Whatever you've been told, Nick, we're not barbarians here. We're simply government employees working on research projects which we hope will benefit not only the nation but all of mankind. The intention with the Genesis subjects at this stage is to monitor and, if need be, stabilise the condition of those of you who are here, and then to provide you all with training which will enable you to control and – but only if you wish it – enhance the abilities you have. After that, the future will be in your hands. If you wish to help your government by becoming a psychic operative then you will be given that opportunity. If, however, you simply want to go back to your own life, then that will be arranged.'

Nick scrutinised her face, but it was unreadable. After a moment he said, 'Is it really as easy as that? I mean, if we did decide that we wanted to go back home, wouldn't we be a dangerous liability, a security risk? How do you know we wouldn't go blabbing to everyone we met, sell our story to the papers?'

Jenna spread her hands as if to indicate she had nothing to hide. 'You can be made to forget,' she said simply.

Forty-Two

Over the course of the next two weeks, Nick was subjected to so many tests – both physical and psychological – that he began to feel like a laboratory rat. The information extrapolated from a session in Jaws, attended by the delightful Dr Swanwick, was evidently not deemed to be enough, because in addition he had his heart rate monitored as he jogged on a treadmill, his brain activity scrutinised as he sat at a computer screen and attempted to solve a succession of mathematical, logistical and lateral problems, and various fluids extracted from his body at such regular intervals that he remarked to Sasha, at the end of the fifth day, that they were taking the piss in more ways than one. Each afternoon he also attended a one-hour session with a tall, bald psychotherapist called Dr McGovern who reminded him of the giant in *Twin Peaks*. There, Nick talked about anything and everything – his childhood, his parents, his drug use, his time in prison, his job and his various relationships – with Sasha, with Linsey, with other women he had dated, with people in general. McGovern encouraged him to 'freewheel' as he called it, punctuating Nick's ramblings with questions. His favourites were: 'How did that make you feel?' and 'What were you thinking of while this was happening?'

Eventually, inevitably, they got on to the subject of Nick's vision in the Gridlock and all that had come after it.

'Did the vision excite you or thrill you at all?' McGovern asked.

'No *way*,' said Nick, appalled at the very idea.

'How *did* it make you feel?'

'Shocked. Sickened. Horrified. Confused. I didn't know what was happening.'

Each evening, and sometimes during the day, Nick and Sasha were allowed to visit each other. Though he had different wall-paper, different curtains and a different mural painted on the wall where the window would be, the layout of his suite was in all other respects identical to hers. It was not, however, on the same floor; his suite was on a lower level. He had asked for, and been given, a computer, an exercise bike and a laser-disc player. Almost daily he would add to the list of CDs, films, books and magazines that he wanted, and these would be procured for him, usually within twenty-four hours. Nick had cheekily asked Jenna if he could keep the laser-disc player when all this was over, expecting a polite refusal, but she had simply shrugged. 'I'm sure that can be arranged.'

Despite the tests he was being subjected to on a daily basis, it quickly became obvious to Nick that he was coping with the situation much better than Sasha was. He loved his life in London, but two weeks into his enforced stay at the Chicken House, the only thing he was *really* missing was going to gigs. He had spent a great many wild nights in the capital's pubs and clubs in the past, but he was no longer the social animal he had once been. He enjoyed his own company and had become quite content to spend long periods of time on his own, working, reading, listening to music, watching TV – most of which he could do here just as easily.

Sasha, however, he knew, was desperate to get back to her old life, and not only because she was worried about Linsey. Back in London she had her studies, and a large circle of friends whom she saw most nights. She had always liked places where there were a lot of people, places that buzzed – pubs and restaurants, packed movie theatres, heaving concert halls. But she loved fresh air too. She adored the countryside, and regularly at weekends would go walking with friends, or down to the coast to windsurf. The Chicken House was anathema to her.

Faced with her resentment and aggression – and her hatred for Jenna – Nick felt almost guilty. Certainly, being the age she was, she had far more to lose than him (and certainly, when he was seventeen, he'd have felt just as indignant and stir crazy as she was feeling now), but surely if anyone should despise Jenna for the way she had duped them, it should be him. Oh, he felt a certain amount of bitterness, certainly, but his overriding emotions were

283

disappointment and even embarrassment at the way he had greedily taken every scrap of bait she had dangled before him. When he saw her now it made him feel sad and foolish rather than angry. When he spoke to her he even found himself trying to recapture a hint of the warmth and closeness that they – in his estimation, at least – had briefly shared.

After a couple of weeks at the Chicken House, his relationship with his daughter had grown edgy, uncomfortable. One evening he picked up the phone on the table beside his enormous double bed and dialled 731. After four rings, Sasha, sounding weary and depressed – which was how she sounded recently when she wasn't angry – picked up the phone. 'Yeah?'

'It's me,' Nick said, trying to instil some enthusiasm and energy into his voice in the hope it would rub off on her.

'Oh, hi.'

'Well, don't sound so pleased to hear from me,' he said, 'or is it just that you were expecting a call from Brad Pitt?'

He was dejected to hear silence instead of laughter on the other end of the line. Then she said, 'Sorry, Dad. I'm just tired.'

'What have you been doing today?'

'Nothing much.'

'What does that mean?'

'Just . . . sitting around. Listening to music. You know.'

'Have you been swimming?'

On a higher level (Nick guessed that it was about halfway between his floor and ground level) was a fully equipped leisure centre which Jenna had told them they were free to use at certain times. All either of them had to do was dial 500 and someone would arrive to escort them. Twice Nick and Sasha had swum together and several times – usually during Nick's afternoon session with Dr McGovern – Sasha had swum alone.

'No,' she said, as she had said for the past four days now.

'Why not?' asked Nick, trying to keep his voice light.

'I didn't feel like it.'

'So basically all you've done is sit and stare at the walls all day?'

'More or less.'

'Why, Sasha?'

'Because there's nothing much else *to* fucking well do, is there?' she said, suddenly aggressive.

284

Nick took a deep breath, trying to stay calm. 'Yes, there is. You *know* there is, Sasha. It's up to us to keep our minds and bodies active.'

'Why? What's the point?'

'What do you mean, *what's the point?* There's every point. You think it's better just to give up?'

'We might as well. I mean, it's not as if we're ever going to get out of here, is it?'

'Of course we are. Don't be ridiculous.'

'If you believe what that bitch tells you, Dad, then you're the ridiculous one, not me.'

Nick felt his own anger and frustration struggling to break out, but the last thing he wanted was for this to degenerate into a situation where he might say things he would regret later. 'Look, Sash, we've been given no reason to believe that they won't keep their word and let us go once all this is over. All right, so they've lied to us to get us here, but that's only because it wasn't a good idea for us to know the truth while we were wandering around London. Whatever happens, we've got to stay optimistic, Sash. We can't just give in. I thought you were stronger than this. I thought you were the sort of person who always fought for what you believed in, who always made the best of things.'

'Yeah, well, it just goes to show that you don't know me very well, doesn't it?'

Nick felt the remark hit home like a poison dart. He clenched his teeth briefly. 'I don't think that's true, Sasha. I think you're just going through a bad patch. It's understandable.'

She grunted, but said nothing. After a few moments he said, 'Look, why don't you come down for some pasta and a film? I got a new laser-disc today: *Bullitt* – I remember you saying that you'd never seen it. We could watch that together or we could just talk – whatever you want.'

She sighed as if he were some thick-skinned guy who was pestering her for a date. 'I don't think so, Dad. I don't feel like it.'

'Go on. I hate to think of you alone and depressed in your room.'

'Like I said, I'm tired, Dad. I just want to sleep.'

Nick was aware that his and Sasha's conversation was almost certainly being monitored, but he was frustrated enough not to care. 'So that's it, is it? You're giving up. You're letting these people win. If Jenna's as bad as you say, then don't you realise she's probably watching you at this moment, laughing her head off, thinking how bloody easy it was to grind you down, break your spirit? Not that they even had to try very hard. You've done it all by yourself.' He paused, then said, 'I'm really disappointed in you, Sasha. I thought you had more fight in you than this.'

He wasn't entirely sure whether he was trying to snap Sasha out of her torpor or merely unburden his own anxieties: if the former, it didn't work. Sasha just sounded weary. 'Yeah, well, you were wrong, weren't you?' she said and put the phone down.

Nick rang back immediately, but she didn't answer. He considered ringing Jenna's number, 340, and asking if she could check on the security cameras to make sure Sasha was okay, but in the end he decided against it. He didn't want Jenna to become his confidante, his sounding board. Despite the past and his tenderness for her, he wanted to establish an emotional distance between them. He lay on the bed, feeling the poison of the conversation churning inside him; the phone call had soured his whole evening. He had been planning to eat, watch *Bullitt*, listen to some music and maybe even start working on a novel he had been mulling over for years – one based on his experiences with drugs and prison and the music world – but he didn't feel like doing any of that now.

Maybe he ought to call for an escort to go to Sasha's room, speak to her face to face. He had seen her fury and frustration growing daily, but this lethargy was new and it frightened him. If she was like this after two weeks, what would she be like after a month? Two months? Perhaps he ought to speak to Jenna about the possibility of them letting Sasha go. After all, it was him they really wanted; what use was Sasha to them now, except perhaps as a lever to get him to co-operate, which he was doing without argument in any case. Jenna had admitted to him that when Sasha had first arrived at the complex, they had analysed the results of her session in Jaws and had initiated a preliminary series of tests to ascertain whether Nick's artificially created abilities had been implemented into his genetic code to such an extent that they had become hereditary. This appeared, however, not to be the case; so what objections could they honestly have to letting her go? If nothing else, Linsey needed her. Surely they couldn't be so hard-hearted as not to acknowledge that?

286

He picked up the phone and dialled Jenna's number, but was informed that she would be unavailable until the following day. Nick hesitated for a moment, again wondering whether to ask for an escort to take him to Sasha, but in the end said, 'Okay. Thanks,' and put the phone down. In the end he watched the film, nibbling titbits from the fridge, and then went to bed. In the morning he would sort everything out, he promised himself.

The next thing he was aware of was the sound of his door buzzer. Instantly awake, he sat up, blinking the glue of sleep from his eyes as two people entered the room. One was a middle-aged woman in a white lab coat whom he had never seen before, and the other was one of Nick's regular escorts, an Arsenal supporter called Ben.

'What's going on?' Nick asked, not exactly alarmed but wary.

Ben gave the impression of being skinny because he was so tall, though in truth his upper arms were twice the circumference of Nick's and his hands were like shovels. He had a ginger crewcut, a pockmarked face and scars around his eyes that Nick assumed had been picked up in fights. He would have been fearsome if he hadn't been so cheerful and if his enthusiasm for Dennis Bergkamp's goal-scoring prowess hadn't been so endearingly boyish.

'Morning, Mr F,' he boomed. 'Big day today.'

'Is it? Why?' Nick asked, half-expecting Ben to tell him that Arsenal were playing AC Milan in Europe that evening.

Instead the middle-aged woman stepped forward and extended a hand. 'Hi, Nick, I'm Dr Farrow,' she said in a New York accent. 'I'll be overseeing your preparation training for today.'

'Preparation training,' said Nick blankly. 'What's that?'

'It's the next stage on from all the needles and machines we've been subjecting you to these past couple of weeks. Well, okay, we'll still have to hook you up to the odd machine – but it's interesting and kinda fun. Plus you get to meet the others.'

'The *others*?' said Nick. 'You mean the other . . .' unable to think of how to refer to them, he finally blurted, '. . . Russian children?' and immediately felt foolish.

Dr Farrow, however, merely nodded. 'The Genesis subjects, yes.'

'Genesis subjects. Right. So . . . are you wanting me to start right away? I mean, what time is it?'

287

'Six a.m.,' said Farrow. 'An ungodly hour, I know, but we got a whole lot to get through today. But look, take a shower, get dressed, have some breakfast. We'll be back in a half-hour.'

She and Ben moved towards the door. Farrow had her hand on the handle when Nick spoke. 'Er . . . is there any chance of seeing Jenna before we start? I really need to talk to her.'

'I'm afraid Jenna's not around just yet. Maybe later,' Farrow said. She smiled, then she and Ben exited.

Nick looked at the phone on his bedside table and thought briefly about calling Sasha to see if she was okay. However, waking her up at such 'an ungodly hour' – as Farrow had referred to it – was not the ideal basis for the heart-to-heart he felt they needed. He got up, showered, dressed and slowly ate a bowl of muesli with chopped banana, sitting in the armchair beside the dressing table and allowing the Verve's *Urban Hymns* to provide a backdrop for his thoughts. He was nervous and, he had to admit, excited about the day ahead, but he wished it had come at a different time. He didn't think Sasha would do anything foolish – but then he had never thought she would respond so negatively to their . . . he hesitated to call it incarceration because their captors were so accommodating, but he supposed that was what it was.

The door buzzed as he was finishing his tea. He swallowed what remained in one gulp and stood up.

Nick's corridor, like Sasha's, was self-contained, closed off at either end, which meant that the first part of any outing started with a short stroll across the grey-carpeted corridor to the lift. Today the lift ascended past the point where Nick normally got out – so far past, in fact, that he was beginning to wonder whether he was being taken back up to the surface when it came to a sedate stop, the doors gliding open.

He was ushered into a large, airy, high-ceilinged room, reminiscent of a hospital foyer. There were coffee and snack machines against the walls and a liberal scattering of comfortable seats. Wide corridors led off in several directions. And there were people – more people than Nick had seen since he had entered the Chicken House – milling about, some wearing suits, some white lab coats like Dr Farrow, and some dressed casually, in jeans and sweatshirts. One young guy, sitting on a seat and eating a Danish pastry whilst peering intently at a sheaf of notes in his lap, was wearing a Manic Street Preachers' *Everything Must Go* T-shirt, which Nick found ridiculously reassuring. Perhaps he wasn't so far from home, after all.

'The heart of the complex,' Farrow explained. 'This is where it all happens. Shall we?' She gestured to the right and they walked towards a set of brown double doors which people were bleeping through almost constantly, the keycard/combination/hand-print sequence as mesmeric as a factory production-line.

Farrow performed her own security clearance routine and they passed through into a wide corridor whose walls were studded with closed, unmarked doors and from which sprouted several tributary corridors. Farrow acknowledged the greetings of several people as they moved along this main corridor; none of them questioned Nick's presence, nor even so much as gave him a second glance. This seemed to confirm what Nick had gradually come to realise, which was that either the Genesis Project was simply one amongst many equally prominent research projects going on here, or it was so secret that only a select few were privy to it. When he had first arrived at the Chicken House, his assumption had been that the installation had been built solely to house the project, but it had not been long before he realised how pointless it would have been to maintain such a vast installation purely to monitor a project that had been in an apparently dormant state for the past thirty years.

Three-quarters of the way along the main corridor, Farrow turned right into a narrower corridor, then left, then almost immediately right again. Finally she stopped at a door and produced her keycard. Moments later she was holding the door open. 'After you, Nick.'

Nick walked into a small room sparsely furnished with a desk, a wooden armchair with leather upholstery and a couch like the one in Dr McGovern's room. The only other item was a small lamp sitting on the desk, its already weak light smothered yet further by a dark conical shade. The walls of the room were painted dark blue; the carpet was of a similar colour. Nick felt a little nervous. The place reminded him of an interrogation chamber in a Nazi war film. Farrow and Ben entered behind him, and Farrow closed the door, shutting out the light from the corridor.

'Are we going to have a seance?' Nick asked, trying to keep his voice light.

289

Farrow chuckled. 'Not today, Nick. Before we start your full training programme, it's important that you learn how to fully relax, how to become aware of yourself, how to focus your mind.'

'I'm a pretty relaxed sort of person already,' Nick said.

'Well, that's good. That gives us a head start. But you see, Nick, however relaxed you *think* you are, your mind is still full of the clutter of day-to-day living. By our nature as human beings, we're constantly thinking about what we're going to do next, what duties we have to perform. We spend an awful amount of time and energy assessing our own concerns and the concerns of others. Our brains receive and process constant input. Everything we see, hear, touch, smell and taste is subjected to the most intense analysis. We divert energy and constantly pump out signals from our brains simply to make our bodies work. Often we're focusing on so many things that our central focus – the real core of our being – is dispersed.

'What you have to learn, therefore, Nick, before you can use the abilities that have been given to you, is how to rediscover that focus by blotting out all other stimuli. Sweeping aside all the clutter. We do this first of all simply by teaching you how to relax. You see, those receptive to ESP, as you are, are attending to very weak signals, to the energy that we create with our thoughts and emotions and which are beyond the perceptive abilities of most people. After a short session here, therefore, I'll introduce you to the Ganzfeld Technique, which is a mild sensory-deprivation procedure. What this does is to heighten the perception of the hidden signals by eliminating the signals that usually take precedence.'

'So what happened when I had my vision?' asked Nick. 'I mean, I was still receiving signals from outside then.'

'Well, that's one thing we're trying to find out and rectify,' Farrow said. 'The vision you received was like . . .' She paused, then said, 'Think of it as a dangerous surge of electricity. You were lucky that it didn't blow any of your fuses. In some of the Genesis subjects, similar experiences sadly did.'

'Michael Mercy and Mark Cotto.'

'And others. By the time we realised what was happening, seven of our subjects had destroyed not only themselves, but others too.'

'*Seven?* So there's only . . . what? . . . seventeen of us left?'

'Well, sixteen at most, though we only have eleven of you here. One of our subjects tragically died in a car accident at the age of fourteen. Five more are still to be accounted for.'

Hallett, plus four others, thought Nick. He remembered Hallett telling him that he had fixed up new lives, new identities, for other psi-humans.

'Okay, so how do we start? Do you want me to lie on the couch?'

'Please.'

Nick did so, feeling nervous and self-conscious.

'Now put your hands down by your sides, uncross your feet and close your eyes. That's good. Now I want you to take slow, deep breaths. Breathe right down into your lungs, then let it out. Think about your breathing; concentrate on it. Try to put everything else out of your mind. Let's keep that going for the next few minutes. Slow, deep breaths. That's good!'

Nick was not sure how long the initial session lasted. After a while, drifting along, guided only by Farrow's voice, time seemed not to matter. She pinpointed every part of his body – his crown, his temples, his jaw, his shoulders, his spine, his limbs, his solar plexus – and encouraged him to relax them one by one. At her behest, Nick imagined tension streaming from his finger-tips and toes like ectoplasm, imagined himself walking on a beach, the sand between his toes, the soft rush of the waves in his ears, and then strolling through a forest, smelling the pine and watching the sunlight flitter through the gaps in the leaves above.

Finally, in a voice which had changed from that of a tough New Yorker into a slow, mesmeric drawl, she said, 'Okay, Nick. Now I'm going to count up to five. When I reach five, I want you to take a deep breath, open your eyes and slowly sit up. One . . .'

The space between each number was a soothing, delicious eternity. When she reached five, Nick did as she asked without question, opening his eyes and sitting up, his body feeling as relaxed as he could ever remember.

'How are you feeling?' she asked.

'Fantastic. I'm looking forward to tomorrow already.'

She smiled. 'Soon you won't need me to guide you. You'll be able to achieve a state of total relaxation all by yourself.'

Though relaxed, Nick did not feel at all tired. Indeed, he felt newly energised. He swung his legs from the couch and grinned. 'Okay – what's next?'

Next was what Farrow had referred to as the Ganzfeld Technique. Nick was led along more corridors until they came to a room that was slightly larger than the one they had just left. The dominant feature of this room was a large tank with a lid made of some strange, black, non-reflective material. Nick thought at first it was rubber, but on closer inspection he realised it was more like fibreglass, with a smooth, almost velvety texture.

The tank was linked to a generator and, via several lengths of thick grey cable, to various items of monitoring equipment. Farrow lifted the lid, inviting Nick to look inside. He saw that the interior of the tank had smooth, curved walls. It was as if he were looking into the cross-section of a black bubble. Perhaps because the light in the room was shining above the tank's interior and not directly on to it, looking down into the tank made it seem oddly depthless. When he peered hard, Nick could see a treacly substance shimmering somewhere below, snatching half-slivers of light and reflecting them back at him. Perhaps this should have provided him with the sense of perspective he needed, but in fact the substance merely seemed intangible, near and yet far away, like clouds he had watched whilst lying on his back as a boy, which he had reached out for, half-believing that they were close enough to pluck from the sky.

'Weird,' he said. 'It's like an optical illusion.' He drew back, looking again at the exterior of the bath. 'Does the inside of this thing go below floor level?'

'No,' said Farrow. 'As you say, it's an optical illusion. In fact, it's a sensory illusion. Once inside you'll feel as though you're floating in space. You'll see nothing, hear nothing, feel nothing, smell nothing, taste nothing. You'll feel as though you're composed of pure thought.'

'Like an out-of-body experience,' said Nick.

'Yeah, I guess so – though like I say, you won't see anything except for what's in your own head.'

'Sounds scary.'

Farrow laughed. 'Not at all. It's very relaxing. Just think good thoughts.'

A few minutes later Nick was ready. Farrow had directed him to a curtained-off alcove where he had removed his own clothes and donned a lightweight wet suit which had perhaps a dozen leads trailing from small circular sensor pads attached to it, both front and back.

'Here you go,' said Ben, standing beside the tank. 'I'll give you a leg up.'

He cupped his hands and Nick plodded barefoot towards him. The suit had left his hands, feet and head exposed. When he asked Farrow about this, she told him that the suit was not intended to protect him; its purpose was simply to enable them to monitor his bodily functions and responses whilst in the tank.

With Ben's help, Nick clambered up and on to the rim of the tank. Sitting on the side, he extended his feet carefully, still not entirely sure whether the bottom was further away than the outer shell suggested.

Then his toes slid into a gelatinous substance. He had expected it to be cold but it was, in fact, pleasantly warm. He paused a moment, then slid his foot in further until the substance had enclosed his ankle.

'What *is* this stuff?' he asked curiously.

'We call it Sleep Gel,' said Farrow. 'It's a combination of relaxants. It gives off an odourless vapour which acts as a mild sedative, and in this semi-liquid form it'll give your body a buoyancy that'll enable you to fully relax – rather like floating on the Dead Sea.'

'What's it made of? Chemicals?'

'Not at all. Natural ingredients right down the line. It's non-addictive, non-carcinogenic – believe me, Nick, it will do nothing but good to your body.'

'Okay, you've sold me,' Nick said, lowering himself gingerly into the goo.

'Right, before you lie back and relax,' Farrow said, 'I want you to do me the favour of plugging yourself in. On each side of you are two rows of sockets – tiny little holes in the wall. There are three holes in each row, so six on each side. You got them?'

Nick reached out and ran his hand over the velvety interior of the tank to his right. 'No, I don't think—' Then his index finger encountered a small hole ringed with metal. 'Oh, yeah. Here they are.'

'Great. The leads on the back of your immersion suit go into the bottom row of sockets and the leads on the front go into the top.'

293

'Right,' said Nick. He sat down, the gel moving around him like thick soup; the sensation was peculiarly pleasant. For the next couple of minutes he fumbled with the leads, trying to fit them into the correct sockets. At last he was finished. 'I think that's it. Now, a couple of hours on Regulo Seven should do me nicely.'

Farrow laughed. 'Okay. Now lie back, close your eyes and relax. Don't worry about the gel getting in your hair and on your skin – you can have a hot shower later. And try not to worry about the lid coming down. Remember, we'll be monitoring your physical responses closely. If we detect any indications of distress, we'll pull you out immediately. Okay?'

'Fine, but I don't think I'll have any problems. I'm not the claustrophobic type.' He lay back, the gel moving sluggishly and soundlessly around him. Once his weight was evenly distributed, the gel lifted his body up so that no part of it was touching the bottom or sides of the tank. It was a blissful sensation. He felt completely weightless. 'It's like floating on air,' he murmured.

'We're going to put the lid down now, Nick, okay? When we do that the darkness will be absolute.'

'Fine by me,' Nick said, thinking that the vapours that Farrow had mentioned must have started working already; suddenly even speaking seemed like too much of an effort. He closed his eyes and for a few seconds saw an orange glow behind his eyelids before blackness closed over it like an eclipse. Briefly he opened his eyes again, but as Farrow had promised, the darkness inside the tank was total. As she had also promised, he could hear nothing, smell nothing, taste nothing. He was quickly losing all sense of the weight and functions of his own body. It was as though the messages that passed from his brain to the rest of him – his heart, his stomach, his bowels, his bladder, the muscles in his limbs – had completely ceased. As if he were, very pleasantly, paralysed.

This is nice, he thought, and wondered whether dying would be like this, his mind drifting in a void, the messy and binding impedimenta of life fading to insignificance. Already his anxieties seemed inconsequential, each problem, each irritant, each niggle of doubt like single knots from a tangle that was being deftly unpicked. He could feel his mind stretching, expanding, using the emptiness, the *purity*, of the void to rid *itself* of impurities, and thence to push out, explore beyond its accustomed realm, unencumbered by the clutter of living. Nick already felt sure that

294

somewhere, close by, he could sense the timeless and perfect workings of existence.

Suddenly orange light, harsh as acid, flooded through the thin curtains of his eyelids, coating his vision. With it, Nick felt his consciousness shrinking, diminishing, being sucked back into the bottle of his skull. Physically he became aware of himself once more: the dryness of his mouth; the heaviness of his bladder; the queasiness of disorientation in his stomach. His eyes scrunched open and the orange light became a white pain that jabbed at his eyeballs.

'Just give yourself a moment, Nick,' he heard Farrow say. After the pure silence of the void, the sound of her voice was ugly and dull. 'Allow yourself time to come round.'

Nick wanted to give himself more than a moment. He wanted to recapture the glorious sense of nothingness that had been snatched from him. Yet although the gel still sought to caress and soothe and support his body, the degree of interference from outside was now too distracting. He sat up, the gel slithering down his back, running in thick treacly trickles down his face. He could feel the pumping of his own heart and it discomforted and depressed him, for it now seemed less like a life-source and more like a great weight pinning him to the corporeal plane.

'That's it, Nick,' he heard Farrow say. 'Take it easy.'

He struggled to his feet, his body feeling like a clumsy burden that he was finding it difficult to manipulate. After the warmth of the gel the room seemed to contain a chill that clung to him, seeping through the rubbery suit.

'Don't try to climb out,' Farrow said, as if he had been attempting it. 'Ben here will help you. First, though, we'll have to get you unplugged. Do you think you can do that for us?'

Nick looked down at himself and saw that the leads attached to his suit had been stretched taut by his standing up. He looked like Gulliver trying to escape from the ropes of the Lilliputians. He looked up at Farrow again and in a voice that to him sounded weak, drained of vitality, said, 'Why do I have to get out? What's wrong?'

'Nothing's wrong, Nick,' Farrow said. 'Everything went fine.'

'But I've only been in here a few minutes.'

Farrow shook her head slowly, sympathy and understanding on her face. 'No, Nick. You've been in there for two hours.'

Nick looked at her in disbelief. 'You're kidding!'

'I'm not. Look at the clock on the wall.'

Nick did as she asked and saw that it was almost ten thirty a.m. When they had come in here, it had been a little after quarter past eight.

'It's a set-up,' he said. 'You moved the hands.'

'For what purpose?'

'I don't know. To . . . to disorientate me.'

'And why would we want to do that, Nick?'

'I don't know. Maybe it's part of some kind of experiment.'

Farrow smiled. 'I understand your confusion, Nick. It's a very common reaction, especially after a subject's first experience in the tank. But I promise you, we have absolutely no reason to want to disorientate you. I mean, think about it – what would be the point? Okay, so you're confused – what then? You switch on the TV or the radio and immediately the deception falls apart.'

Nick frowned. 'But I was sure I'd been conscious the whole time I was in there.'

'You probably were.'

'But I *can't* have been! The whole thing went by so fast. It seemed like . . . not much more than the blink of an eyelid.'

Farrow held up her hands. 'I'm not going to argue with you, Nick – you have to deal with this in your own way. What I *would* like you to do for the next hour or so, however, is to acclimatise yourself again, ease yourself back into the real world. My guess is that you're feeling a little down right now?'

Nick nodded. 'Everything seems small and petty and sort of trapped. And everything around me – all this – seems flat and dull and . . . I don't know. Oppressive somehow.'

'Well, that's natural. We can have a coffee and talk about that. What's important, Nick, is getting your preparation training right, which means doing it at a pace you're comfortable with. If you're not happy at any time, you just tell me and we'll try to fix it, okay?'

'Okay.'

After he had unplugged himself, showered and changed, Nick, Farrow and Ben sat drinking coffee, and Nick tried to articulate to Farrow what he had experienced in the tank. The doctor seemed pleased with what he was telling her. A couple of times she nodded and murmured her approval.

Because the time for Nick had seemed to pass so swiftly in the tank, it only took him a couple of minutes to relate what had happened. When he was done, Farrow slapped her hands down on her knees. 'That's great, Nick! You're making excellent progress.'

'Am I?' said Nick, surprised.

'Oh yes. You've already recognised the potential in your own mind and you've embraced the opportunity to work on it with no resistance whatsoever. Many subjects are frightened of what they are shown they can achieve at first.'

'And with good reason, considering that quite a few of them have been destroyed by their abilities.'

'Those were not controlled circumstances though, Nick. Those guys were not given time to acclimatise. Their abilities were not drawn out slowly and carefully, a little at a time – they were yanked out violently, creating a lot of mess and trauma.'

Nick thought briefly of his dormant ability like a fat white worm coiled around his internal organs, a parasite that had to be coaxed gently into the open. The image made him feel slightly sick.

'So how are you feeling now?' Farrow asked, sounding genuinely concerned.

Nick shrugged. 'A bit deflated.'

'Do you feel this morning's session has been beneficial?'

'Oh, yeah.'

'In what way?'

'My mind feels sharper. More focused. Like you say, I feel that the potential is there.'

'That's great,' said Farrow again. She tipped back her head and swallowed her last mouthful of coffee. The gesture had an air of finality about it, and what she said next confirmed that. 'Okay, Nick, I'll see you tomorrow morning and if you feel up to it we'll go through this whole routine again. And now, if you're ready, Ben will escort you to the main complex and you'll get a chance to meet the other Genesis subjects and see the project in action.'

'You're not coming?' asked Nick. Somehow he felt Farrow was his ally and he would have welcomed her support.

'No, I'm just . . . Think of me as your personal trainer, toning you up for a role in a movie. Once I've finished with you, I hand you over to the producer and the director and the crew and you get to work with the other actors.'

'Right,' Nick said. 'Well . . . see you tomorrow.'

'You bet,' said Farrow.

Forty-Three

Ben escorted Nick along more corridors until they emerged into a wide, tall-ceilinged one that ended in a pair of large, white double doors. Most of the doors they had passed after leaving Farrow had been unmarked, but this one had the words RESTRICTED ACCESS printed across it in large red letters. There were more security cameras in evidence here than Nick had seen previously. Ben paused and waved to one of them, then produced his keycard and went through the usual routine. For several seconds after Ben had placed his hand on the illuminated panel Nick thought that the doors were not going to open. Then they did, sliding apart slowly and smoothly, and Nick and Ben passed through into a short corridor that looked like a spaceship airlock in a science-fiction movie. At the far end was another pair of double doors, glimmering like a mirage in the harsh, blue-white light; Ben and Nick walked up to them. It was not until the doors behind them had closed that this second set of doors began to open.

They passed through into a warehouse-sized hexagonal room, constructed on two levels. The upper level – ten or fifteen feet above Nick's head, and with a rail running all the way round it – seemed to serve both as observation platform and central operations section, white-coated lab technicians moving back and forth, monitoring and operating banks of equipment. Floor-level was dominated by a dome-like chamber constructed of triangular panels of a transparent material. Inside the chamber was a sort of podium, and perched atop the podium was an orange.

The surviving subjects of the Genesis Project, aside from Hallett and those he had sent beyond the reach of the Illuminati, were seated in a rough circle around the chamber, staring intently at the orange. Their foreheads were adorned with sensor pads, trailing wires, which were hooked up to portable monitors. The Genesis subjects consisted of five women and five men, all of whom were around Nick's age. Although he could hear the metal walkway above him creaking as people moved about, there was an air of expectancy and concentration in the room which discouraged normal speech.

Leaning forward until his mouth was close to Ben's ear, Nick whispered, 'What's going on?'

Ben half-turned, his shrug mimicked by his raised eyebrows. 'No idea, mate, but if we stand here long enough one of these doctor geezers is bound to come and tell us.'

Nick looked again at the Genesis subjects, scrutinising their faces one by one, half-expecting long-suppressed memories to stir in his mind. But they were all strangers to him – the thin-faced woman with the curly black hair, the fat man with the bushy dark beard and glasses, the attractive woman in the blue mohair jumper, the rather effete-looking man with the mop of wispy blond hair, his physical frailty emphasised by his white T-shirt.

In his peripheral vision, Nick saw something happen to the orange. Had it been his imagination, or had it seemed somehow to bend, to be pulled briefly out of shape? He glanced at the Genesis subjects again and saw the concentration intensify on their faces, saw the attractive woman narrow her eyes and bare her teeth, saw sweat dribble down the fat man's face into his beard. All at once the realisation of what they were trying to do jumped into his mind as if someone had murmured it in his ear.

They're trying to peel it. They're trying to peel the orange with their minds.

Feeling an odd squirm of excitement and something like awe, he himself concentrated on the orange, imagined it shedding its skin in one long fleshy spiral. He saw the orange bend again, saw it *warp*, as if it were being pulled by enormous forces in two opposite directions.

And then it exploded, filling the air with a fine spray, hurling wet gobbets of soft, juicy flesh in all directions, spattering against the interior panels of the dome like bugs coming to grief against car windscreens. Almost in unison the Genesis subjects slumped like marionettes. Several of them groaned. All of them looked exhausted or defeated or both.

Nick had instinctively stepped back as the orange exploded. Now he blinked in astonishment at the mess dribbling down the inside panels of the dome. A bald man with a thick moustache and a neat dark suit clanged down a set of metal steps that linked the two levels of the room.

'That was good,' he claimed effusively. 'That was close. You almost got it that time.'

One of the Genesis subjects – a handsome man with slicked-back hair, wearing a green jacket and a white collarless shirt – paused in the act of lighting a cigarette and made a caustic response. 'Bullshit. We're like little kids with ladybirds. No matter how hard we try to be gentle, we always end up squashing the fuckers.'

'You need more time, that's all,' the bald man said. 'It's like learning to drive a car – you simply need to practise, to hone your skills. Remember, only a few weeks ago the orange simply sat there; you couldn't even make it tremble. You've come a long way, Mr Lousada. Believe me, before long you'll be able to perform open-heart surgery using only your mind if you should wish to.'

'I'll have died of old age before then,' Lousada retorted. 'We all will.'

'Nonsense. You're frustrated, that's all, and that's understandable.'

Lousada took a drag on his cigarette, then gestured round at the others. 'And what if we all want out? What if we decided here and now that we'd all had enough and we wanted to go home? Would you try and stop us?'

'Well, I'd try and dissuade you, certainly. It would be a shame to see such painstaking and what I believe will be ultimately successful research go to waste.'

Lousada shook his head. 'You're full of bullshit, Pemberton. You adopt this nicey-nicey approach with us to get us to co-operate, but the fact is, if we all decided to jack it in, then things would turn ugly pretty quickly, wouldn't they? You'd start threatening us, maybe hurt us a little, remind us that we're your prisoners and that if we don't toe the line we're never going to get out of here. Well, let me tell you something, Pemberton – all of you. We might be the little kids playing with the ladybirds, but you're the ones playing with the matches. You don't know what you're fucking dealing with here. You're creating weapons that

300

pretty soon you won't be able to control. I mean, what's to stop any of us doing to your brain what we did to that orange, huh? You tell me that.'

Pemberton smiled nervously and glanced at Nick, evidently embarrassed that the newcomer was having to witness Lousada's outburst, that this was his introduction to the group. Attempting to make it sound as though Lousada were joking, he smiled. 'Now why would you want to do that, Greg? I mean, we're all on the same side here. We're working towards a common goal.'

'Fuck you, Pemberton! Your little brainwashing techniques – be as nice as pie and give them everything they want – might work on these other feebs, but they don't work on me. I was taken from my bed at gunpoint in the middle of the night. My wife ended up in hospital, her brain shot to fuck, because of you bastards.'

'Come on, Greg – that's hardly fair. As we explained, the reason you were taken at gunpoint was because we believed your life was in jeopardy from whatever criminal or political faction had carried out the psychic assault on your wife. It was simply the quickest and most efficient way to get you out of there.'

'Bollocks. You fucked up my wife's brain because she knew too much. You wanted to keep her quiet.'

'That's not true, Greg.'

'No, of course it isn't,' Lousada sneered. He took another drag on his cigarette. 'You still haven't answered my question, Pemberton.'

'Which question was that, Greg?'

'What would happen if we decided to give your brain the same treatment as that orange?'

'I really don't think the query merits an answer.'

'Oh, I think it does.'

But it wasn't Pemberton who replied. From the opposite side of the room, from behind Nick, a woman said loudly, 'Such behaviour would be considered extremely unpatriotic and met with ultimate force. Is that what you want to hear, Greg?'

Nick turned and saw Jenna standing in front of the silently closing doors. She was wearing a charcoal-grey pin-striped suit, complete with waistcoat. Nick hated to admit it, but she looked bloody sexy.

Lousada grinned slowly, cigarette smoke curling in front of his eyes as if trying to form itself into a mask. 'Well, look who it is –

Jenna, the Chicken House bike. How many free rides have you given today, Jenna?'

Jenna regarded Lousada coolly. 'I hardly think you're in a position to question my morals, Greg.'

'I'm not *questioning* anything. I *know* you're a slut,' Lousada said, and chuckled unpleasantly. 'Ultimate force eh? I guess we all know what that means.'

'It means that any unpatriotic behaviour will be viewed as an act of terrorism and will result in the project being terminated.'

'And us along with it,' said Lousada.

Jenna smiled. 'But of course it won't come to that, will it, Greg? I'm sure you people would not wish your husbands and wives and sons and daughters and mothers and fathers to discover that you've been traitors to your country.'

'Fuck you, Jenna,' said Lousada.

'Never again, Greg,' she responded sweetly.

There was a palpable tension in the air. Pemberton looked miserable, perhaps he believed he would be blamed for the situation and was waiting for a reprimand. The Genesis subjects for the most part were still and wide-eyed, frightened of drawing attention to themselves. Even the scientists on the upper level had stopped what they were doing and were watching proceedings apprehensively.

Lousada grunted and indulged himself in his cigarette, evidently content for the moment to have had his say. As if nothing had happened, Jenna turned to Nick. 'And how are you this morning?'

'Oh . . . fine,' said Nick. He nodded in the direction of the dome. 'That was all very interesting.'

'Which part? The demonstration, or Mr Lousada's little tantrum?'

'Both.'

She smiled and leaned forward, lowering her voice. 'Mr Lousada likes to stir up trouble. There's always one. It makes him feel important.'

'But surely we *are* all important?'

'Oh, absolutely. No denying it. But you're all *equally* important, Nick, and I don't just mean the eleven of you, but everyone involved with this project. This is a team effort. Everyone in this room has a vital role to play.'

302

'So if Mr Lousada's so unhappy with everything, why does he stay here?' Nick asked, lowering his voice to a murmur.

'He stays because he knows he has the gift and he wants to learn how to use it.'

'But isn't it dangerous to teach him if he's so . . . unstable?'

She shrugged. 'We'll see. Sometimes rogue elements can be useful. However, if we decide at a later date that Mr Lousada is still too much of a loose cannon, then he'll undergo regression therapy.'

'Sounds painful.'

Her smile widened. 'Not at all. He'll simply be returned to the state you were all in before your abilities began to break through. His real memories will be repressed and replaced with false ones.'

'And what about his ability? What will you do with that? Cut it out and keep it in a jam-jar?'

'We'll block it. To put it simply, we'll build a mental wall around it. And then we'll observe Mr Lousada closely to ensure that the wall remains solid.'

'You can do that?'

'Oh, yes. It's a relatively simple and harmless procedure.'

'But what if Mr Lousada doesn't want you to mess with his mind? What if he just wants to pack up and go?'

Jenna shrugged. 'Then that would be a mistake on his part. His ability is still unstable. It might well destroy him.'

'But that aside, if he wanted to go, right here and now, would you let him?'

Her smile became shrewd, a little playful. 'You're testing me, Nick. You're still not sure our motives are entirely honourable, are you?'

He shrugged, a little embarrassed. 'I just want to get things straight, that's all.'

She reached out and touched his hand in what seemed a genuinely affectionate gesture. The feel of her flesh on his sent a pleasant tingle through his body. But he still wished she would take her hand away.

'That's okay,' she said, 'you can ask as many questions as you like. We want to be as open and honest with you as possible. In the *hypothetical* case of Mr Lousada, well . . . We're not devils here, Nick, but we can't afford to be angels either. We care about the individual, of course, but the needs of the many must take precedence over the needs of the few.'

'So what does that mean?' said Nick. 'You'd get rid of him?'

Jenna laughed. 'Good God, no. We'd *force* him to have the treatment, that's all, possibly under sedation. It would take longer that way, of course, but if that was what it came to . . .' She shrugged.

'And then you'd let him go?'

'Absolutely. We would sedate him and fly him back to England. He'd wake up in his own bed with no memory of ever having been here.'

'And what about his wife?'

'As Mr Pemberton explained, his wife was nothing to do with us.'

'But how would you explain her condition to Mr Lousada?'

Jenna shrugged. 'We'd implant a false memory. Greg would remember his wife having a seizure, collapsing with a brain haemorrhage – something like that.'

'And what about these political factions that Mr Pemberton mentioned?'

Her reply was casual. 'He'd have to take his chances with those. Of course, we would provide him with whatever protection we could.'

Nick wanted to ask Jenna about the sexual side of her relationship with Lousada, but couldn't think what to say without making himself sound hurt or bitter or betrayed. He wondered if she'd been fucking Greg at the same time she'd been fucking him. He wanted to ask whether her time with him had meant more to her than her time with Greg, whether he'd been a gentler, more considerate – hell, *better* – lover than Lousada.

Pathetic, Finch, he told himself savagely. *Bloody pathetic*. He kept the questions locked inside him and the moment passed.

'Right,' Jenna said, 'I think it's time for you to become acquainted with the people you'll be working with.'

She introduced him to Pemberton, the head of the project, describing him as 'a brilliant scientist, the foremost authority in his field.' Nick shook Pemberton's limp hand, oddly reassured by the man's apparent lack of confidence, by the look of uncertainty in his eyes. To him, Pemberton looked like a man who had suddenly been cast into a situation in which he was out of his depth, a man who found the level of responsibility he held daunting in the extreme.

Of the Genesis subjects, Nick remembered only a few names. The bearded man, who greeted him perfunctorily, and whose hand was as sweaty and clammy as gelignite, was called Mark Brown; the attractive woman, who smiled and gripped his hand as if she'd finally found a kindred spirit after weeks of searching, was called Julie Lean; and the thin-faced, dark-haired woman who greeted him with the words, 'All right, pet?' in a musical Geordie accent, was called Ellie McKee. There was Greg Lousada too, of course, who shook his hand as if trying to prove a point, and who smirkingly intoned, through a veil of cigarette smoke, 'Welcome to the village of the fucking damned.'

'We'll take a break now, everyone,' Pemberton said. 'After lunch we'll try some visualisation exercises.'

The Genesis subjects peeled the sensor pads from their heads, stood up and stretched.

'Actually,' Nick said to Jenna, 'there was something I wanted to talk to you about.'

'There was something I wanted to talk to *you* about,' Jenna said.

'Oh?'

Jenna placed her hand on his again. Her face was etched with concern. 'I'm worried about Sasha, Nick. As you know, we brought her here to keep her safe, but I'm afraid she's not coping with confinement too well. If you and she are agreeable, I think we should take her home.'

Forty-Four

It's them, Sasha thought. *They're doing something to my mind.*

It was an instant of utter clarity amid a stew of befuddled theories and half-made connections. When – an eternity ago now – she
had first arrived at the Chicken House she had been frightened,
had even despaired on occasion; yet she had been defiant too, full
of fighting spirit, of thoughts of vengeance and escape. How could
all that have slipped away so quickly? How could she have
become so fogged, so indolent, unless they had done something to
make her so?

Her sleep patterns had become erratic. She had lost all sense of
time. She slept when she was tired, which now seemed to be
constantly, and each time she woke up it was as though a fat black
cloud were descending on her mind, crushing any resistance
beneath a weight of confusion and depression. At first she had
tried to fight the effects of the cloud, but little by little it had
become heavier, denser, until now the easiest option was simply
to give in to it. When she wasn't asleep, therefore, she simply sat
and did nothing, meekly allowed the insidious lethargy that had
infiltrated her like a virus to clog her thoughts, dismantle her
personality, insinuate its dark nothingness into her brain.

How were they doing it? she wondered distractedly. Was it
something in the air, or in her food? Even now she almost didn't
care. It seemed to take too much effort to think about.

And yet it was the first independent thought – the first spark of
individuality – she had had for what seemed like days, and so she
forced herself to cling to it, tenaciously. Afraid of letting this
glimmer of rebellion slip, she made herself visualise an image of
Jenna's face, of the woman's smug, superior smile. Using that as

a spur, the vague sense of indignation in her mind blossomed into a glowing red coal of anger. With enormous effort she channelled her thoughts, made herself imagine Jenna sitting in front of a bank of TV screens, watching her and laughing at her apathy, making snide and disparaging comments to a bevy of sniggering, dark-suited men clustered around her like groupies.

Sasha knew that sometimes people snapped; that disturbed people, mentally unstable people, could experience surges of rage that transformed them from quiescent, mild-mannered individuals one moment to rampaging beserkers the next. She would never have believed herself capable of such behaviour. She had always been too focused, too self-aware, too in control of her emotions.

Now, though, with the image of Jenna holding fast in her mind, the glowing red coal suddenly and shockingly erupted into a white-hot flare of rage that engulfed her completely. Instantly her indolence was burned away, but it was not clarity of thought that replaced it. Indeed, her fury overwhelmed her mentally even as it empowered her physically, reducing her to little more than a focus for its own terrifying energy.

Barely aware of what she was doing, Sasha jumped to her feet. A sound was coming from her throat, an animal-like ululation, an uprising of raw emotion. Though she heard the sound, it seemed to be coming from a long way away. *That isn't me*, a detached portion of her mind assured her.

The force that had hold of her body made her run at the television and push it over, made her lift the music system above her head and smash it to the floor. These acts of destruction did not sate the frenzy but merely fed it. Over the course of the next few minutes, systematically and conclusively, Sasha trashed the suite. She ripped the covers from the bed and shredded the pillows with her teeth; she smashed crockery; tore the shower unit from the wall in the bathroom; threw bottles of sauce and jars of preserves and cartons of milk against the walls until the wallpaper was dripping and spattered and stinking of jam and vinegar, pesto and salsa, curry paste and mustard.

Finally, drenched in sweat, her blonde corkscrew curls swinging across her vision, errant strands sticking to her face, she lurched back to the kitchen. She wrenched out a drawer, cutlery clanking and jangling to the floor. She bent and selected two things, one for each hand: a marble rolling pin and a large carving

307

knife. She swung and took out one of the security cameras in the kitchen with a single blow. The second took three blows, the third likewise. One by one, from the kitchen to the main room to the bathroom, the security cameras fell, smashed into submission by Sasha's bludgeoning arm. She didn't slow down even when something went *zing* in her shoulder like an elastic band snapping, accompanied by a hot hiss of pain. She swung and swung, smashed and smashed, until her world consisted solely of her pounding heart, her screaming muscles, the crunch of metal and the tinkling of glass.

The last camera to die was the one above the wrecked shower, which took six blows to disable. At last, however, it fell, and as it did so Sasha felt the strength drain out of her. And as her strength ebbed, so the pain replaced it in hot, twisting knots, making her cry out, sink to her knees amid the debris. For several long minutes the pain was so bad that she thought she would pass out. She leaned over until her forehead was touching the floor, and there she stayed until she sensed movement in front of her.

She looked up and saw a man standing there, his face expressionless. He was a big man with a bristle of ginger hair and a complexion cratered with pockmarks. Sasha knew she had seen him before, knew he had even told her his name, though for the life of her she couldn't remember it. She looked at the man and he looked at her, and an eternity passed in which it seemed they were frozen there, cursed by the fact that neither would be able to move until the other spoke.

Then, as if in slow motion, the man held out a hand. 'Come on, Sasha,' he said, his voice soft and soothing, 'let me help you up.'

He seemed to take her lack of response as compliance and stepped forward. Sasha's mind was blank; she honestly didn't know what she was going to do until she did it, and so was as astonished as he when, as he reached cautiously down towards her, she brought up her arm and lashed out at him.

She was doubly astonished to see the sleeve of his jacket, the sleeve of his white shirt and the skin of his arm spring apart simultaneously in a neat, ruler-sharp line. There was an instant during which nothing seemed to happen. And then blood jumped from the slit she had made with the knife she had forgotten she still held in her hand, so much of it that within seconds it had turned his arm

308

red and was running in rivulets into his palm, dripping from the ends of his fingers on to the floor.

The man gritted his teeth and flinched back, grunting. Instinctively Sasha jumped to her feet and darted past him, through the open door of the bathroom and into the main room. For a second the stench of the liquid foodstuffs running down the walls made her head spin, then she bolted for the door which he had left ajar.

Plunging through the door she turned and slammed it behind her, then ran across to the lift. Hardly thinking what she was doing, she started pressing random buttons on the security keypad beside the doors before giving up and slamming her hand against it in frustration. Hearing sounds from her suite, she abandoned the lift and ran to the double doors at the end of the corridor. Not even bothering with the security panel this time, she began to kick and pound at the doors, only now noticing that somewhere – probably as she'd been fleeing the suite – she had discarded the rolling pin and the knife.

Part of her knew that the doors were made of thick steel or some equally impenetrable substance, but her attack on them nevertheless continued unabated for what to her seemed like many minutes. Indeed, it may well have continued indefinitely – or at least until she collapsed from exhaustion – if someone hadn't barged into the back of her and knocked her over.

She sprawled on her stomach on the grey carpet, but before she could roll over to see who had attacked her, a crushing weight fell on her back, pinning her to the ground. She was aware of hands grabbing her wrists and pinning those to the ground too, but it wasn't until more hands grabbed her ankles and her thighs and the backs of her knees that she realised she was fighting more than one person. Then, filtering through a buzzing curtain of interference, she heard voices, male voices. One, speaking directly into her ear, sounded reassuring. 'Come on, Sasha, take it easy.' Another was more urgent. 'Hold her still. Just hold her still.'

Sasha tried to wriggle, to escape, but the weight on top of her was immovable. She felt her ribs being crushed against the floor; when she tried to draw a breath pain shot through her lungs. She began to panic, tried to cry out, but she had no space, no free air, to do so. She tried to twist her head but someone was pressing it into the carpet.

309

She felt hands fumbling at her waist. Then, to her horror, she felt her leggings and her knickers being yanked down to her knees.

They're going to rape me, her mind screamed, the thought high and sharp and full of terror. *Oh, God. they're going to rape me and I can't do anything about it.*

Her terror was mercifully short-lived. For several awful seconds she expected to feel them pulling her legs apart, but the next thing she experienced was a brief stinging pain in her left buttock.

Bee sting, she thought, then almost instantly realised that she'd been injected with something, that all they had really wanted to do was subdue her.

Thank God, she thought, *thank God, thank God*. She felt relief washing over and through her, sweeping her away as her world melted into grey.

Forty-Five

By the end of the following week, Nick's life had settled into a routine that – though he felt more than a twinge of guilt about his lack of resistance – he had no particular desire to break out of. He tried to assuage his guilt by assuring himself that his compliance was not because his time in the Chicken House had become comfortable, but because it had become dynamic, fulfilling, exciting. His preparation training had continued apace, and his response to it, or so Dr Farrow assured him, had been excellent. He thought of himself as a rare plant that was being nurtured and coaxed into producing the most fabulous blooms. After each session with Farrow and each period spent in the Ganzfeld tank he felt the tightly clenched leaves of his mind yielding a little more, the buds within swelling, gaining strength, pushing themselves into the light.

Each afternoon he joined the other Genesis subjects in the Central Research Unit as they attempted to control and focus the abilities that were being drawn from them. So far Nick had been requested to do nothing more than observe, though he had been informed by Farrow that he was almost ready to join the others in their endeavours. Sometimes the Genesis subjects were set similar tasks to the one Nick had seen them trying to perform the first time he had entered the CRU. Their progress was perhaps best described as slow but steady. Now, when asked to peel an orange, they no longer made it explode – at least not immediately, nor so spectacularly. Now bits of peel and pith jumped from the orange in random slivers and chunks before the entire fruit, evidently unable to withstand the barrage of psychic energy being directed at it, collapsed in a squelchy mess as if stamped on by some invisible boot.

Not all the experiments that Nick witnessed had been directed at fruit. On several occasions the group had been asked to try to influence the behaviour of animals. These experiments had met with only moderate success. Animals with a modicum of intelligence – monkeys and dogs, for instance – responded well to psychic commands, whereas others – rabbits, birds, rodents – responded either intermittently or not at all.

This afternoon, for the first time, Pemberton had asked the group if they were willing to participate in an experiment involving another human being. Several of the Genesis subjects, wires trailing from the sensor pads on their foreheads, looked doubtful.

'What sort of experiment?' Ellie McKee asked.

'Oh, it's nothing to become alarmed about, I assure you. The aim would merely be to ascertain how adept you are at projecting certain simple images into the mind of a non-psi.'

'What kinds of images?' asked Jason Westmoreland, a very tall, prematurely balding man with a gentle face.

Pemberton shrugged and smiled in that uncertain, slightly ingratiating way of his that always reminded Nick of a schoolboy trying a little too hard to be accepted by his peers. 'Oh – shapes, colours, numbers. Nothing too complex to start with.'

'Who's the . . . volunteer?' asked Julie Lean. Nick wondered whether her slight hesitation had been because she had been tempted to use the word 'victim'.

'It's me,' said a voice from above their heads. Nick looked up to see a white-coated scientist standing on the metal walkway, identifying himself with a raised hand. The man was in his forties, a little overweight, with black wiry hair. Nick had seen him pottering around before, but the man had never spoken, and Nick did not know his name.

'Andrew has offered to enter the lions' den,' Pemberton said, raising a hand like the compère of a variety show as the scientist descended the metal stairs.

'It won't be dangerous, will it?' Julie Lean asked anxiously.

Pemberton's laugh was obviously meant to sound carefree. 'Not unless you mistake his mind for an orange and try to peel it.'

A couple of people smiled uncertainly, but nobody joined in Pemberton's short-lived rattle of laughter. Nick glanced at Greg Lousada, half-expecting him to make some cutting comment –

although Lousada had been oddly subdued since his outburst the previous week, making Nick wonder whether privately he had been given some sort of dressing-down, admonished for undermining morale.

A little reluctantly, after Pemberton had assured them that the experiment would cease if Andrew showed even the slightest signs of discomfort, the psis agreed to go ahead. Andrew was given a drawing-pad, a black marker pen and a packet of coloured felt-tips. Two men carried a stool and a table into the dome and Andrew went inside and sat down, elbows on the table, pad and pens at the ready in front of him. He looked more relaxed than the psis, each of whom were given a large brown envelope.

'If we could bring the lights down a little and put a spotlight on Andrew,' Pemberton said to the gallery.

The necessary adjustments were made. 'Very theatrical,' one of the psis – it may even have been Greg Lousada – murmured.

Pemberton smiled. 'It may look dramatic, but it's simply to help you focus. Soon you'll have no need of such artificial aids to concentration.' He stood up straighter and pressed his hands together; he looked like a teacher at the head of a classroom where pupils were about to take an exam. Nick almost expected the scientist to say, 'Right, class – you can turn your papers over and begin. Remember to read the questions carefully, and good luck.'

'The envelopes you hold in your hands contain numbered sheets of card, on each of which is a simple image,' Pemberton said. 'What I want you to do is look at the images and try to project them mentally into Andrew's mind. He will then draw or write down the images he is receiving on his pad and we'll compare them. It's as simple as that. Does anyone have any questions at this point?'

No one did, so they began. Sitting behind Mark Brown, Nick was able to see the images as they were drawn from the envelope. The first was of an aeroplane, simply depicted. Each of the psis gazed at Andrew, their faces for the most part calm, blank. Pemberton moved from foot to foot and tried not to look tense, though his eyes roamed restlessly from one individual to another, flickering towards Andrew at intervals to see what effect their combined scrutiny was having on him. Pinned by his cone of light, the volunteer's face appeared chalky, though his features

313

were composed. He sat, unmoving, for two or three minutes, and then at last he picked up the marker pen and began to draw.

When he had finished he put down the pen and raised his thumb. Pemberton returned the gesture and the scientist lifted his pad. He had drawn an aeroplane almost identical to the one on Mark Brown's card.

These minor wonders were becoming almost daily occurrences in Nick's life, yet they never failed to give him a little thrill of excitement, of awe. Pemberton grinned. 'Well done, everybody. Let's try another one, shall we?'

The next image was a clown's face. Andrew did not get this one quite right, but he was close enough – he drew the face of a grinning man wearing a top hat. There then followed a green triangle, reproduced by Andrew within seconds, a teapot, also reproduced successfully, and then a tree that Andrew, after some deliberation, interpreted as a lollipop.

Unless the volunteer had some prior knowledge of the images on the card, the experiment could not be seen as anything other than an unmitigated success. The coloured shapes – a blue square and a red circle followed the green triangle – he reproduced almost as soon as the psis had taken the cards out of their envelopes. The only image he had any real difficulty with was that of a cat, whose ears and whiskers he interpreted as two pointed hills, with lines possibly intended to represent furrowed earth beneath them. The only image that provoked an intense reaction from the scientist was the final one. This image, in a departure from the previous simple line-drawings, was a more detailed depiction of a tarantula viewed from above, its legs outspread, its body etched with black lines intended to represent bristling hair.

Only seconds after each of the psis had drawn the image from their envelopes, Andrew leaped up, his chair falling over. Nick started, his concentration broken, as Andrew swiped frantically at the front of his white lab coat. The psis looked at the scientist and each other with bewilderment and concern. Julie Lean was blinking as though roused from sleep; the frail, blond-haired man, Chris something, wrapped his thin arms around himself and hunched forward as if he suddenly felt cold.

Pemberton stepped forward and raised a hand. 'All right, people – we'll leave it there. Could we have the lights back up please?'

314

The lights returned to normal. Inside the dome Andrew had moved away from the table and the overturned chair, his mouth open and chest heaving as he took deep breaths.

Pemberton opened the door of the dome and leaned in. 'Are you all right, Andrew?'

The scientist looked at him, puffed out his cheeks and expelled one huge breath as if ridding himself of the last of his panic. Then he nodded and walked across to Pemberton who reached out and helped his colleague over the dome's threshold as if he were a frail old lady.

Andrew glanced round at the psis sheepishly, shame-faced. 'Sorry about that, everyone,' he said, clearly embarrassed. 'It was that last image. I suddenly got this idea in my head that a bloody big spider was jumping at me. It's silly, I know, but I've always been terrified of spiders. But I'm all right now. Nothing to worry about.'

'My dear Andrew,' Pemberton said, 'I'm so sorry. I had no idea you were scared of spiders. If I had I would never—'

Yes, you did, Nick thought suddenly, the insight so fierce that it drowned out the rest of Pemberton's words – in fact, for a split-second he thought he might actually have spoken out loud. He stared at Pemberton and it was suddenly as though he were looking right into the man's head. Nick's own mind felt clear and sharp, almost sinewy, the mental equivalent of an athlete's body. However, he was not sure whether he was genuinely reading Pemberton's mind, or whether the man was simply a bad liar. Certainly he didn't *feel* as though he were mind-reading. He was not picking up images or words; it was simply instinct. He simply *knew* that Pemberton had included the image of the spider because he was aware of Andrew's phobia and wanted to see what effect it would have.

Wondering whether any of his fellow psis had had a similar insight, he looked around and caught Julie Lean's eye. The way she raised her eyebrows at him seemed to suggest that she knew exactly what his unspoken question was; more than that, she was responding in the affirmative. Nick had never seen any of the other psis outside the CRU, had never had the opportunity to speak to them, yet for all that he felt – perhaps not unsurprisingly – an affinity with most of the group. He wondered how many of them felt the same as he did, how many knew the full story of why they were here.

As usual, however, there was no opportunity to discuss the situation. Pemberton clapped his colleague companionably but dismissively on the shoulder. 'Excellent work, everyone,' he declared. 'I think we'll leave it there for today. Go back to your rooms, relax, get a good night's sleep, and then we'll pick this up again tomorrow.'

Back in his room Nick felt restless, out of sorts. He realised with surprise that this was the first time he had felt less than content since Jenna had informed him that Sasha had been flown back to London last week.

'When?' he had asked, surprised. It had been the evening following his second day of preparation training, the day after Greg Lousada's outburst. In the thirty or so hours following Nick's conversation with Jenna in the CRU, when Jenna had pre-empted Nick by expressing her concern for Sasha's welfare, Nick had tried to ring Sasha several times, to no avail. A couple of times he had also rung Jenna, asking to be escorted to Sasha's suite, but Jenna had apologetically informed him that Sasha had specifically requested that she be left alone. Then, the following evening, Jenna had turned up at his suite to say that Sasha had gone.

'We flew her out this morning. She'll be back in London by now.'

'But . . . but she *can't* have gone,' Nick replied. 'She didn't even say goodbye.'

'I know. She felt bad about that, but she said she couldn't face it. She told me to tell you that she loved you and that she would see you soon.'

'But she wouldn't have gone without saying something,' Nick persisted, a little plaintively.

Jenna pulled a sympathetic face. 'She was depressed, Nick. It wasn't doing her any good being here. I think she thought that if she came to see you, she wouldn't be able to leave.'

'*I* wouldn't have made her stay,' Nick said indignantly.

'I'm not suggesting that. I think she would have made herself stay. I know it's hard on you, but I think what happened was for the best.'

Nick wondered what Sasha was doing now, how Linsey was coping with her blindness. He hoped the two of them were safe in London from whoever their enemies were. Personally he still couldn't work that one out: couldn't decide who were the bad guys and who the good, or even whether such labels should apply. Maybe they were *all* bad guys, or maybe none of them had intentions that you could actually describe as evil. Maybe the Illuminati, Hallett's mob, whoever else was involved (if, indeed, there *was* anyone else) all saw themselves as good guys, albeit ones who had to resort to ruthless methods in order to achieve their objectives. Maybe, as in war, they considered the occasional atrocity to be necessary in order to achieve a greater good.

Then again, some of the things that had happened seemed pointless, irredeemable. What could possibly have been achieved by blinding Linsey, for instance? That, to Nick, appeared to be nothing more than an act of hideous and gratuitous cruelty. And then, on a smaller scale, there was the question of what Pemberton had done that afternoon, deliberately including the spider image simply to observe the effect it would have on his arachnophobic colleague. Was such ruthlessness acceptable, even in the interests of science? Would Pemberton have felt any remorse if the shock of receiving the psychic transmission had been powerful enough to send Andrew mad, or worse? Or could he have known in advance that the effect would be relatively mild? There was surely no precedent for such an experiment, so could there have been any way of calculating the outcome? Nick thought back to what Greg Lousada had said during his outburst a week ago, likening Pemberton and his colleagues to a bunch of kids playing with matches. How accurate was that? he wondered. Could it be that Pemberton was not ruthless but simply irresponsible? Wondering about the real motivations of the people who lived and worked here made Nick realise how little he really knew. Jenna had told him that he could ask as many questions as he liked – and he *had* asked many questions – but how did he know that the replies he received were truthful ones?

Finally, unable to relax, to clear his mind, he put in a request to go swimming, and Ben appeared ten minutes later and escorted him to the leisure complex. Nick swam lengths for over half an hour. By the time he finished his lungs were aching, but he felt better. He still didn't have any answers, but the physical exercise had made him feel calm again, prepared to bide his time. After all, what else could he do? There was no point kicking up a fuss, especially since his anxieties were based almost solely on what-ifs and maybes.

'Did you see the game on Sky last night?' Ben asked as they stood together in the descending lift.

'No. Who was playing?'

'*Who was playing?* It was only the Gunners, wasn't it? We only won three bleeding nil at Coventry! Jesus, Nick, you was in that room with a TV and you didn't even watch the Gunners go back to the top of the league! If I had my way, that'd be a criminal offence.'

Nick grinned at the man's indignation. 'Sorry, mate. I forgot it was on.'

'*Forgot it was on!* Bloody hell, that's like saying you didn't buy a turkey 'cos you forgot it was Christmas.' The lift stopped and the doors opened. 'You want to get yourself sorted out, mate. You want to get your priorities right.'

He patted Nick condescendingly on the back of the head with one of his shovel-like hands.

As soon as Ben's hand touched him, Nick felt a rush of sensations cram into his brain with such force that it seemed his skull would split in two. After the initial shock he became aware that he was occupying a body that was not his, a body that he realised, after some confusion, was in fact Ben's. Looking out of Ben's eyes, the first thing he saw was Sasha standing naked in front of him, an expression of utter horror on her face. Nick barely had time to register that he was standing in the bath in his London flat before he was lashing out with his fists, viciously and efficiently punching Sasha in the face, smashing her nose and splitting her skin, bludgeoning her to the ground.

Then the scene changed and he was in a different bathroom, looking down at Sasha as she knelt in front of him. This time she looked wild, animal-like, her hair, dark and greasy with sweat, hanging over her face, her eyes like black, glinting beads. He stretched out a hand to her; and suddenly *she* was lashing out at him, her teeth bared and gleaming with spittle, something flashing in her hand. He felt a pain so swift and hot it seemed to sizzle across his skin. And then the scene shifted again and he was one of several people pinning Sasha to the floor, crushing her small body beneath his weight, enjoying the savage, almost sexual thrill of the power that he had over her.

Finally – one scene sliding seamlessly into the next – he was looking down at Sasha lying in a hospital bed, her face deathly-pale apart from the blue tinge of the almost-faded bruises around her closed eyes. She had an IV drip in her arm and her chest was rising and falling spasmodically as she snatched shallow breaths from the air. He was aware that his – or rather Ben's – arm was still hurting; he was holding it to his chest, his right hand supporting it. His clothes were covered in his own blood and he was feeling a little light-headed. Jenna was standing on the other side of the bed. She said to him, coldly, 'Go and get that arm seen to before you pass out. And be more careful next time.'

Then the images were gone, dragged from his mind like a hood being pulled from his head, allowing the light back in. Slowly Nick became aware that he was on his hands and knees on the grey-carpeted floor of the corridor, his head bowed and his stomach churning as if he were about to throw up. Someone was speaking to him, but the buzzing rush of blood in his head made the words fuzzy, distorted.

'Nick,' the voice was saying, 'Nick, mate, are you all right?'

Nick shook his head like a dog with a flea in its ear and dropped back on to his heels, using his arms to push himself into a kneeling position. He saw Ben reaching towards him, evidently intending to haul him to his feet.

'Don't touch me!' Nick snapped, venomously enough to make the big man blink in surprise and rear back. Nick felt a surge of hatred, a desire to strike out, which was almost instantly superseded by a rational inner voice urging him not to reveal what he had discovered. It was hard, but he somehow managed to hide the fact that he was boiling with rage inside. He even made himself smile.

'Sorry,' he said, 'it's just . . . I felt really faint and sick for a minute there.'

'No problem,' said Ben. 'Overdid it a bit with the swimming, I suppose.'

'Yes,' Nick replied. 'Yes, I must have done.'

He took a deep breath, then made himself stand up quickly before Ben could step forward to help him. He stood aside while Ben opened his door, then walked into his suite.

'Can I get you anything?' Ben asked. 'Cup of tea? Maybe something a bit stronger?'

'No, I'll be fine, honestly. I'll just sit down for a bit.'

319

'All right. Well, if you need anything, or you feel a bit dicky, give us a bell.'

'I will,' Nick said and jerked a thumb at the nearest security camera, 'although I think someone'll notice if I collapse.'

As Ben left, closing the door behind him, Nick shuddered, releasing his pent-up feelings of anger and revulsion. He thought about what had happened out in the corridor, thought about his discovery that Ben was the man who had assaulted Sasha. Jenna had always denied that the Illuminati had had anything to do with Sasha's beating, had always claimed that they did not employ such brutal tactics. So if she had been lying to him about this, what else might she have been lying about? Perhaps she had been lying about the whole nature of the Genesis project. Perhaps the project had *always* been viewed as a long-term experiment. Maybe as children Nick and Mercy and Julie Lean and Hallett and the rest had been planted with seeds that it had always been known would not bear fruit for decades.

These speculations fluttered briefly in his mind, but dominating them was the knowledge that Jenna had lied to him about Sasha. He knew now that his daughter had *not* gone home, that she was still here, somewhere in the complex. From Ben's thoughts Nick had been able to glean that she had had some sort of breakdown, that she had attacked Ben and had tried to escape. She had been restrained and sedated, though what had happened since then was anyone's guess. Nick's priority now was to decide how to go about handling this. Obviously he had to be careful. The last thing he should do was let it be known to Jenna how he had come by the information.

Indeed, because of *what* he had discovered, it had been easy to overlook the incredible fact that he had discovered it at all. He wondered whether the Illuminati were aware that sooner or later each of the psis would experience the kind of psychic breakthrough that he had just had. He wondered whether they were waiting for it to happen, whether they had taken measures to deal with it. Or were they truly unaware of the nature and power of the forces they were dealing with here? Were they simply lighting matches and hoping that they would be able to contain the fire if and when it erupted into life?

If so, then for Nick and the rest of the psis the prospect was an encouraging one. It gave them hope, gave them a weapon to fight with. He thought of Andrew, of the way he had reacted to the image of the spider. Was it possible that with a little more practise, a little more discipline, he and his fellow psis could influence the thinking of the Illuminati? Could they do it with enough force, enough authority, or indeed enough subtlety, to bend Jenna and Pemberton and the rest to their will? Certainly, if placed in the position where they were forced to try such a thing, there would be no room for error. He recalled Jenna's response when Lousada had asked Pemberton what was to stop them destroying his brain as they had destroyed the orange. *Ultimate force.* Isn't that what she had promised to unleash upon them?

Nick knew that if he was going to use his gift, he had to understand how it worked; more precisely how he could make it work for him. He thought of the nature of the images he had unwittingly extracted from Ben's mind. Why, of all Ben's thoughts and memories, had *these* particular images passed across? They were pertinent to him, certainly, but what difference did that make? Was it that these thoughts had been foremost in Ben's mind when he had touched Nick? Had he been consciously thinking of Sasha in Nick's presence, perhaps wary of making a slip? Or had the psychic part of Nick's mind instinctively and instantaneously plucked data that was relevant only to him from a tangled jumble of thoughts and memories? What would happen if he touched Jenna's hand and consciously focused on Sasha's present whereabouts and condition? Would she be aware of his intrusion? Would she feel his mind fumbling around, trespassing in her own?

Suddenly he knew what he had to do. He picked up his phone and stabbed in the number that would get him through to Jenna. A woman – not Jenna – said, 'Yes?'

'I'd like to speak to Jenna, please. This is Nick Finch.'

'I'm afraid Jenna is unavailable at the moment,' the woman said.

'I need to speak to her now,' Nick said calmly. 'It's urgent. Tell her that I know Sasha's still here and I want to see her.'

'Wait a moment,' the woman said, her voice noticeably more wary. There was a long pause, during which Nick tried to remain focused. At last Jenna came on the line.

'Hello, Nick. What can I do for you?'

'I know Sasha's here,' he repeated. 'I want to see her.'

Jenna sounded as unruffled as ever. 'What makes you think she's here?'

'I don't *think* she's here – I *know* she's here.'

'All right then. How do you *know* she's here?'

'Ben told me.'

There was the barest pause, and then Jenna said, 'I see. And when was this?'

Nick was all too aware that every second of his life had been filmed and recorded over the past few weeks and that they would be able to check whatever he told them. However there was one place where the ceilings were high and the security cameras therefore perhaps not close enough to pick up lip movements, where there might just be enough background noise to muffle the occasional snatch of speech.

'In the swimming pool,' he said confidently. 'I said something about how I'd always enjoyed swimming with Sasha and he said perhaps we'd be able to do it again when she got better. When I asked him what he meant he tried to cover it up, but he's not a very good liar. I know she's here, Jenna, and I want to see her.'

Jenna gave a small sigh. 'Okay, Nick – sit tight. I'll be round in five minutes.'

It was more like ten before the door buzzed and she entered his suite. Knowing that she may well have checked out his story and discovered that he was lying, and feeling edgy because of that, Nick decided to go straight on the attack.

'Why did you lie to me, Jenna? Why did you tell me you'd taken her home?'

Jenna raised her hands. 'Relax, Nick. I'll explain everything.' She sat on the bed. She looked relaxed, guileless. 'The reason we didn't tell you that Sasha was still here, Nick, was because we didn't want to distract you from your preparation training by worrying you unduly. The fact is, the very day I voiced my concerns about Sasha, she went ballistic. She smashed up her room and when Ben went in to calm her down she attacked him with a knife. For her own safety as much as for the safety of others, we were forced to restrain and sedate her.'

'And she's still here?' said Nick.

'Yes. Our aim was to make her better and then take her home without telling you. Maybe that was wrong, but we really were

322

trying to spare your feelings. We decided that what you didn't know couldn't hurt you.'

'Very thoughtful,' he said drily, 'but did it not occur to you that Sasha might have needed me?'

'Sasha is under sedation.'

'What, *still?*'

'Yes. Dr Ryder, who has been monitoring her condition closely, seemed to think it necessary.'

'But you can't keep someone under sedation for a whole week just to keep them quiet!' He pushed himself up from his chair. 'I want to see her now.'

He expected Jenna to offer some reason why he couldn't, but she simply said, 'Certainly. Come with me.'

They crossed to the lift, ascended several floors and walked along a number of corridors. Finally they rounded a corner to see a white-coated man in his forties with frizzy hair and a hang-dog expression standing outside a half-open door, evidently waiting for them.

'This is Dr Ryder,' Jenna said. 'Dr Ryder, this is Nick Finch – Sasha's father.'

The two men shook hands. Pushing the door to the room wider, Ryder said, 'Your daughter's in here, Mr Finch. You won't get much response from her, though, I'm afraid.'

The room was small, well-lit, sparsely furnished. Nick crossed to Sasha's bed, appalled at her pallor and her stillness, at the IV tubes in her arm, up her nose.

He took her hand, which was cold, as if she'd been outside without gloves on a winter's day. He felt his emotions, which until now he'd managed to conceal beneath a mask of composure, beginning to break through, and swung angrily to confront Ryder. 'She looks terrible! I want you to stop pumping this shit into her right now.'

'With all due respect, Mr Finch,' Ryder said, 'we've tried reducing her medication on several occasions, but she just becomes violent.'

'So what's your plan?' snapped Nick. 'Keep her under until her brain turns into vegetable soup?' Before Ryder could respond, he turned to Jenna, who was standing by the door.

The sight of her – unconcerned, even bored – incensed him; the last of his composure cracked into brittle pieces and fell away. All

323

at once he was as furious as he could ever remember being, more so even than when he had confronted Hallett after watching Jacobs die. His voice harsh, he said, 'If Sasha isn't conscious the next time I see her, you can stick your fucking Genesis project up your arse. I wouldn't co-operate even if you tortured me. Do you hear?'

Jenna nodded, unperturbed. 'Of course, Nick. There's really no need to resort to threats. Dr Ryder, I want you to act on Mr Finch's request immediately.'

'What if she becomes violent again?' Ryder asked.

'Try *talking* to her,' Nick snapped. 'My daughter's not an animal. She's an intelligent human being.' He turned back to Jenna. 'I want to visit her every day until she's better.'

Jenna smiled sweetly and nodded once more. 'Of course, Nick,' she repeated. 'Whatever you say.'

Forty-Six

From today, Farrow had told him, he would cease to be merely an observer; he would become an active member of the group. Yet it was not this that caused Nick's body to tingle with excitement as he was led into the CRU. Last night, lying in bed, he had come to an important decision. No longer would he accept what Jenna, the mouthpiece of the Illuminati, told him; no longer would he allow himself to be seduced by the cosy, comfortable, carefree existence they had created for him here. If nothing else, yesterday's experience with Ben had taught him that the Illuminati were not to be trusted. It was time, therefore, to take matters into his own hands, to try to establish a link with his fellow psis. Of course, he still had no real idea of the extent of his capabilities and ought, therefore, to prepare himself for failure, yet even so the prospect of trying, of doing something proactive rather than reactive, filled him with nervous excitement. What added to his nervousness was the knowledge that he would have no time to dither, to choose the right moment. He would have to act before the sensor pads were attached to his head and the monitor switched on: for once that happened, his brain activity became public property, and any unauthorised attempt to use his ability would not pass unnoticed.

Most of the other psis were already there, taking their places, when Nick arrived. The fat, bearded, sullen Mark Brown and a couple of others were already having the sensor pads attached to their temples by white-coated lab assistants. Nick had banked on the fact that Greg Lousada, as usual, would be the last to sit down, defying the NO SMOKING signs to have a final cigarette before work began. Aside from this token act of rebellion, however, Lousada seemed as subdued as he had been since his outburst on

325

the first day Nick had entered the CRU. There was a brow-beaten, defeated air about him. Nick's intention was to find out why, but first he had to establish a link. Not knowing quite how to go about it, he stared fiercely at Lousada, concentrating on his face. In his mind he simply chanted the phrase *Are you okay?*, repeating it silently over and over. He had no idea whether this was the correct approach. Despite the successful psychic projection experiments he had witnessed, and the progress he had made in his preparation training, in his heart of hearts Nick did not really expect anything to happen.

He was therefore delighted and astounded when Lousada suddenly reacted as though someone had reached between his legs from behind and grabbed his balls. His eyes widened and he jerked upright so violently that a quarter-inch of ash tumbled from his cigarette to create a grey smear down the lapel of his jacket. Nick gritted his teeth. *Don't make it so obvious,* he urged silently. *Don't let them guess.*

Whether Lousada picked up on his message, or whether it was his own presence of mind that helped him to recover so quickly, Nick was not sure. But Lousada glanced quickly around to ensure his reaction had not been observed, casually brushed the ash from his lapel, then glanced idly across the room. His eyes met Nick's and his lips twitched upwards in a tiny, conspiratorial smile.

Are you okay? Nick asked again, imagining the words crossing directly into Lousada's mind.

Lousada raised his eyebrows and gave the tiniest shake of his head. All at once, in his own mind, Nick sensed the man's reply. It was an odd sensation. He didn't hear a voice, nor did he picture the response in the form of words, yet he knew exactly what Lousada was thinking: *I've been better.*

'Mr Finch,' a lab assistant suddenly said behind him, 'would you take a seat?'

'Er . . . sure,' Nick said, smiling. As he sat, he glanced at Lousada again. *Later,* he thought.

Lousada took a last pull on his cigarette, then dropped the butt on the floor and stamped on it. As he exhaled a column of smoke he gave the minutest of nods.

Forty-Seven

Nick listened hard, but could hear nothing at all. He wondered how many of the scientific and security staff remained in the complex at night. *They must all have quarters here*, he supposed; unless he was much mistaken, there was nowhere else for them to go. He suspected even Jenna's flat in London had been a place acquired by the Illuminati for her short-term use while she ensnared him and possibly others. He wondered if she *did* have her own home somewhere, and what it was like. He wondered if she had a boyfriend or a husband, maybe even children. He couldn't imagine it – she seemed to dedicate too much time to her job to allow room for anything else – but you never knew. Maybe they had family quarters here, schools, shops, cinemas, restaurants. Not just a military and medical research complex, but a whole city beneath the earth in the middle of nowhere.

He lay in bed, staring up into the darkness. Without a window, without street lamps and stars and the moon, the darkness in his room at night was absolute. He guessed the security cameras still worked though. They wouldn't leave something like that to chance. *Under cover of darkness*: the phrase was simply not applicable here. They were watching him, listening to him, every minute of the day, though unless they were merely toying with him they seemed to have accepted his explanation for how he knew Sasha was still here.

To be honest, he didn't know what he was waiting for – the right moment, he supposed, though exactly what that meant he had no idea. Perhaps he was scared of failure; or perhaps he was afraid that the instant he started to project, to try to get through, they would *know* somehow. Perhaps alarms would go off and security guards would burst in, pointing guns at his face, shining bright lights in his eyes.

He smiled at the image, and then instantly killed the smile, thinking that it would alert them, that they might wonder, watching him, what that sudden smile was for. Closing his eyes felt like shutting the doors on them, pulling the curtains across the windows so that they couldn't see in.

Now was as good a time as any, he thought. He pictured Greg Lousada's face, pictured Greg lying in the darkness, just like he was. *Greg, are you there? Greg, are you there?* He repeated the words over and over in his mind, beaming a mental radio signal across the airwaves.

Nothing happened. Minutes passed. The message became a meaningless mental chant, an incantation. The words in themselves seemed to become devoid of significance and yet to retain some form of arcane power, like an occultist's spell to summon demons. As in the Ganzfeld tank, Nick felt his mind opening up, felt as though he was gradually unlocking the gates to the infinite inner universe of thought and possibility.

Then he was travelling, his mind rushing through the vast blacknesses opening up before him. There was a definite destination in sight, yet his conscious mind had no idea what it was. It was his instinctive mind that was leading him unerringly towards it. He travelled for a long time. There was no sensation except that of moving forward.

And then all at once he was hurtling down, swooping like a bird of prey.

He was not aware of the darkness parting, but suddenly he was looking as though from a great height at a bed and a sleeping figure within it. The figure's sleep was restless – brow furrowed, duvet rumpled, arms and legs bent almost into the shape of a swastika. As if breaking through a curtain of static, Nick suddenly heard his own thoughts, still transmitting the same message, over and over: *Greg, are you there? Greg, are you there?*

And although the figure was sleeping, Nick heard the reply of its unconscious mind: *Yes, I am.*

Whichever part of Nick had broken away from his physical body to come here – his mind, his soul, his astral being – came to a halt a few feet above the bed in which Greg Lousada slept.

Abruptly, as though sensing his presence, Lousada rolled on to his back and opened his eyes. Instinctively recognising the moment of vulnerability between sleeping and waking, the moment when secrets might be revealed, Nick projected an urgent message: *Shut your eyes. Don't say anything.*

He was not sure whether Greg had heard him. For several seconds he did not respond. Then Nick heard, or rather sensed, his reply: *Nick? Is that you?*

Yes. Yes, it's me. How are you? Are you okay?

No words this time, but merely emotions, despair and fear primary among them. And then suddenly, with no sense of interval, no intermediary phase, Nick was somewhere else.

Just as yesterday, when he had slipped unwittingly into Ben's mind, Nick suddenly found himself in an unfamiliar body, looking out through someone else's eyes. He was a passenger in Greg's mind as Greg sat in a chair in a darkened room, staring at a TV screen. There were other people in the room, at least two of them, but they were shadowy figures. All of Greg's attention was fixed on the screen, and as he watched through Greg's eyes what was unfolding there, Nick felt Greg's emotions, felt terrible, sickening horror coursing through him, wave after wave of it.

Greg was being shown video footage, filmed by someone holding a camcorder, of three masked men terrorising an elderly couple. The couple, in their late sixties, were lying on the floor of what was evidently their lounge, their hands tied behind their backs. The old man looked dazed, blood matting his white wispy hair and trickling down into his ear; the woman was sobbing hysterically, breathlessly, her left eye so purple and swollen that it looked as though a plum had been rammed into her eye-socket. Around them their lounge was being systematically destroyed, ornaments swept to the floor and smashed, paintings yanked from the walls and hurled across the room, upholstery ripped to shreds, furniture kicked and stamped to matchwood. The grainy, jerky quality of the film only seemed to add to the mayhem, to the sheer, sickening cruelty of the scene. The destruction went on for several minutes – they seemed like an eternity. Then, finally, one of the masked men turned towards the camera, said something which the blurry, achney sound quality made incoherent, then laughed echoey. Nick found himself tensing, shrinking back, his balls – *Lousada's* balls – crawling up into his stomach as the man

329

stomped over to the elderly couple which all at once Nick knew were Greg Lousada's parents. The man stood over the bound and cowering couple. Then he unzipped the black jeans he wore, took out his cock and began to piss on them, spraying it around so that it covered them both, laughing as urine splashed on the woman's face and she gave little whimpering screams, as though the warm piss were burning her skin like acid.

The film ended there, to be replaced by crackling grey static. A man stepped forward and switched off the TV. Nick felt Greg's emotions as though they were his own. He felt so devastated, so appalled, so *soiled*, by what he had seen, that he couldn't even speak. He was aware of a second shadowy figure, just behind and to his left, moving to stand in front of him. He turned his head – and saw Jenna, barely able to conceal her amusement.

His voice felt as though he had to dredge it up from some deep and rusty chamber. It scoured his throat as he croaked, 'You bitch!'

Jenna laughed. She was in high spirits. 'Now, now, Greg! Don't tell me you haven't learned your lesson. My boys can always go back and finish the job, you know.'

Greg said nothing, though Nick felt his murderous hatred like a bristling, twisted ball of white-hot razor wire in his skull and stomach. Jenna pulled up a plastic chair and sat right in front of him, their knees almost touching. 'You brought this on yourself, you know, Greg,' she said reasonably. 'We tried to be nice to you, gave you comfortable quarters, all the luxury items you could wish for – and what happened? You threw it right back in our faces. Now, if you'd expressed your grievances to me in private, things would have been different. We could have talked the matter through, sorted everything out, like civilised human beings. But you didn't do that, did you? Instead you tried to rock the boat, stir things up, upset everybody else – and not for the first time. You're a shit-stirrer, Greg, and I'm afraid that's simply not acceptable around here. There's far too much at stake for that sort of behaviour. So I'm afraid sometimes, to bring people like you back into line, we have to hit them where it hurts, target their vulnerable areas in order to avoid the situation getting out of hand. It's not pleasant – in fact, sometimes it's downright unsavoury – but it's necessary, Greg. I'm sure you can see that, can't you?'

330

Greg didn't reply. He couldn't. His fury was like a rock in his throat. Unperturbed, Jenna went on. 'I hope you'll regard what happened to your parents – and don't worry, they weren't hurt *too* badly – as a warning. A little nudge back on to the straight and narrow. I'm sure you wouldn't want anything like that to happen again, would you, Greg? And you know, to be frank, neither would we. I mean, it would be terrible if your . . . um, wayward behaviour, shall we say, forced us to pay a visit to your sister Alice and her eight year-old daughter, don't you think?'

Greg's (Nick's) throat was still so constricted that it felt as though someone were trying to strangle him. Yet this time he managed to squeeze out a few words. 'You . . . leave them . . . alone!'

'We have every intention of doing so, Greg. As long as you're a good boy you have my word they will never come to any harm.' She smiled and looked thoughtful for a moment. 'Do you know what I think all this aggression of yours stems from, Greg? Sexual frustration. You're just uptight because you're not getting any.'

She reached out and placed a hand on his crotch. 'Would you like me to remedy that situation for you, Greg?'

'No,' he croaked.

'You're just being polite. It's no trouble, really.' Her voice hardened a touch. 'Why don't you just close your eyes and think about your parents? This won't take long.'

She unzipped him and reached into his boxer shorts, her hand closing around his cock. Again, Nick experienced Greg's emotions as if they were his own: he felt sick, humiliated, but physically he couldn't fail to respond. His cock was already hardening in Jenna's hand. She gave a cold, superior smile and began to wank him off.

It was not a sexual experience, was nothing so much as a callous and functional display of her power over him, yet although he sat with his teeth gritted and his stomach in knots, Nick knew that Greg could do nothing to prevent his orgasm building inside him. Coming was like vomiting in a public place after too much alcohol: a bitter relief yet degrading nonetheless. Then Greg (Nick) slumped forward with a groan, his legs hollow and brittle, hands tightly gripping the arms of the chair. Jenna shoved him upright again, then smeared his sperm across his face and into his hair. The sneering triumph on her face made her look ugly.

331

'You can only push us so far, Greg,' she muttered into his ear. 'You may be valuable to the project – but you're not indispensable. Remember that.'

She wiped the last of the sperm on her hand down the front of his shirt, then stood up and walked out of the room.

Forty-Eight

The second day he went to visit her, Sasha was awake. Yesterday she had still been woozy, drifting in and out of consciousness, reminding Nick distressingly of how his mother (his *adoptive* mother, he couldn't help reminding himself) had been in the last days of her illness. When he went in today, though, Sasha was lying quietly, staring up at the ceiling. She looked serene. There was nothing to suggest she had been violent, or would become so. When he entered the room she moved her head a fraction of an inch to look at him and offered a wan smile.

'Hi,' he said, speaking in a hushed voice as if she were some rare and highly strung creature he didn't want to startle. He moved to the chair beside her bed. 'How are you?'

'Fine,' she murmured. 'You?'

'Oh, *I'm* fine. Do you remember anything of what happened?'

'I really lost it, Dad. I wasn't myself.' She paused, and lowered her voice even more. 'I think they were putting something in my food.'

He smiled, imagining the circular eye of a security camera burning into the back of his head. 'Oh, I don't think they'd do that, Sash.'

Her smile was tired but sceptical. 'Wouldn't they? I wouldn't put it past them.'

He reached out and took her hand. It was cold, and suddenly seemed as small as it had when she'd been six years old and he'd held it to cross the road. 'You were depressed, that's all. Being like that can do funny things to your head, make you feel that your mind's not your own. The time I spent in prison was a constant battle against depression. There were times when I used to think I was going mad.'

The bitterness in her smile faded to tenderness, which he presumed was for what she saw as his naiveté. 'I was depressed, all right, but it was artificially induced. I know myself, Dad. There's no way I would have gone downhill so quickly. I'm tougher than that – as you said.'

He matched her smile with his own. 'I don't want to argue with you, Sash, but I'm sure you're wrong. These are not bad people.'

'They brought me here at gunpoint, Dad.'

'For your own good.'

She closed her eyes, then opened them again in a slow blink. When she spoke she sounded, not scornful, but merely disappointed. 'You really believe that, do you?'

'I do, Sash, yes. We're doing great work here, and I don't mind admitting it's something I'm proud to be involved with. It may sound corny, but I really am convinced that we're at the forefront of man's next stage of evolution. What we're doing here will have far-reaching effects for the future of humanity.'

'Yes, but what kinds of effects, Dad?'

'Good ones. Only good ones.'

She looked at him sadly. A little colour had returned to her cheeks now, though she still looked pale, and when she spoke her voice was soft. 'Oh, Dad. They've really got to you, haven't they?'

He squeezed her hand. 'I'm sorry you feel this way, Sash – but trust me. I know what I'm doing.'

'Do you?'

'*I* think so, yes.'

'I hope you're right, Dad, I really do.'

'I am,' he said. 'I know I am.'

She gave another slow blink and expelled a long, sighing breath. 'You're tired,' he said. 'I'll go now and let you sleep. I'll come and see you again tomorrow.'

'That'll be nice.' She looked at him with sudden intensity, as if she wanted to commit every detail of his face to memory. 'Be careful, Dad.'

'I will,' he said. 'Don't worry.' And as he leaned forward to kiss her, he moved his left hand, which up until now had been lying idly on the bedspread, to Sasha's, to the hand that he was

334

already clutching with his right, so that it would look as if he had taken her small hand in both of his as a gesture of affection. He loosened the fingers of his left hand and pressed the small square of paper he had been clutching in his palm against the undersides of her fingers, hoping she would realise what he wanted her to do. She didn't fail him. She closed her fingers around the paper and drew it into her palm without a flicker of surprise or puzzlement showing on her face.

He said goodbye, promised again that he would see her tomorrow and left. For a long time Sasha lay on her back, eyes closed and breathing deeply, pretending to be asleep. Though the sedative still lingered in her system, the adrenaline surge caused by the note-passing incident made her body jitter with anticipation. Finally, hoping that her supine form was not being observed too closely, she let out a deep sigh and rolled languidly on to her side, her hands delving beneath the sheets in such a way that, if she opened one eye to a tiny slit, she could see her hands, which would be concealed from the camera by a raised edge of sheet. She forced herself to count slowly to six hundred, and then eased the square of paper out of her palm and unfolded it.

It was a four-line note written in block capitals, the lines slanting oddly towards each other at the ends as if they had been written under cover of darkness. The note read:

DON'T WORRY, SASHA,
I'VE GOT A PLAN TO GET US OUT OF HERE,
BE READY OVER THE NEXT FEW DAYS.
ALL MY LOVE, DAD.

Forty-Nine

It was like an internal bee sting, a sharp fizz of pain in his cerebral cortex. It woke Hallett, made him sit up in bed before he had even opened his eyes. Without legs that movement required more control of the stomach muscles than it would for an able-bodied person; but Hallett, despite his bulk, was in good shape. He worked out every day, continually pushing himself beyond the pain barrier. One positive legacy of his accident was his incredibly high pain threshold; another was his ability to remain cool and alert in situations that reduced others to heart-pounding panic. Within two seconds, therefore, even as his eyes opened and were peering to penetrate the darkness, Hallett was already shrugging off the disorientation of being snatched into wakefulness and was taking stock of his surroundings.

The air was cool, though there was no breeze, which meant that none of his windows had been opened. The room was silent, and reaching out mentally Hallett could discern no unfamiliar or hostile presence within his immediate vicinity. Yet *something* had woken him; the sting of pain in his head had left an imprint of itself behind. Though the threat was unknown, he did not yet allow himself to become anxious about it, and even when something moved on the other side of the room, he jerked not in fear but in surprise, for he knew that the closest living presence was several rooms away.

As his hand moved to the switch of his bedside lamp, Hallett scanned the area mentally, *viciously*, but came up blank. The movement – a kind of slow, clumsy unfurling, as if something unused to being upright were attempting to stand – had occurred between the door and an Elizabethan armchair that he had bought at auction because he liked the shape of it. Was it his imagination, or was the darkness oddly dense there, like thick smoke or black, unshifting fog? He barely had time to consider the matter before his stubby thumb found the rectangular stud of the lamp switch.

The darkness fled from the light in a strangely solid way that made Hallett think of shiny black cockroaches scuttling for cover. In fleeing, it left something behind; something that now fixed on Hallett in his bed and took a lopsided lurch towards him.

It had once been a man, though it was now shrivelled by fire, blackened and charred and still smoking. Its clothes and its skin had become indistinguishable from one another, both reduced to scraps of ash which clung to its stick-like bones and brittle grey skull. Its eyes and nose were holes in its face; its teeth jutted from the lipless cavity of its mouth. As it took another lurching step towards him, it reached out its arms towards Hallett as though to embrace him, or perhaps in silent accusation.

Hallett could not remember the last time he had been afraid – perhaps he never had, not truly. The emotion that gripped him now, therefore, pulling his stomach into a tight knot, draining warmth from his extremities and moisture from his mouth, was unfamiliar and alarming yet seemed inextricable as a race memory.

He let out a half-strangled cry and reached with both hands to grab the right-hand side of his mattress. Frantically he hauled up the corner and grabbed the automatic he kept there. When he turned back, the incinerated corpse of Gary Jacobs had taken two further steps towards his bed. Four more and those spiky twig-fingers would be close enough to scrape across his flesh.

Hallett let off a shot, the gun's retort spanking his ears in the confines of the room. The bullet passed through the centre of Jacobs' chest as if he weren't there and smashed a huge chunk of plaster from the wall beside the door. Hallett let off another shot; this time the bullet passed through Jacobs' eye socket like smoke. It was this – the realisation that the creature stumbling towards him was as physically insubstantial as thought – that finally brought Hallett to his senses.

He remembered the sting of pain in his head that had woken him. He had assumed that to be of his own making, a premonitory warning that something was amiss, but what if there was an outside influence at work here? He had scanned the room, but he

337

hadn't looked inside his own head; he had thought that he knew himself well enough for that to be unnecessary. But he did so now, and discovered a slight pressure in his mind, *so* slight that it was akin to a hand resting lightly in the small of his back, only noticeable if you knew it was there.

Furiously he shrugged it off. It was as easy as brushing an insect from his sleeve. Instantly the vision of Jacobs faded, leaving no residue of itself behind. When Mad Dog burst in through the door a split-second later, swinging his gun from side to side, Hallett was so wound up that he almost shot him. Mad Dog stopped dead, eyes widening at the sight of the gun pointing at his face, at Hallett's expression of twisted fury.

'Hey, boss, take it easy,' Mad Dog said, raising his hands, pointing his own gun at the ceiling. For two seconds an insane light danced in Hallett's eyes, then he slowly lowered his gun.

Mad Dog swallowed. 'What's happening, boss? You okay?'

'I'll kill them,' Hallett muttered through gritted teeth, bubbles of foam collecting at the corners of his mouth.

'Kill who, boss?'

Hallett glared at Mad Dog. 'Whoever did this to me. I swear to you, Mad Dog, I'll find them, and when I do I'll fry their fucking brains.'

Fifty

Three days later, Sasha was deemed well enough to return to her room, which had been restored so thoroughly to its original state that she could almost have believed her violent breakdown two weeks earlier had been nothing but a bad dream. Meanwhile, Nick and his fellow psis had moved on to what Nick considered the real stuff – or at least the beginnings of it. They still did the relaxation and visualisation exercises, still attempted mentally to influence the behaviour of both animals and humans, but now an extra ingredient had been added to the pot. Yesterday Pemberton had held up his hands. 'Ladies and gentlemen, today I would like to move on to the next stage of your training. I know we're moving quickly, and that you have still to master many of the basic control skills that you will need if you are to use your abilities to their full potential, but I nevertheless believe it necessary at this point to introduce you to a technique known as remote viewing, which some of you may already have heard of. For those who haven't, what it involves is this . . .'

He spent the next few minutes explaining how the technique worked. Then he gave each of them an artist's sketchpad and a black felt-tip pen and ordered that the lights be turned down low. He told them to spend a few minutes emptying their minds of extraneous clutter and to prepare themselves to receive the information he was about to give them.

Time passed. The silence and the motionlessness of everyone in the room seemed to stretch the minutes into a timeless somnolence that became more and more difficult to break. When Pemberton did finally speak, the texture of the silence was such that his measured voice seemed to acquire a rich and intoxicating

339

quality, each syllable seeming to drip slowly into Nick's mind like smooth, thick honey.

'It has recently come to our attention,' he said, 'that Iraqi jet fighters have once again been impinging on Kuwaiti air space – just as they did several years ago. The purpose of these flights is currently unknown, though over the past three months they have been occurring with increasing regularity. Additionally, a larger than average number of Iraqi diplomats stationed throughout Europe and the United States have recently returned to Iraq, claiming that their presnece is required to deal with domestic matters. Two weeks ago an American intelligence agent, Jim Strang, was sent into the field to gather information about these activities. For the first ten days of his mission everything ran smoothly – but four days ago radio contact with Mr Strang was lost. What we would like you to do today, ladies and gentlemen, is to focus on a series of co-ordinates I am about to give you – I should explain that these co-ordinates are randomly selected, intended to be used as nothing more than a focus, a trigger, a psychic map reference if you like – and try to establish Mr Strang's current whereabouts and state of mind. If any information does come to you concerning Mr Strang, and there is certainly no guarantee that it will, it may do so in the form of images and signs, in a confused and jumbled mass of odd notions, symbolic ideas, inspirational flashes. Anything that seems significant – even if you don't understand it – should be noted down. It doesn't matter what it looks like on paper – numbers, words, pictures – even the smallest, most obscure details can sometimes turn out to be important. So, ladies and gentlemen, here are your co-ordinates . . .'

Pemberton enunciated a series of eight numbers and immediately Nick felt himself slipping inside his own mind, down into the interior. Pemberton had said the numbers were randomly chosen, yet they nevertheless seemed to act as a combination, to open a door and release Nick's innermost thoughts. His surroundings bled away and he found himself rushing like a comet, soaring through the stratosphere. He had no notion of time. From receiving the co-ordinates to achieving this state seemed to have taken no more than seconds, but past experience had taught him that it could just as easily have been hours.

The images he received that day – a building with a cross on it

340

(a church or a hospital); an impression of severe head pain, a thin man with a black moustache shouting and kicking; a stench of petrol fumes so overwhelming that he thought he was going to die – came instantaneously, out of nowhere. Though intense they were as fleeting as blinks.

When he came to, groggily, as though waking from an alcohol-induced sleep, he found that the impressions and images he and his fellow psis had experienced – some of which were shared, some of which were unique to particular individuals – enabled them to build an approximate picture of Strang's current situation. All agreed that after being captured he had been beaten and kicked so savagely about the head that his captors had been forced to provide him with hospital treatment. They had transported him by strapping or tying him to the underside of a car or truck. He was now in a small place, very possibly in a well-populated area, but well hidden; perhaps somewhere underground, a basement maybe, though not a prison, less official than that. His injuries were causing him great physical discomfort and he was scared – though Ellie McKee said she believed very strongly that he was scared more for his family than for himself.

After the remote viewing session Nick felt exhausted. He was covered with a layer of sweat so rank that the first thing he did when he got back to his room was to shower and change before collapsing on to his bed and sleeping solidly for four hours. Now it was the next day and, as ever, Nick and his fellow psis had done a few preliminary mental exercises and were now being asked to try to re-establish psychic contact with the mind of Jim Strang.

As Pemberton gave them the co-ordinates, Nick glanced meaningfully at Julie Lean and she acknowledged the look with one of her own. This time Nick did not allow himself to slip into the semi-comatose state that precipitated the ability to remote-view. He glanced around the circle. Ellie McKee offered him a barely perceptible smile; Greg Lousada actually winked. For a second Nick thought he was going to grin, which might have given the game away, but by staring into space in what he hoped was an approximation of the remote viewing state and clenching his teeth hard, he was able to keep his face expressionless.

After a while Nick began to feel his limbs becoming tense. He wished Julie would get on with it, yet at the same time he admired her restraint. He began to worry about the wink Greg Lousada had given him. If they hadn't spotted it now, would they do so later, when they reviewed the film? Perhaps their suspicions would be roused by what Julie was about to do. If they also saw Greg wink, they would surely realise it was a put-up job. Then what would happen? Would Nick and his cohorts be interrogated? Would the Illuminati realise what a huge can of worms they had opened here and terminate the experiment?

Stop it, he told himself. *You're getting paranoid, you're letting your imagination run away with you.*

The thought was still in his mind when Julie Lean screamed.

Although he had been expecting it, Nick jumped, which he supposed was no bad thing. He looked up, trying to adopt a dopey expression to make it seem as though he were waking from a trance. He hoped the depiction of his brain activity wouldn't give him away for the last few minutes he had been fully conscious and alert when he should have been quiescent, introspective.

Julie leaped to her feet, knocking her chair over, and tore the sensor pads from her temples. 'I can't do it,' she sobbed. 'I can't take it any more. I'm so tired.'

She collapsed so convincingly that for a moment Nick wondered whether she was not acting after all. Dry-mouthed, he stood up, turning to Pemberton who was coming down the steps.

'We're *all* tired, Mr Pemberton,' he said, trying to sound weary, at the end of his tether. 'The training has been moving so quickly. We need a break.'

Pemberton stared at him, then at Julie. He looked alarmed, uncertain. Nick felt sure that their little performance would not have convinced Jenna, but Pemberton was a softer touch.

'Please, Mr Pemberton,' Nick said again, 'we're no good to you in this state. We're exhausted.'

Pemberton hesitated a moment longer, then nodded. 'All right – you can take the rest of the day off. Perhaps I *have* been pushing you a little too hard lately. I'll arrange for you to be escorted to your rooms.'

Back in his suite, alone, Nick closed his eyes and quickly established a link with Julie Lean. It was less than a week since he had first 'spoken' to Greg Lousada, but already telepathic communication was becoming second nature to all of them. It was like riding a bike; once you got the knack of it, progress came in leaps and bounds. The speed at which they were learning – at which their minds were expanding to encompass these new abilities – was frightening in a way, but Nick wasn't frightened. He knew how powerful they were becoming: what a threat they might be capable of posing to the Illuminati.

Well done, Julie, he thought.

The reply came back almost immediately: *Thanks*.

This time Nick sent out a general enquiry: *Is everybody ready?*

The affirmatives came back in an overlapping collage of thought so intense it was almost like sound. *Yes-es-yes-ye-yes-es-yessss*.

Fifty-One

Despite his boyhood accident, Hallett knew what it was like to walk, to strut, to run. He knew what it was like to kick a man, knew the savage joy of stamping on somebody's face, grinding their bollocks beneath his heels. Mad Dog was comfortable with his boss's intrusion, though Hallett never overstepped the mark. He had his pride and his standards, and as such was only an occasional and always very courteous passenger in the head of his right-hand man.

Mad Dog trusted him implicitly, Hallett knew that, and Hallett in turn knew that he could rely on Mad Dog, knew that his lieutenant would protect him with his life if called upon to do so. The first time Hallett had seen Mad Dog he had been a skinny seven-year-old kid called Leslie White, which had not been a good name for a black kid to have on that particular estate. Indeed, it may well have been his name which had contributed to the fact that little Les White had been lying beside the swings on the concrete surface of a kids' playground, getting the shit kicked out of him by a couple of NF skinheads.

Hallett, sixteen at the time, had been wheeling himself past the playground on his way home from his friend Dave McNeill's house. He had recognised the skinheads instantly: the Gibson twins, slow of thought and speech, with dull, dead eyes, matching swastika tattoos on their foreheads and a mother who looked and smelled as if she had just crawled out of a swamp.

Hallett didn't like the Gibson twins: they were cunts and bullies, and a few days earlier they had shouted some sexual remark after Hallett's mum in the street which she had said was too disgusting to repeat but which Hallett had extracted from her mind anyway. A group of kids were standing around the Gibson

344

twins (who were a few years older than Hallett, nineteen or twenty), some silently watching the systematic kicking their young playmate was receiving with wide eyes and blank expressions, and some urging the skinheads on with shrill, prepubescent cries: 'Kick him in the head'; 'Kill the wog bastard'.

Living on the estate, Hallett was inured to violence, but something about the brainless, brutal way the Gibson twins kept kicking and kicking even though the skinny kid was silent and unmoving spurred him into action. That, combined with the need to seek vengeance on his mother's behalf. Changing course, he wheeled himself down to the playground where everyone was too engaged with the attack to notice him. At least until he shouted, 'This is about your fucking level, isn't it, you cunts?'

Some of the kids turned, evidently relieved at the intervention, though their faces fell when they saw that he was just a teenager in a wheelchair. The Gibsons ceased their kicking and turned to him in the slow, stupid manner in which they did everything except inflict violence on others – which they did with impressive energy and ferocity.

'Huh?' one of them said.

'*Huh*,' Hallett imitated. 'Sorry, fuck-face, was I speaking too fast for you?' Before either of them could respond he continued. 'You've proved you're both men by kicking the little kid's head in, so why don't you come and have a go at me now? I mean, I'm only a fucking spasmo in a wheelchair. I reckon both of you together should just about be able to handle it.'

The Gibson twins looked at each other, each hoping that the other had managed to grasp the meaning of the words that Hallett had machine-gunned at them. Then the one who had grunted, evidently the mastermind of the family, said, 'Why don't you just fuck off, you spazzy shit-head?'

'Yeah, why don't you . . . go and look for your legs or something?' the other added, inspired by his brother's dazzling wit to make his own contribution.

Hallett was too angry and weary and just plain contemptuous of the twins to trade insults with them, so he made them hit each other instead. The dull, moronic hatred on both their faces became a dull, moronic surprise that was funny enough to make Hallett give a bark of laughter when one of them turned and unexpectedly punched the other right in the centre of his face.

345

He left the twins trading punches whilst the other kids looked on in bewilderment. Manoeuvring himself from his wheelchair, he scraped the skinny black kid up off the concrete. Helped by those of the kids who were not too engrossed in the twins' incomprehensible fist-fight to tear themselves away, Hallett took the black kid home, where his mum tended to his injuries and made him a cup of tea. The kid didn't speak until the mug of hot liquid was being pressed to his lips, and then he grimaced. 'What's this?' he murmured.

'It's tea,' Hallett said. 'It's got sugar in it. It'll make you feel better.'

'Got any Coke?' the kid asked.

Twenty years ago now, that encounter had been. Twenty years of friendship and loyalty, of working for each other, looking out for each other – though in truth it was Mad Dog who did most of the work and Hallett who did virtually all of the looking-out. He was looking out today, though, in a different kind of way, looking out through Mad Dog's eyes, sharing his vision, his perception. It was nothing special – a routine bit of business, that was all, a little reminder for a bad payer – but Hallett knew he would enjoy it. Mad Dog's head was a good place to be, a familiar and warm place, and of course there was always the prospect of a bit of action to spice things up.

He was with Mad Dog as he walked into the snooker hall with Sherman in tow, with him as he accosted the owner and an argument ricocheted between them. He was with him too when the owner pulled a shotgun from behind the bar where he was standing and pointed it at Mad Dog's stomach, felt Mad Dog's momentary surprise and alarm, soothed it with one brief mental caress, like smoothing out a wrinkle in a tablecloth with one sweep of his hand. Chanelling his ability through Mad Dog, Hallett made the snooker hall owner turn the gun around and put the barrel in his own mouth, made him reach down and grasp the trigger, made him tighten his finger on it . . .

Then the pain came again, though this time it was less like a bee sting and more a blistering attack which tore into his mind. It was so powerful and so unexpected that Hallett was thrown into a dark and churning confusion, and for a vital few seconds contact with Mad Dog was lost.

346

Fifty-Two

Until Hallett was torn from his mind like a large scab being ripped from an internal wound, Mad Dog had been enjoying himself. He had never liked Bob Winston. The guy was a mouthy fucker and a racist bastard. Although Winston had never revealed his political leanings outright, Mad Dog could tell he was a Nazi by the way he looked and moved and spoke, by the company he kept, by his clientele. After twenty-odd years of being called nigger and spade and coon, you just *knew* who to trust and who was out to get you. Men like Winston had a stink about them like diseased shit.

Not that Mad Dog gave a fuck; it was a long time since he had let petty-minded bigots like Winston worry him. Still, it was nice to get one over on them, nice to rattle their cages and see them snarl, nice to think of them all twisted-up inside with the knowledge that some wog, some jungle-bunny, had got them by the short and curlies.

He had sauntered in that day as if he owned the place, knowing it would wind Winston up, Sherman trailing him like a pet Rottweiler spoiling for a fight, a role he played to perfection despite his mental failings. The few guys who were playing snooker looked up at him as if he were a walking bad smell as he strolled between the tables; they clutched their cues like weapons.

Mad Dog and Sherman walked up to the bar where Winston, wearing a brown short-sleeved shirt that looked fit to burst beneath the weight of his enormous gut, was talking to two guys perched on stools. The guys were both thick-set and scruffy, both drinking pints of lager and smoking Rothmans. Mad Dog gave them the once-over. Their expressions were hostile, but they posed no threat.

347

'What do you want?' Winston said, decidedly unfriendly. He was an ugly fucker with a lumpy face, and hair that looked as if it had been cut by a blind man with a knife and fork.

'You know what we want,' Mad Dog said wearily.

'Do I?' said Winston, raising his eyebrows.

One of the men sitting at the bar snickered. Sherman gave him a withering look.

'You're a week late with Mr Hallett's money,' Mad Dog said. 'He's not a happy man.'

'Well that's tough,' said Winston, 'because I haven't *got* his fucking money.'

'Then get it. Sherman and I will have a game of snooker while we're waiting.'

'I've not got it and I'm not gonna get it. You can tell your Mr fucking Hallett that our agreement is at an end.'

'I don't think so,' said Mad Dog mildly, 'not if you want to stay in business.'

'*I* think so,' said Winston, lifting a shotgun from behind the bar and pointing it at Mad Dog.

Mad Dog felt a momentary jolt of shock and surprise, not because Winston was pointing a shooter at him – he'd had guns levelled at him many times before – but because he'd underestimated the man, had always assumed he lacked the bottle for anything more than threats and bluster. If Hallett had not intervened at that moment and cleared Mad Dog's mind in order to channel his own energies through it, Mad Dog knew that his shock would have been followed by self-reproach at his unprofessional lack of foresight.

However, he suddenly felt his mind flooded with his boss's incredible energy, felt it sluicing through him like a warm balm, pouring invisibly from his eyes and nose and mouth, entwining itself around Winston's brain, tightening its grip, strangling the thoughts inside the man's head and implanting new instructions.

He saw the familiar fleeting expression of fear and astonishment scuttle across Winston's features; and then his eyes glazed over and Mad Dog knew that he was Hallett's puppet, body and soul.

The two men drinking at the bar watched with stupid disbelief as Winston slowly turned the gun around, pointed it up at his face and pushed the barrel between his lips. Mad Dog knew that

348

somewhere, tucked away in a little pocket of his mind, Winston would be terrified, and though he always tried to maintain his cool in these situations, the thought amused him so much that he couldn't help grinning.

Hallett was not going to let Winston kill himself, Mad Dog knew; he was simply going to frighten him, teach him a lesson. Hallett was not cruel or sadistic – he was a businessman, pure and simple. He merely did what needed to be done and the only time he took extreme measures was when there was no other alternative.

Winston reached down, his eyes full of disbelief and fear, groping for the trigger, unable to stop himself. His finger found it, tightened on it, Hallett toying with the man, teasing him. Then, suddenly, without warning, Mad Dog felt Hallett's presence being torn from his mind.

The pain was so intense that he fell to his knees, certain that his brain had ruptured. It took him a few moments to realise that although his eyes were open, he could see nothing but a swirling red-black darkness. The acute pain lasted for only a few seconds before it began to ebb, but it left Mad Dog feeling sick and weak. Trembling, he brought his hands up to his face, sure that his eyes would be leaking blood. They weren't, but his skin was greasy and clammy with sweat.

'Mad Dog. Hey, man, you okay?' The words seemed to boom slowly into his throbbing mind like distant underground echoes. Part of Mad Dog resented the intrusion; he wanted to give in to his pain, curl himself up in it . . .

He felt hands on him, attempting to haul him to his feet. Though he groaned, he tried to help them, to plant his feet on the ground, but his legs were hollow tubes of rubber. At that moment sparks of light began to pierce the darkness filming his eyes; his vision was returning. The light that came into his eyes seemed to provide him with a little strength. He could feel his legs again now. At first they felt like soup, but already he could feel them hardening, strengthening, becoming more able to take his weight. The light was shredding the darkness and shapes were forming, colours focusing into concrete reality. A block of green was the baize on a snooker table; a fuzz of red a man's shirt. Mad Dog's thoughts reassembled like film footage of an object that had been dropped and smashed, played in reverse. His first concern was for his boss:

349

what had happened to Hallett? Was he in trouble? Then he remembered his own predicament, remembered that Winston still had a gun in his hands and was no longer under the boss's control. It was this realisation that focused his mind in double-quick time. A quick blink and a shake of the head and suddenly his faculties were fully restored.

Winston did indeed have the gun in his hands. But the barrel was no longer in his mouth but pointing up at the ceiling. Winston was blinking at the gun as if he had no idea where it had appeared from. Then sensing Mad Dog's gaze, he looked from the gun to the black man and his face twisted into an expression of rage and fear.

It was the fear rather than the fury, Mad Dog knew, which made the man dangerous. Mad Dog's sense of self-preservation kicked in and raising a hand he began to speak in a low, soothing voice.

'Now, come on, Mr Winston – don't do anything crazy. Don't do anything you'll spend the rest of your life regretting. I mean, hey, think about it, I'm not worth spending ten years in—'

Winston jerked the barrel of the gun down so that it was once again pointing at Mad Dog's midriff and yanked back on the trigger.

Mad Dog folded in half as his digestive system and the bottom part of his rib cage disintegrated. He was dead even before he had hit the ground, even before his blood had finished raining down on the surrounding snooker tables, staining the green baize. The half-dozen players in the room dived for cover, perhaps believing they were next. One of the two men sitting at the bar opened his mouth as if he had just witnessed a miracle; his cigarette dropped unnoticed into his lap.

Sherman looked down at the twitching remains of his companion and absently wiped a hand across his face, turning the spots of blood into smears. 'Fuck,' he said. Then, as Winston dropped the gun, which clattered on to the bar, and swayed back as if about to faint, he turned and ran, pumping his legs as fast as his bulk would allow him.

Fifty-Three

The deed had been done; now it was simply a case of waiting to see what Hallett's reaction would be. The two phases of the plan – first the psychic attack, then the appeal for help – had been Nick's idea. Some of the others had been unwilling at first to use their abilities to terrorise, particularly one of their own, but Nick had assured them that a simple cry for help, if sent alone, would fall on deaf ears. First, he told them, they had to make Hallett believe that his own position was in jeopardy, had to give him cause to retaliate; that was why they had tapped into the fear centres of his mind whilst he was asleep. Now they had followed that up with an admission of responsibility for the attack, albeit tempered by the claim that their captors had forced them to carry it out against their will. On this second occasion Nick and the others had left their minds open as a gesture of good faith, to show Hallett that they wanted him to come and find them before they were forced to attack him again. Now they were waiting, Nick all too aware of how ruthless Hallett could be, of the appalling risk they were taking.

He recalled again the sensation of Hallett's mind becoming aware of his and the other psis' presence inside it that first time. When he had felt Hallett begin to fight back, experienced the first spasm of pain in his mind like the onset of migraine, he had hurriedly ordered his fellow psis to withdraw, to break the connection. Even after what he had learned about Hallett, Nick had been surprised by the man's strength. Instinctively he knew that Hallett had managed to swat them from his mind merely by flexing his mental muscles. What damage might he have done to them if they had given him time to recover his mental faculties?

Were they capable, even if they combined their strength, of holding him off? Or would he simply burn out their brains, reduce them to cabbages, one by one?

Hopefully he and the others would never find out the answer to that. Nick's gamble was that their telepathic explanation for the first attack would cause Hallett to view it as a declaration of war, not by them but by the Illuminati. Hallett was ruthless and cunning, but he was also intelligent and, in his own way, fair-minded. Surely he would realise that Nick and his fellow psis were simply instruments of the Illuminati, slave labour, their talents exploited, coerced to perform tasks against their will?

And if Hallett fell into line, what then? Before suggesting the plan, Nick had thought long and hard about it, had tried to make himself view the situation as Hallett would, based on his limited knowledge of the man. He knew that a battle with the Illuminati was a conflict that Hallett had successfully managed to avoid for a long time, either because they'd been unable to track him down or because they couldn't stomach the fight. And yet, by the same token, he knew that if such a conflict was presented to him as an inevitability, then Hallett would not shirk from it.

The way Nick saw it, Hallett had three alternatives: he could psychically seek out and destroy all those he considered a threat to him – which would include not only Jenna and her ilk, but also Nick and his fellow psis; he could psychically destroy the Illuminati and leave Nick and the others to sink or swim inside the Chicken House; or he could mount a combined psychical and physical assault on the Chicken House and, if successful, rescue the psis at the same time.

Nick was hoping – praying – that Hallett would go for the third option. He tried to convince himself that he had good cause to be optimistic. He knew that Hallett was a man who hated leaving loose ends, who liked dealing with his problems not only head-on but hands-on – hence the vicarious thrill he got from cadging a lift inside Mad Dog's head, allying his mental power to his right-hand man's physical presence and mobility, factors denied him by the loss of his legs. Nick felt sure that, if he really wanted to, Hallett could run his various rackets simply by seeking out the minds of those who fell within what he perceived as his jurisdiction and planting suggestions in them – but where would be the fun in that? No, Hallett got off on strutting his stuff, on the gut fear invoked in

352

opponents by the size and influence and sheer physical meanness of the firm or mob or whatever he called it that stalked the streets of *his* manor in *his* name. Hallett was one of the old school. Long-distance, push-button conflict was not for him. He liked to smell the blood, taste the terror.

It was for this reason that Nick believed Hallett would not be satisfied until the Genesis project had been well and truly wiped out, until he could stand in triumph at the edge of the smoking crater in the ground that had once contained the Chicken House. However, he thought there might be another reason why Hallett would come to the Chicken House in person. What was it he had said to Nick during the brief period of time that Nick had spent under his protection? That he viewed the Genesis subjects as his brothers and sisters? Words to that effect, anyway. Despite his ruthlessness, his awesomeness, Nick knew that Hallett also possessed a sense of justice (warped though it might be), honour and loyalty; as such his abiding hope was that the man would arrive here not only on a mission of destruction but also on a mission of mercy.

'Cry havoc,' he murmured wrily, 'and let slip the dogs of war.' He shuddered, then put on some Van Morrison and lay back on his bed, closing his eyes, concentrating hard on the man's voice and his lyrics and the arrangement of the music.

He had considered other options before suggesting the attack on Hallett, but had been able to come up with nothing more than half-measures, temporary solutions. He had wondered, for instance, how much influence he and the other psis could exert over the minds of their captors, whether they could bend them to their will, force them to release them, take them home. But even if they could do that, how many people would they have to control in the long run? The threat would always be there; nowhere would ever be safe. They would have to be on their guard every minute of every day, constantly looking over their shoulders, vulnerable through their families and friends, perpetually concerned for their safety.

No, contacting Hallett – giving him a kick up the pants and then apologising for it and pointing him in the direction of the real enemy – was the only way. Drastic, reckless, perhaps even suicidal, but their only realistic chance of total freedom.

He had been listening to the music for perhaps twenty minutes, allowing the bitter-sweetness of Morrison's voice to carry him away, when he felt what could only be described as a tickling sensation at the back of his brain.

Hallett, he thought, his eyes popping open, upper body springing into a sitting position as though someone had lifted his shirt and dumped ice cubes on his naked stomach. He looked quickly around as if expecting the man to be in his room, then belatedly remembered the cameras and tried to make it look as though he had woken from a bad dream.

Had he spoken Hallett's name aloud? He didn't think so, though he couldn't be sure. He tried to think of a similar-sounding word which he might have blurted in the throes of nightmare if they questioned him about it later. He felt the tickling sensation again and realised that someone was softly, timidly, speaking his name. He tuned in:

Who's this?

It's Mark Brown, Mr Finch. I'd like the chance to speak with you alone, if I may?

Nick pictured the large, sweaty, bearded man, who always went along with the consensus of the group, but rarely contributed to their telepathic discussions. When his opinion was sought, he responded in as few words as possible; indeed, this request he had made was the longest sentence Nick had ever known him to use. He had always thought the man to be surly and solitary, uninterested in establishing a relationship with his fellow psis. But now he sounded hesitant, even wary.

Of course, Nick responded. *What is it?*

I have a confession to make, Mr Finch. I've been afraid to tell you before, but I simply can't live with it any longer.

What sort of confession? Nick asked, wondering ominously, with the part of his mind he had quickly learned to shield, to reserve for his innermost thoughts, what terrible thing Mark Brown was about to reveal.

There was no immediate response, and Nick began to wonder whether the man had withdrawn from his mind. For several long seconds he was not even aware of Brown's silent presence. Then, abruptly, there was a blurt of words that felt oddly like a bubble swelling and bursting inside Nick's head:

I was the one who blinded your wife.

The words came in such a rush that Nick didn't grasp the

meaning of them at first. When he did he felt shock stealing through him, freezing him, numbing his ability to respond.

She's not my wife, he thought instinctively, forgetting to shield the thought.

He felt Brown's dismay and confusion at his apparent cold-heartedness and struggled for something more appropriate. Pressing his fingers to his forehead as though it would help him hold his thoughts together, he managed to formulate a reply:

I'm sorry – it was just the shock, what I meant was . . . we never married – though that's irrelevant. What I should be asking is: why? Why did you blind Linsey? What happened?

Nick could feel Brown's discomfort and shame; it pulsed through his mind in waves, left a metallic taste in his mouth. The man's thoughts were hard to latch on to, little more than a mental mumble.

I made her blind herself. I put certain . . . ideas into her head. I was the first psi to arrive here and I was tricked by Pemberton. He told me it was a harmless experiment, that no one would get hurt. I didn't even realise what I'd done at first. It was only later, when I started to piece everything together, that it clicked. I feel so ashamed. I have the blood of innocent people on my hands. These people, Mr Finch, they're evil. They're turning us all into murderers.

Evil. Murderers. Nick thought of Hallett and his entourage, advancing through the night like avenging angels towards the Chicken House, and wondered, just for a moment, whether he had done the right thing. What if Hallett didn't win? What if he and his people were overwhelmed by the forces of darkness that operated here? What if the Illuminati captured Hallett, the most ruthless and powerful psi of them all, and found a way to use him for their own ends?

Everything will be fine, he thought; and realised he was attempting to reassure himself as much as anyone else.

PART FOUR:
THE DEVIL'S
PLAYGROUND

Fifty-Four

The two men appeared as tiny black specks at the edge of the circle of searchlight beams that surrounded the Chicken House and extended a mile into the desert. It was Midge Ellison who saw them first. He, Dave Russell and Rob McKinley were playing cards when he glimpsed a smudge of movement in his peripheral vision. He turned his head and his eyes widened. 'Bloody hell,' he said, 'would you look at that?'

Dave glanced at him, suspecting some cheat's ruse, but Rob followed his gaze. The way the Glaswegian's head lurched forward and his spotty, pale face appeared to gawp convinced Dave to look too.

'Jesus!' Rob exclaimed. 'Where the fuck have they come from?'

Midge licked his lips nervously. 'They can't have come all the way out here by accident. They must be hostile.'

Dave Russell, the most composed of the three corporals, and at twenty-four the oldest, shook his head. 'Not necessarily. If they were hostile they wouldn't just come walking towards us like that, would they? I mean, it's going to take them ten minutes to get here. They must know that we can pick them off any time.'

'Maybe it's a trick,' said Rob, buttoning his tunic as if about to go on parade.

Dave stood up and reached for the binoculars that sat on the shelf beneath the gatehouse's large window of reinforced glass, facing out on to the desert. He wiped dust from the eye-pieces with his thumb and held them to his face. He watched the figures' slow progress for a minute or two. 'I'm pretty sure they're unarmed.'

Rob grinned and reached for his SA80. 'Easy meat.'

Dave shook his head. 'Fucking Jock psycho. Midge, give Wanks a call. See what he has to say.'

Midge grimaced but nodded; Sergeant Banks would not appreciate being woken up at three fifty-one a.m., but in this situation there was no alternative. He put the call through and spoke to his superior for several minutes. Throughout that time he kept an eye on the two approaching figures. They became a little more distinct, though they didn't appear to get much closer.

'What did he say?' Dave asked when Midge replaced the receiver.

'He said to play it by the book. One of us go out and challenge the men, the other two stay here. Any trouble, we hit the alarm.'

'Okay,' said Dave. He had known the procedure anyway, but it was good to get it officially confirmed. 'I'll go out.'

'Don't you think we should vote on that?' Rob said, his voice thickening with aggression.

Dave glanced at Midge. 'No, I don't. This is no time to get bolshy, Jock.'

'You're the one getting bolshy, telling us what to do. Who the fucking hell do you think you are?'

'*I* think Dave should be the one to go out too,' Midge said.

Rob glanced at him scornfully. 'Oh aye? Up his fuckin' arse, are you?'

'Come on, Jock,' said Dave, 'you wanted a vote and you've got it – two against one. Now, do you want Wanks to find out that we let those guys get too close because we were arguing the toss like fucking schoolkids?'

Rob glared at him wordlessly. Dave knew the guy was a liability, but he tried not to let it worry him. He would have to watch his back for the next few weeks, but that was no big deal. 'All right,' he said, 'you two stay alert, okay?'

Rob remained silent, but Midge nodded. 'We will. Good luck, Dave.'

'Cheers.'

Dave opened the door and went outside, the metal steps creaking beneath his weight as he descended to ground level. It was bloody cold, the chill night air pressing hard against his cheekbones, making them ache. A scorpion reared up at him and Dave ground it to mush beneath his boot. The two men were closer now, though still in silhouette, their shadows thin black trails behind them. One of the men was swinging his arms around his body, evidently trying to keep warm. Both of them were trudging rather than walking speedily – though Dave, remembering Rob's words, wondered whether their show of tiredness was intended merely to catch him off-guard.

'No bloody chance, boys,' he murmured, cradling his SA80 in the crook of his arm. Dave was a sensible bloke, but he had had it drummed into him that the Chicken House was an ultra-high-security installation. If the two guys did anything even slightly suspicious they would be crawling round the desert like wounded crabs, trailing blood from the stumps of their legs.

It was another five minutes before the men became more than silhouettes. As they got closer, the powerful security lights shining out from the installation scrubbed them clean of the shadows that had been clinging to them. Dave looked up at the gatehouse and saw Midge watching the men through the binoculars. He himself could now see them clearly enough to tell that the man swinging his arms around his body was tall and rangy with a long, bony face and dark, neatly cropped hair, and that his companion was a chubby man with a shaved head and a goatee beard.

Both men appeared to be in their early to mid-thirties. The rangy man was inappropriately dressed for the desert at night, wearing only a pale green T-shirt on his upper body. The chubby man's attire was not much better, a thin cotton jacket over what appeared to be a white polo shirt.

Dave waited until the two men were within hearing range and then he shouted, 'Please halt and stand still.'

The men did so, screwing up their eyes to see who had shouted, the chubby man using his right hand as a visor.

'Hello,' the chubby man called a little hesitantly. 'Are you English?'

Ignoring the question, Dave shouted, 'Please state your identity and your business here.'

The chubby man indicated his companion, who Dave could see was shivering. 'This is Professor Patrick Beaumont and my name is Charles Nicholls. We're archaeologists. You might have heard of us?'

'No,' Dave said.

'Ah,' said the chubby man. 'Oh, well, it doesn't matter. The thing is, we were excavating a site not far from here and on our way back to camp our jeep died on us. We decided to walk the last five miles or so, but we somehow managed to get lost. We've been walking for . . . how long is it now, Patrick?'

'Seven hours,' the man muttered.

'Seven hours,' confirmed the chubby man. 'We saw your lights and decided to head for them. We had no idea what we would find here.'

'This is a high-security military installation,' Dave said.

'Yes, we guessed that from all the . . . er . . .' The chubby man gestured at the barbed-wire-topped chain-link fence, then suddenly swayed and put a hand to his head. 'Forgive me – we're both exhausted and very cold. Is there any chance you could help us, do you think?'

'Just a minute,' said Dave. He took a radio from the breast pocket of his jacket and pressed a button. 'Midge? Are you receiving me?'

'Yes, Dave.'

Quickly Dave related what the man had told him. 'Put a call through to Sergeant Banks, would you, and ask him how we should proceed?'

'Will do, Dave. Out.'

The chubby man took several steps forward. Shoving his radio back into his pocket, Dave raised his gun threateningly. 'Please stay where you are, sir. The matter is being dealt with.'

The chubby man looked at him, an odd, dreamy expression on his face, and then he tilted his head up to regard the gatehouse. 'No calls,' he murmured.

The man's manner was so strange that Dave couldn't help following his gaze. The gatehouse was a well-lit box on a raised platform with large, reinforced-glass windows on all sides which allowed whoever was on duty to have an extensive view of the surrounding area. Dave saw Midge standing inside the gatehouse with the internal phone raised halfway to his ear, a puzzled expression on his face, as if he had forgotten something important. Then, moving like an automaton, Midge replaced the receiver and straightened up. For several seconds he stood motionless, staring into space. So did Rob McKinley, who was standing behind him.

'What's—' Dave began, but no sooner was the word out of his

362

mouth than Midge and Rob suddenly convulsed, their arms jerking up, their heads snapping back as if they were having fits. Both men crumpled to the ground simultaneously, disappearing from view beneath the level of the windows. Dave, though astounded by what he had witnessed, reacted quickly: he swung round, his SA80 already pointing at the two men, and pulled the trigger, intending to cut them to ribbons where they stood. Or at least, he *tried* to pull the trigger, but he suddenly found that he couldn't move. Impossible as it seemed, his entire body was locked. He couldn't so much as twitch as eyelid.

The chubby man smiled at him dismissively, then walked up to the first of the two fences surrounding the installation and curled his fat fingers through the chain-link. The barrel of the SA80 was still pointing at his stomach at a distance of no more than six feet, but the man didn't seem to mind.

'Don't be afraid, Dave,' he said in a soft, somehow distant voice. 'We are your salvation. Open the gates for us, would you, and don't try to pretend that you don't know where the key is because we all know there's one in the safe in the gatehouse, don't we?'

Dave found his head jerking in an involuntary nod and realised that the man was playing with him. Although he couldn't move of his own volition, he was still breathing, could still feel his heart beating in his chest. Yet the functions felt strange, unnatural, as if his body were being kept alive by artificial means. He still retained his senses and his conscious thoughts, but he had the distinct impression that he was sharing those thoughts with another presence. He could feel it scrabbling in his mind, rifling through his memories. It was not exactly an uncomfortable feeling, but it was alarming nonetheless, as though his skull were a chimney flue and the other presence a trapped bird.

'Off you go then, Dave,' the man said gently, and Dave found himself letting his weapon drop from his grasp. Then he turned about, and moving like a robot marched up the metal steps and into the gatehouse. Immediately he felt the warm air puffing from the fan heater, which would have been welcoming after the cold if it hadn't been for the circumstances, and if Midge and Rob hadn't been lying dead on the ground, their limbs sprawled wildly as if they had dropped while dancing, their eyes open and glazed, their faces contorted, ugly, bestial.

Midge had a trickle of blood running from his ear that had formed a small pool on the ground beside him. The bottom half of Rob's face was entirely coated in blood; at some stage his tongue must have seethed from his mouth, and his teeth had clamped together during his convulsions, almost severing it.

Dave moved across the room to the safe and tapped out a six-figure number on the keyboard beside it. There was the clunk of metal and the safe opened. Dave reached in and took out a bunch of keys, then marched out of the gatehouse, down the steps and across to a double gate set into the inner chain-link fence. He unlocked the four heavy-duty padlocks there, tugged free the massive steel chains threaded between them. Then he unlocked the two bar mechanisms, top and bottom, and swung them free. He opened the gate, scrambled down into the ditch, walked across it and scrambled up the other side. The outer fence had a similarly secured gate to which he applied his keys. A minute later he tugged the gate open and the two men stepped through, the fat man reaching out almost tenderly to stroke his cheek.

'Thank you, Dave,' he said. 'Now, I know your brain is steeped in the poisonous thoughts of the Old Ones at present, but in due course you'll see that you've done the right thing in throwing open the gates of Hell to the righteous. When judgement comes you'll receive your reward in the Great Kingdom.'

He ambled through, followed by the rangy man, who put his face aggressively close to Dave's. 'We've arranged to meet some friends here, pal, so pull the gates shut, but leave them unlocked, then follow us.'

Dave did as ordered, pulling the gates shut then following the two men up the steps to the gatehouse. He noticed that the fat man moved quickly despite his bulk and that the tall man was no longer shivering.

Inside the gatehouse the two men bent to the corpses of Midge and Rob and began to strip them of their uniforms. Watching them, Dave felt anger burning inside him. He eyed Rob's SA80 on the floor not three feet away, and tried to will himself to move towards it, but to no avail. The two men stripped down to their underwear, then put on the uniforms of his dead colleagues. Midge's uniform was too short at the wrists and ankles for the rangy man, Rob's too tight for the fat man, but from a distance they'd be passable. As the two men clattered down the steps, urging Dave to follow, Dave wondered whether their movements had been captured on camera and therefore observed on the monitors in Security Control, inside the main bunker. If so, wouldn't it look as though he were the intruders' accomplice, their inside man? He could only hope that the oddness of his movements would convince the security staff that he was being controlled in some way.

Then again, it was equally likely that the mens' breaching of the outer shell of the compound had so far passed unobserved. The main bunker was considered well nigh impregnable, and Dave knew for a fact that the monitors which relayed movements from outside the bunker were only glanced at occasionally. Most of the security staff's attention was focused within the bunker itself. Dave was not entirely sure what went on in there, but the rumour was that the government had some pretty important prisoners banged up inside who required almost constant observation. He wondered what the men meant to do, wondered how much they knew of the compound's internal security system. He wondered too who they were (from the look in the fat guy's eyes and the way he spoke he'd guess they were from some sort of terrorist religious cult, like those Waco nutters), and, more to the point, how they were controlling him. Was it some nerve weapon he had never heard of, some sort of gas, or maybe even some drug that they had somehow managed to inject into his system – with a tiny dart from a blowpipe, perhaps? Would they dispose of him, as they had disposed of Midge and Rob, when he was considered no longer useful? Unable to move of his own free will, he was more angry and frustrated than scared. He wouldn't mind going down – if only he could go down fighting.

Casually the two men, with Dave in tow, strolled across the concrete, chalky under the white glare of the security lights, towards the main bunker. It was a long walk across a large open area, but the men appeared not to be in any particular hurry. Nor did they seem to feel a need to conceal themselves, which gave Dave cause for hope. Most of the people who worked here were asleep at this hour, but if the guys in Security Control were doing their job properly then the men would be intercepted by a heavily armed reception committee any minute now.

Dave remembered the last conversation he had had with Joanna, his fiancée, before they had flown him out here:

'Will it be dangerous? Is that why they won't tell you where you're going?'

'No, of course not. In fact, we've been told this is the easiest three months we'll ever get paid for. Piece of piss, Sergeant Corby said . . .'

A few minutes later they reached the doors of the main bunker, Dave cursing inwardly. What were the security guys fucking about at? Were they treating this whole thing as an exercise, seeing how far these men could get? Didn't they realise his life was in danger?

'How do we get in?' the rangy man asked.

'Mr Hallett will show us the way,' the goateed skinhead said, and smiled beatifically. He looked at Dave, his eyes glazing over, and Dave felt the faint, disconcerting scrabbling in his head once again.

After a few moments the scrabbling stopped. 'He doesn't know,' the chubby man said.

'So what do we do now?'

'We look further afield. Have faith, Mr Clark.'

The chubby skinhead seemed to go into a kind of trance, his eyes fixing on a point somewhere in the middle distance. For perhaps two minutes there was silence, then, abruptly, he grinned.

'Yes,' he hissed. 'There. Come to me. *Come to me*.'

Fifty-Five

Nick dreamed that he was small, a child, a toddler even. He was picked up by someone bigger and older and stronger than he was and hurled through the air. He flew backwards, then slammed into a hard surface, the breath rushing out of him. The impact in his dream was so great that Nick jolted awake – only to find that he was indeed being crushed down into his bed by an unbearable force, a force not physical but mental, like a massive weight in his mind.

Then the feeling, the presence, moved away and Nick sat up and shuddered, staring into the darkness, feeling like a deep sea diver in murky water who has seen a dark and ominous shape pass by above his head. Fearful of attracting attention, but desperately needing to know whether the others had experienced a similar sensation, he sent out a general request:

Is everyone okay?

Almost immediately his mind was filled with a babble of fear and confusion, of emotion so raw that he winced. Then the distinctive shape of Ellie McKee's thought-patterns rose from the cacophony:

What was *that?*

I don't know, answered Greg Lousada, *but it was fucking powerful.*

And angry, Jason Westmoreland added.

Yes, I felt its anger too.

And it knows we're here, Julie Lean cut in, and her thoughts seemed wavery, fragile, like a fearful, timid voice. *It knows we're here, and it's playing with us.*

367

Fifty-Six

When Pemberton arrived to open the door to them he was jerking like a marionette, his eyes swimming with fear. He knew only too well what was happening, how they were controlling him, but Sherman gleaned (through Mr Hallett) that the scientist, despite his professional status, had lacked the imagination and intelligence to foresee such an eventuality. He had no empathy with human emotion. He was an idiotic genius, a brilliant simpleton. Sherman grinned at him. 'Don't worry, Mr Pemberton. We've come to take away your pain.'

Mr Hallett took over then, speaking through Sherman's mouth. He instructed Pemberton to take them by the most covert route to the security control area, which the scientist was now in the process of doing.

The place had several names: Chicken House, Zone X, Kingdom of the Old Ones. Sherman had to concede that it was an impressive structure. He could understand only too well how the gullible and feeble-minded had been tempted to give their souls over to it. If it hadn't been for the frailty of the humans who served it, the place would have been well nigh impregnable. When they had entered the vestibule beyond the steel doors that led into the complex, it had appeared that the lift at the far end was the only means of entry into the lower reaches of the complex; but then Pemberton tapped a certain sequence of numbers into the keypad beside the lift door and placed his hand on the attendant panel, whereupon an entire section of white wall slid back to reveal a narrow stairwell.

'Nice one,' Clark said, nodding, and the four of them began to descend, Pemberton and the soldier leading the way.

368

It was quiet on the stairs, aside from a very faint humming that seemed to come from deep within the walls. Sherman glanced up at the myriad security cameras, all too aware that every inch of their descent was being observed by the many-eyed beast. However he was not unduly worried; he knew he was in the grip of destiny. Besides, he had faith in Mr Hallett. He knew that Mr Hallett thought of everything; he overlooked not a single detail. What had happened to Mad Dog in the snooker hall had not been Mr Hallett's fault. Mr Hallett had been distraught at Mad Dog's death, but had assured Sherman that he would not be caught unawares like that ever again, that he would avenge himself on those responsible. Already Sherman himself had had the pleasure of tying Bob Winston up in a sack with a couple of anvils and dumping him in the deepest part of the Thames. Winston, though, was simply an underling. The Old Ones held ultimate responsibility, which was why Sherman was here, deep in their domain, all too willing to seek them out and strike at their heart.

Abruptly there was a clatter of boots on the stairs above and below, a warning shout. 'Stay where you are! Put your hands in the air!'

Armed soldiers swarmed on to the stairwell from both sides, surrounding them, SA80s pointing at their heads. Sherman had the briefest of impressions that Pemberton was so terrified he would have shat his pants had he not been in thrall to Mr Hallett. And then a tsunami of devastating psychic power rushed through and out of him, and split into separate columns, each of which – like intelligent and personalised heat-seeking missiles – targeted a different soldier.

The soldiers quivered and dropped dead where they stood, as if subjected to a blast of intensely lethal gas. Sherman stepped out of the way as one of the soldiers behind them pitched forward and tumbled down the stairs, lifelessness reducing him to nothing more than a flesh-and-blood mannequin. Some of the soldiers leaked blood from their noses, their ears, their mouths. They dropped their weapons, which clattered noisily to the ground, and then they slumped on top of them with a series of dull thuds. Within seconds the massacre was over. Sherman felt dizzy, but otherwise unharmed. He blinked down at the soldiers. 'A terrible vengeance shall visit them from on high,' he said softly. 'Let's go.'

They continued their descent, the heap of dead men at the bottom of the stairs so compacted that the quartet had to use them as stepping stones. Through Mr Hallett, Sherman could feel the emotions of their captives, could almost see the colour of their feelings like thick, oily paint in his mind. Dave Russell's anger was a dark, rich purple; Pemberton's fear and physical revulsion yellow as pus. A few minutes and several floors later they reached their destination.

Pemberton used his security clearance to unlock the only door on the otherwise featureless landing. The door was made of thick, solid steel, like that of a walk-in safe. The scientist had to put all of his weight behind it, and even then the door only groaned open slowly.

The gap between door and frame was perhaps a foot wide when the stillness was punctured by three shots in quick succession. Sherman knew guns, knew the firing pattern of an SA80, and was diving to the floor even as the spanging whine of ricocheting bullets was followed by a trio of hammer-like cracks as they embedded themselves in the walls. He felt Mr Hallett swamping his mind, taking over, assessing the situation, and he marvelled at the quick clarity of his thoughts. It suddenly seemed obvious that in the corridor beyond the metal door another group of soldiers were waiting in ambush and one of them, composure perhaps stretched to breaking point by viewing the camera footage of his comrades' deaths, had been unable to prevent his finger nervously squeezing the trigger of his gun.

Sherman felt the force rushing through and out of him again. He rolled over on to his back, opening his mouth wide, as if that would allow it easier access. Another silent massacre ensued, the only indicators of its success the soft thump of falling bodies. Then the silence closed in again and Sherman – together with Clark, who had also thrown himself to the floor – climbed slowly to his feet.

'Do you think they're all dead?' Clark hissed.

'Let's find out, shall we?' Mr Hallett said, speaking through Sherman, making him grin savagely at Pemberton.

Sherman felt Mr Hallett giving a little push, and suddenly Pemberton, his eyes full of terror, was walking like a wind-up doll to the steel door and shoving it all the way open. Mr Hallett made Pemberton march through the open door and into the middle of

370

the corridor beyond. Sherman felt that Mr Hallett was almost disappointed when the scientist was not cut to ribbons by machine-gun fire.

After a few moments Sherman and Clark, with Russell leading the way, also stepped through the metal door into the corridor. Here was a similar scene to that on the stairs; soldiers lying dead, sprawled across each other, blood leaking from facial orifices. The soldiers had been guarding a set of imposing-looking double doors, again constructed of solid steel. Pemberton was urged forward towards them, Sherman aware of the man's abhorrence at having to step on and over the heap of strewn corpses.

'Piece of piss,' Clark muttered as Pemberton again used his security clearance to open the doors for them. They stepped into a shorter corridor and were confronted with another set of double doors. Again Pemberton used his security clearance and these too yielded.

Sherman, under Mr Hallett's influence, got Pemberton to push one of the doors open a crack and then belched forth another blast of power. This time Sherman almost imagined he could *see* the power as a thread of thick grey mist that streamed from his mouth and curled through the gap between the doors like a vast, ghostly snake. When thirty seconds had elapsed he got Pemberton and Russell to shove the doors open further and step inside. Clark waited for ten seconds, then nodded to Sherman and slipped inside after the two men. Sherman brought up the rear.

Once inside the doors, Sherman knew they had pierced the Devil's heart. This was Security Control: from here they had access to all of the Chicken House's security systems. The place resembled a brightly lit control suite in a TV studio. It was not a big room, but it was crammed with banks of screens, control panels, computer terminals. The four-strong team who had been manning it – scientific rather than military personnel – were huddled behind a chair in the corner of the room. They were dead, their brains burnt out by the advance guard of psychic power that Mr Hallett had unleashed on them. The man at their head, perhaps the most senior of the four scientists, had evidently seen himself as the protector of the others. He had thick, dark-red clots of blood in his beard, and a revolver was still clenched in his right hand.

Clark looked around at the array of complex-looking equipment in bewilderment. 'I wouldn't know where to start in here.'

371

Sherman looked glassily at Pemberton. 'These are the Devil's toys. He will play with them for us.'

He indicated the scientist and felt Mr Hallett stirring inside him again, using his mind as a transmitter to relay his instructions into the receiver of Pemberton's brain. Sherman did not actually *hear* Mr Hallett's instructions in his head, but he understood almost on an instinctive level what Mr Hallett was telling Pemberton to do. He wanted the scientist to override the computer security system and open all the doors, both internal and external. Additionally he wanted all the lighting within the complex to be extinguished.

Although Pemberton did not resist Mr Hallett's instructions, Sherman gathered that he had a problem with them nonetheless. The gist was that what Mr Hallett wanted was regarded as an emergency procedure and needed the security clearance codes of *two* senior personnel to implement it. The dead men were no use; although their keycards and their hand-prints could have been used, the identification codes they carried in their minds were irretrievable, dissolved to mush with the rest of their thoughts. Sherman sensed Mr Hallett's frustration, but knew his boss was already on a quest, his mind roaming through the complex in search of a solution.

Less than five minutes later the solution appeared in the form of a dishevelled little man with bare feet who shuffled through the half-open double doors into Security Control wearing green-and-white-striped pyjamas. The man was in his sixties, his wispy white hair sticking up in tufts, his face creased, his eyes puffed with sleep. He was clutching his keycard like a confused pensioner with a bus pass. He shuffled over to a keypad situated on one wall even as Pemberton was moving across the room to another.

The two men swiped their cards, tapped in their identification codes, had their hand-prints recognised and approved. Pemberton then moved across to a computer terminal and began to tap in commands, his fingers moving rapidly. Sherman watched him, stealing occasional glances at the screen, though only fleetingly; he didn't want to be infiltrated by the occult symbolism of the Old Ones that he knew would be swarming through the veins of this place like a viral infection.

Abruptly, after several minutes' work by Pemberton, the room and the corridor beyond were plunged into darkness, save for the

372

ethereal glow of computer terminals. Two seconds later the emergency lighting flickered on, intermittently placed lozenges of light bathing the room in a dim red glow. Sherman turned and smiled at Pemberton, at Dave Russell the soldier, at the sleep-befuddled man.

'Thank you, gentlemen,' he heard Mr Hallett saying, 'you've been most helpful.'

Then Mr Hallett's power gushed through and out of him once more and the three men convulsed. Blood burst from Pemberton's nose, appearing black in the dim red light; his legs buckled and he pitched forward on to his face. Dave Russell's back arched and he folded up without a sound. The little man simply crumpled, his head thudding against the floor, blood trickling from his mouth.

Sherman turned to Clark, his bared teeth shining a slick rose-red, his fat face florid, eyes glittering like rubies. Raising his hands as though exhorting the heavens, he hissed, 'From the darkness shall come forth light.'

Fifty-Seven

Despite coming from what had in the past been labelled a broken home – and being forced to hump around the crippling psychological baggage that everyone automatically assumed would be a by-product – Sasha could honestly say that the only real trauma she had ever experienced in her childhood was as a result of her friend Moira Jarvis's suggestion that the two of them sit up one Friday night to watch *Appointment With Fear*.

Both Sasha and Moira had been nine at the time, and for a while their lives had seemed to run parallel. Moira had been living upstairs with her odd, vague mother, her father apparently having deserted them for a 'Jamaican woman' when Moira was three. (It was only when she was fifteen that Sasha had learned from Linsey that Moira's mother had been an alcoholic and that the 'Jamaican woman' her father had run off with had been a sixteen-year-old pupil at the school where he had been headmaster. Apparently it had caused quite a scandal at the time, the story appearing on the front pages of several national newspapers – publicity which had eventually forced the couple to flee the country. Linsey, when Sasha asked her, had not been sure whether Moira's mother's alcoholism had driven her husband away, or whether it had resulted from his desertion – though she suspected the latter.)

In any case, for the two-and-a-half years that Moira and her mother lived in the flat above, Sasha and Moira became the best of friends. One Friday night Linsey had had to go out – perhaps she was working, or had a date; at the age of nine such details passed you by – and so she asked Moira's mother whether she could look after Sasha for the evening. As the two girls played board games on the lounge carpet, Moira's mother sat and watched TV, and

374

presumably – Sasha only remembered her as a vague presence in the background – drank herself into near-oblivion. The only thing Sasha did vividly recall about her that night was when she rose unsteadily from the settee and blearily announced that she was not feeling very well and was going to bed. Sasha had never known an adult go to bed before a child – *her* mother would certainly never have dreamed of letting her have the run of the place – and for a moment she felt an urge to run after Mrs Jarvis as she tottered from the room, to drag her back and say, 'But you can't go to bed yet! You're a grown-up!'

She didn't, of course, but even now she could recall the cold shock, the near-panic, of the moment. It was Moira's casual response to the situation that had made her calm down before she could embarrass herself. Sasha quickly concluded that her friend must be used to her mother going off like this. For almost as soon as the door closed behind Mrs Jarvis, Moira jumped up. 'Let's have a feast,' she said.

Sasha watched as Moira confidently beetled round the kitchen, gathering together cheese and biscuits and cake, pouring Coca Cola into glasses from a large plastic bottle in the fridge. Back in the lounge, as the two girls were munching away – Sasha a little guiltily, half-expecting Mrs Jarvis to burst into the room at any moment and demand to know what was going on – Moira raised her eyebrows. 'Shall we watch *Appointment With Fear*?' she asked slyly.

The fearful thrill Sasha felt was exactly the same as the one she was to experience seven years later when Linda Hartson offered her ecstasy in front of all her friends at the sixth-form Christmas party. On that occasion, despite the pressure of her peers, she had had the presence of mind to resist; but seven years earlier, intimidated by Moira's confidence, she could only mutter, 'I don't know.'

'Oh go on,' Moira said, 'it'll be a laugh.'

'Mum doesn't let me watch horror films.'

'Yeah, but she's not here, is she? You don't have to tell her.'

'What if your mum comes in and sees us and tells my mum?'

'She won't. My mum'll be out like a light now until the morning.'

'How do you know?'

'I just do.'

Sasha had been too ashamed to admit how apprehensive, even scared, she was. She had never seen a proper horror film before and was terrified that the images on the screen might prove too much for her to bear.

In the end, though, Moira ground her down, and at eleven a.m. the two girls settled down to watch the film, Sasha clutching her glass of Coke as if it were a lucky charm.

To this day, she couldn't remember what the film was called, and try as she might she had never been able to track it down. All she knew was that it was about a ravening, sub-human psychopath who beheaded his victims, and that it had a far more terrible effect on her than she could even have imagined.

She and Moira watched it to the end, but long before then Sasha was rigid with terror. When the film was over she could do nothing but sit on the settee, trembling, too traumatised by the experience even to speak.

She supposed her mother had come home soon after that and had taken her downstairs to their own flat. Sasha had a vague recollection of trying to act normal, of holding back her real emotions so that Linsey would not suspect what she had done. Once she was in bed, however, all Sasha's emotions came flooding out. She cried hysterically, almost retching with terror at the memory of what she had seen. For weeks afterwards she suffered terrible nightmares, insisted on sleeping with the light on, became frantic on the couple of occasions on which her mother – still not knowing about the film – told her not to be silly and turned off her lamp in exasperation.

Oddly, though, the thing that frightened Sasha the most during this time was not the memory of the grunting killer with his axe – though that was bad enough – but of the severed heads of his victims. Sasha became terrified of opening a cupboard or wardrobe, of looking under her bed, for fear of discovering a severed head there. She developed an unhealthy terror of closed curtains, because in the film the husband or wife of one of the victims had drawn back the curtains to reveal their spouse's head hanging by its hair, spinning slowly on a length of twine like some grotesque Christmas bauble. Even now, anything to do with decapitation brought back that crawly, nauseous dread, a remnant of that unreasoning terror.

All of this – the memory and therefore the fear – was in Sasha's mind when she came awake with a jolt as though someone had touched her face. It was as if she had been remembering it, reliving the experience in her sleep. Had she dreamed about it? She had come awake with such a wrench that she couldn't remember.

It was dark, without moonlight or street lamps to temper the blackness, and the air had that faint plasticky, recycled odour that she only noticed immediately upon waking, when her senses were particularly attuned.

If it had been morning – or rather, if the lights had been on – she would have pushed aside her night-fears as easily as her duvet. In the darkness, though, it was harder to rationalise them away. With nothing else to focus upon, they seemed to grow, to take on a life of their own. She knew she wouldn't sleep again until she had exorcised them with light and perhaps a cup of tea.

Instinctively she reached out a hand to the lamp on her bedside table. She knew the exact shape and position of it by touch alone, knew where the switch was. On this occasion, however, her fingers touched not the lamp's hard curves but what she felt sure was human hair.

She let out a little scream and snatched her hand back, in the process dislodging the object. She heard a thump as it hit the carpet, and then a smaller, softer sound which she could only imagine was the object rolling a little way across the floor before coming to rest. Fear danced inside her; she fought to contain it, to keep it from blossoming into terror. *You will not get hysterical*, she told herself firmly. *You will not get hysterical. You are not the hysterical type.* She didn't know what would be worse – sitting here in the pitch-blackness with only her burgeoning imagination for company, or turning on the light and finding out what it was she'd knocked off the bedside table.

She decided light was better; there was nothing to be gained from sitting in the blackness. After all, it wasn't as though she could stay in bed until dawn broke, because daylight and fresh air were alien concepts down here. No, she was just going to have to be brave. She was going to have to reach out again, find her lamp and turn it on. Her rational mind told her that it wasn't as though she would touch the thing again, not now she had knocked it on to the floor, yet all the same her heart began to beat faster as she stretched out her hand in the darkness.

Her fingers seemed to stretch an awfully long way before they encountered a hard, cool surface which she knew immediately was her lamp. She fumbled upwards until she had the switch beneath her thumb, licked her lips, took a deep breath and clicked it down.

Nothing happened.

She was gripped fleetingly by panic. And then she thought, *The bulb's gone, that's all. It's nothing to get worked up about.* She would just have to switch the main light on. The switch was by the door, no more than half a dozen steps away.

Yet for a few more seconds she remained where she was, and tried to convince herself it was not because whatever she had knocked to the floor was lying on the carpet between her and the light switch. At the back of her mind, however, was a little voice she could not fully contain, the voice of the little girl she had been not so many years ago. 'I don't want to put my foot on the floor,' the little voice wheedled, 'I might step on its—'

Shut up, shut up, Sasha told herself, *don't think about it.*

'—face.'

Fuck, Sasha thought; she almost said it out loud. *What did you have to think that for?* Suddenly angry, she threw back her covers and swung her legs out of bed, telling herself that she knew roughly where the bloody thing had fallen, for Christ's sake; it wasn't as if she couldn't avoid stepping on it.

Besides, she reasoned as she took an exaggerated step forward, she had been half-asleep, still wrapped in whatever dream had awoken her. Wasn't it likely that what she had touched was merely Flop's fur and her imagination had done the rest? Yes, now she thought about it, it seemed *more* than likely it had been nothing more than her beloved old rabbit. She would be laughing in a minute at what a prat she had been.

She padded to the light switch, her feet encountering no obstacles on their short journey. As she pressed the switch down she twisted round to look at the spot beside her bed where she imagined the object to have fallen. She screwed up her eyes, anticipating the light, but again nothing happened. She remained sealed in darkness.

The little girl's voice cut through her surprise before she could stop it. 'It's turned off the lights. It can see me in the dark but I can't see it and it's coming for me . . .'

378

Power cut, she thought savagely, like an angry mother scolding a child. *It's hardly surprising out here, they've probably got their own generator, it's bound to go wrong now and again.* She refused to look beyond this possibility, refused to consider anything except what she should do next. Get back into bed and wait for them to sort it out? No, hold on: she had some candles in the kitchen, a packet that had been in the drawer with all the other paraphernalia when she had arrived.

She crossed again to the bed, wading through the darkness, eyes straining as she peered ahead of her, though she couldn't see her feet at all. She told herself she was silly to regard her bed as if it were a sturdy raft in shark-infested waters, but she was grateful to flop on to it nonetheless, to grab her duvet and pull it over her legs and up under her chin. For a moment she toyed with the idea of pulling her duvet right over her head and curling into a ball, but she knew that if she did that she would be powerless to prevent the object on the floor getting into bed with her, if only in her thoughts. She had to take action.

At least the kitchen was on the opposite side of the bed, well away from the thing on the floor. She got out and made her way over to where she pictured the kitchen doorway to be, moving slowly and waving her arms in front of her, partly to prevent herself banging into anything, partly because she was half-afraid something would reach out of the blackness and touch her face.

She tried to stifle her imagination, but it refused to be stifled. She couldn't help imagining a huge, ape-like figure standing silently beside the kitchen doorway, a dripping axe hanging from its hand, patiently waiting for her to blunder into its deadly embrace. She told herself not to be stupid, that if there *was* someone or something else in the room with her it would be as blind as she was. But then her imagination out-trumped her again, made her remember *Silence Of The Lambs*, Clarice Starling stumbling through the darkness whilst the killer watched her every move through infra-red goggles.

Sasha felt the hairs prickling on the back of her neck. All at once she was absolutely certain that someone was standing behind her in the blackness. She whirled round, arms pinwheeling in frantic karate chops; but there was nothing. Her hands swished soundlessly through cool air, the movement so violent that it jarred her shoulders.

379

When she turned back she wasn't sure if she had moved far enough or too far. It wasn't that big a room, but for some reason she had completely lost her bearings. She pointed herself in the direction in which she thought she needed to go and moved forward slowly, almost in a half-crouch, hands held out as before.

A few feet away, down to her left, at floor-level, something rustled.

Sasha's whole body clenched, except for her heart, which surged and began to hammer painfully. Her instinct was to run away, or at least snatch her feet up off the ground, but in the darkness she could do neither. Instead, like a deer which has heard a noise in the woods, she stood stock-still, too scared to move or make a sound, too scared even to breathe. Her mind was racing, trying to make sense of what she had heard. The only thing the sound reminded her of was a sheet of stiff cellophane unfurling slowly after it had been screwed up into a ball.

She listened hard for any further sound, but the silence was so absolute that she could hear only the faint rush of her own blood in her ears. Finally she lifted her right foot slowly off the ground and took a step forward, wincing at the almost infinitesimal *shhh* of carpet fibres yielding to her weight. After several more painfully slow steps her knuckles brushed against something and she stopped, drawing her hand back. After a short pause she extended the hand again and felt a cool, hard, flat surface: the wall. But which one?

Placing both hands on the wall, she moved along it to the right, like a mime artist operating in slow motion. Her room had become an alien landscape to her; she could not work out which wall this was, or where it might lead. Presumably she was still in the vicinity of the kitchen, unless she had somehow managed to double-back on herself and make her way round the end of the bed without bumping into it. It was unlikely, but the darkness seemed to shred her reason, to make anything seem possible. She kept imagining that her bare foot was going to bump against the object she had knocked to the floor, that at each step her toes would encounter the tickle of human hair.

And then her hand came up against a thin ridge that she realised was a doorway. The kitchen doorway. She felt her way round it, the carpet beneath her feet giving way to cold lino. She sidled to her left, reaching out her hand – and there was the fridge. She groped for the handle and tugged the fridge open, and was almost relieved when the interior light failed to come on.

Definitely a general power cut then, she thought. She had not been singled out for special treatment. She closed the fridge door as quietly as she could and stood for a moment, thinking. Did the air-filtration system run on electricity? Were they all going to suffocate? She sniffed the air and it seemed reasonably fresh – but then again, how long would it take to get stale in a massive place like this? Surely they wouldn't have put all their eggs in one basket – they were bound to have some sort of back-up system. It would be a major *faux pas* to have a single generator that controlled the lights, the air, the door locks and everything else, not to mention all the important experimental projects that were going on all over the complex, that presumably relied on a constant power supply.

No, it was just some glitch. Some technical problem. Nothing to worry about. They would sort it out soon enough. In the meantime she'd light a few candles, convince herself that her fears were due to nothing more than an overactive imagination and sit tight.

She felt her way along the kitchen counter to the gas cooker. Would that be affected too? she wondered. She located one of the knobs and the ignition button with her hands and twisted the former whilst pressing the latter. There was silence; of course, the ignition button also needed an electrical supply to work. She groped above her head, picturing a box of matches on the shelf there, and a moment later her hand closed around it. She struck one of the matches and the kitchen blossomed into wavering life. To save matches and free her hands, she turned on the gas again and applied the flame to a ring. There was a whoosh, and suddenly the darkness was further punctured by a lily-pad of blue flame. It didn't provide much illumination, but gave a sketchy, blue-limned impression of the shape of the room. Sasha shook out the match, then looked round quickly, and was relieved to find she was alone, at least in here. The main room beyond the kitchen threshold was still thickly clotted with shadow, but she could just about make out her bed as a dark bulk against a darker background.

Sasha opened a drawer beneath the sink, lines of blue light reflected in the curves of the stainless steel, and found a pack of eight white candles. She tore the pack open, grabbed a candle, lit it with the flame from the gas cooker and jammed it into the neck

381

of one of three empty Grolsch bottles sitting on the draining board. As she picked up the bottle and turned to carry it into the main room, her stomach began to knot and twist at the prospect of what she might see in there. She turned off the gas cooker and was left with the candle light, which, although more penetrating than the blue gas-flame, was less steady. She moved slowly out of the kitchen and into the main room, the flapping candle light making the walls look as though they were stretching like rubber, making the shadows at the edges of the light move like prowling animals. Her double bed with the duvet bunched on top of it resembled a lunar landscape, but the floor on the far side – where the object she had dislodged from her bedside table had fallen – remained within a dark block of shadow cast by the bed.

Taking a deep breath, she walked towards her bed and climbed up on to it. As she moved across the mattress on her knees, holding her candle out before her, so the band of light on the far side of it grew thinner. *Whatever you see*, she told herself, *don't panic. Don't drop the candle*. Her stomach felt alive with movement as she leaned over, holding the candle in front of her, warm wax dribbling down the glass and fanning out across the dam of her fingers. Now the shadow on the far side of the bed shrank back and she could see the whole of the carpet.

There was nothing there.

The sound of relief that came from her throat was almost a sob. All at once Sasha was shaking, as if her nerves contained by the tension in her belly had now been let loose. The white light quavered, jittering on the walls, causing the shadows that it couldn't altogether dispel to swell and diminish as if the darkness itself were breathing rapidly. Sasha swung her legs round and placed her feet on the floor so that she was sitting on the edge of the bed. She leaned forward and placed the Grolsch bottle on her bedside table, beside the lamp.

As she drew her hand away from the bottle, something rolled out from beneath the bed and bumped against her ankle.

Sasha looked down and saw part of a whitish dome, almost completely obscured by tentacle-like swirls of long dark hair. Something seemed to glint beneath the hair; something like an eye.

Her scream was raw and hot and coppery as blood in her throat, and hurt her head so much with its sudden ferocity that it seemed for a moment to obscure her vision. She ran blindly across the room to the door and tugged at it without thinking. It opened, but it didn't occur to her to be surprised until she was outside in the corridor. Then she paused only briefly, the thought barely registering through her terror, before blundering across to the lift and unthinkingly banging the keypad beside the door with the flat of her hand.

That's no good, you silly cow, she thought vehemently, and swung away from the lift, looking for another means of escape. As she turned she saw a glimmering band of whitish light bisecting the red emergency lighting that drenched the corridor and realised that, in her panic, she had left the door to her room open. She ran across to it and leaned forward to clasp the handle, unable to resist glancing into her room as she did so. What she saw almost froze her. A dark, roundish object was rolling across the carpet towards her. As Sasha stared at it, it seemed to sense her, for suddenly it began to pick up speed, moving quickly now, evidently anxious to reach the door before it closed. Sasha gave a blurt of sound too feeble to be termed a scream and yanked the door shut. Two seconds later something bumped against it from the other side.

There was a part of Sasha that wanted to sink to the ground, curl into a ball and pray for it all to go away. It was only her desire to put as much distance as possible between her and the thing on the other side of the door that kept her going. She ran down the corridor to the fire door, grabbed the handle affixed to its steel surface and tugged hard, praying that whatever had disabled the lock on her door had done the same here. To her immense relief the door shifted a little. She gritted her teeth and heaved with all her strength. The door, bank-vault thick, slowly swung open.

Beyond it, again soaked in red emergency lighting, was a landing and a staircase. Sasha slipped through the gap and began to lope up the stairs, taking them two at a time. She wondered which floor Dad was on, wondered whether he knew about the lights and the locks. She also wondered briefly what she would do when she got to the top of the stairs, then pushed the thought to the back of her mind. There was no point planning anything; she would have to play it by ear. For all she knew this could be some sort of test, a game they were playing with her. Jenna was probably sitting watching her on a screen somewhere, drinking tea and laughing her tits off.

Something grunted, pig-like, on the stairwell, cutting in on her thoughts. Sasha looked up and saw a huge looming shadow, the emergency lighting making it look like a flow of gravity-defying blood, moving up the wall and not down it.

She froze, sinking to her haunches, like an animal trying to make itself as small a target as possible. The shadow swayed, ballooned, and then the figure that had made it appeared at the top of the stairs.

It did not seem to have a proper face, just a shifting blur of darkness through which could be seen the glint of eyes and of big white teeth clamped in a grin. The tall, broad, ape-like figure grunted and sniggered and began to descend towards her, its head waggling on its shoulders. Sasha tried to move, but couldn't; some force greater than she was had paralysed her body. Her eyes, stretched wide, shifted from the indistinct face of the nightmare man she had last seen when she was nine years old, and focused instead on the figure's right hand – and on the enormous, dripping axe that dangled from it.

Fifty-Eight

Jenna had been eighteen when she saw her first dead person. She was a rookie police constable in Manchester and she and an older male colleague broke into the basement flat of a man who was wanted for questioning in relation to drugs offences, but who had not been seen for several weeks.

The man had been in the flat all right, lying face up on the bed, but he had been in no state to talk. His body had been discoloured and hideously bloated, the flesh like soft black cheese, rotting away. The stench had been so awful that Jenna had immediately thrown up. She had continued to retch even when her stomach was empty and the only thing coming from her mouth were threads of bitter-tasting drool. The worst thing of all had not been the body itself, but the maggots that crawled all over it, packing its eye sockets, writhing in its hair. Even to this day, Jenna vividly remembered the sight of the man's tongue, black and swollen and lolling from his mouth, encrusted with tiny white eggs. She had seen plenty of corpses since, and the sight of death no longer bothered her, but from that day she had always hated maggots. The mere sight of them brought on feelings of nausea and panicky revulsion.

So when she woke with the conviction that something was wriggling on her face and in her hair, she sat bolt upright, then jumped from her futon in the dark, scrabbling at her scalp. She thought she heard the sound of several small objects pattering to the floor, but she couldn't be certain. Unerringly she reached out in the darkness for the lamp, constructed of bamboo and ricepaper, sitting on the small cabinet beside her futon. Jenna had excellent spatial awareness, an ability which she credited to her devotion to *feng shui*, by which one found inner peace through the correct arrangement and manipulation of one's immediate environment. Certainly Jenna felt at one with herself and the universe. Despite her phobic reaction to maggots, she had never had nightmares about them before – in fact, she never had nightmares about anything – and had certainly never hallucinated that they were crawling on her skin.

Her fingers found the lamp switch, which she pressed; there was the usual click, but nothing happened. Jenna took a deep, slow breath, then walked across the room in the dark, neatly side-stepping her rowing machine, and found the main switch with her outstretched fingers. As soon as she pressed that switch, and still the room remained steeped in darkness, she knew for certain that something was badly wrong.

She stood for a moment, thinking, moving rapidly through the possibilities. Then she crossed to her futon once again, sat down and pulled open the topmost drawer of the bedside cabinet. It slid open smoothly, almost silently. She put her hand in – and then snatched it back with a gasp. The drawer was full of what felt like a writhing mass of maggots.

Jenna breathed deeply and steadied her thoughts, calming her heart in four beats, then cautiously extended her hand once again. This time she felt what she expected to feel: a drawer empty apart from her gun and her torch. She took out her gun, transferred it from her right to her left hand, then reached in again for the torch. She pointed it in front of her and turned it on.

Hundreds of fat white maggots were writhing on the carpet.

Jenna's breath quickened again; her instinct was to flinch away from the sight, but she managed to catch herself, to sit perfectly still. Her hand barely shaking, she clicked off the torch, then sat for a moment in the darkness, filling her lungs with air, expelling it slowly.

She knew what was happening. It was what she had feared might happen all along, what she had warned them would happen if they rushed headlong into this project without imposing any proper safeguards. The psis had become too powerful to be contained and were now fighting back with the only weapon at their disposal. She pictured the condescending expressions of her so-called 'superiors' – out-of-touch old men who had spent most of their lives in laboratories and behind desks, studying journals and reports instead of interacting with people – as they pooh-poohed her warning that their proposed implementation of the Genesis project was simply a way of providing the lunatics with enough firepower to take over the asylum.

'But why should they?' they had argued. 'If we treat them well, if we convince them that we and they are working together, for the good of the country, why should they turn against us?'

She had called them naive and blinkered, but her words had been so much water off a duck's back. She had suggested drugging the psis to keep them docile, but they had said that this would affect the preparation training, that if the psis were to realise their full potential their minds had to be alert at all times.

'And if they *do* realise their full potential, what's to stop them getting inside all of our heads?' she had asked frustratedly.

Their so-called solutions had seemed simplistic to her, ill-conceived.

We'll only give them the ability to do so much, they had said. *We'll make them trust us, and if that doesn't work we'll threaten to harm their families if they don't co-operate. We'll make them rely on us for their food and light and air, their means of survival. We'll isolate them physically, give them nowhere to escape to. We'll install a fail-safe mechanism so if the worst comes to the worst, gas will be pumped through the ventilation system, rendering the psis unconscious. We have many weapons, Jenna, many ways of bending our friends to our will.*

'But that's just it, isn't it?' Jenna had argued. 'The question of *will* is the crux of the matter. What if we open Pandora's box and find that we can't contain what's inside? What if *our* will becomes *their* will? What then?'

Round and round her arguments had gone, in ever-decreasing circles. And they had continued to smile and nod and to tell her that it *wouldn't* happen, it *couldn't* happen, that she was worrying unduly.

Except that now it *was* happening – and who was expected to deal with it? *She* was. Not them, sitting there looking on in their ivory tower, tutting and shaking their heads like disapproving grandparents observing the antics of recalcitrant children. Jenna wondered how far it had gone, how powerful the psis had really become. Where this might lead now was anybody's guess.

She switched her torch on again. There was not a maggot to be

387

seen. As always her room was spotlessly clean, immaculately neat. She dressed quickly – grey sweatshirt, black leggings, Reebok trainers, gun holster. Then, weapon in hand, she moved across to the door, listened for a moment, then plucked it open and stepped into the corridor, immediately swivelling in an arc, gun at chest level.

She was alone and the immediate area was quiet, though Jenna knew only too well that the place was heavily soundproofed, that a person could sit and read in silence in one room oblivious to somebody screaming for mercy in the next. Moving like a puma, swiftly but so lightly that she made almost no sound at all, she padded along the corridor – the emergency lighting making the grey carpet look drenched with blood – to the steel door at the end that led out on to the emergency stairs. She had considered using the lift for maybe a second before rejecting the idea. It was too confining. It would only make her vulnerable.

She was reaching for her keycard when a thought struck her and she gave the door a tug. It opened – which meant that the psis had overridden the security systems. They were probably roaming all over the complex now like a pack of escaped laboratory rats; which, Jenna thought, was more or less what they were. Not that their physical liberty worried Jenna unduly: their danger lay in the damage they could inflict mentally, and she was all too aware that an attack on that score could come from anywhere at any time. They were just as dangerous in their rooms as out of them. Jenna could only hope that she would have enough mental strength of her own to overcome whatever they might throw at her.

Her quarters were situated not far below ground level, but instead of heading up and out, abandoning the complex to the psis, Jenna moved on to the staircase and began to head down, towards the central control area. She hated being involved with failure, even if it was not of her making; her aim, slim though her chance of implementing it may be, was to minimise the effects of the catastrophe as far as she could. If possible she wanted to get the security systems running again, reactivate all the internal locks and contain the psis within the complex. If she managed to get that far, she would then be in a position to operate the fail-safe mechanism and flood the complex with knock-out gas. Of course, this plan relied on the hope that the psis were not powerful enough to have an overview of the minds of everyone within the

388

complex; obviously, if they knew what she was thinking, they would stop her. And what her superiors would do to contain the psis' abilities once they came round (aside from killing the psis and thus terminating the project, which would have been Jenna's solution) was anybody's guess. But that wasn't her problem right now.

She moved down the stairs, gun at the ready, keeping low and grabbing what cover she could. Five floors down from her own she saw a mass of dark shapes huddled on the stairs and froze into place, keeping her gun trained on the mass until she could discern exactly what it was. Little by little she was able to pick out details in the dim light: here the white oval of a face, there a hand, there a discarded firearm. She sidled closer, scanning the huddled shapes for any sign of movement, but seeing none she moved closer still, gun arm steady as a rock, eyes darting to take in new details until they became clear.

Finally she was standing right over the heap of bodies, face grim, mind working. She crouched and turned a couple of them over, trying to ascertain how they had died. There were no immediate marks or wounds aside from trickles of blood from mouths, noses, ears. Had the psis really done this? Even if they had the combined ability to inflict such devastating physical damage, were they capable of being so ruthless? There must be two dozen dead men – maybe more – on this landing and the one below. Had this massacre been an accident – a panicked response by a group which didn't know its own strength – or was there some other factor at work here, some rogue element that even she had not foreseen?

Whatever the answer, one thing was certain – she couldn't afford to take any risks. These men had been killed instantaneously: not a single one had had time to respond to being attacked.

She continued her descent, moving slowly, taking nothing for granted. She had gone down three more floors when she heard a sound on the stairwell below her. She crouched down and sidled around the bend in the stairs, hugging the wall, gun arm ramrod-straight.

On the landing at the bottom of the stairs, she could see a figure. It seemed to shuffle, to move awkwardly, perhaps wounded or disabled. As though sensing her, it raised its head.

And suddenly Jenna was eighteen again, but this time the bloated, fly-blown corpse on the bed was not playing by the rules. It was below her in the red-soaked dimness, placing one elephantine foot on the bottom stair, extending a splitting, swollen, black-fleshed hand to grip the stair-rail and haul itself up. It seemed to wheeze as it came, foul air belching from its decaying lungs, but that was not the worst thing about it. The worst thing was the maggots, dozens, hundreds of them, that cascaded from its yawning mouth in a steady stream, that tumbled from its eye sockets and down its cheeks like solid, wriggling tears.

Fifty-Nine

It's playing with us was the last message that formulated in Nick's mind before, right on cue, it found them again. This time it seemed to pounce, as if the energy generated by their collective communication had attracted it. All at once it felt to Nick as though hot knives were sliding into his skull, dissecting portions of his brain. Within seconds the pain had become so excruciating that he passed out.

When he came to he had a splitting headache but knew instinctively he was alone. He lay for a few minutes in the darkness, groaning softly, nursing his psychic hangover. Could the presence he had felt – they had *all* felt – have been Hallett? He didn't see how it could have been anything or anyone else. The man's power was frightening, phenomenal, and despite the message they had sent apologising for their initial attack on him and begging for help, it seemed he was not in a forgiving mood. However, Nick supposed he ought to view the fact that he was still alive as encouraging. He tried to pull his throbbing thoughts together to decide on his next move. The best thing would be to try to get in touch with Hallett, let him know Nick's whereabouts – if he didn't already. Then he ought to sound the others out, find out what their feelings were about how to proceed.

Using his mind felt as painful as coughing with badly bruised ribs, but Nick gritted his teeth and forced himself to send out a message. *Mr Hallett, are you there? Mr Hallett it's me, Nick. Can you hear me?*

There was no response. Nick tried again, each word he formulated feeling like someone pressing down hard on an internal injury, making him dizzy and nauseous.

Finally he gave up and lay back on his bed for a few minutes, exhausted. Either Hallett couldn't hear him, or he was choosing

391

not to respond. As soon as he felt able, Nick sent out a general message, asking whether everyone was okay: he thought he detected a murmur of response but he couldn't be sure. Were they all unconscious, or afraid to draw attention to themselves, or had the blistering psychic attack wounded their minds so severely that their powers were temporarily (or permanently?) nullified? He braced himself against the pain and tried again, but again received nothing but a murmur, a tickle so light that its source could not be identified. He gave up – it was pointless splitting his head in two for nothing – and forced himself to get out of bed. He padded through the darkness to where he knew the door of the bathroom was situated; he may as well down a couple of paracetamols. They might not do any good, but at least they wouldn't do any harm.

He frowned when he clicked the switch outside the bathroom door and the light failed to come on. He paused for a moment in the doorway, then turned and headed in what he thought was roughly the direction of the main door, waving his hands in front of him as if in an attempt to scoop the darkness aside. Eventually he reached the wall and groped along it until he found the door, and then the light switch beside it.

When he pressed it, the room stayed dark. Nick's heart skipped with both hope and fear. Could this be an indication that Hallett was actually here? Had he somehow disabled the systems, cut off the power, plunged the whole complex into darkness? If the lights were off, did that also mean . . .? He put out a hand to the door, found the handle, turned it and tugged. It came open so smoothly and unexpectedly that Nick almost overbalanced. There was a red glow in the corridor outside; at first, with a shock, he thought that Hallett had set the place on fire, trapping them all underground. Then he realised that the glow came from lozenges of emergency lighting, situated at intervals along the wall.

Trying to ignore the pain in his head, Nick sent out another message, instructing the others to use the stairs and head upwards, to congregate at ground level, just inside the main entrance. Again he felt a slight buzz; it may or may not have been an acknowledgement. His own plan was to pick up Sasha en route to the surface. Even though his escort had always concealed the floor button from him on the occasions when Nick had visited his daughter, he was pretty certain that Sasha's room was four floors above his.

He walked to the end of the corridor, opened the steel door and stepped out on to the landing. The place was eerily quiet, though he supposed it *was* the early hours of the morning. Most of those who had living quarters within the complex – and he had no idea how many did – were probably still asleep. Unless of course Hallett had done what he did to Jacobs on a massive scale, which Nick – thinking of people like Jo Swanwick and Dr Farrow, who seemed nice enough despite the circumstances in which he and they had been thrown together – sincerely hoped was not the case.

He began to head upwards, alert for any sound, any movement, coming from the floors above. He heard and saw nothing; reaching the landing three floors above his own, he was beginning to wonder whether he was alone in the complex, whether everyone else had somehow been spirited away while he slept. Then the steel doors abruptly swung open and a figure plunged through the gap, falling to the floor in front of him.

Nick quickly realised that the figure posed no threat. All the same, he couldn't help but be disturbed by the man's behaviour. He was tall, willowy, somewhere in his sixties, with grey hair sticking out at crazy angles, and a grey moustache. He was bare-foot, wearing a pair of maroon silk pyjamas, and was currently scrabbling on the floor and batting at his head with both hands, screaming, 'Get them *off* me! Get them *off* me!'

'Are you all right?' seemed an inappropriate question, but Nick found himself asking it anyway. The man ignored him, indeed seemed oblivious to his presence. Nick hesitated, then moved forward and placed what was intended to be a reassuring hand on the cowering man's shoulder. 'Hey,' he said softly, 'it's ok—'

'*Get them off me!*' the man screeched again in utter terror, twisting away from Nick's touch as though his fingers were red-hot pokers. All at once he stared straight at Nick, his eyes wide. He was shaking. The corners of his mouth were white with froth.

Nick felt sure that although the man was looking straight at him he was seeing something else altogether, something so night-marish that he had lost all reason. There was no consoling him. The man needed something stronger than words.

'I'll get help,' he muttered, and edged past the man, who continued to crawl and writhe about the floor, clawing at himself as if he were being attacked by rats or scorpions.

On the next floor up – Sasha's, he hoped – he noticed that the steel door leading to the corridor was ajar. Perhaps Sasha was already out, he thought, and heading towards the surface – unless her aim was to come and find him first. But if so there was surely no way they could have missed each other. He tried not to think of the danger she might be in; tried not to think of the way Hallett had made Jacobs burst into flames just by willing him to; tried to tell himself that the man on the landing below had just been in the wrong place at the wrong time. After all, Nick was okay, wasn't he? *He* hadn't succumbed to whatever had caused the man in the maroon pyjamas to lose his mind.

But then the man in the maroon pyjamas was not a psi. Like Sasha, he did not possess Nick's mental strength. In an attempt to stifle his anxiety he shoved the door open a little further and marched into the corridor. He heard the steady *thud . . . thud . . . thud . . .* before he realised where it was coming from.

At first he thought the dark shape at the opposite end of the corridor was a shadow in a doorway; then he realised it was a person. The person (Sasha?) was facing the wall, reminding Nick incongrously of playing hide and seek as a kid, of being 'on' and turning to count to a hundred whilst everyone else ran to hide. The sight of the figure had stopped him momentarily in his tracks, but now he began to move forward again. He opened his mouth to say his daughter's name, but some doubt prevented him from speaking, and as he got closer to the figure he saw why.

This was not Sasha; indeed, the figure did not look even remotely like her. This was a man, tall and broad, with short-cropped hair, dressed in what appeared to be a dark suit. Nick was more than halfway down the corridor now, almost parallel with the closed door of Sasha's room. All at once he realised what the man was doing, what was causing the steady thumping sound. The man was drawing back his head, then nodding it sharply forward, unflinchingly and methodically slamming his face into the wall.

Then all at once the man stopped. He paused for a moment, and although Nick couldn't see his expression he regarded the wall with what seemed to Nick like puzzlement. Opposite the man's face, Nick could see a dark patch which looked black in the red light. Slowly the man turned his head. His face was a mask of blood. The expression he wore caused the hairs on Nick's back and arms to quill: it managed somehow to convey both terrible fear and maniacal glee. For a few seconds Nick and the man looked at each other, Nick not daring to move, to breathe. Then the man turned back to the wall and the thudding began again.

Nick shuddered. He moved quickly across to Sasha's door, opened it and slipped inside. The light from a candle in a Grolsch bottle on Sasha's bedside table caused shadows to swell and fall in a silent black tide. 'Sash,' he hissed, moving across to the bed and putting out a hand to touch the curled-up figure that was lying there. He touched the figure's shoulder – and it deflated beneath his grip. It was not a figure at all, merely the bunched-up duvet which had been left in such away that it looked as though it were covering a shoulder, a head. Nick skirted the bed, peering at objects that were no more than darker shadows than the ones around them. The kitchen was empty, the bathroom too. Sasha was not here.

He went back out into the corridor, where the thudding sound had now become a little squishy, and hurried across to the steel door. He all but ran up the next two staircases, simply to put distance between himself and the madness behind him. Finally he made himself slow down, caution superseding his revulsion once again, and for the next few minutes, during which he ascended six more floors, he saw and heard nothing.

And then, climbing the stairs up to the next floor, he suddenly stopped. Had he heard a small sound – a *tiny* sound – somewhere above him? It was so faint that it was not difficult to convince himself that he might have imagined it; but he thought he had heard an animal, whimpering.

He stood, holding his breath and listening hard, for almost a minute. He was wondering whether he should move on when he heard it again. Yes, it was definitely whimpering: Nick got the impression that the sound was being made by someone or something who either lacked the energy or was too afraid to produce a louder noise. It was close, certainly no higher than the landing above him. He continued his ascent, fully expecting to find yet another stranger cowering in a corner, terrified of shadows.

What he did see when he rounded the corner on to the next landing caused him to stumble with shock. The strength drained from his legs and he had to reach out to the banister rail for support. On the landing a few feet away from him, curled up into a ball, making small, animal sounds of fear, was Sasha. Above her, at the top of the next flight of stairs, standing rigid, arms extended stiffly, a gun clutched in her hands and pointing at the top of Sasha's blonde head, was Jenna.

Jenna had a crazed expression on her face. Her teeth were clenched, her eyes wide and glaring. Even in the red light Nick could see that she was gripping the gun so tightly her knuckles had been squeezed into bloodless points. Despite his wobbly legs he knew that he had to do something. Another three seconds and his daughter's brains would be spread all over the wall. Gathering all his strength he lurched forward. 'Jenna, *no!*' he shouted, holding up his hand like a traffic policeman.

Jenna jumped as though she'd been snapped from a trance, then instinctively jerked the gun up and pulled the trigger. The noise was unbelievable in the confined space. Nick's skull rang with it, and his teeth ached as though his nerves were vibrating. He looked at Sasha. She was still curled into a ball, her hands wrapped around her head. They were both unharmed. The bullet must have missed them, had perhaps embedded itself in the wall behind.

Then he felt a strange sensation in his arm: a cold, aching numbness that almost immediately changed to a burning tingle, radiating out from his hand and sweeping through his body. Suddenly feeling sick and faint, he turned his head and looked at his still upraised hand. The bullet had drilled a hole right through the centre of his palm. Already the cuff of his denim shirt was soaked with blood.

Dreamily Nick looked up and saw that Jenna was adjusting her aim, pointing the gun at Sasha once again. He had no doubt that she intended to pull the trigger, that unless he acted now he would not have saved his daughter's life, but merely postponed her death. Desperately, ignoring the raging pain in his hand, he hit Jenna with a mental barrage, a psychic punch, hoping that Hallett had not killed his power, that there was at least enough gas left in the tank to scramble Jenna's brain, to disable or confuse her.

To his horror, the effect proved far more devastating.

Jenna suddenly convulsed. She threw up her hands as if she were having a fit, the gun flying from her grasp in an arc and striking the wall before bouncing to the floor with a clatter. Blood gushed from her nose and ears and mouth as her head became one huge haemorrhage. Even as she fell, graceless as a sack of rocks, Nick knew that it was over. Jenna – who he had once thought of as his friend, who he had once spent a night with, drinking wine and pouring out his life story, who he had once made love to – was dead before she hit the ground.

Sixty

He wanted to pass out then, wanted to close his eyes and let it all go. He was not entirely sure whether the waves of nausea he felt sluicing through him were due to the skull-splitting agony in his head, the burning pain in his hand or the terrible guilt he felt at murdering his former lover. If it hadn't been for Sasha, curled up like a frightened animal, he may have simply laid his head on the cold concrete and allowed himself to be washed away in the torrent of his own misery.

But concern for his daughter overcame his own physical pain, his own self-loathing. Though he dropped to his knees, his legs for the moment unable to support him, he made himself crawl across to Sasha, whisper her name.

She seemed oblivious to his presence, her body trembling as though she was freezing-cold. Her eyes, glimpsed between the arms that she had wrapped protectively around her head, were wide and staring but oddly unseeing, as if they were the twin lenses of a projector, externalising whatever nightmares were being played out inside her mind.

Nick spoke her name again, and again she didn't respond. He reached out with his uninjured left hand, and gripped Sasha's right wrist. As he tried to tug her arm away from her face, he saw her fingers tighten in her hair. He gritted his teeth and tried again, and, slowly, was able to lever her arm away from her face. He saw her features tighten, saw her staring eyes flicker towards him – and suddenly she was spitting and screeching and clawing at him, fingernails like talons, tearing at his eyes.

Nick lurched away, losing his balance, rolling over on to his back as one of Sasha's fingernails scraped across his cheek. Nick

397

had to put up both hands to defend himself, and within seconds both he and Sasha were covered with the blood still pouring from the hole in his palm.

'Sasha!' Nick shouted at her, desperately attempting to fend her off, his own voice grating in his head, 'Sasha, *stop*! It's me! It's Dad!'

She seemed not to hear him. Nick felt his own movements becoming slower, weaker, felt the greyness of unconsciousness seeping around the edges of his senses. My God, he was going to pass out and his own daughter was going to tear out his throat like a werewolf as he lay helpless. He rolled on to his side, curling up into a ball, his hands and arms coming up to protect his face and head just as Sasha had hers a few moments before. As he felt himself beginning to drift he wondered whether this was *his* nightmare, whether in fact none of this was really happening anywhere but in his own mind.

And then it seemed he *was* dreaming, and in his dream he heard Sasha's voice calling to him. She sounded confused, lost; frightened. 'Dad,' she called. 'Dad, is that you?'

In his dream he nodded. 'Yes,' he whispered.

He felt hands on his body, not clawing and tearing this time, but stroking, soothing. 'Dad, wake up. What's happening? Oh, my God, Dad, there's blood. Where's all this blood coming from?'

With a jolt Nick realised that he was not dreaming. His eyes sprang open. Sasha was kneeling beside him, hands held up like a surgeon awaiting gloves, looking down at herself with horror. Nick's blood on her baggy checked shirt looked like car oil under the red light.

He felt sick and dizzy and his head was cracking open. 'My hand,' he croaked. 'Jenna . . . shot me.'

Sasha gazed at him in disbelief for a moment, then she gasped. 'Oh, God, Dad.' Nick's hand was now a pulsing bulb of pain on the end of his arm. It was so tender that even Sasha's gentle fingers as she took it to examine it felt like whacks from a hammer. He screamed, his back arching involuntarily.

Sasha's face crumpled with distress. 'I'm sorry, Dad. I'm so sorry.'

For a few seconds the pain was too acute to allow Nick to respond. Then, as it ebbed a little, he managed to whisper, 'It's okay, it just . . . it *hurts*.'

398

'I know, Dad, I know, but I've got to stop the bleeding. I'm going to have to tie something around it, all right?'

Nick wanted to tell her no, to leave it alone, but somehow he had to rise above this if he didn't want to pass out from loss of blood. For Sasha's sake, if nothing else, he somehow had to get himself into a fit state to accompany her up to the surface.

'Okay,' he whispered. 'I'll try . . . not to scream . . . too loudly.'

She tried to smile at that, but couldn't manage it. She rooted in the pockets of her jeans in the hope of finding something to use as a tourniquet, but came up with nothing more than a screwed-up handkerchief. Discarding that, she attempted to tear a strip off her shirt – but the material wouldn't budge, no matter how much she yanked and pulled. 'This always looks so easy in the movies,' she muttered. 'Hold on.' She lifted the corner of her shirt to her mouth and began to tear at it with her teeth.

Nick felt the threat – or promise – of unconsciousness pricking at the edges of his senses again. He closed his eyes. It felt better that way, the pain not disappearing but receding slightly, muffled by the grey gauze of encroaching sleep.

'Okay, Dad, are you ready?' Each syllable that Sasha uttered was like the boom of a drum in his mind. Nick drifted to the surface of consciousness again, the pain climbing with him.

'Yes.'

'I'll be as gentle as I can.'

He had to clamp his teeth together to stop himself from crying out as she took his hand once more. Burning waves of pain raced up his arm and engulfed his whole body. As she began to wrap the ragged strip she had finally managed to tear from her shirt around his hand, sweat sprang out all over him and his legs jerked as electric shocks of pain spasmed into them. Somehow, though, he managed to keep reasonably still until she had finished the job. Then he slumped back to the floor, gasping, sweat sizzling on his face, big clots of darkness sailing across his inner vision, inviting him to jump aboard.

Sasha allowed him a little time – though nowhere near enough – to recover. Then she said, 'Dad? I think we'd better be going.'

He rolled slowly on to his back and looked at her. She looked exhausted and scared, her torn shirt spattered with blood – but her overwhelming expression was one of concern for him. 'Do you think you can walk?'

He wanted to laugh at that: the idea was ludicrous. Did she have no idea how much pain he was in? But he didn't want to disappoint her. 'I think so . . . Just give me a minute.'

He concentrated hard on drawing together every ounce of strength in his body, on trying to deny the pure liquid pain that pulsed through his veins in place of blood.

'I'm ready,' he said at last – although he wasn't, not really. 'Could you help me up?'

Sasha wrapped both arms around his good arm and helped him to his feet. As he stood upright, Nick felt as though blood were draining rapidly from his head and legs, coagulating into a heavy, doughy mass in his belly. He started to sweat again. For a few seconds the world blanched and span away and he was certain he would pass out.

'Come on, Dad,' he heard Sasha say, her voice echoing as though from the end of a long tunnel, 'just lean on me. You'll be all right in a minute.'

Nick took deep breaths, forced himself to resist the urge to sink back down to his knees, and after a minute or so the dizziness passed and his legs began to feel more sturdy. Together he and Sasha moved slowly to the stairs and began to climb them, Nick looking no further ahead than the next step, and the next, and the next.

All at once Sasha tightened her grip on his arm and she stopped abruptly. 'Oh, no.'

Nick blinked. 'What is it?'

'There's a body on the landing.'

He looked up. At first glance the body, lying on its face, seemed shapeless, like a heap of dark blankets; but then he saw the legs, one with its knee bent, and the dark hair fanning out, matted with the blood that was pooled around the head, giving the odd impression in the semi-darkness that it was twice as large as it should be.

Nick swallowed, licked his lips. 'It's Jenna. I didn't . . . I didn't mean to kill her. But she was going to shoot you. I had to . . . do something.'

'Shh,' Sasha soothed, 'it's okay, Dad.' She was silent for a moment and then she spoke again, and there was a rasp of bitterness in her voice. 'She deserved it. For all she'd done, she deserved it. She only got what was coming to her.'

He didn't reply. They edged past the body and carried on up the stairs, moving slowly, like two infirm pensioners attempting to escape from an old folks' home in the middle of the night. As they progressed, the minutes drifted by and they lapsed into silence, too raw with the horror of their own recent emotions to speak. It was not *quite* silent in the complex: occasionally they heard a distant wail, or scream, or shout of fear. The place was full of nightmares – or perhaps, thought Nick, it was occupied by one vast nightmare which each person was living in their own way. Everyone must be affected by it, everyone except the psis, which accounted for the reason why none of the security or military staff had made their presence felt.

'How are you doing, Dad?' Sasha asked eventually, and Nick wondered whether his feet had been dragging, whether he had been starting to lean too heavily on her arm. In truth, the slow, repetitive rhythm of their progress had had an almost soporific effect on him and, despite the effort it took to climb the stairs, his mind had begun to drift again, so much so that when Sasha spoke it took him a moment to remember where he was.

'Oh . . . fine,' he said vaguely. 'How about you?'

'I'm doing okay, Dad. We can't be that far from the surface now. How's the hand?'

Nick looked at the blood-soaked wad of material wound tightly around his hand and tied in a frayed knot at the wrist. The hand itself felt hot; he could feel it throbbing, like a secondary heart.

'Okay,' he said. 'The pain's eased a bit.'

He wasn't sure whether that was true, whether it wasn't simply the pain in his head which was not so acute. However, he did feel a little better than he had before, not so nauseous, not so dizzy. They rounded another bend in the stairs and Sasha stopped, squeezing Nick's arm.

'My God.'

The words were not spoken so much as breathed. Sprawled on the stairs in front of them, heaped on the landing above, were at least twenty or thirty dead men. They were wearing military uniforms and had clearly been armed at the time of their deaths – the guns they had carried were lying under and around their bodies.

'They've been shot,' Sasha said, her voice small and stricken. 'Every single one of them – shot in the face. Oh Dad, it's *horrible*.'

401

'Yes,' Nick said numbly, 'it is. But . . . I don't think they've been shot.'

The scene of carnage made him feel ill all over again, but Nick made himself crouch down to examine the nearest body more closely. At last, aided by Sasha, he straightened up.

'There's definitely been some sort of . . . battle here, but these men weren't shot. There aren't any bullet wounds.'

'But look at all the blood!'

'I know, but when I . . . stopped Jenna from hurting you, she bled too – from her nose and her mouth. It was as if she was . . . haemorrhaging internally.'

'So these men were killed by . . . what? Psychic forces?'

'Looks that way,' said Nick.

'God. All these people . . .' Sasha looked at her father as though she were seeing him in a new light. Her voice was terse, and she was unable to prevent an accusatory tone from creeping into it. 'Did your *friends* do this, Dad?'

'No!' said Nick firmly. He looked again at the bodies strewn before him and although his voice faltered, he said again, 'No. I'm sure they didn't.'

Sasha was silent for a moment. Then she said, 'They might have acted in self-defence. I mean, if the soldiers were prepared to shoot them . . .'

Nick shook his head; his fading headache flared briefly back into life. 'No. I think this is more likely to be Hallett's work.'

'*Hallett?* Who's he?'

Nick sighed. He had not had the chance to tell Sasha about his time with Hallett because of the problem of being continually observed and overheard. In his present state the prospect of launching into a long explanation of Hallett's background and current exploits seemed an impossible task. 'He – looked after me for a couple of days before I came here,' he said after a moment. 'He's another psi, the strongest of us all. The Illuminati either don't know where he is or won't touch him – the only reason they got me was because I left Hallett's protection and came here voluntarily when I heard they'd taken you.' He paused. 'Mr Hallett is . . . I suppose you'd call him a gangster, though not to his face. He's built up a large organisation over the years.'

'You make him sound like the Mafia,' Sasha said.

Nick shrugged and gave a wry smile.

402

'So what's he doing here now?' Sasha asked.

'We made him an offer he couldn't refuse.'

Sasha looked at the dead soldiers again. Eventually, her voice full of horrified wonder, she breathed, 'These people – the Illuminati – really had no idea what they were unleashing here, did they?'

'No, I don't think they did.'

Sasha turned and looked at him. Nick felt discomfited by the directness of her gaze. 'So what happens now, Dad? I mean . . . if we get out of here, what happens? Things can't ever be the same again, can they? Not after this.'

Nick didn't answer immediately. Eventually he murmured, 'I honestly don't know, Sash. I don't know what's going to happen. All we can do is keep going, hope things work out.'

'Yeah,' she sighed, 'I suppose so. Come on then. The first thing we've got to do is get past this lot.'

Negotiating a route through the corpses was almost unbearable. At the top of the stairs the bodies were so densely packed that Nick and Sasha had no choice but to clamber over them, stepping on backs and arms and legs, slithering on patches of blood that had burst from ruptured organs, leaked out through various bodily orifices. By the time the ordeal was over, Sasha was pale and shuddering; Nick's teeth were gritted, his face creased in distress. As they left the bodies behind, Sasha gave one final almighty shudder, as though sloughing off her revulsion like a layer of unwanted skin. 'I never, *ever*, want to do that again,' she said bleakly.

Nick felt too sick to respond. He only hoped that there were no equally unpleasant ordeals awaiting them. They lapsed into silence as they began to climb the stairs once more. As they neared the top, Nick felt his back hunching over, his head drooping a little further forward with each step. He was exhausted and still in a great deal of pain. He wanted to stop and rest more than he had ever wanted anything else in the world, but he was afraid that if he did he would not be able to summon the strength to get up again. Beside him Sasha was plodding on doggedly, her arm linked with his, which further encouraged him to match her pace. He didn't want to be a burden.

He was watching his feet, willing them to lift themselves for another step, and another, and just one more, when Sasha suddenly announced, 'We're here.'

A little dazed, he looked up. Sure enough, the landing above them lacked the usual right-hand curve on to the next flight of stairs, ending instead in what appeared to be a blank wall. Nick looked along its length for a door, but couldn't see one. 'It's a dead end,' he said.

'It can't be,' said Sasha in disbelief. Gently she disengaged her arm from his and ascended the final few steps on to the narrow landing in front of the wall. She placed her hands on the wall and gave an experimental push, then walked from one end to the other, examining it, paying particular attention to the corners.

'There's a gap on both sides where the walls meet,' she said, 'a crack that goes all the way up. It's only narrow – I can't even get my fingernails into it – but these walls are definitely not joined together. There *must* be some way through.'

'Is there not a – a button, or a panel or something?' suggested Nick, gripping the banister, and trying desperately to resist the temptation to sink to his knees.

'Not that I can see. I wonder how thick this wall is.' She gave a number of experimental taps and, to the surprise of them both, the taps were almost immediately answered from the other side.

Sasha looked wide-eyed at Nick for a second, then put her mouth to the wall. 'Hello,' she called. 'Who's there?'

A man's voice, louder than expected, replied. 'Who's *there*?'

'I think that's Greg,' Nick said. 'Greg Lousada. He's one of the psis.'

Sasha called, 'Is that Greg Lousada?'

The voice sounded surprised. 'Yes. Who's that?'

'It's Sasha Finch. Nick's daughter. I've got Dad here with me, but we can't get out.'

'Hang on,' called Greg. His voice became muffled as he turned away to talk to whoever was with him. There was a shuffle of movement close to the wall, a few seconds of near-silence – and then the pin-thin crack at the right angle of the two walls on the right-hand side began to widen.

Sasha stepped back and Nick shuffled forward to the top of the stairs as the crack of darkness became a band and then a column. All at once the fingers of several hands appeared, curling around the section of wall they were tugging back like a warehouse door, attempting to gain a better grip. The appearance of the fingers was

404

followed by the appearance of a face in the gap, florid and pink-eyed under the emergency lighting.

'You took your time,' Greg Lousada said. 'Well, come on then, look lively. It's not easy holding this bloody thing open, you know.'

Sasha glanced back at Nick to see if he needed help, but he waved her through and then followed. They emerged into the vestibule beside the main entrance to the Chicken House. Only now did it occur to Nick that, when he had last been here, many weeks ago, the vestibule had appeared to contain no means of access to the lower floors other than the lift. Now, of course, he understood why. He glanced to his left as he emerged and saw four of the psis struggling to keep the gap wide enough for them to slip through. One of them – Mark Brown, who had confessed to being responsible for what had happened to Linsey – was puffing out his bearded cheeks in his exertion, so much sweat rolling down his face that he appeared to be melting.

Trying not to look as exhausted as he felt, Nick grinned and clapped Mark Brown on the shoulder with his good hand. 'Okay – we're through. You can let go now.'

With a collective grunt the psis let the section of wall go. It began to rumble back into place as though propelled by powerful springs, then all at once there was a metallic screeching sound as if thick, high-tension metal cables were shearing apart. The sliding length of wall shuddered and then ground to a halt, leaving a foot-wide gap.

Greg Lousada, all but devouring a cigarette, said wrily, 'You've bust it now. That'll have to come out of your pocket-money.' He nodded at the blood-soaked rag around Nick's hand. 'What the hell happened to you?'

'I had a bit of an argument with Jenna. She had a gun – I didn't.'

'Is she still prowling around?' Chris Kingsley, the thin, blond-haired man asked, glancing nervously about him as if he expected Jenna to pop up from nowhere.

'No,' Nick said, his hope that he wouldn't have to elaborate dashed by Sasha who declared, almost proudly:

'Dad killed her!'

Greg Lousada raised his eyebrows, his cigarette momentarily forgotten. 'You bastard,' he said.

'It was in self-defence,' Nick protested. 'I didn't mean to kill her, I just meant to put her out of action. If I hadn't done something she would have shot both of us.'

'You misunderstand me,' Lousada said mildly. 'You're a bastard because you got to the bitch before I could.'

'Yeah, well. It's over now,' Nick mumbled.

'Not yet it isn't,' said Ellie McKee. 'Our next job is to think of a way of getting out of here.'

She gestured towards the smaller steel door set into the two larger ones at the far end of the vestibule. Through there, they all knew, was fresh air and a night sky none of them had seen for weeks – but the doors were firmly closed.

'I presume you've tried opening them?' said Sasha.

Most of the psis nodded, but Greg Lousada said laconically, 'Do you know, we never thought of that.'

Sasha gave a tight smile. Nodding at the section of movable wall she asked, 'How did you get through there from the other side?'

'We came prepared,' said Julie Lean, and held up her hand, in which she held a carving knife, the blade snapped neatly in two. 'I got this . . . this . . . it wasn't really a message, more like a *feeling* in my head. Very faint. It woke me up after the terrible pain that knocked us all out. Somehow I just *knew* that the power was off, that my door was unlocked and that we should all head up to the surface.'

'That was me,' said Nick. 'I sent that message. I wasn't sure if anyone heard it.'

Julie Lean smiled gratefully at him, then continued. 'I was scared, so I brought this with me out of my kitchen – though whether I'd ever have been able to make myself use it is another matter. It turned out that one or two of the others had done the same thing – perhaps we're getting to the stage where we subconsciously pick up on each other's ideas. We managed to get the blades into the crack and make a big enough gap to get our fingers in to pull it open.'

'Wouldn't you have used your powers if you had been threatened or attacked?' asked Sasha.

'I don't know. My head was hurting – and besides, I didn't know what I would be capable of doing in that kind of situation. I still don't.'

'So you didn't kill the soldiers?' said Sasha. 'None of you?'

406

'No,' said Ellie McKee. 'Most of us saw them, though. Horrible.'

'I think we're all capable of killing,' said Nick. 'We just have to be desperate or angry enough to do it.'

'Cool,' said Lousada, then spread his hands innocently as one or two of the others glared at him. 'What? I just meant, it might prove useful.'

'It's not something to be abused, Greg,' said Ellie McKee sternly. 'We're not psychos.'

'Hey, I know that. What do you take me for?'

Tactfully, nobody answered.

'Has anybody seen any sign of Hallett or his men yet?' Nick asked.

There was a general shaking of heads.

'Maybe he's been and gone,' suggested a thick-set man whose name was John Pierpoint and who Nick thought looked the most Russian of all of them.

'Yeah, perhaps he just cracked the place open like a nut and buggered off,' Greg elaborated.

'I don't know,' said Nick. 'That doesn't sound like him. I can't believe he'd leave something only half-done.'

'Look, why don't we all concentrate on getting out of here for now and worry about this Hallett bloke if and when he shows up,' said Sasha.

'Any suggestions on *how* to get out of here?' asked Ellie McKee. The look she gave Nick made Sasha wonder whether she was deferring to him not because he had only just arrived and might be able to bring something fresh to the discussion but because she – and possibly some of the others too – saw him as some kind of leader.

Much as she loved her dad and admired his many undoubted qualities, Sasha had never viewed him in this vein, and certainly not in his present dishevelled and exhausted state. Feeling, not for the first time in her life, somewhat protective towards him, she said, 'Why don't you try using your powers to open the door? I mean, you can damage living tissue, so who's to say you can't damage other things as well?'

'We're talking two-foot thick reinforced steel here,' Chris Kingsley said, as if she were mad.

'So? There's no harm in trying, is there? If all of you combined have a go . . .'

407

'Yeah, why not?' said Ellie McKee. 'My headache's more or less gone now. I'm ready to give it a shot.'

Around half of the others looked dubious but shrugged and moved forward instinctively to form a tighter-knit group. At least, Sasha thought, their physical positioning would help give them a psychological focus. They fell silent as they stared at the door, utter concentration on their faces. Sasha stood off to the side, her gaze alternating between the door and the group of psis. She noticed that her dad's eyes were half-closed and hoped he wasn't succumbing to the tiredness caused by his blood loss and earlier mental exertion.

For a few minutes nothing happened. Then, abruptly, the smaller door set into the two larger ones slid smoothly open. Sasha was surprised. She had not expected this. She had expected something less neat – the metal door to buckle and melt like wax, or to crack and splinter like dry, brittle wood.

Perhaps everybody else was as surprised as she was, because for several long seconds nobody moved. Sasha felt a waft of fresh, cold air and gulped it in greedily. As if drawn to the promise of more, she took a step forward.

And then the doorway was filled by a dark, bulky, almost square shape, which paused on the threshold for a moment as if surveying what was inside before trundling into the room.

Sasha's initial thought was that this new arrival was some kind of machine, some piece of military hardware, perhaps even a robot. Then, as it moved further into the vestibule and red light slid over it, her eyes made sense of the sight. She was looking, not at a machine, but a man in a wheelchair whose legs ended at the knees. Despite this, the man's broad shoulders, bullet-like head and large hairy hands which gripped the wheels of his chair and propelled him forward made him appear powerful, ape-like.

As his gaze moved over her Sasha shivered – and then swallowed hard as more men entered the vestibule. There were four of them, built like gladiators in grey suits; each of them carried a machine-gun. They came to flank the man in the chair, and as Nick took a step forward, they raised their guns and trained them on him.

The man in the wheelchair raised a hand and the four gladiators lowered their weapons.

'Hello, Mr Hallett,' Nick said, his voice sounding lost and small in the high-ceilinged room.

There was no smile of greeting from the man in the wheelchair. He stared back at Nick, stone-faced and unblinking for what seemed an uncomfortably long time. Then in a gruff, quiet voice, he said, 'Do you know what you've done, old son?'

Nick licked his lips. 'I . . . we called you here. We needed your help.'

Hallett shook his head as if Nick's voice were an irritating fly in need of swatting. 'You've killed my best friend. Not only that, but you've drawn me into a war I didn't want to fight. Now that, son, is unforgivable.'

Nick looked confused. 'Killed your best friend? I don't know what you mean.'

'Mad Dog's dead,' said Hallett, 'and it's all down to you, Nick. You broke my concentration with your pathetic little whinge, as a result of which Mad Dog took a bullet in the gut. That man was a brother to me. He trusted me to protect him. How do you think that makes me feel?'

Nick raised a trembling hand to his head and ran it through his hair. His voice wavering, he said, 'I'm really sorry. I didn't mean for that to happen. It's just . . . we were desperate. We didn't know what else to do.'

Hallett placed a finger to his lips and Nick fell silent. 'I'm not interested in your excuses, old son. Nothing you say to me can justify what you did. I offered you my help once, and you rejected it. From that moment on the problem became yours to deal with.'

'But I only rejected your help because of Sasha,' said Nick. 'I couldn't abandon my own daughter, could I? In that situation you would have done the same thing.'

'No, son. They dangled the bait, and you took it. I would never have shown that kind of weakness. Once you show weakness, that's it. You're lost, you can't help yourself any longer – just as you can't help yourself now.' He shrugged. 'Course, I'm not saying I don't sympathise with your situation. You had a tough decision to make. But life's full of tough decisions and sometimes sacrifices have to be made. When you've decided on one direction, son, you have to stick to it. You can't rely on others to come and drag you out of the shit.'

'But they were making us attack you,' said Nick desperately, then tailed off as Hallett shook his head.

'Don't take me for a tosser, Nick. I know this was all down to you. Part of your little plan to drag me out here.'

'But you came all the same, didn't you?' Nick said hopefully.

'I came for my own welfare, son, not yours. I couldn't afford to ignore the kind of shit that you and your friends were throwing at me.'

'Yeah, but . . . it's not worked out too badly, has it? I mean, I can't see the Genesis Project carrying on after this, and we've all managed to come out of it more or less unscathed.'

Hallett shook his head. 'Sorry, son – but it doesn't work like that. You've caused the death of a friend, and by dragging me out here, involving me in a high-stakes war I didn't want to fight, you've put everything that I hold dear at risk. Now, just because we're brothers of a kind doesn't mean I can forgive you. You've got to be punished. I'm sorry, Nick, but that's the way it is.'

Nick looked nervously at the men holding the guns. 'Punished how?'

Hallett didn't answer his question directly. Instead he waved a hand at the other psis clustered behind Nick. 'I know this lot were also involved in what happened, but as you were the ringleader, old son, and because of the bond between us, I'm prepared to be lenient. Your mates can go.'

No one moved. A couple of the psis looked at each other, uncertain of what to do.

'Well, go on then, if you're going,' said Hallett irritably. 'I'm offering you your freedom. No tricks.'

Still no one moved. They seemed to be waiting for something to happen. It was Greg Lousada who finally took the initiative. Stepping forward, he said firmly, 'We're all in this together. We only go if you let Nick come too.'

Hallett shrugged. 'Have it your way. It's no skin off my nose. Sorry about this, Nick, old son – nothing personal, you understand.'

His calm, relaxed demeanour didn't change, but suddenly Nick doubled over as if he had been kicked in the guts. He fell to his knees as blood gushed from his nose and trickled from one of his ears. The other psis looked on, so taken aback by the abruptness and ferocity of the attack upon him that they were transfixed. It was Sasha who reacted first, running forward to protect her father physically, as if from flying shrapnel. 'Make him stop, for God's sake!' she screamed at the other psis. 'Make him stop!'

She wasn't sure what happened next, but all at once her father gasped and slumped to the floor, as if released from the mental vice in which Hallett was crushing him. She glanced up at the psis. As one, they were glaring at Hallett, their faces clenched in concentration. Sasha twisted to see Hallett's reaction. His own face was contorted with the effort of trying to overcome the psis' combined strength. Behind him she was puzzled to see his men standing immobile, and then she realised that they were unable to raise their weapons, their muscle locked by the psis' power.

She felt her father stir beneath her, try to raise himself up on his good hand. She helped him, supporting him, holding him upright. He didn't clamber to his feet, but remained on his knees. He raised his head and looked at Hallett, blood smeared around his nose and upper lip, forming two thread-thin lines from his ears.

'Mr Hallett,' he rasped, 'it doesn't have to be like this. We've got a common enemy. What's the point of fighting amongst ourselves?'

Hallett gave no indication that he had heard Nick. His heavy features were set in a frozen, feral snarl.

Nick tried again. 'Can't you see we're at deadlock? Our combined strength now is more than a match for yours, but we don't want to fight with you. You're one of us. We should be helping each other.'

Was Hallett silent because he couldn't respond, or because he wouldn't? Nick looked at Sasha, saw the uncertainty he felt mirrored on her face. He reached up to touch her cheek in a gesture of reassurance and suddenly it occurred to him that whereas everyone else appeared to be locked into immobility, he and Sasha were relatively free to move around. What did this suggest? Presumably that Hallett did not have sufficient mental strength to incapacitate them in the same way that his own men were incapacitated. This undoubtedly was an advantage, but how could they make it work for them? They could use physical violence against Hallett, of course, bludgeon him into unconsciousness. Nick had no doubt that if the roles had been reversed Hallett would have done the same thing to him without a qualm. But there was no way he could bring himself to be so ruthless, so cold-blooded. It was Sasha who came up with an answer of sorts.

'I'll disarm Hallett's men while I still can.'

'Good idea,' said Nick, and Sasha scuttled forward. As she moved from one grey-suited man to the next, however, it quickly became clear that her plan was not to be so easily realised.

'Their hands are like concrete,' she gasped, trying in vain to prise one of Hallett's men's fingers from his gun. She tried for a moment longer, her teeth gritted with effort, then made a hand-flapping gesture of exasperation and gave up.

'So what do we do now?' she asked.

'Why don't you get out of here?' Nick said. 'Get out of the line of fire. You can wait for me on the other side of the compound.'

'No way! I'm not leaving you.'

Nick hesitated a moment. 'I've recovered a bit now. Maybe I should join the others, help to try and overcome Hallett rather than just holding him at bay.'

Sasha gave a worried frown. 'Are you sure you're up to it? The man just tried to fry your brain. He might have . . . I don't know . . . done some damage.'

Before Nick could answer, Mark Brown gave a groan that sounded almost wistful. Then his eyes rolled up into his head, and he fell to the ground, almost taking Julie Lean with him.

Instantly Nick felt fresh pain sizzling through his head, as if someone were trailing a red-hot poker across the surface of his brain. He cried out, his good hand going to his head, his body spasming in agony. The psis too showed signs of distress, unable to compensate for Mark Brown's sudden absence as Hallett took advantage of the broken link in the chain. Julie Lean's eyes fluttered like the wings of trapped butterflies; a number of the psis uttered moans of pain and one or two even tottered.

Sasha flung herself to the ground beside the big, bearded man and began to shake him. 'Wake up! Come on, wake up!' she shouted. Gaining no immediate response she turned again to the psis. 'Come on you lot – concentrate. Plug the gap.'

Whether in response to her words, or whether they were simply finding their feet again after the setback, the psis slowly rallied once more and Nick felt Hallett's painful mental grip slackening. Feeling battered, bruised and dizzy, his hand a permanent throbbing ache, he slowly turned his head to look at his attacker.

He saw immediately that the delicate equilibrium had not quite

412

been restored. Although the psis were keeping Hallett mentally cornered, their mental influence was no longer powerful enough to extend to his men. Infinitesimally slowly they were moving, beginning to raise their weapons. It was an eerie sight, like watching soldiers from some legendary army coming gradually to life after a centuries-long sleep.

Desperately Nick added his own mental power to that of his colleagues, but his beleaguered mind was weak, tired, unable to reach its full potential. Sasha was still trying desperately to rouse Mark Brown, but he appeared dead to the world. Meanwhile Hallett's men continued to move, degree by painstaking degree, despite Nick's attempt to pour everything he had, every ounce of willpower left to him, into a frantic effort to freeze their limbs once more.

How long, he wondered, would it take them to raise their weapons to chest height, to take aim, to apply enough pressure to the triggers for the guns to discharge? Two minutes? Five? Ten? However long it took, the outcome was inevitable and unavoidable. Sooner or later Nick and his colleagues would be cut down in a hail of machine-gun fire and there was nothing they could do about it. If they moved physically against Hallett, their concentration would be broken and the gangland boss would unleash a mental hurricane which would slice them apart.

They had lost. Strong as he and his colleagues had become in the past weeks, Hallett was stronger, and he was slowly wearing them down. To Nick, attempting to hold Hallett at bay was akin to carrying a heavy armchair on his back. You could do it for a little while – you might even feel comfortable with the weight at first – but carry it for any length of time and finally, inevitably, your muscles will start to ache, your knees to buckle.

Nick's mental muscles were aching now and still the men flanking Hallett were slowly, slowly raising their guns. Out of the corner of his eye he saw Sasha crouching over Mark Brown, trying in vain to wake him. He wanted to tell her that it was over, that she should get away while she still could, but he couldn't find the energy even to speak. He felt the vice tightening around his mind once more, felt the threat of unconsciousness prickling at the edges of his senses.

As he felt himself on the verge of slipping away he thought: *At least we tried.*

413

Sixty-One

Finally abandoning her attempt to wake Mark Brown, Sasha stood up, feeling anguished and helpless. It was clear that Dad and his friends were losing, that it would be only a matter of minutes before Hallett's men cut them down in a hail of machine-gun fire. Her dad's face was contorted, his lips drawn back from gritted teeth, his eyelids fluttering as though he too were about to faint. A number of the other psis didn't look too good either; a couple of them only seemed to be standing upright because they were leaning against their neighbours.

But what could she do? How could she change the situation? There was only one possible solution – she had to hurt Hallett, put him out of action. He was not vulnerable mentally, at least not to her, so she had to harm him physically.

Unlike her father she had no qualms about doing so. When it came to a choice between hurting the man who was prepared to massacre her dad and a bunch of other people, or standing by and watching that massacre take place, there was simply no contest. Sasha would do whatever was needed to save her father's life. Quickly she looked around for a weapon, though she would be more than prepared to batter Hallett into unconsciousness with her bare fists if needs be.

She saw something glinting on the floor in the red light; realising what it was, she rushed to pick it up. It was the carving knife with the broken blade that Julie Lean had shown them when she had been explaining how the other psis had made it into the vestibule. Sasha scooped it up and, without giving herself time to reflect on what she was about to do, raised it above her head like a psycho in a horror movie and charged at Hallett.

It was maybe twenty strides to the figure in the wheelchair. For the first ten or twelve Sasha was running freely, unencumbered, picking up speed. Then suddenly she hit a wall, or a web – invisible, sticky, clinging. She felt herself slowing down, her muscles turning to lead, her breathing becoming laboured. Five yards from Hallett she ground to a stop. She could go no further.

Evidently the man had thrown up some sort of mental barrier around himself to protect his physical body. Whether it was an automatic defence mechanism or a specific response to her attack was immaterial. The fact was, it was there and there was no way she could penetrate it.

She backed up, slowly and painstakingly at first, as though moving through treacle, and then more freely as Hallett's circle of influence began to fade. All at once the last constraining strands of Hallett's web released her and she stumbled backwards. She lost her footing and plumped unceremoniously on to her backside.

Immediately she jumped to her feet, panic leaping inside her. She had lost precious seconds in her fruitless attack, during which Hallett's men had raised their weapons a few millimetres higher. She calculated that if they fired them now the bullets would rip up the ground directly in front of the psis. Drawing back her arm she threw the knife at Hallett. That at least – presumably because it was inorganic – was not hampered by his psychic barrier. However, it failed to hit him, instead clattering against the side of his wheelchair and raising a bright wink of a spark in the gloom before bouncing harmlessly away.

What could she do now? She dithered for a moment, at a loss, and then an idea sprang into her head and she turned and ran, heading for the gap in the wall that led on to the stairs.

She squeezed through the gap and raced down the stairs, taking them three and four at a time, almost falling headlong on several occasions. Within a couple of minutes she had covered the distance that it had taken her and Nick ten times as long to travel going the other way.

Finally she rounded a corner and came upon the sight she had been both dreading and desperate to see. The dead soldiers, heaped and sprawled across one another like so much rubbish waiting for collection. She scanned the area; for several panic-stricken seconds she could not find what she wanted. Then she saw one: a gun – a smallish machine-gun – lying at the tip of the

415

outstretched fingers of a young soldier, as if he had been trying to reach it when he died.

Sasha snatched it up, shuddering; she half-expected the dead man to make a grab for her wrist as she bent to steal his property. The gun felt strange in her hand, heavy and dangerous. Holding it a little awkwardly, away from her body, she turned and began to lope back up the stairs, panting and sweating with tension.

Oddly it was turning her back on the mass of dead human flesh – now no longer people, but just objects, unfeeling or heaps of dirty laundry – that sent ripples of gooseflesh down her back. She used the fear as a spur to increase her speed, though by the time she reached the top – despite the urgency which drove her – she was exhausted, her legs shaking with effort. She lunged for the gap in the wall, at first making the mistake of trying to squeeze through with the gun, getting it jammed, and having to back up and re-manoeuvre. As she shoehorned herself out and then dragged the gun after her, she half-expected to be greeted by the chatter of machine-gun fire.

She ran forward on trembling legs, trying to familiarise herself with the weapon as she did so. If she was going to use it she could no longer treat it as some repugnant item she was only carrying out of necessity. She knew guns had safety-catches, but wasn't sure what one looked like – she could only hope that this gun was already primed and loaded. She decided it was best not to tamper with the thing. After all, she might easily find herself putting the safety-catch back on, or pressing the magazine release button and causing the curved bit at the back (that she knew, from watching movies, contained her ammunition) to drop off and clatter to the floor.

Hallett's men now had their weapons pointing at the psis' chests. It could only be a matter of seconds before they were able to exert enough pressure on their triggers to strafe her dad and his friends with deadly fire. Still running, Sasha levelled her own weapon at Hallett. And then it hit her, like a sudden curling skein of freezing fog – a cold paralysis in her arms and hands, an inability to jerk her finger back on the trigger of her gun.

'No!' she screamed. She was still running forward, was parallel with the psis now, but remembering the treacly psychic web surrounding Hallett, she abruptly clumped to a halt. She tried desperately to make her hands work, to override the psychic thread that Hallett must have cast in her direction. Presumably he had been able to deflect a little of his power away from the psis because of their gradually weakening state. Sasha cast a desperate look at them. They looked drawn, exhausted! Her dad was slumped on the floor, semi-conscious. Mark Brown was still stretched out next to him like a fat brown bear, his eyes closed.

Suddenly Sasha felt a fierce, panic-fuelled hatred for the fat man who, by passing out, had broken the link in the chain and thus allowed Hallett to press home his advantage. Because of Brown they would all be dead soon, their brains and hearts and lungs torn apart by chunks of high-velocity metal. Oblivious to the fact that she was moving into the firing line, she ran across to Mark Brown and kicked him in the thigh. He groaned.

'*Wake up!*' she screamed at him. '*Wake up, you fat bastard!*'

She kicked him in the stomach. He groaned again; his eyelids fluttered, and he tried to turn over, to protect himself.

'Oh, no you don't,' she snarled at him, and nudged him hard in the back of the neck with her foot. He raised a hand to try to push her away. She kicked out at it, then prodded him again, this time in the back of the head. 'I'm not going to stop until you wake up,' she shouted at him.

He opened his eyes. His voice was thick, blurred. 'Wassappenin? Leave me alone.'

'We need your help,' Sasha shouted, leaning down towards him. 'If you don't snap out of it in two seconds we'll all be dead.'

Her words seemed to get through. He didn't snap out of it in two seconds, but he recovered pretty quickly. He looked up at the flagging psis, at Nick wallowing on the ground, trying desperately to remain conscious, his bandaged, blood-soaked hand clutched to his chest. Then he twisted his head and looked at Hallett in his wheelchair, the gangster's face set, his eyes fixed in murderous concentration. Finally he looked at the men flanking Hallett, the business-ends of their AK47s seeming to point right at Mark's face like black, unblinking eyes.

Sasha saw Mark Brown's body go tense, saw his eyes behind his spectacles widen. She got the impression that he had released something – a sort of psychic bolt – directly at the man in the wheelchair.

Hallett flinched, drawing up his shoulders, gripping the arms of his wheelchair, but he seemed to accommodate this fresh attack

417

without too much difficulty. However, he was momentarily forced to divert his attention away from Sasha. She felt the paralysis leaving her hands, heat flowing back into them. Without hesitation she pointed the gun at Hallett and pressed the trigger.

The gun chattered three times. Hallett was slammed back into his chair, head whiplashing like a crash-test dummy's. He hit the back of the chair with such an impact that he rebounded forward, plunging to the floor face-first. He didn't put up his hands to protect himself; they trailed behind him like so much dead-weight. His head struck the floor with a clunk, like a dropped coconut. After a few seconds, as the sound of gunfire faded into silence, blood that looked like sump oil began to creep out from beneath Hallett's body to form an ever-widening pool across the floor.

Sixty-Two

The weight of Hallett's mind was bearing down on Nick with increasing pressure, squeezing slowly but inexorably through the thinning veil of resistance that the psis had thrown up in desperate defence. *Maybe dying won't be so bad*, he thought as he lay on the ground, curled around his injured hand. It couldn't be worse than a lot of the shit he had had to endure in his life – the grinding dependency on drugs and drink, the nightly beatings in prison. Indeed, he had wished himself dead more times than he could recall, and now death, if it came, would simply be an end to all of that and to all of this: a release from the pain and the fear.

He closed his eyes, hoping that if he gave himself up to it without resistance it would be over quickly. In his semi-conscious state he heard a series of cracks; he thought it might be the sound of his earthly bonds twisting and breaking, like the roots of some enormous tree. Perhaps it was, for the next instant he was flying, his mind soaring, making him giddy. *I've died*, he thought, awestruck, and wondered whether anyone down on Earth could see his immortal soul leaving his irreparably damaged body.

His euphoria, though glorious, was short-lived. Nick's heavenbound thoughts reached an apex and then plummeted once more. And despite his light-headedness he realised that he was still not free of the throbbing pain that radiated out from his injured hand and ground in his bones, like little spurts of polluting effluent into crystal-clear water, or of the nauseous curling in his stomach, or the ache of exhaustion in his limbs.

He opened eyes which felt raw and hot and dry. He saw Hallett's men, bathed in red light, standing with their mouths

419

agape and their machine-guns held slackly in their hands, the barrels drooping, pointing at the floor like wilting erections.

He also saw that Hallett's wheelchair was empty; it was as if the man had got up and walked. And seeing this, Nick suddenly realised exactly why he felt light-headed. The crushing weight of Hallett's mind trying to force its way into his brain like powerful fingers tearing into a piece of soft fruit had stopped. Oddly, it was as if this realisation suddenly enabled Nick to see the broken body of Hallett himself. He was lying on his face on the floor in front of his chair, blood fanning out from beneath his body. Whether it was his physical stillness or the absence of his presence Nick was not sure, but he had no doubt that the man was dead.

He levered himself into a sitting position with his good arm as he took in the wider picture. Sasha was standing with a gun in her hands and a shocked expression on her face; the psis were standing in a motionless group, Mark Brown hunkered in front of them like the captain of the team waiting for someone to bring a trophy to place at his feet. The church-like silence of the place was suddenly broken by Sasha, who gave an exclamation of repugnance and flung the gun away from her as if it had begun to squirm in her hands.

It was the sound of the gun clattering to the floor that jerked Hallett's men from their stupor. Though he did not yet feel fully alert, Nick read their intentions even as they were forming in the mens' minds and moved to counter their actions. As the men jerked their guns up once more and curled their fingers around their triggers with real purpose, they were hit with another psychic barrage, once again locking their limbs.

'No you don't, lads,' Greg Lousada muttered.

'Can you make them drop their guns this time?' Sasha asked shakily.

Nick imagined the mens' hands as if they were his own, imagined himself opening them, letting the guns fall.

The men opened their hands and the guns fell.

Sasha ran forward to collect them up, then carried them to the corner beside the lift and dumped them there.

As if in unspoken agreement, the psis released Hallett's men, who looked back at them without fear, rubbing their wrists and flexing their hands. 'I think we need to talk,' Nick said. Getting no response, he blundered on. 'We didn't want this – this violence.

420

We didn't want to have to kill anyone. We didn't want to kill Mr Hallett, but he gave us no choice. You do see that, don't you?'

Still the men said nothing.

Ellie McKee stepped forward. 'We're not your enemies. Your real enemies are the people who run this place. We're just ordinary people who want to get out of here, who want to go back to our families and our normal lives.'

'Won't you please help us?' said Julie Lean piteously.

One of the men, his long hair tied back in a ponytail, spat contemptuously on the ground. 'Why should we?'

'Why *shouldn't* you?' retorted Sasha. 'Like the lady said, we're not your enemies. If you don't help us, we'll be stranded here.'

'You think we give a shit?' one of the other men said.

'You *should* give a shit,' Greg Lousada suddenly snapped, making Nick turn his head to look at him. 'We've asked you nicely and it obviously isn't getting through – so let me put it another way. You saw what we did to your boss. You've felt our power. If you don't help us, we'll fry your fucking brains.'

Ponytail shook his head. 'You haven't got the bottle, man.'

'Just fucking try me,' Lousada said quietly.

There was a ten-second stand-off, Ponytail and Greg Lousada attempting to stare each other down. Then the silence was broken by one of the other men, his voice uncertain. 'There's a whole army of us out here. You can't take us all on.'

Greg's voice was quiet, oozing with conviction. 'Oh, yes we can,' he said. 'We can fill your heads with nightmares. We can tear you apart from within.'

Nick saw the man who had spoken last glancing fearfully at his comrades. For all their bravado, he suspected that without the focusing influence of their leader these men were at a loss what to do. They were used to taking orders, not making decisions. Their overriding desire in this situation was simply not to be seen to lose face.

'Look,' he said reasonably, 'all we're asking for is a lift home. Once we're in England we'll go back to our normal lives and you'll never see us again.'

Hallett's men glanced at one another, then Ponytail gave an abrupt nod.

'All right,' he muttered. 'Come with us.'

Sixty-Three

The plane was not quite as luxurious as the one Sasha had arrived on, but it was impressive nonetheless. She wondered whether Hallett had owned it or had simply hired it for the occasion. If he'd been planning to return all his men to England by air once the operation was complete, then he would have needed several such planes. What was it one of his bodyguards – the most self-doubting and probably therefore the most intelligent – had said? *There's a whole army of us out here.* So how many was that exactly? Fifty? A hundred?

She wondered whether Hallett had gathered his 'army' together in London and flown them over, or whether he had recruited them as mercenaries from the local underworld community. Not that it mattered – it wasn't her concern, not now. What she ought to be thinking about – all she really *wanted* to think about – was getting home and seeing Mum and somehow trying to claw her way back into her old life.

She turned her attention from the window, where she'd been staring at the unbroken blackness outside, to her dad, sitting beside her. The young man who had carefully cleaned and was now rebandaging Nick's hand seemed an incongruous component in Hallett's criminal machine. He was slight, blond-haired, handsome, friendly, articulate. And yet he had evidently not been here under duress or false pretences, for when he found out about Hallett's death he had looked genuinely stricken. He had released a deep, groaning exhalation of grief and covered his face with his hand, remaining in that position for a couple of minutes before looking up, his eyes tearless but his face blotchy. 'I don't believe it,' he had said, in a voice that was gruff and faint and hollow with emotion. 'I mean, it's . . . well, I mean . . . what happened?'

Sasha had looked him in the eye and had said, a little defiantly, 'I killed him.'

'You!' he exclaimed, regarding her as a little boy might regard someone who has performed an astonishing conjuring trick. 'How?'

They told him, Sasha and Nick doing most of the talking, one or two of the other psis chipping in from time to time. Nick sat beside the young man and placed a hand on his arm, as though he were an old friend. 'We're not proud of what we did, Ray,' he said, 'but Mr Hallett gave us no choice. We tried to speak to him, to reason with him, but he wouldn't listen. In the end it came down to a straight decision between him and us. I mean, what else could we do?'

He sounded regretful, battle-weary, sounded almost as if he were asking Ray for forgiveness. Ray simply looked at him in wonder.

'But Mr Hallett was so . . . so *strong*.'

'So are we,' said Greg Lousada. 'We're stronger than he must have thought we were. Working together we were more than a match for him.'

'You do see that we had to do what we did, don't you, Ray?' Nick said again. 'We didn't want to kill Mr Hallett, it was nothing personal, but he made us do it. We all feel pretty sick about it. You *do* see that, don't you, Ray?'

Ray looked at him a moment longer, then slowly nodded. 'Yes. I can't hate you for surviving. Mr Hallett always admired survivors. Come on, let's have a look at that hand of yours.'

That conversation had taken place four hours ago in one of the outbuildings – a mess-hall – on the compound that Hallett had earmarked as a makeshift medical facility for those among his men who might get injured during the conflict. It was a measure of the overwhelming success of Hallett's operation that when the psis had entered the building, led there by Hallett's bodyguards, they had found Ray alone, sitting with his feet up, drinking a cup of tea and reading the *Independent*.

Hallett's bodyguards – who, given their employer's abilities, had surely been superfluous, little more than show, even though in the end they had almost tilted victory Hallett's way – had left, grunting that they needed to report back. Ray and the psis remained in the building: talking, drinking tea, a number of the psis resting their heads on the formica-topped tables and drifting into fitful sleep for the next two hours. Eventually the door opened and a number of tough-looking men in charcoal-grey suits entered, faces grim, like pallbearers at a gangster's funeral. One of the men, dressed differently to the others in an ill-fitting military uniform, was Sherman. He was red-eyed, as if he had been crying. He looked at Nick sadly.

'We'll take you home,' he said, 'but don't expect any favours once we get back to England.'

'We won't,' said Nick.

'Right. Let's go, then.'

The men led the way outside. The psis, after looking at each other uncertainly, followed, Ray bringing up the rear.

They stood outside the building for fifteen minutes or more, like early arrivals at a football match waiting for the stadium to open. It was a cold night, a breeze blowing up off the desert. For the first six or seven minutes no one said anything until eventually the silence became so tangible that it seemed thick enough to chew on. Eventually Greg Lousada asked the question that had been jammed in Nick's throat like a stone for several minutes.

'So what exactly are we waiting for? A number ten bus?'

'Plane,' Sherman said, and looked up at the sky. 'It'll be here soon.'

Nick couldn't believe how little activity there was. Apart from themselves there was not a soul to be seen. Encouraged by Greg's example he cleared his throat. 'So, have you . . . er . . . finished up here?'

Sherman turned his head slowly and looked at him. Not for the first time Nick felt uneasy at the almost child-like intensity of his stare. Sherman nodded slowly, the overhead arc-lights making the white curl of scar tissue gleam on the crown of his shaven head. 'Oh, yes,' he said softly. 'The area has been sterilised.'

'Sterilised?' said Sasha. 'What do you mean?'

Sherman turned his attention to her. 'This is the Devil's playground. It's no coincidence that the main complex burrows deep into the earth. Everything it contains is sponsored by the Black Budget – it has the stink of the Old Ones about it. We've done

424